John Flood   5/78

D0593820

John Fiske 6/3

THE BEST PLACE TO BE

HELEN VAN SLYKE

The Best Place To Be

Doubleday & Company, Inc., Garden City, New York
1976

All of the characters in this book are fictitious, and any resemblance to actual persons, living or dead, is purely coincidental.

Library of Congress Cataloging in Publication Data

Van Slyke, Helen, 1919–
  The best place to be.

  I. Title
PZ4.V2777Be [PS3572.A54]   813'.5'4
ISBN 0-385-01429-5
LIBRARY OF CONGRESS CATALOG CARD NUMBER 75-40748

"The Perfect Year" by Lois Wyse in Chapter 32 is reprinted with the kind permission of the author. Copyright © 1968 by Lois Wyse

COPYRIGHT © 1976 BY HELEN VAN SLYKE
ALL RIGHTS RESERVED
PRINTED IN THE UNITED STATES OF AMERICA

For my mother, with love and gratitude.

Chapter 1

There was something almost indecent about a man like Sean Callahan dying at the counter of a dry-cleaner's shop in that circumspect suburb of Cleveland called Shaker Heights.

When the police came to the front door of the big house on Malvern Street to tell Sheila that her husband was dead of a heart attack, she stared at them wordlessly and then began to laugh. Not because it was funny or because she was glad. Neither was true. Her laughter was an involuntary reaction to the ridiculous circumstances under which death came to Sean. Such a stupid, mediocre end shouldn't have happened to the handsome, virile, unpredictable man who'd allowed her to share his life for twenty-seven years. He should have died as he liked to live, with a flourish. Given a choice, he would have gone dramatically. Lost at sea, perhaps. Or killed navigating an impossible turn in his Mercedes-Benz on the snake-like road from Algiceras to Marbella. Or, even better, Sean would have opted for a headline death at the hands of a jealous husband.

It was a cruel joke on Sean, expiring wordlessly on a hot August afternoon in a stupid little store, waiting to pick up his tan gabardine suit. Sheila wondered whether, at the moment it was happening, he knew. If so, he must have been fearfully angry. So angry it was a wonder he hadn't frightened death away with one of his towering Irish rages.

The young policemen did not find her laughter unusual. Hysteria, they thought. They'd seen it before. They stood quietly, with carefully composed expressions of sympathy on their faces and circles of sweat under the armpits of their blue shirts, waiting for the shock to subside, hating the news they were forced to bring. They knew Mr. Callahan. Everybody did. A big, hearty, outgoing man with enough charm to talk himself out of a speeding ticket and, people said, into the bed of any woman from the Gold Coast to Chagrin Falls. A classy guy, though, the cops agreed on their way to his house. Tough to go so young. Only fifty-three. And one hell of a big, strong hulk of man. Jesus, you never know, do you?

When Sheila became quiet they told her that her husband had been rushed to the hospital but too late. He was there now, they said, waiting for unnecessary but official identification. Did she want—that is, could they take her . . . ?

"No, thank you. I'll call someone. Thank you, officers. You've been very kind."

"If you'd like us to get someone to be with you, Mrs. Callahan . . ."

She shook her head. "I'll be fine. My brother-in-law will come. And my children." She smiled now, quietly. It was ridiculous. As though she was comforting and reassuring these strangers. Playing the old game. Sheila the unflappable. Sheila the tower of strength. Sheila pretending there was nothing she couldn't take, whether it was Sean's unfaithfulness or Sean's untimely death. She wished they'd go away. "Thank you again," she said for the third time, as though they'd caught a burglar or found a lost dog.

"We're very sorry," the younger one said. "Everybody liked Mr. Callahan."

"Yes. I know."

They went away, finally, the squad car disappearing slowly down the curved driveway. She tried to think what to do first, commanding her mind to perform in an orderly fashion. The clock on the mantel said half-past two. Sean's brother, Terry, would just be getting back to his office after lunch. He could be at the hospital from downtown in about thirty minutes. Probably he'd send Margaret over to be with her in the meantime. Sheila wished he wouldn't. She didn't want her sister-in-law around, briskly taking charge. But it was unavoidable. While Terry saw to the "arrangements," his wife would take over the house in that infuriatingly competent way of hers. Just as, Sheila thought, she'll take over my life now, if I let her.

It was so quiet in the house. Soon it would be noisy. Everyone would arrive as quickly as they could when she called. She pictured them all there. Sean's parents flying in from their retirement condominium in Sarasota; her own mother, Rose, coming from New York; Sean's closest friend and lawyer, Bob Ross, and his tart-tongued wife, Emily; Sheila's dearest friend Sally Cantrell. And, most of all, the children. In her mind she saw her eldest, Patrick, already as serious as the doctor he was in training to be. Pat. Hard to believe he was twenty-six years old and married. It seemed only a minute ago that she was pregnant with him, barely three months after she and Sean were married. Maryanne, the "middle child," had come two years later. She was a handful from the start and she was a handful today. The rebel of the family, Sheila thought. Her and her damned defiance. They'd tried so hard with Maryanne. Earlier in her life, Sean had been able to get through better than Sheila had, but later neither of them really reached their daughter. Maryanne would come. Please God she wouldn't bring Rick Jawolsky, the young rock musician with whom she shared an apartment in Ohio City, on the West Side.

She had to call them all and tell them their son, son-in-law, brother, friend, father was dead. The only one who wouldn't be notified by phone was her youngest. Tommy would be coming home from his ball-game in a very few minutes. She'd have to look into the sensitive, loving face of her fifteen-year-old and tell him about Sean. She knew how he'd react, this half-man, half-boy. The deep blue eyes, so like his father's, would cloud over with sadness and concern for her. He'd be the quietest of them all, his understanding the deepest, for he was her darling, her baby, her life. The "accidental" child born nine years after Maryanne, the one they hadn't really wanted, was the one who had brought the truest joy Sheila had ever known. She loved him so much. And now she had to take care of him alone. God knows how well Sean provided for us, she thought. He never discussed money or the future with her. Maybe Terry knew. Or Bob Ross.

The clock said a quarter to three. She couldn't just sit there in a kind of fuzzy bewilderment. There was the hideous present and the unpredictable future to be dealt with. She dialed Sean's brother. Without preamble she said, "Terry, Sean's dead." And then disjointed, almost automatic answers to his questions, as though she were an automatic recording device on a telephone. Heart attack. About two o'clock. Hospital. Margaret. Yes. Thank you, Terry.

She should call the others. Let Margaret do it. What difference did another half hour make? Not aware of what she was doing, she went into the kitchen. Tommy was always hungry when he got home from school. She began to make a peanut-butter sandwich. Halfway through, she carefully put down the knife. Tommy hated peanut butter. It was his father who loved it.

And then there was an angry voice screaming in the empty house. A bitter, out-of-control voice.

"Damn you, Sean Callahan! Damn you to hell!"

It took her a few horrified seconds to realize that the voice was her own.

It was as she knew it would be. Tommy came in, whistling, throwing his baseball glove on the hall chair, yelling "Mom? You home? What's in the fridge?" She was sitting in the breakfast room, waiting for him. One look at her face told him something was terribly wrong. He didn't cry when he heard about his father. It occurred to her, almost with shame, that she hadn't cried either. She supposed her face was like Tommy's, frozen in disbelief, stunned by the incomprehensible fact that Sean, so bursting with life a few hours ago, was now a still thing in the hospital morgue. It had no reality at that moment. It was a statistic, a head-shaking, almost impersonal tragedy, like the ones reported every day in the *Plain Dealer*. For a few seconds they simply stared at each other, the boy and the woman. And then, almost simultaneously, they broke. Holding each other tightly, they sought comforting warmth. Sheila cried and Tommy awkwardly patted her hair and said nothing. She smelled the boy-smell of the baseball field, felt the still-skinny young arms holding her protectively, heard the deep breathing that determinedly held back the tears.

"I'm sorry, Tommy," she said, finally, sinking back into the chair.

Sorry for what? For crying? But that was absurd. She was expected to cry, to welcome the release it brought. Sorry her husband was dead? Of course she was sorry. Sorry for Sean, for his children, for herself. Sorry he'd died in such a stupid, undramatic way. Sorry they hadn't had the life she'd hoped for. Even, insanely, sorry she hadn't offered to pick up his gabardine suit, as though if *she'd* been there death would have been foiled by the appearance of the wrong victim.

Tommy slumped into the seat opposite her. "I know, Mom."

But he didn't know. He'd never know what life with Sean Callahan had really been. He saw what the world saw—the ultimate charmer, the big spender, the "professional Irishman" who was "the fun one" in the Callahan marriage. Tommy surely didn't know about the women, many of them their friends, who went to bed with Sean while Sheila pretended, to everyone except her husband, that she didn't know. Tommy did know that the unaware husbands of these women admired his father, not for his great business success but for his eternally unworried attitude, his love of adventure, his enjoyment of pleasure which was in such direct contrast to their own concerned, conventional, thoughtful-of-tomorrow lives.

Neither Tommy nor the others knew what sheer hell Sean Callahan was to live with. It was more than his monumental temper which Sheila, in her own way, could match. It was his refusal to grow up. Strangely, their biggest fights had not been over women but over security, or the lack of it. They had the house and Sean made good money in his real estate business. They lacked for nothing because Sean spent every penny he made, whether in a wild-cat oil scheme, an extravagant trip to Europe or a show-off dinner party under an elaborate canopied tent in their garden. He refused to discuss anything as distasteful as old age or sickness or, God forbid, death. He even managed to make Sheila feel guilty about her "middle-class mores."

"Life's for livin', darling," he used to say. "Stop worrying about tomorrow. We're blessed. Nothing bad's ever going to happen to Sean Callahan and his family."

But it had. To him and, Sheila suspected, to the rest of them. She should have been grieving for her husband and thinking of the hundred things that must be done in the next three days. It was sinful of her to be remembering the irresponsible part of Sean. She should be cherishing the happy times, the joyous memories of which, in fairness, there were many. For in spite of it all, she'd loved this lighthearted, amorous, irresponsible man. Even now she felt the prick of guilt. I should have made him smoke and drink less, get more rest, have regular checkups. Maybe this wouldn't have happened if I'd been more understanding. Stop it, Sheila! Sean wouldn't have done any of those things no matter how much you nagged.

It crossed her mind that Sean never thought of his own death. Nor, really, had she. If anything, she'd imagined he'd outlive her. She had even, occasionally, pictured him as a widower, going through the dramatics of bereavement for a while and eventually, secretly, enjoying release from a wife who was too practical, too boringly worried about his escapades and his improvidence.

So much for all that. He was gone and she was a widow. She looked at Tommy who was staring out of the window at the swimming pool, probably remembering the many times he and his father had roughhoused in those waters.

"It's going to be all right, Tommy," she said. "We'll miss him, but life's for the living. We're blessed. Your Dad always said so."

Chapter 2

        The rest of that hot, steamy day and evening was a blur. Margaret arrived from her house only three blocks away and, as anticipated, took charge. After a quick hug for Sheila, a sympathetic pat on the cheek for Tommy, and a few quickly wiped-away tears, Margaret Callahan proceeded with the business of organizing her brother-in-law's wake and funeral and her sister-in-law's participation in it.

"Have you called everyone?"

Sheila shook her head. "No one."

"Don't worry. I'll do it. Terry's gone to the hospital, you know that. I'd better get in touch with Father Reilly right away. Let's see. It's Monday. The services should be Thursday morning. We'll need to arrange the time at the church. Terry will see to the rest. He'll know what's appropriate. Now, about notifying people. I'll get hold of Pat and Betty and Maryanne first, of course. And your mother. And Jean and Bill in Sarasota. . . ."

"No," Sheila said.

Margaret stared at her. "No? What do you mean, 'No'?"

"I want to call Jean and Bill myself. They've lost their child. And I'll call my own children. If you do the rest I'll appreciate it, Margaret. But not those calls."

"But you're not expected to . . . That is, they'll understand that you're in no condition to . . ."

6

"No, Margaret. Not those calls."

Her sister-in-law shrugged. "All right, dear. As long as you think you're able." Margaret tugged the jacket of her pants suit into a straight edge at the bottom. The gesture was so typical, Sheila thought idly. Everything about Margaret was a straight line from here to there. How boring it must be for Terry to live with such an efficient woman. More boring than it was for Sean to live with me. Not true. Sean was never bored. Angry, often. Impatient, frequently. But never bored.

Margaret's involuntary gesture made her think of clothes. "You *do* have something for the funeral, Sheila? A black dress, I mean. Probably we'll have to get a veil."

Ridiculously, Sheila wanted to laugh. Those closest to Sean did not even know he was dead and Margaret was concerned about widow's weeds. She'd be concerned about a dozen other outmoded things, too. They might as well get those straightened out now.

"I have a black dress," Sheila said. "And I won't wear a veil, Margaret. Dark glasses will do. And while we're about it, I don't want any public viewing of Sean. Not even by me. Tell Terry I want the casket closed. Sean would have hated being stared at." Her own calmness amazed her. It was an instinctive thing. She'd have to suffer two evenings at the funeral parlor, greeting her husband's friends, accepting their condolences. She'd have to go through a mass and a burial. But she'd not have it all turn into a ghoulish display of the man who was always restless, even in his sleep, and who'd be outraged to be seen in a state of helpless passivity. She didn't want to remember him immobile and silent. No one should remember Sean Callahan that way.

"I do think his parents and his children—" Margaret protested.

"No," Sheila said again. "No one."

"It's up to you," Margaret said disapprovingly.

In the background, Tommy listened quietly, taking no part in the conversation between his mother and his aunt. But when Margaret turned away, he nodded solemnly at Sheila. You're right, the nod seemed to say. Don't let her stampede you.

In two minutes she was through to Jean Callahan in Florida. She was fond of both of Sean's parents, fonder, she thought guiltily, than she was of her own mother. The senior Callahans had taken adjustment gracefully. There'd once been a lot of money in the family. Sean and Terry had grown up in one of the great houses on South Park, had gone to the best schools, had expected to be like their father—"well off," if not rich. But Bill Callahan, in his own way, had been as impractical as Sean. His big job at Public Steel paid him handsomely, but his retirement, though adequate, was not lavish. He'd made foolish investments which brought little income. Ten years before, at his mandatory retirement age, Bill and Jean sold the big house for far less than they expected to get for it and bought a small, pleasant condominum in Sarasota. They were comfortable and independent, but Jean did her own housework and Bill played golf on the public course. They asked nothing from their children, but regretfully they could offer little except love and devotion to their sons and daughters-in-law and grandchildren. They were cheerful and entirely uncomplaining about their reduced mode of life. They had each other and a family of whom they were proud. They'd seen Terry establish a lucrative law practice in Cleveland and watched Sean operate a one-man real-estate business that seemed to provide more than enough security for Sheila and the children. Devout people, they gave thanks for their blessings. Real tragedy had never struck until now.

Sheila tried to keep her voice steady but gentle when Jean answered the phone. "Mother Callahan," she said, "are you alone? I mean, is Dad there?"

The unusual beginning of the call instantly alerted the elderly woman. "Yes, Dad's here. What's happened, Sheila?"

"It's Sean." Sheila took a deep breath. "He had a heart attack this afternoon."

"Oh, my God! How bad is he?"

Margaret was right, Sheila thought. I can't do it. But then she gripped the telephone tightly and said, "It was instantaneous, dear. Sean's dead."

There was only a terrible gasp on the other end of the wire and then Jean said, "Are you all right, Sheila? Darling, is someone with you?"

"Yes, Tommy's here. And Margaret. And Terry is seeing to things."

"What about Pat and Betty and Maryanne?"

"They don't know yet. I called you first."

She heard her mother-in-law fighting for control. "We'll be on the first plane tonight. Bill will call back and let you know what time we arrive. Perhaps Terry or Patrick can meet us. I—I have to hang up now, Sheila. Be brave, sweetheart. We'll be with you very soon."

How marvelous she is, Sheila thought as she quietly replaced the receiver. I wonder if I'd be as strong if someone called to tell me about Pat or Tommy or Maryanne. I wouldn't be. I'd think of my own loss first, not be concerned about others, as Jean Callahan is. Her heart must be breaking. Her first-born, her beloved, laughing, invincible son dead and yet she worries about me. Suddenly all the strength seemed to leave Sheila. She couldn't go through it again. She couldn't say the words even to her other children. Margaret was right. She was in no condition to track them down and tell them about their father. She couldn't face the certainty of her own mother's hysterical reaction. She couldn't speak to Sally Cantrell or Bob Ross. Let Margaret do it. Let everybody do everything while she simply sat and tried to absorb the enormity of her loss. It was selfish and cowardly of her, but what difference did it make how they heard about Sean? No matter whose voice spoke the words, the fact remained unchangeable. He was gone. And for the first time in her life she had to figure out the future for herself, by herself.

Patrick, tall and handsome in his crisp whites, answered the page for "Dr. Patrick Callahan." He took the call at the nurses' station, expecting it might be Betty saying she was detained at the West Side Community Health Service. It wouldn't be the first time either of them was late getting back to the apartment. Betty was a good wife, he thought. The salary she made as a caseworker at the city-run center wasn't much, but it made all the difference. They couldn't live on Pat's pay as an intern at the Cleveland Clinic, and they'd agreed two years ago when they married that Betty would keep on working while he finished his training. Some day I'll make it up to her, Pat told himself. She'll be a rich doctor's wife with a house in Gates Mills or Chagrin Falls. An even better house than the one his parents had in Shaker Heights.

"Dr. Callahan," he said professionally into the phone.

"Patrick? It's Aunt Margaret." The voice was efficient, precise. "You're needed at home right away. It's your father. He's gone."

For a moment Pat didn't understand. "Gone? Gone where?"

"He's dead, Patrick. A heart attack this afternoon. Your Uncle Terry is seeing to things, but you should be here with your mother. Will you get hold of Betty and come as soon as possible? Your grandparents are on the way from Florida; you may have to meet them at the airport tonight."

He was speechless. In his work he was used to the death of strangers, used to the grief of the survivors. But at the hospital he was reasonably unemotionally involved, even with the saddest cases. This was the first time death had touched him personally and his Aunt Margaret was announcing it in the way she might have summoned him to usher at a wedding.

"How is Mother?" he asked finally. "Is she all right? Is Tommy okay? Have you reached Maryanne? My God, Aunt Margaret how did it happen?"

"Everybody's taking it well," Margaret said. "It happened in a second, apparently. At the dry-cleaner's on The Square. They say he never knew what hit him, Patrick."

"I'll get hold of Betty and be there shortly. Tell Mother to hang on, will you?"

"She will. She's a strong woman."

Is she? Patrick wondered after he'd talked to a horrified Betty and received the Chief Resident's condolences and permission to take off. How strong is Mother? Married at twenty, never on her own in her whole life, left with a house to run, and a teen-aged boy to raise and educate, how will she cope? He doubted that his father had left much of an estate.

9

Even Sean's lawyer, Bob Ross, had once confided to Pat that his father was irresponsible about money. "He acts as though he's going to live forever," Bob had said. Pat remembered laughing. "That tough Irish bastard probably will," his son had answered. He'd believed it. And so, he was uncomfortably sure, had Sean.

Maryanne heard the telephone ringing but she just turned over in the big bed and ignored it. Telephones bored her. For that matter, almost everything bored her except listening to rock music, smoking pot, and having sex with Rick. In that order. If I'm this bored at twenty-four, Maryanne thought, what will I be at forty-four? Who cared? With a little luck she'd never make middle age. Damn that phone. Would it never stop? Angrily she reached for it, intending to take it off the hook and go back to sleep. Beside her, Rick snored gently. She looked at the clock. Four-thirty in the afternoon. Who'd call at this hour? Didn't they know that musicians and their chicks slept all day? She was about to drop the receiver on the floor when she heard an urgent, uptight voice saying, "Maryanne! Maryanne, are you there? It's Aunt Margaret! Maryanne!"

Oh, no, she thought. Not the Shaker Heights clan in pursuit again! Couldn't they understand that she'd kicked all that? It was a long, long way from Hathaway School for girls to this ninety-dollar-a-month pad in Ohio City, the twenty-block West Side area that people were trying so damned hard to turn into another quaint little Georgetown. It was a long way from the Shaker Country Club to those dear little dives in the inner city where she spent every night listening to Rick Jawolsky play electric guitar. Sometimes Rick let her sing with the band. She supposed that's what she wanted to do—be a girl singer with a really good group. Maybe cut records and get on the charts. Be famous and make a lot of money and die dramatically at thirty. That was her fantasy, except she was usually too stoned to do much about it. Her voice wasn't half-bad, husky and sexy, but better suited to the ballads of the forties than the Nashville sound of the seventies. Probably she'd never make it. It didn't really matter. Reluctantly, the low-pitched voice responded lethargically to the urgency of the caller's.

"Hi, Aunt Margaret."

"Maryanne! Thank God! I thought you'd never answer! Maryanne, something terrible has happened. Your father is dead. You must get out here right away!"

Maryanne stared stupidly at the telephone. "Dead? What is this, some kind of sick joke?"

There was a brief, shocked silence on the other end.

"It's hardly the kind of thing one makes jokes about," Margaret said coldly. "He had a heart attack this afternoon. I'm making the calls for your mother. She wants you here. And," pointedly, "*alone.*"

Even now, the disapproval in her aunt's voice was unmistakable. They could never understand, any of them, what had happened to Maryanne. How could they? She didn't really understand it herself. She only knew she didn't want to be like the women in the world she grew up in, the "safe" women with their phony religion, their domineering husbands, their good works, and their boredom. Even her mother, who was less rigid than most, did "what was expected of her." Maryanne and Patrick knew about their father, his unfaithfulness and his selfishness. Only Tommy was unaware of the pretense of normalcy that existed in the Callahan household. Pat had reacted by opting for "respectability"—an early marriage to a bright girl and a well-planned future as a doctor. She'd gone the other route, seeking complete freedom, whatever that was. She wondered whether Pat was pleased with his choice. She wasn't exactly thrilled with hers. Sometimes she thought she'd chuck it all and try to make something of her life. Maybe get into the Woman's Movement and try to do something about chauvinists like her father. And then she'd think, the hell with it. The Sean Callahans of this world with their double standards and their single-minded wives were what people admired and emulated and who was she to try and change it?

And yet in her way she loved them, these upper middle-class parents of hers. Even when she hurt them, when she angered Sean and baffled Sheila, she wanted to tell them that she was searching for herself. Drugs made it easier, though she wasn't on the hard stuff. Pot took her into herself, introspective and dreamy and content for a little while. The sparsely furnished apartment represented a nose-thumbing gesture at the manicured lawns and polished-silver houses of Shaker Heights. Even Rick, uncouth and careless as he was, was more honest than her father. She'd taken him to her parents' house only once. That was enough for all of them. Rick had gone out of his way to be outrageous and Sheila had been overly polite to hide her distress. Sean, for once, had been silent and surly. They'd never gone back. And Aunt Margaret had made it patently clear that Rick was no more welcome now than he'd been when Sean was around to glower.

"I'll be there in a little while," Maryanne said.

Margaret's voice dripped with sarcasm. "That's very kind of you, I'm sure." And hung up without another word.

Maryanne lay staring at the ceiling. Then she nudged the man beside her. "Wake up, Rick. I have to go home. My father died."

He turned over and opened a bleary eye. "Hey, that's heavy, baby. I'm sorry. You want me to go with you?"

She shook her head. "I guess I'll have to stay a few days."

"Sure."

"But I'll be back."

Methodically, Margaret stayed on the telephone, the composed bearer of bad news. She caught Bob Ross just as he was leaving his office, heard his unbelieving "No!" and then the disciplined inquiries about Sheila and about what he could do.

"Terry's taking care of the arrangements," Margaret said, "but maybe you'd call the newspapers, Bob. You know what to say." She gave him details of the hours the family would "receive" at the funeral home, the time of the service, already established with Father Reilly. "I think it would be good to ask for donations to the Heart Fund in lieu of flowers, don't you?"

"Yes. How's Sheila taking it?"

"She's in shock, naturally. She wanted to call everyone herself, but after she spoke to Sean's mother she realized she couldn't handle it. She's lying down now."

"And Tommy?"

"I don't know. He's in his room. But he's just a boy. He'll get over it quickly."

"I'm not so sure. He's at a rough age for something like this. And he loved Sean."

Margaret bristled. "We all did, Bob."

"Of course. I didn't mean it that way. Hell, Margaret, Sean and I grew up together. He was best man at my wedding. God, you never know, do you? Emily and I will come over tonight if that's okay. You think Sheila's up to it?"

"I think so. The children are on the way and so are Jean and Bill. I'm going to call Sheila's mother now, heaven help me. I suppose she'll fly in from New York tonight."

"Has Sally been notified?"

Margaret wrinkled her nose. Sally Cantrell was Sheila's best friend but Margaret had never liked her. Sally, Margaret thought, was a fool. Letting Fred Cantrell have a divorce to marry that snip twenty-five years younger than himself. So he provided well for the woman who'd been his wife for twenty years. Did a gorgeous house in Gates Mills and a whopping alimony settlement make up for being alone at forty-five, humiliated and husbandless? Sally had always been so damned independent. Maybe if she'd been a little less so she'd still have Fred Cantrell. I never could understand why Sheila thinks she's so terrific, Margaret told herself. She's chic and witty, I suppose. But she's still a fool.

"No," Margaret said now in answer to Bob's question. "I've been too busy rounding up the family and I still have Mrs. Price to go. Maybe you'd call Sally for me, Bob? Or ask Emily to?"

"I'll call her right now."

I'll bet you will, Margaret thought. Half the married men in Shaker Heights would like a legitimate excuse to call Mrs. Cantrell.

"If she wants to come over," Margaret said, "I suppose you'd better let her. *Sheila* probably would want her."

And *you* don't, you bitch, Bob said silently. All of you are secretly jealous of that nice woman who refuses to feel sorry for herself. You wish in your rotten little hearts that you had half her class. Or Sheila's. Fred Cantrell wanted out, dumb bastard, to marry that little sexpot. And Sally wouldn't try to hold a man who didn't want her. That was the difference between Fred and Sean. Sean never wanted out. Sheila would have let him go if he had. Sean wanted it both ways—a perfect wife and as many other women as he chose. And that's the way he had it, right up to the end.

He looked up Sally's number. She'll be better for Sheila now and in the days ahead than any of her so-called "women friends," he thought. Better than that overbearing Margaret, God knows. And much better than my unloving, acid-tongued wife.

Rose Price's response to Margaret's call was instant hysteria followed by indignation. Margaret tried to break the news gently to Sheila's mother, but the moment Rose grasped what was being said she began to scream and sob. The crying and shrieking lasted for a few seconds before Rose realized that she was hearing about her son-in-law's death second hand. Outrage followed.

"Why are *you* calling me? Why isn't my own daughter telling this terrible thing to her mother? Where is Sheila? Put her on the line. I want to speak to her!"

"Please, Mrs. Price. Sheila wanted to call you herself, but she's just not able to speak to anyone."

"I am not *anyone!* I'm her mother!"

"I know. Of course. We're just trying to spare her. That's why I'm notifying the family and close friends for her. I'm sure you'll want to come right away. If you'll tell me what flight you'll be on, we'll meet you."

"You put my Sheila on the phone! How do I know *she* isn't dead too and you're not telling me?"

"Don't be foolish, Mrs. Price. You know that if . . ."

"I don't know anything except that Sheila isn't telling me herself that her husband has passed away! I don't want such news from you. You get her. Now!"

Angrily, Margaret put down the phone and went to get Sheila who was lying on her bed, eyes closed.

"Sheila? Are you asleep?"

"No."

"Your mother's on the phone. She insists upon talking to you. She's afraid something has happened to you."

Sheila rose wearily. "I was wrong not to call her myself. It must seem heartless. I've been lying here worrying about Patrick and Maryanne, too. Have you reached them?"

13

"Yes. They're all on the way."

"Thank you, Margaret. I couldn't have managed it. But I should have called Mother myself. It was just that after Jean . . ."

"I understand. Everyone does."

Sheila was trembling when she picked up the phone. "Mother? I'm sorry I didn't call you myself. It's been such a shock. Are you all right?"

"How can I be all right when my only child's husband is lying dead? When I don't even know if you're alive?"

"I'm sorry," Sheila said again. Even then she realized she was doing what she'd been doing for most of her forty-seven years: apologizing to her mother, feeling guilty for no logical reason, even asking whether Rose was all right when it should have been the other way around.

Rose was slightly mollified. "You poor, poor child," she said. "Tell me how it happened."

"Didn't Margaret tell you?"

"I suppose so. I was too upset to listen."

For once, Sheila resisted. "Mother, I just can't go through that now. We'll talk when you get here. What plane will you take? Sean's parents are arriving tonight."

"Naturally, you called *them* first."

Damn it, she said silently, I don't have strength to argue with you about such pettiness. "Of course I called them first. It's their son, for God's sake!"

"Don't swear, Sheila. It's unbecoming. Particularly now."

Sheila waited.

"I'll have to call about plane schedules," Rose said finally. "I don't see how I can start out this late. It's nearly six o'clock now."

"There's a United flight that leaves from LaGuardia at eight-fifty in the morning. Sean used to take it. It gets you to Cleveland at ten-eighteen. Why don't you get that one?"

"I don't know. Maybe I should come tonight. I won't sleep a wink anyhow."

"Take the morning flight, Mother."

"Well, all right. Will someone meet me?"

"Yes, dear. Of course. Try to get some rest."

"I'll never close my eyes. And I'll be afraid to take my sleeping pill. I might miss the airplane." Rose paused. "You'd better take a pill, Sheila. The Callahans won't expect you to wait up for them."

"I'll be all right, Mother. We'll see you in the morning."

Sheila hung up. Rose hadn't really asked about her or the children. She was much too self-absorbed. Why do I expect her to change? Sheila wondered. Why can't I change myself?

14

Chapter 3

For the next few days, Sheila had the sensation of drowning in solicitude. It was ungrateful of her to feel that way, she knew. People meant well, but there were so many of them. Fortunately, or unfortunately, the house was big enough to hold them. It was a sprawling house with four bedrooms and baths on the second floor, a downstairs den with a convertible couch and an attic finished as "servants quarters." In the years since Pat and Maryanne left home, this had been converted into a private "apartment" for Tommy. They'd never had "live-in help," and it had been ideal for a boy thirsting for his first taste of privacy. She and Sean had shared the master bedroom and used the adjoining room (once Tommy's) as a dressing room and bath for Sean.

Her mother was ensconced in that room now; the senior Callahans had the third bedroom and Pat and Betty settled into the fourth. There was no need for her married son and his wife to stay in the house; they lived only fifteen minutes away. But they wanted to stay and she could think of no tactful way to refuse. Maryanne moved into Tommy's quarters and the boy bunked on the convertible in the den.

Between the "temporary live-ins" and the constant flow of visitors, Sheila was not allowed one moment alone, except to sleep. Even when she locked herself in the bathroom, Jean or Betty or Rose or even a surprisingly docile Maryanne would tap lightly on the door to ask if she was all

15

right. What did they think she was going to do—kill herself in grief? They knew better. They were simply watching over her, some with sincere concern, others with the mistaken idea that the bereaved must not be allowed to "feel lonely." The widow, convention dictated, must be kept endlessly occupied, constantly surrounded, and tenderly reassured. They had no idea what a strain it was for her to "bear up" for their sake. They fussed over her, asked her a hundred times a day whether she was "all right," and she reassured them, wanly, that she was.

Of course, in many ways, emotionally and practically, it was good that they were there. Betty was invaluable in helping Annie Winchester, the Callahans' long-time daily housekeeper, make beds and straighten up rooms. Annie even volunteered to cook during this period, and Betty assisted. Sheila was grateful. God knows how she'd have coped with this houseful of people otherwise. Patrick was calm and sensible, making her take it easy, very much the comforting doctor-son who had already developed a "bedside manner" that worked even on the woman who'd given him birth.

Maryanne was the biggest surprise. She had arrived neatly dressed (in itself a happy change) and without Rick. Most of all, she seemed to have left her hostility in Ohio City. For those three days she was the Maryanne her mother remembered—pretty, soft-spoken, and gentle. It won't last, Sheila told herself. When this is over she'll go back to that futile, inexplicable life she's chosen. But for now it was good to have her daughter near her, sharing the loss. She hoped, knowing the chances were slim, that Maryanne would stay on after it was all over. If they could only spend a little time together, quietly, perhaps they'd find some kind of communication. Perhaps, as two adult women, they could come to understand each other.

The children were shocked and saddened by their father's death, concerned for Sheila's well-being. But they'd go away again, their mother knew: Pat and Betty back to their jobs and their own circle of young friends; Maryanne to whatever self-destructive pattern she had chosen for whatever reasons. In a few days only Tommy would be left. Tommy who was the most silent, the most apparently grief-stricken of them all. He stayed out of the house most of the day, sat with them at the funeral home on Tuesday and Wednesday evening at the prescribed seven to nine visiting hours, and then retreated immediately to the den with Mr. Magoo, the lovable sheepdog who was his best friend and bedmate.

Jean and Bill Callahan were—there was no other word for it— magnificent. It was, Sheila decided, more than their deep religious faith that sustained them. They were strong and disciplined people, products of generations of good breeding with a sense of fitness and dignity. Their sorrow was all the more pathetic for their efforts not to burden their son's widow with their own grief. Sheila felt very close to them. She

16

sensed that they instinctively knew Sean had been a trial to her. But they also knew that she'd loved him and been right for him. They were grateful to her. Not that she wanted gratitude but it was good to know they could accept their son's frailties, as she had, and still feel love for him, as she had.

Her own mother was something else. Rose had been outspoken in her opposition to Sheila's choice of a husband from the very first, and over the years she'd seen no reason to change her views. Until now. Now that he was dead, the son-in-law she'd called weak, impious, irresponsible and unfaithful suddenly became, in her mind, a fine figure of a man, a devoted father, and a wonderful husband. It was Rose, not Sheila, who wore unrelieved black and sat holding court in the funeral parlor, tearfully accepting the pat expressions of condolence from Sean's friends. It was Rose who had to be helped into St. Dominic's for the mass and who seemed closest to collapse at the graveside in Calvary Cemetery.

Saddened and distraught as she was, Sheila could not help being fascinated by Rose's performance, especially in contrast to Jean Callahan's own quiet sorrow. Watching her mother, Sheila realized Rose was enjoying the attention, totally involved with her prominent role as the widow's mother, making the most of this brief moment in the spotlight. I know it's unconscious, her daughter thought. She'd be horrified if she knew she was relishing her part in this drama. How dull her life must be. How much she must need to feel important. But how irritating it is to watch her carry on as though she'd lost the person she loved most in all the world. Hating herself for it, Sheila said as much the day after the funeral, after the Callahans had gone back to Florida and Pat and Betty had returned to their own apartment.

Sheila and Rose were alone in the living room. Tommy was off somewhere and Maryanne was packing the few things she'd brought, preparatory to returning to her life with Rick. There'd been no question of her staying. That had been established the day before, quickly and abruptly.

Rose, still dressed in deep mourning, sat in the big chair by the fireplace, the one Sean liked when he was home. For once she was not talking, but she sighed regularly and deeply, occasionally wiping her eyes with a black-bordered handkerchief. Suddenly Sheila couldn't stand it.

"Mother, I don't mean to be unkind, but why are you taking on so about Sean's death? You never liked him. Dying hasn't made him a different man."

Mrs. Price was genuinely shocked. "Sheila! How can you say such things? Sean had his little ways but he was a good person at heart. He was good to you and the children. He was loved and admired by his friends. He was a respected member of the community. I was proud to have such a son-in-law."

Sheila spoke very softly and deliberately. "Your son-in-law," she said with a trace of irony, "was an exciting, provocative, and popular man. In his own way he did love the children and me. But you seem to have forgotten, Mother, that in twenty-seven years you and Sean scarcely exchanged a civil word. You were never proud of him in life. Why has he become a saint in death?"

Rose stared at her. "I can't believe this is my daughter speaking. Her with a husband not cold in his grave! Sheila, are you so hard, so unfeeling? Don't you grieve for your husband, God rest his soul? Didn't you love him, the way I loved your father?"

"Yes, I loved him. And sometimes I hated him. I'm going to miss him terribly but I can't beatify him because he's dead. Sean was what he was, Mother. Wonderfully gay and attractive, glamorous, glorious to know, and hell to live with. I lived with him for twenty-seven years and I'd have lived with him for another twenty-seven if that was the way it had been intended. But for most of those years I also saw him as he was—immature, selfish, and thoughtless, for all his charm. He wasn't as bad as you always made him out to be. But he wasn't as perfect as you're painting him now. Don't do it, Mother, please. It's degrading to you, insulting to Sean, and painful to me."

Rose burst into tears. "How can you hurt me so? Don't you know I can't sleep at nights worrying about what's going to happen to you? I know what it's like to be a widow. It's a terrible, lonely life, Sheila. How do you think a mother can rest, knowing her only child is all alone in the world? Do you think there'll be a moment's peace for me from now on?"

Sheila was silent. Rose did not see that she was thinking of herself. *Her* worries. *Her* sleepless nights. Her own self-pity. She'd never understand any of that and Sheila would never be cruel enough to tell her. She's seventy-five years old, Sheila thought. A different generation. One that wasn't brought up on Freud and Philip Wylie.

"I'm sorry, Mother. I know how concerned you are."

I'm doing it again, Sheila realized. I seem to have spent my whole life saying I'm sorry for things that I have no reason to be apologetic about. I've lived with this ridiculous sense of obligation to everyone. To Mother. To Sean. Even to my children. They all, deliberately or not, manage to make me feel guilty, as though somehow I've failed them. I'm never again going to feel everything is my fault. I've said my last "I'm sorry," unless there's really something for me to be sorry about. She waited for Rose to accept what would be the final *mea culpa*. And Rose did. She dried her eyes and managed a brave, forgiving smile.

"It's all right, darling. I know you wouldn't say those terrible things unless you were so upset. It's all part of your grief. I know how much you loved Sean and how lost you are without him. Just the way I was when your sainted father died. We're exactly alike, Sheila dear. I understand what you're going through."

18

No, you don't understand, Sheila thought. And we're not the least bit alike. You bossed my father, nagged him, probably suffered his lovemaking as your duty. I suppose, in your way, you loved him, and you *have* been lost these past ten years with no one to humor you and cater to you as that dear, patient man did. But you never had a marriage like mine, stormy, frustrating, unpredictable. Sean and I battled. You and Dad only quarreled now and then, and most of the fighting was on your side. My father was faithful, tolerant and a little frightened of you, probably. He left you modestly but amply provided for, which was expected of him and important to him. It was stupid of me not to find out more about our finances. I don't know how, or if, Sean has provided for Tommy and me. But I know that he could lift me to glorious heights with his passion and drive me to despair with his headstrong ways and his ridiculous dreams. I'll miss him. God, yes, in spite of his faults I'll miss him. I'll miss his lovemaking and his laughter and his big, boisterous physical presence. But I'll live, Mother. I'll find my way without him. Don't identify my thinking or my widowhood with yours. They're very different.

"We're going to be all right, Tommy and I," Sheila said finally. "Pat and Maryanne will be nearby. And Sean and I had good friends like the Rosses and Sally Cantrell. And of course there's always Terry and Margaret." She paused. "I know you're anxious to get back to your own home, Mother. Don't worry about leaving us. We're going to manage. Everyone has to. You know that firsthand."

Rose looked surprised and hurt. "I'd planned to stay on a while. I thought you'd need my help and I was perfectly willing. Of course if you don't want me . . ."

"It isn't that I don't want you," Sheila lied compassionately. "It's just that we all have to pick up our own lives again. You have yours in New York. You'd be miserable in Cleveland without your church work and your bridge club and the friends you've known all your life. And I have to find out where I stand. Bob Ross is waiting to sit down with me and tell me exactly what Sean left. He has a copy of Sean's will and he's a good lawyer. It's a blessing to know that he's also such a good friend."

Rose sniffed. "Bob Ross. I never understood why Sean had him as a lawyer. Seems to me he'd have been better off with his own brother."

"Sometimes it's easier not to deal with family. At least that's what Sean thought. And Terry and I agreed. Emotion can cloud even a good legal mind like Terry's. Bob was almost like a brother to Sean anyway. Without the blood ties."

"And I suppose that nasty Emily Ross was like a sister."

"She may not be endearing," Sheila admitted, "but she's been a good friend, too."

"I never got that impression."

"Mother, I don't know what you're talking about."

"Sheila, you watch out for that woman. She's no friend. She's jealous of you. You be careful about seeing Bob Ross. She'll think you're trying to take her husband."

"Mother! That's absurd! Sean and I were with Bob and Emily all the time. They were our best friends!"

Rose hesitated. "I didn't want to say this to you, but it's my duty. I've heard rumors every time I've visited you these past years. I know Emily Ross was crazy about Sean. I wouldn't be surprised if she even tried to get him to sleep with her."

Sheila began to laugh.

"I fail to see what's so funny," Rose said.

"It's funny because if Sean had wanted to 'sleep with her,' as you put it, he would have. She wouldn't have had to try very hard. She wasn't his type, Mother. Nor he hers. I doubt any man is but Bob. Emily may be hard to take but she has a bright, attractive husband, a nice house, two grown kids. She wouldn't have thought twice about Sean as a lover. And she certainly has no reason to be jealous of me."

"Hasn't she? She's plain and you're pretty. You're unattached now and personally I don't think that husband of hers is in love with her and she knows it. You mark my word. Emily Ross is dangerous."

Sheila sighed. "Mother, you're wrong. And I really don't want to talk about it any more, if you don't mind."

"Very well. You're a grown woman."

Yes, I am, Sheila thought. So won't you please treat me like one?

Before the girl left, Sheila and Maryanne did talk, though it was a short and basically unsatisfactory exchange, with Sheila sitting on Tommy's bed, watching her daughter toss the few clothes she'd brought into the canvas duffel bag she used as a suitcase. Somehow the scruffy zippered tote seemed symbolic. There was a beautiful matched set of Vuitton luggage on the shelf of the closet in Maryanne's old room. It had been an extravagant gift to her three Christmases ago when Sheila and Sean had thought she'd want a trip to Europe after graduation from college. Maryanne hadn't wanted any of it. Not the expensive luggage or the trip or any of the "status symbols" that were important to her parents. By that time, in her last year of school, she was into a new group of friends and viewpoints. Two weeks after graduation she moved out of the house. And a month after that she moved in with Rick.

Sean had greeted the defection with outrage and threats that she'd never see a penny from him, no matter if she was starving. Sheila had tried to understand, which was impossible, and to reason, which was futile. Two years later she was still trying, with the same lack of success. She had continued to see Maryanne for lunch whenever she could, choosing a "neutral place," some anonymous restaurant. She'd been terrified that they would lose all touch with their only daughter. Sean saw her only once, on that distasteful evening she'd brought Rick to the house. He never had contact with her again, and he was bitter about her until the day he died.

Watching her now, Sheila tried once more to get through the barrier that was more than an age difference.

"You've been wonderful these last few days, Maryanne. I hate to see you go."

There was a fraction of hesitation before Maryanne said, "Tommy needs his own room back."

Was there a hint of regret in her voice, Sheila wondered? Would she welcome some face-saving way to come home?

"Yours is still here." Sheila spoke carefully. Please say you'll stay, she silently begged. Please get out of that world before something terrible happens to you. I won't ask you to come back out of pity for me, or because your father is no longer around, angry and unforgiving. I want you to come for your own sake and, yes, for mine as well. I want us to redis-cover the kind of mother-daughter relationship we once had. Or what I thought we had. But it was no use.

"Sorry, Mom."

In spite of herself, Sheila couldn't resist. "What is it you're searching for, Maryanne? What kind of life do you really want? What's made ours so distasteful?"

Maryanne stopped putting things in the bag and turned to face her mother.

"I just don't care about the same things you do," she said kindly. "I don't want a husband and a proper house and children and country clubs and committees and community living. It's phony and pointless. The same people. The same weekend plans and vacation trips and holiday gatherings. It's mediocre, Mother. And I detest mediocrity. It's stifling and dull. Not for you, maybe. You're used to it. For you it's safe and comfortable and secure. But for me it's zombieland."

Sheila was angry. "That seems to me a highly opinionated and quite ig-norant point of view. How do you presume to know what makes me feel safe and comfortable and secure? How do you know I've ever felt that way?"

"Haven't you? All the trappings of middle class are here, Mom. They've been here since Day One."

"Does that make them bad?"

"Not for you. For me. I want to be free. I like not knowing what to-morrow will bring."

Sheila didn't answer. She couldn't say that all the outward manifes-tations of security were a facade. She'd never felt truly secure in her whole married life. Maryanne didn't know that one day the Callahans were rolling in money and the next Sean had lost it all in some ridiculous investment or harebrained scheme. She'd kept that from the children, never wanting them to feel threatened in any way. Yes, Maryanne was right. Sheila would have loved to have felt safe and comfortable. Maryanne would have been highly surprised if she knew that her mother never had.

"Oh, I know Dad was a bad boy about other women," the girl went on, almost casually. "But he still had the instincts of a suburban householder. He never really wanted to be free, any more than you did. If either of you had, you'd have been divorced long ago." She half-smiled. "And don't tell me about your religion, Mom. That wouldn't have stopped you or Dad if you hadn't been perfectly content in this rich little rut."

"And your way is better," Sheila said, denying it by her tone. "A cheap apartment, an occasional job, sloppy clothes, a totally unstructured life that doesn't seem to be going anywhere."

"You forgot to mention a horny, uneducated Polack," Maryanne said, sarcasm in her voice.

"That, too. Is that unrealistic, irresponsible attitude, your precious 'freedom,' Maryanne? We're in the 1970s. I thought flower children were out of fashion."

"I don't give a damn about 'fashion.' It's meaningless. Everything's meaningless. The whole damned world is without value."

"But not without values, darling. People still want accomplishment and pride in themselves and love. Most of all, love."

"At least I have that."

"No," Sheila said. "I don't think you have. Not with Rick, anyway. Sex is what you have. Not love. At this point in your life, the only love you have is here."

There was no answer. Sheila rose slowly from Tommy's bed. "Thank you for these last three days, anyway."

"Are you going to be all right?"

"Yes," Sheila said. "I'm going to be fine."

Chapter 4

She hadn't been sure at all that she was going to be fine, emotionally or financially, and when Bob Ross came over the next night after dinner her worst suspicions about the latter were confirmed.

After all the legal gobbledegook, the situation was quite evident. She had twenty-five thousand dollars in life insurance, two thousand dollars in a joint checking account, and a house she owned free and clear. Sean's estate was like Sean's life, an unrealistic legacy that mirrored the attitude of a man who was sure that tomorrow would never come.

"In a word," Sheila said, trying to sound unworried, "I'm in lousy shape."

"Well, it could be worse," Bob said. "but I can't say it's rosy. After all the debts and taxes are settled, you won't have much money."

"But at least I have the house."

"True. You can live rent free. Except for taxes and upkeep, of course. That takes cash. And no matter how cleverly you invest it, the interest on what Sean left won't bring in enough for your needs and Tommy's."

"Should I sell the house?"

"I wouldn't rush into that, Sheila. The market for big places like this one is very soft. Besides, it'll be harder because there's no mortgage."

"Harder? I thought it was *good* not to have a mortgage. My God, Bob, I was brought up to think that burning the mortgage was the biggest thing in everybody's life!"

"Not any more, unfortunately. Anybody who buys nowadays is looking for an existing mortgage at a low rate. They don't want to start financing at the present high ones."

"But didn't Sean know that? He was in the real estate business!"

Bob just looked at her. Knowing Sean, it was a stupid question.

"All right," she said. "Don't remind me. Sean never thought about things like that in relation to himself. Where his own life was concerned, he wasn't a very practical man, was he? And that's the understatement of the week."

"I tried to talk to him about it, Sheila. Many times. I felt a responsibility as his lawyer, as well as his friend."

"And he told you to buzz off—or words to that effect."

Bob smiled. "Something like that."

"What am I going to do, Bob? Can we sell the business?"

"We'll try. But don't get your hopes up. There's nothing to sell except 'good will' and a few secondhand desks. Of course, we'll get out of the lease on the office right away. And I guess we can raise a few bucks on Sean's Mercedes-Benz. You won't need a second car and you have the station wagon."

"It's peanuts, isn't it?"

"Yes, dear, I'm afraid it is. Can Sean's family help?"

"Jean and Bill? No. They just about get by themselves. And besides I wouldn't ask them."

"What about Terry? He's doing well."

She shook her head. "He can't be expected to be responsible for his brother's widow and his young nephew. It wouldn't be fair. I know he'd do it, but even if *he* didn't mind, Margaret would resent it and I wouldn't blame her. In her place, I'd probably resent it too. Besides, Bob, I don't want charity. I'm forty-seven years old and able-bodied. I'm not trained to do anything, but God knows I should be able to keep Tommy and me fed and housed and clothed. I'll have to get a job. Some kind. Any kind. Even if it doesn't pay much, it'll be enough to buy groceries for Tommy and me." She paused. "I'll have to take Tommy out of University School, won't I?"

Bob tried hard not to show how sorry he felt. Goddamn Sean Callahan! If he'd only listened, just once, when I tried to give him some advice.

"Afraid so," Bob said now. "But Shaker Heights High is a good school. Always has been. One of the finest in the country, scholastically speaking."

"But what about college for Tommy?"

"Honey, that's three years away. Who knows what can happen by then? You may be a big, successful career woman. Or, more likely, you'll have remarried. You're a beautiful woman, Sheila. I don't anticipate you'll spend the rest of your life alone."

Even now, her humor came through. "You wouldn't be so sure of that if you'd been talking to Sally Cantrell. She's much more beautiful than I, childless and richer. And since her divorce she swears she hasn't met a single man who isn't married, unsufferably spoiled, or gay." Sheila smiled. "Anyway, that's the last thing I'm thinking of now. Maybe ever. The first thing is to find work. Any ideas, Bob?"

"I'll check around. There are bound to be openings. Seems to me all the lawyers I know are constantly looking for secretaries. Would a job like that interest you?"

"It would interest me, but unfortunately I couldn't qualify. Sean and I were married when I was twenty, you know. I worked at odd jobs a couple of years after I got out of high school, mostly selling at Lord & Taylor."

"I thought you met Sean when you were working in a real estate office in New York and he was in town for a convention."

"I did. But it was just a temporary job as a typist. I only had it a few weeks and I don't know how I ever got it. I don't, for sure, know how I *kept* it! I was a terrible typist. I think the man who hired me thought I had good legs. Anyway, Sean came along and you know him. He never waited for anything he wanted. A long-distance romance wasn't for him. Before I knew what happened I was married, living in Cleveland, and pregnant with Patrick. The rest, as they say, is history."

Bob was quiet. "I'm not going to be hypocritical and tell you not to worry. You know you have problems. But you'll make it, Sheila. We both know that. You'll get a job. And meantime, if you need a little something to tide you over for a few months . . ."

She interrupted. "That's dear of you, but no thanks. Not unless we're starving. And we won't starve. Not if I have to sell my lily-white body. Assuming anybody would want it."

"I don't think that would be a problem, but I hardly think it's a solution. Not for you."

"I'm only trying to be funny. And making a damned bad job of it, I must say. I'll tell you the truth. I'm scared to death. I never felt so confused and helpless in my whole life."

"Sheila, dear, you have friends. Don't forget that. Not just Terry and Margaret and Emily and me. *Lots* of people who love you and who will help you every way they can."

"I know. And I appreciate it."

(So much for you, Mother. Emily Ross *is* a friend. Her husband just said so.)

But it was not Emily or Margaret to whom she turned when she needed another woman with whom to talk out her problems. It was Sally Cantrell. And it was not just because Sally was her best friend or because she, too, was husbandless. Sally had that rare combination of good sense and an upbeat attitude toward life that made people feel good just to be around her. Even Sean had liked Sally, and he never cared much for any of Sheila's women friends unless he was sexually attracted to them. No doubt he was attracted to Sally, but she was one of the few who would have laughed at him if he'd suggested anything. She was much too loyal to Sheila to go to bed with her husband. Sean knew that. He probably knew it so well he never even tried. And besides Sally's sense of loyalty, Sheila had always had a hunch that she was the only other one who saw through Sean, the only one who recognized how immature and vain he was. She never came right out and said that to Sheila, but somehow Sheila knew and was strangely glad that someone else was not blindly taken in by all that charm. It was a crazy kind of thing to take comfort in, but Sean Callahan's wife did then. And his widow did now.

She remembered conversations she and Sally had had a couple of years ago when the Cantrells had been divorced. Fred's radical move after twenty years of marriage had been a juicy topic from downtown Cleveland to Chagrin Falls. His male friends discussed it over steak sandwiches in Marie Schreiber's Tavern, shaking their heads in amazement that the sonofabitch had the guts to do it. They were slightly envious of his courage and more envious of his money. Most of them stayed married out of habit and the awareness that they couldn't afford divorce with its double household expenses and alimony. Fred Cantrell could handle both an unsettling change in life style and the financial drain that went with it. They expressed reluctant admiration over their prelunch martinis and said well, hell, a man only had one life. Might as well get what he wanted out of it. If he could.

The wives in the Cantrells' circle were indignant, not because they cared that much for Sally but because they felt threatened, as though a single defection could set a trend. The consensus was that Fred was making a fool of himself. Nearly fifty years old and losing his head over some sexy little thing half his age! There certainly was such a thing as male menopause, they agreed. He'd regret it. Give him a year, six months maybe, and he'd be wishing he was back in Gates Mills where he belonged.

They were also much nicer to their husbands for a few days after they heard about the Cantrells; more attractively dressed in the evening and more accommodating in bed. The men, aware and amused, enjoyed these "second honeymoons" while they lasted, knowing full well that things would soon return to normal. "Normal" was a wife in shirt and pants instead of a slinky housecoat when they got home at night. Normal was getting out the ice yourself, instead of finding a set-up cocktail tray. Normal was sex once a week, maybe twice, with a routine partner who didn't go for those "weird practices."

Through all the speculation and nervousness, news of which inevitably

26

reached Sally, she said nothing to any of them. Except to Sheila. To her friend she talked freely, with no great bitterness but with a degree of harshness and almost detached understanding.

"I don't hate him, you know," Sally had said, "but I don't intend to make it easy for him. Except for having a husband, I don't plan to make any great changes in the way I live. I'm keeping this house and the help and the country-club membership and all the other amenities. I have no intention of crawling into a shell. I'll entertain and travel and do exactly as I did when I was married." She stopped abruptly. "Damn it, Sheila, who do I think I'm kidding? I hate the idea of being divorced. I'm forty-five years old and I thought my life was planned till death did us part. He's made me feel inadequate in some crazy way I can't fathom."

"You're not the one who's inadequate," Sheila had said. "Fred is. He's scared of aging. He's trying to reassure himself that he's still attractive to other women." She paused. "Sean has the same fears."

"I know. But he'll never be so drastic about it. Hell, I could have forgiven Fred some little fling. Even a series of them. Men need that, especially in their middle years, for their flagging egos. What I can't really accept is his stupidity. He could have had it like Sean—both ways—the comfortable, easy life with me and the clandestine little side excursions with girls young enough to be his daughters. But not Fred. He had to advertise his virility. That's what it amounts to, you know."

"I suppose it does," Sheila had answered, thinking of Sean. "Not that he had to. There aren't any secrets in the Cleveland suburbs."

Sally had laughed, a mirthless, disenchanted laugh. "No, there are no secrets. Everybody knows who's sleeping with whom. But the reaction is a kind of resigned tolerance on all sides. Like that's the way it's supposed to be. Even the wives who know it's happening to them pretend it isn't because it's not publicly announced. It's only when somebody like Fred ups and walks out that women get nervous about their own marriages. Until then you think it could never happen to you. Like a car accident or cancer. When it happens close to home, you get the jitters. I'm seeing it already, Sheila. Some of the people Fred and I saw constantly are already backing off from me. The women are, I mean. It's not only that I'm an 'extra woman.' I'm a menace in their midst. Presumably available to their husbands. And most of all I'm a constant, disquieting reminder that the 'dalliance disease' sometimes can be fatal." She lit a cigarette. "Sometimes I think about moving away from here. Starting over someplace else where the natives are friendly. But then I think, why should I? This is my home. I like it here. Besides, where would I run to? Just be glad you have Sean, kiddo. He may not be perfect, but as they say about mountains, he's *there*."

Driving across the flat, hot Ohio countryside toward Sally's house, Sheila remembered that conversation and others that were more or less

27

repetitions of it. Well, Sean wasn't there any more. He hadn't divorced her but he'd left. Even more irrevocably than Fred Cantrell, though not by choice. Maybe in a way it's easier to be widowed than divorced, Sheila thought. The humiliation isn't there and perhaps the sadness is less hard to bear, knowing there is no way you could have prevented it, and knowing there is no hope you could ever get him back. Divorcées grieve, too. Though the ones with pride, like Sally, never let the world know.

Aside from herself, she doubted that anyone knew how Sally felt. She was always so chic, so quick with the repartee, so able to laugh at anything, including herself. She even talked about her divorce dispassionately and easily in public. Not the way she talked about it to Sheila.

"I'm part of the new social syndrome called 'the middle-aged split,'" Sheila had heard her say at parties. "Have you kept up with the latest statistics? My dears, there's an absolutely *alarming* new outbreak of divorce among couples who've been married twenty or thirty years! It's the very 'in' thing to do. Personally, I think in time there won't be any such thing as marriage. Or if there is, it will come with a five-year-option clause, renewable upon review, like an employment contract."

Such flippancy amused the men and angered the women who made her pay for her irreverence by inviting her to fewer and fewer parties, excluding her, almost pointedly, from the social gatherings in which she and Fred would automatically have been included. Sometimes Sheila thought Sally deliberately provoked these results. Once, shyly, she even voiced her suspicions.

"Of course I do it on purpose," Sally had said. "It's part of the rotten side of my nature. I'm amused when I see all those smug, sure-of-themselves, wifely faces go blank when I rattle off that nonsense about late-in-life divorce. Not that it isn't true, but it probably won't happen to them. I just can't resist stirring up their complacent souls now and then. They get nervous indigestion every time this piece of living proof walks into their living rooms. That's why I get asked out less and less in our little closed-corporation community."

"But you're punishing *yourself*," Sheila had protested. "Maybe your first thinking was right, Sally. Maybe you should move away."

Sally shook her head. "No way. Look, luv, a fifth wheel is useless most of the time but every spare tire has its day. Who knows? One of these inflated marriages may go flat and I'll be right on the scene to jack up the lonely husband. That sounds terrible to you, doesn't it? I think it's realistic. I'm not out to wreck anybody's home. You know that. You probably also know that half the righteous husbands in our set have been eager to offer consolation on a temporary basis. I'm not buying that, either. But what sense is there in my moving away from the few good friends I do have—like you—and trying to make new ones? Where do you go looking for eligible men? Nope. I'm standing pat. I have no money worries and my chance for remarriage is better here than anywhere. If there is any chance at all."

Turning the station wagon into the gate marked "Cantrell," Sheila felt a surge of affection and admiration for Sally. She had never found her friend's reasoning cold-blooded. She'd always thought that if the same thing happened to her—if one day Sean got really intrigued with one of his affairs and wanted out of their marriage—she'd do just as Sally had: Stay where she was and not uproot her life and the children's in some frantic search for a "new existence." But she'd known it would never happen that way with Sean and her. He really loved the comfort of his home. He'd never elect to leave. Besides, Sheila thought wryly, he couldn't have afforded it.

She hadn't seriously considered that Sean would die or that she would now, a week later, be turning to anyone for serious advice about her own empty life. Sally had been marvelous during the unreal days after Sean's death. She'd arrived that first evening and (deliberately?) thanked Bob Ross for "calling her and sparing Margaret the trouble." She'd been good with Maryanne who liked her and had even won over Rose who had always regarded her with suspicion. Through it all, she'd stayed close to Sheila, never intruding with knocks on the bathroom door, but letting her know, just by her calm presence, that hers was a shoulder for leaning and, when Sheila was ready, an ear for listening.

They talked now over lunch in Sally's big, handsomely equipped kitchen with its wall of gleaming copper pots and its big windows half-covered with hanging containers of ferns and geraniums. The cook served them on delicate Spode dishes, leaving extra iced tea in a Waterford pitcher before she discreetly vanished. It was all gracious and unpretentious, eating in the kitchen, and yet every detail bespoke elegance and money. For a moment, Sheila felt a pang of envy. I must be terribly mercenary, she thought. I'm saddened by the loss of Sean, but I'm consumed with worry about how I'm going to survive. If only my future were as secure as Sally's.

She explained to her friend exactly where she stood, financially. "What am I going to do, Sally? There's practically no money. I have the house, and though God knows Tommy and I will rattle around in all that space, it looks like it'll be cheaper than any other place I could live. Besides, Bob Ross says it's no time to sell." She paused. "And I'm like you. Even though I'm 'transplanted' from New York, this is my home after twenty-seven years. I don't want to leave it. It's Tommy's, too. He's feeling displaced enough, losing his father. I don't want to take him away from the neighborhood he feels secure in. Terry thinks I'm wrong. He says I should get rid of the house, invest the cash, and take a small apartment."

"Terry Callahan is a pompous ass," Sally said, "Even Sean knew that. He wouldn't even use his brother as his lawyer. All that nonsense about 'emotional ties' that they gave us as an excuse was just so much family face-saving! You listen to Bob, Sheila. I'm sure he's right. Trying to sell in this market would be asinine. Besides, people have the damnedest ideas that changing the place you live is the magic answer to everything, as though new surroundings erase old memories. That 'fresh start' business is baloney. Your life has been uprooted enough. You don't need to compound the confusion by going into a strange situation. There's comfort in familiarity, my girl. Take it from one who knows."

Hearing her own instinctive feelings confirmed gave Sheila a sense of relief. She wanted to stay in the big, sprawling house. It was as though she couldn't remember ever living anywhere else. Even as a girl in New York she'd never liked apartments. The impersonality of boxes of rooms within other boxes of rooms always depressed her. She'd never really admitted it until now, but Sean's lyrical description of the "wide open spaces" where they would have their own house and garden, where they would drive cars instead of taking subways, where their children could bike to schools and country clubs and Scout meetings—these things were not the reason for marrying him so quickly but there was no question that they nudged along her decision. She'd loved Sean, that was primary. But she'd also loved the picture of life he'd painted. And for the most part it had come true. She'd had all those things and more. She'd run her house, cared for her children, and still had time left over for what Sean called her "do-gooder" activities. She served on the boards of the Cleveland Clinic and the Cleveland Playhouse and was active in The League of Women Voters. Over the raised-eyebrow objections of Rose Price and the senior Callahans, she'd worked at the Christmas Boutique that raised money for Planned Parenthood. She'd wanted to join the Ludlow or Lomond associations which were dedicated to keeping a racial balance in Shaker Heights by encouraging white families not to move out as black ones moved in. But Sean had objected. "Not that it's a bad idea," he'd said. "God knows we don't want this to become a black community with property values going to hell. But having my wife take an active part in anything so controversial could backfire on my business, Sheil. I'd rather you didn't get mixed up in that."

So she hadn't. There'd been plenty else to keep her busy. She'd have to give up all those things now, she supposed. What strength she had left after a day on a job (assuming, please God, she could get one!) she'd need for housecleaning and cooking. She'd have to let Annie go. Just as she'd have to let her country-club membership go. And Tommy's private school. And Lord knows what else.

"Well, at least I can try to hang on to the house," she said now. "But wherever I live, I'm going to need income. I don't even know where to begin to look for work." She frowned. "Even Sean, the perpetual optimist, could see a recession coming . . . prices and unemployment rising.

Costs are up and jobs are down . . . like the Bronx and the Battery and the world's a helluva town." She managed to smile. "He considered the economy a personal affront, rather than a national problem. At least in the last year of his life there were no wildcat schemes to eat up our capital. But that's only because there was no capital to eat up." Sheila paused. "I sound terrible, don't I? Sean gave us everything we wanted, always. It's rotten of me to blame him now."

Sally was silent. Sean's widow had every right to blame him for his extravagance, his lack of foresight. But there was nothing to be gained by dwelling on that now. Let her remember the high spots, Sally thought. God knows she had enough low ones. She tried to sound optimistic and efficient.

"Let's run over your skills," she said. "At least that should give us a direction."

Worried as she was, Sheila had to laugh. "My skills? They're absolutely wonderful! Let's see. I can drive a car, clean a house, darn socks, play fair golf and bad bridge, sit on committees, cook a gourmet meal and, according to my husband, be quite good in bed. I also can read and write and nearly manage a checkbook if I concede that the discrepancy between the bank's figures and mine will inevitably prove *them* right. Oh yes, I was a salesperson. And a typist once, for about two weeks, twenty-seven years ago. I doubt that my proficiency, nonexistent then, has improved with disuse. In a word, my friend, I can't really do a damned thing. Except I *have* to."

Sally looked thoughtful. Sheila was right. She'd have little chance of getting an office job in competition with all those pert young things with their up-to-the-minute skills. Maybe she could be some kind of receptionist, but Sally had heard somewhere that even receptionists these days were required to type well. Cooking. That's what Sheila did best.

"Cooking," she repeated aloud. "You're a superb cook. The best meals in Cleveland are served in your house."

Sheila looked at her. "Are you suggesting I hire out as a cook?"

"No. Of course not. But how about a cooking school? A real gourmet number with the classes held in your own kitchen? I'll bet we could get eight or ten women right around here to sign up tomorrow! And the thing would build. I'm sure it would. There's nothing like it in this area that I know of. What do you think? Isn't it a *brainstorm?*"

For a moment Sheila was tempted, but then she shook her head. "It would be great. I'd never even have to leave the house. But it's too risky, Sally. I need the security of a job where the paycheck comes in every week, not the nervousness of wondering where the next batch of students is going to come from. It might work, but it might not. And I don't dare make even the minimum investment in equipment and things I'd need to handle eight or ten women. No, it's a *real* job I need. Probably my best chance is selling. At least I did that in New York when I was a kid. I have some experience in that area, antiquated as it may be."

"Selling what?"

"I don't know. Anything. Clothes, probably."

"Sheila, you can't! Have you any idea what it would be like to be on your feet all day in a store, lugging dresses in and out of fitting rooms, putting up with rude, thankless women in dirty girdles?"

"You make it sound so attractive."

"Well, dammit, I'll bet it is just like that!"

"Nevertheless, I think it's my only option. Maybe I won't have to sell clothes. Maybe I can sell cosmetics or household stuff. Anyway, stores are always advertising for help. With my lack of qualifications I'd better go where the opportunities are. I'll try Higbee's first."

Sally's voice was practically a wail. "But you'll have to go downtown every day!"

"Lots of people do. The Rapid Transit is only a block from my house."

"But you won't make enough money to live on!"

"Sally, dear, I won't make a lot of money, but surely enough to keep Tommy and me alive. That's exactly what I have to face at the moment."

Her friend grasped at a last straw. "Maybe you could take over Sean's real-estate business and run it."

"No chance, dear. I don't know a thing about real estate. I wouldn't even know how to get a license. Besides, Bob thinks we may be able to sell the 'good will' to somebody." She leaned over and hugged her friend. "Thanks, Sal, for listening. Getting a selling job has been in the back of my mind for days, but I needed to explore it. I don't see anything else I could hope to do. Let's just hope this works."

"Look. Don't rush into anything. If you need some money . . ."

Sheila shook her head. "You and Bob. You're both so generous. But borrowing from my friends isn't the answer. I will admit, though, it's a big load off my mind to know there are people I could turn to in case of some real emergency, like sickness. I appreciate it. I really do. More than I can tell you."

It isn't fair! Sally thought, watching her friend drive away. She gave so much and ended up with so little. It would have been better if Sean had gone off like Fred did. At least he'd have had to support his ex-wife. And he'd have managed. He'd always managed to get what *he* wanted—the expensive cars, the golf clubs, the trips. He was strictly a live-for-today fella. He'd have gotten up alimony and child support too, if that's what it took for his gratification.

"You really were a bastard, Sean," she said aloud. And then she laughed at her own foolishness. "But you had style. Nobody could deny that."

Chapter 5

Fifteen is an awkward age, especially for "privileged" children. They are neither babies nor adults, midway in adolescence, experiencing "grown-up" feelings, emotionally, intellectually, and sexually, yet bound by lingering infantile selfishness, bewilderment, and the limited experiences of a short, sheltered span of life.

Tommy Callahan was at this typical stage of development in the summer of 1973, and though his father's unexpected death was something he understood and accepted (his generation saw a lot of dying, violent and otherwise, on TV screens and in PG-rated films), the effect of it on him and his future left him frightened and insecure. He was sorry his dad was dead, though he would have been sorrier had it been Sheila. He'd always felt closer to her. Sean had been so overpowering, so goddam *male*. Not that Tommy was effeminate, but he'd known for a long time that he'd never be the football hero his father had envisaged, or the race-car driver or even the scratch golfer Sean expected. His father was not a passive member of the household, like the fathers of most of the kids he knew. Sean yelled a lot and demanded things *his* way and sometimes Tommy wanted to yell back. But now that he was gone, Tommy had a sinking feeling that the props had been knocked out from under his life. His and his mother's.

With unusual insight, he sometimes wished that his parents had treated

33

him *more* as a child than they did. He supposed it came from his being born so much later than the others, this habit of speaking to him almost as a third and equal member of the household. He'd always felt that so much was expected of him, not just physically, in terms of his father's visions, but in the kind of understanding and adjustment they seemed to take for granted he possessed. Tommy knew, better than they, that he was a kid, with a kid's limitations. Most of his friends' parents were maybe ten years younger than his own. Most of his friends were the eldest children in the family, not the baby, as he was, with a grown-up married brother and a crazy sister who acted like some nutty eighteen-year-old girl instead of a twenty-four-year-old woman.

To him, Sean had seemed old. In his fifties. And even Sheila, at forty-seven, was a long way from being young. They'd been in their *thirties* when he was *born!* Most of his friends' mothers and fathers were around that age now. They didn't expect their fifteen-year-olds to act like men. Sean and Sheila always had. And Sheila still did. She'd made that clear right after everybody left, sitting him down and explaining their financial problems, saying she'd have to go find a job, taking it for granted (as usual) that he'd comprehend their new circumstances.

In a way, Tommy thought, I guess it's a compliment that she treats me like a grown-up. The boys at University School were always griping that their folks treated them like dumb babies. Some of the boys were, in fact, far more advanced than Tommy. A lot of them weren't virgins, as he was. Some of them smoked grass and drank liquor while Tommy had never gotten further than a few cigarettes and a couple of glasses of beer at parties. Yet they figured Tom's parents were a lot more hip than theirs.

It was goofy. His folks expected him to be a man in conversation and a child in his habits. Sheila was expecting it right now, telling him all this stuff about money and jobs and why it wasn't wise to sell the house and how he shouldn't be upset if he had to transfer to the public high school and probably wouldn't be able to play tennis at the club next summer unless someone asked him as a guest. And at the same time she was worrying that when she went to work she wouldn't be home when he came in from school every day. Like he was some six-year-old who had to be fed milk and cookies. It mixed a guy up. It really did. But Tommy was used to his man-child role.

"It's okay, Mom," he said. "About school and the club, I mean. I'm sorry about the money. About you having to go to work, especially. What do you think you'll do?"

"I'm not sure, Tommy. Probably get a job selling. I don't know much except about running a house and trying to look after all of you. I guess I could work in a store, though. I don't think that takes too much training."

He was very sorry for her. And for himself, too. He didn't want to leave his school and his friends there and all the other stuff he'd always enjoyed. It made him feel bad to see his mother so worried and scared. The pity turned to anger. His father had no right to leave them this way.

"Why didn't Dad think what would happen if he died?" There was antagonism in Tommy's voice. "Why didn't he see to it that you had enough money? You're always talking about how much he loved us and how he wouldn't want us to be unhappy. So why didn't he take care of it when he could? I think he was dumb!"

Sheila was startled, hearing her "baby" speak the same resentful phrases that had (God forgive her) been in her own mind. But he mustn't hate his father or think Sean was a stupid man. She searched for the right words.

"Tommy dear, let's get a few things straight. It's true that your father didn't leave much, but not because he didn't care about us. He was young, darling. Not from your viewpoint, I'm sure, but from his and the world's. He thought there'd be plenty of time to educate you and provide for me. Most men feel that way when they're as vigorous and full of life as your dad was." (What harm in a little white lie? What point in saying to his son that if Sean had lived to be eighty he'd never have left his affairs in an orderly fashion?) "We mustn't blame him for an act of God. That would be unfair to a very loving man. It's bad luck, Tommy, but it happens to people sometimes."

He didn't answer.

"You do understand, Tom, don't you?"

It was the first time he could ever remember her calling him "Tom." It was always "Tommy" or, on the rare occasions when she was angry with him, "Thomas Matthew Callahan!"

"Sure," he lied. "I understand."

Do you? Sheila wondered. I'm not sure *I* do.

When Patrick heard about his mother's precarious state, he wasn't sure he understood either. He knew his father was a hell-with-it kind of guy, but there'd always been plenty of money. Or so he'd thought. It had seemed to be no problem when he chose to study medicine, no limit to the funds available for his college and pre-med and medical school years. His father had even offered to help subsidize him after his marriage. Pat would have accepted the help. It was Betty who resisted. "We can make it on our own," she'd said. "We can't go through life letting your father play big-shot, no matter how well-intentioned his motives."

It had been said in an odd tone of voice, Patrick remembered now. As though Betty knew more than she was saying. In all likelihood she did. Her uncle was a vice president of the bank where Sean did business. Maybe she knew all along that Sean's expansiveness was more bluff than reality, that he lived on a day-to-day basis. If so, Pat thought ruefully, she knew more than the Callahans did. Anyway, he'd gone along with her determination that they be independent of both families and it had

35

worked out all right. It wasn't easy. They just got by. And there was no way he could help Sheila now. He hated to think of her in some hard job, starting out at her age to earn a living because his father really had always pretended, in Betty's words, to be a "big shot." He wondered, for the first time in his life, whether his parents had been happy. They'd always seemed so, with their big house and two cars and their fancy trips and big parties. *Sean* had been happy. Patrick was certain of that. He had everything his own way. Including his women. But Sheila? Did she really forgive his unfaithfulness? And did she know that they lived on the brink of financial disaster? And if she did, why did she choose to ignore it? Didn't she want what every woman wanted—a sense of security?

As he went about his duties at the hospital, Pat's mind was filled with thoughts about his family. Sheila. Could she make ends meet? Tommy. Poor kid, he'd never have the carefree growing up that he'd had. Pat almost dismissed Maryanne as a lost cause. Whatever the cause of her rebellion, early on he'd expected her to outgrow it. She hadn't. He doubted now she ever would. It would be a miracle if she didn't come to some sordid, stupid end, hanging around with the drug pushers and futureless wonders, including that creep she lived with. One more thing for Mother to worry about, Patrick thought. As though she didn't have enough. I really hate my sister. She's the only one of us who could help right now. She could get a decent job, live at home for a while, help Mother with the household expenses and with Tommy. No chance. She'd taken off as fast as she could after the funeral. Back to that crummy pad in Ohio City where she could lie on her back all day and hang around clubs all night like some oversexed, sixteen-year-old groupie. She's sick, Pat told himself. I should feel sorry for her. Maybe Betty could get her to come for therapy at the West Side Community Health Service. It was free. Maybe he'd ask Betty to talk to her and explain it.

The brief moment of hope faded. He knew Maryanne wouldn't have any part of it. She'd had some psychiatric sessions, at Sheila's insistence, when she was still in college. All they'd done was make her more hostile.

The hell with it, Patrick thought. I can write off Maryanne. I hope Mother can.

They didn't know what she felt, any of them. "Smothered" was the only word Maryanne could think of to describe her whole life. Smothered by Catholic girls schools, from Hathaway to Notre Dame. Smothered by the religion and the all-female atmosphere that pervaded them. Smothered by being a "middle child" and the only girl, knowing what was expected of her in terms of a suitable marriage after, possibly, a brief working period. She was stifling in anticipated boredom, in compliments on her beauty (always compared to Sheila's) and clucking predictions by her mother's friends about her future life (also compared to Sheila's). Until she'd taken off and gone to live with Rick, she'd felt imprisoned by Sean's overlove. For twenty-two years he'd been fatuous about Maryanne. That was part of his act, too. Like everything else in his life. As long as I did—or appeared to do—what he wanted, as long as I lived up to his idea of a well-brought-up girl, he loved me. When I broke loose, he was outraged, betrayed. He washed his hands of me as easily as he'd held them out to me all the years before. He didn't see my rebellion coming and when it came he didn't try to understand.

Mother, at least, did both. In the last year at that hated college, Sheila tried, in her own inadequate way, to help. She fought Dad over the visits to the shrink. He thought it was nonsense. For that matter, so did I. And we were right.

She remembered her last conversation with Sheila who still talked about "values" and "pride and accomplishment." And, ludicrously, about "love." How could she have held still for the hypocrisy of her marriage to Sean Callahan? What did she know about love? I'll bet my bottom dollar she's never screwed anybody else in her whole life. Not before she was a "child bride" and not even in the twenty-seven years when she and everybody else knew her husband was getting into everything in sight.

Maryanne propped herself up in bed and lit a joint. It was so soothing, so necessary. She watched the smoke curl seductively from the cigarette. Smoking pot filled her mother's soul with fear. But most of Sheila's friends had been on tranquilizers for years, and took sleeping pills as a matter of course. That was "respectable" in her eyes. Maryanne's way was not.

Respectable was a funny word. It meant you had respect from a phony world that you were, in turn, supposed to respect. You functioned in tandem, legally committed and emotionally estranged. You lived in the right part of town and wore proper clothes and pretended that God understood and forgave your weaknesses. Sheila believed that. Even Sean did, Maryanne supposed. She and Rick didn't. She never would. Nor, she was sure, would the men who would come after Rick. Her parents' generation would never accept freedom. They detested it. It made them nervous.

She wondered what Sheila would do now. Probably marry again as soon as she could. Well, good for her. It's not true that a man (or woman) bitten by a snake is afraid of a piece of rope. Sheila would go looking for another "loving" Sean Callahan, poor stupid lady.

Maryanne laughed aloud. And then without warning she began to cry. For Sheila. For Sean. For the world. But mostly for herself.

It was mid-September before Sheila went looking for a job. She scolded herself for procrastinating even that long, though it was only a little over a month since Sean's death. She should have started out immediately, she thought, looking at the dwindling bank balance, but there'd been so much to do. She'd had to go to University School and tell them

37

that Tommy would not be coming back. She hated that most of all. He'd gone through grade school there and the first year of high school and as she drove toward the big brick buildings and looked up at the graceful white steeple with its big clock, she felt a sense of loss for her son. Why him? she wondered irrationally. The other two had had the best education money could buy. Money, she now realized, the Callahans really couldn't afford. Money that, at least in Maryanne's case, seemed to have been totally wasted.

She knew she was being foolish about where Tommy went to school. Shaker Heights High had always had a fine academic reputation but lately, people said, it had changed. By that they meant that there was a greater ethnic mix, a "different class" of students. There'd been talk about drugs and crime and souped-up cars and sex among these "children," as Sheila thought of them. She worried about Tommy getting involved in this new permissiveness, especially with his father gone and with her anticipated morning-to-night absence from home.

It bothered her less to resign from the country club, a move which did not become effective until the end of the year, since their annual dues were paid through December. Still she felt a compulsion to announce that she'd be resigning her membership and she wondered idly how much she'd miss this part of her life. Not too much, she decided as she drove through the big iron gates. She enjoyed playing golf there and Tommy loved the tennis, but the social part of it had really been for Sean. He shone at the club dances, made some of his best deals (or so he claimed) at the "nineteenth hole" over a few drinks.

Poor Sean, she thought for the hundredth time, how he'd hate this new "austerity program." She was glad he didn't know that the Mercedes was now in the hands of a dress manufacturer who'd bought it for three thousand dollars cash, less than a fourth of its value. Sean would have had a fit. Even Bob Ross thought she could get more for the car if she waited, but she had this urge to get as much cash in hand as she could manage. She admitted it was pure panic and probably foolish, but it was reassuring to have even this tiny, available nest egg which could be put promptly into her checking account. Sheila smiled. The manufacturer himself would have been roundly snubbed by Sean, not only for the ridiculously low offer but for the very idea that one of the "nouveau riche" had purchased his precious car with what her husband always whimsically and mysteriously referred to as "funny money." She supposed he meant money made lately, in businesses Sean considered "unfit for gentlemen"—like dresses and cosmetics and discount stores.

All the people around her had complimented her extravagantly on how well and quickly she'd adjusted, commending her strength, her good sense, and discipline. They'd have been amazed had they known the insane thoughts that went through her head as she moved apparently calmly and confidently into her new life. They'd never believe how

38

frightened and depressed she was. Sometimes, in the middle of the night, she'd awaken and lie hatching impossible schemes. One of them was the idea that all the children would move back into the house. In the dark, it seemed to make sense. Pat and Betty could live rent free, perhaps contributing to the monthly bills. Maryanne could return to the world she really belonged in, eventually find some nice, trustworthy young man. But in the cold light of morning she knew such ideas were ridiculous. The Patrick Callahans wanted—should have—their own home. And Maryanne wanted no roots at all. Sheila was weaving a woman's magazine fantasy of a reunited family, an outmoded Norman Rockwell portrait of generations gathered around the ancestral hearth.

She feared loneliness and hated this feeling of being adrift. It was far too soon to think (decently) of another man in her life. And yet she knew that the time would come when she'd be ready for male companionship. She wondered whether she'd find it. Sally painted a dim picture of the prospect. And even if she did find someone interested in her, she was incapable of imagining herself "dating" after all these years. She'd be awkward, wouldn't know how to act or what to say.

Even before she met Sean there'd been only one "serious" beau in her life. Bill Reardon. They'd lived a block apart, "gone steady" in high school and had continued to date for a year after graduation. Sheila hadn't thought of him in years. She forgot him almost from the moment she met Sean. It had never gotten past the heavy petting stage with Bill. There'd been no sex, though once or twice they'd come perilously close. She'd backed off, frightened by the seriousness of such a step, terrified of pregnancy. How different girls were in 1945. How Maryanne would have laughed at the quivering virgin her mother had been at twenty.

In the beginning, Rose sent her news of Bill Reardon. He'd gone to work as a reporter for the *Daily News* and later had become a top writer for *Time.* Or was it *Newsweek?* Anyway, Sheila's mother had kept her posted for a while on the success of the boy she'd always hoped would be her son-in-law. In recent years Rose hadn't mentioned him. Probably his parents who were Rose's friends had died or dropped her after she became a widow.

No matter, Sheila thought. I don't know why he even popped into my head except as my only experience with "romance" before Sean. There had never been any since Sean. She wouldn't know how to handle a "relationship" if one popped up tomorrow.

But driving back from the club, Sheila did know why her mind was working in this direction. There *was* someone interested in her: Bob Ross. In these past few weeks she'd slowly come to realize that her lawyer and dear friend could, with the least encouragement, become her lover. It was a thought she totally rejected. There'd been nothing overt or even vaguely improper in his actions and sometimes Sheila convinced herself that she was imagining it, mistaking friendship and help for something much more personal. But intuition told her that Bob was attracted to her. It came through in small gestures, subtle phrases, seemingly impersonal kisses on the cheek. He was an attractive man, a wonderful man. She couldn't have gotten through this past month without his guidance. But she couldn't imagine herself having an affair with Bob. It was not her style. In a way, she was surprised to feel so sure that it was his. She'd always taken Bob and Emily for granted, the couple who were the Callahans' best friends and a pair totally committed to their marriage. Funny. She knew Sean strayed. She'd never imagined that Bob did. Or might.

She remembered Rose's warnings about Emily. Did her mother instinctively sense that the Rosses' marriage was not all it seemed? Sheila had laughed at Rose's dramatic suspicions about Emily's attraction to Sean and Emily's envy of Sean's wife. It had all seemed so ridiculous at the time. Perhaps it wasn't. Or perhaps Rose had gotten her wires crossed about who was attracted to whom.

"You must be going crazy, Sheila Callahan," she said aloud. Bob Ross was what he'd been for more than a quarter of a century—a dear, devoted friend. He loved his wife and his family and his friends, of whom Sheila was one. Period.

She let herself into the empty house. Tommy was at school and Annie Winchester came in only one day a week now, to do the heavy cleaning. Sheila couldn't afford her full time and was afraid she'd lose her entirely, but Annie was compassionate as well as practical.

"Don't you worry about it, Mrs. Callahan. There's plenty day work. I'd rather just work for one person, but I'll be able to get other jobs and still come take care of you. You don't think I'd walk out on you after all these years, do you?"

She was a warm, understanding woman, and Sheila was grateful to her. It would be difficult enough, once Sheila got a job, to keep the house even tidy and cook breakfast and dinner for herself and Tommy. I'd hate to be scrubbing bathroom and kitchen floors and doing the washing and ironing at midnight, she thought. Although those are things I know how to do. If I had any sense I'd hire myself out as a dayworker like Annie. At least I wouldn't worry about my housekeeping abilities. The idea of telling Terry and Margaret Callahan, or even Patrick, that she'd decided to become a cleaning woman amused her. She could imagine the expression on their faces as she'd explain to them what she believed—that there was dignity in any kind of work.

Of course she had no idea of going that route. She picked up the paper and began to read the Help Wanted ads. Just as she suspected, the only jobs she might even qualify for were selling ones. And those, as she'd known all along she would, were the ones she circled, clipped, and decided to follow up on.

"How's Shaker Heights High?" she asked Tommy over dinner that night.

"Okay."

"Are the kids nice?"

"I guess so. I don't know many of them yet."

She felt, again, a pang of regret that she'd had to take Tommy out of the school he loved. He hadn't complained. He'd been very mature about it. But very quiet.

Sheila tried to sound cheerful. "Well, honey, we're both in for new experiences, I expect. Tomorrow's *my* big day."

"What's tomorrow?"

"The day I set out to conquer the world. I'm going to start job-hunting."

He didn't look up from his plate. He'd not sounded angry about Sean since that one conversation but she knew he was angry now. The resentment remained. He hated the idea of her having to go to work.

"Mom?"

"Hmmm?"

"If I got a job after school, couldn't we make it? Without you doing that?"

"Darling, no. Anyway, what's so terrible? Millions of women work these days. Even ones with husbands. It'll probably be interesting. I'm kind of looking forward to it."

"Where will you look?"

"Department store, I guess. I thought I'd try Higbee's first."

"*Downtown?*"

"Yes. Why not?"

"Mom, nobody goes downtown. It isn't even safe for you!"

She laughed. "Sweetheart, I promise it's no more dangerous than your riding your bike to school. The Rapid Transit goes right into the arcade under the store. I'm not going to roam the streets inviting muggers. And if one approaches me I'll hit him with my Gucci handbag."

Tommy refused to find it funny. "Why do you have to go looking for a job downtown? Why don't you try to find something in the shopping center out here, close to home, where you could drive back and forth?"

It was a fair question. She couldn't tell him that she didn't want to "wait on" the people she knew; that she preferred to be an anonymous clerk among strangers; that, in a stupid, shallow way, she felt demeaned by her change in status from "wealthy" wife to working widow.

"I think there'll be more opportunities in a big store," she said instead. "Anyway, we'll see. Not to worry, okay?"

"I'll help you with the dishes," Tommy said.

The conversation was over, as far as he was concerned.

"Thanks, love. That would be great."

Chapter 6

Catherine Rawlings got up from behind the cluttered desk in her minuscule, overcrowded office and extended her hand to Sheila.

"Hi. Welcome. Personnel says you're interested in books and people and you've had some selling experience. What more could a book buyer ask?"

Sheila took the strong, firm hand and smiled. If I get this job, I'm going to like my new boss, she thought. Attractive. Fortyish. Direct. She could hardly believe her luck. So far it had all been so quick and easy. Her knees had been shaking that morning as she walked into the main floor of Higbee's. It seemed so big and bustling, so suddenly awesome with its ceiling lined with crystal chandeliers, its counters bursting with merchandise, and presided over by women of all ages who looked alarmingly competent. She'd found the personnel department and timidly asked about openings in the store, fully expecting a brusque rejection. Instead, she'd been treated with kindness and surprising dispatch. She'd filled out an application, worrying over questions like "last date of employment" and flinching a little as she checked "widowed" in the "marital status" column. But the interviewer had nodded approvingly as she looked over the paper.

"I see your hobbies are cooking, golf, and reading."

Sheila nodded. "Cooking isn't exactly a hobby," she admitted. "It's a necessity, but I do enjoy it."

"How about people? Get on well with them?"

Sheila looked puzzled. "I . . . I think so. That is, as far as I know, yes."

"I know it sounds like a strange question," the interviewer said, "but that's what retailing's all about. Anybody can learn to write a sales check, but we're a family store with a very personal outlook on things, and our best stock in trade is a staff with patience and good personalities. You have to really like people and get along with all kinds of them to be able to stand the average customer. He or she is demanding, impatient, sometimes downright rude. It takes a certain personality to deal with that. Of course, not *everybody's* that way. But a lot are, Mrs. Callahan."

Sheila remembered Sally's unflattering description of a life devoted to selling clothes. In a way, this woman was warning her of the same thing.

"I don't remember having a problem with customers at Lord & Taylor," Sheila said. "Of course, that was a long time ago, as you can see. I was just a kid."

The woman dialed an extension. "Kitty? There's a lady here I'd like you to see for that opening you have. May I send her to you now? Good." She hung up. "There's room in the book department for a salesperson. I'd like you to talk with Miss Rawlings, the buyer. If you two hit it off, I'll check your personal references and, assuming you're an upstanding citizen, I imagine you could start work almost immediately. I think you'd like it there."

Sheila felt, as she walked into the big, sprawling book department, that she would like working there. She loved reading, admired writers, and felt strongly about their output. So, apparently, did the people who sold this kind of merchandise. There was something touchingly sweet about a table whose sign said "Hurt books." Not "damaged" or "reduced for clearance." Almost as though the books themselves had feelings.

A smiling, gray-haired lady directed her to the back of the department where Catherine Rawlings shared her office with a "clerical." Sheila stood looking at the volumes stacked on chairs and on the floor, noticing the posters which announced the appearance of visiting authors for book-signing sessions. There was a kind of organized chaos about the little room, but there was nothing disorganized or chaotic about Miss Rawlings who apparently had been filled in further on Sheila while the interviewee was on her way to the department.

"Personnel was very impressed," Kitty said now, confirming those suspicions of a second phone call. "So am I. You picked just the right moment to appear. Our darling Mrs. Jennings retired last week at the tender age of eighty-two." She laughed at Sheila's startled expression. "It's true.

We have no mandatory retirement age here. Nor any hang-ups about hiring mature people. How old are you, Mrs. Callahan?"

"Forty-seven."

"Well, some of us are your age or younger, and some of our 'girls' come to work after their husbands die, or when their kids grow up and move out, or when they can't stand another moment of mind-boggling idleness." She looked searchingly at Sheila. "What's *your* reason?"

"I need a job. My husband died recently and left me a house but very little operating capital. What money there is, I'm trying not to touch. I have a son to put through high school and college."

Kitty nodded. "That's laying it right on the line. But you won't get rich in retailing."

"I know that, Miss Rawlings. Personnel already broke the bad news to me. But I can't expect to walk into a high-paying job, can I? I'm virtually unskilled and I haven't worked for twenty-seven years. I can buy groceries with what I earn. At least, with the way prices are going, I *hope* I can."

The buyer looked satisfied. I don't think this one will be with us for very long, she thought. She'll probably find another husband fast. Still she's bright and honest and undoubtedly will hang around through the Christmas rush, at least. She turned to her clerk. "Natalie, get Dorothy Parker in here, will you?" Kitty smiled. "No, Sheila—you don't mind if I call you Sheila, do you?—our Dorothy Parker isn't the one you've heard of. Not even a relative. She's in her late thirties, I think, and divorced. She's been here two years. She'll be able to answer your questions about rules and regulations, such as they are."

Sheila still didn't believe it was all this easy. "You mean I'm hired, Miss Rawlings?"

"As far as I'm concerned. Unless personnel turns up something unsavory in your past, which I very much doubt. They'll give you a quick training course, how to write sales slips and returns, that kind of thing. Dottie will tell you the rest. All things being satisfactory, could you start next week?"

"Oh yes! Thank you very much!"

"Don't thank me. We need each other."

Dorothy Parker was a petite blonde, smartly but casually turned out, obviously efficient but full of humor about herself and her job. She willingly agreed to help indoctrinate the new member of the staff and jauntily promised Kitty she'd have Sheila "brainwashed" in no time at all.

"I'll start by introducing her to everyone," she told Miss Rawlings. "And then I'll explain about our lavish lunch hour and leisurely cocktail break. Okay?"

"Nobody loves a wise guy," Kitty said, amused. "Don't try to live up to your name. Now get the blazes out of here, will you? See you Monday, Sheila."

"She seems nice," Sheila said as they left the office.

"Rawlings? She's okay. The department does well because she's a terrific promoter as well as a good buyer. Higbee's is a big account in the book trade and Cleveland is a big book-buying town. We get all the hotshot authors here for personal appearances, autographing books in the department, that kind of thing. She's what you call a 'creative buyer.' I mean, she helps arrange publicity for the visiting VIPs, does a big job with the City Club on book-and-author luncheons, spends a lot of her own time on store stuff. Yes, she's fine. Very fair with all of us. Makes allowances for personal problems but doesn't stand for any gold-bricking. You'll work hard, believe it."

For the next hour, Dottie whirled her through the department, introduced her to the other women who seemed pleasant and genuinely welcoming. The "lavish lunch hour" turned out to be forty-five minutes and the "leisurely cocktails" meant a twenty-minute midafternoon coffee break, both to be co-ordinated, timewise, with the other members of the staff.

"Other people's lunch hours are our busiest times," Dottie said, "so we try to go out very early or very late. Let's see. You already know you work one evening a week and after five years you get a week's vacation in winter and two in the summer. Oh yes, you're entitled to a 20 per cent employees' discount on anything in the store, which helps a helluva lot.

"We get a lot of nuts, like one guy who never buys a book but comes in on his lunch hour and reads them free, one chapter per day. There's nothing you can do about a 'browser' like that, any more than you can argue with the mean ones who get the titles all mixed up and then give you hell because you can't figure out what they're looking for." Dottie sighed. "Sometimes they're too much! But generally, people are pleasant. Most of us develop a regular following and keep our own record books so we can call customers when a new title they might like comes in."

"That's surprising," Sheila said, "considering you don't sell on commission. It's nice that you bother."

"It's a nice group. Hardly a lemon in the bunch. Day-to-day they're easy to live with."

She showed Sheila where the various categories of books were located, took her to the area where she'd check in each morning and where she'd be assigned a locker, and ended the tour in the "tube room" where each saleswoman picked up her "money bag" at the start of the day.

"You get thirty dollars every morning for making change and you keep that separate in your cash register. End of the day you return it plus the additional money you've made in sales."

"Why is it called the 'tube room'?"

"I'm not sure. I think it's a hangover from the old days when they used to have pneumatic tubes running through the store and all purchase money and change was sent back and forth to one central cashier. Anyway, it's still called the tube room and it's your first stop every day." Dottie looked at her watch. "I'd better be getting back and you probably have to go to personnel, don't you?"

"I don't know."

"Sure you do. Now that Rawlings has okayed you, they'll give you the official word. See you next week."

"Yes," Sheila said. "Thanks, Dottie. You've been marvelous."

"We'll have lunch. Maybe dinner. I know some fun people."

Sheila hesitated. "Lunch would be great. I'm not sure about dinner. You see, I'm a widow with a fifteen-year-old son in Shaker Heights who has to be fed."

"Fifteen? Good lord, that's not a baby! Why couldn't he get himself a meal once in a while? Don't you ever go out?"

"My husband's only been dead six weeks."

"Oh." Dottie looked embarrassed. "I'm sorry. I didn't know. Well, we'll talk about it another time, okay?"

"Absolutely."

She finished her business with personnel and took the Rapid Transit back home. It was a short, easy ride and a pleasure not to have to concentrate on driving. She read somewhere that Clevelanders traveled one hundred million miles a year on public transportation. The figure stuck in her mind because it was so enormous and because she'd never gone anywhere in twenty-seven years except by car. There's so much I don't know about this town, Sheila thought. I've led such an insular life here. Suddenly she felt high-spirited, stimulated. It was like embarking on a whole new expedition. For the first time since Sean's death she accepted the fact that her life hadn't stopped with his. It was a good feeling. Selfish, honest, and good.

"I think it's absolutely idiotic!" Margaret Callahan addressed the figure shielded by the sports page.

"What is?" Terry answered automatically, his mind still on an article about the Cleveland Browns.

"Your sister-in-law taking a job selling books at Higbee's! Commuting morning and night. And hardly making enough to keep body and soul together. She's dramatizing the whole thing out of proportion, if you ask me. Playing it like the poor little match girl. My God, Terry, she didn't have to rush out and take the first job she was offered! Sean left enough insurance to keep her going for a year, at least!"

46

He lowered the paper. "And after a year, then what? Do you suggest we support her?"

His wife gave a long-suffering sigh. "In a year anything could happen."

"Such as?"

"Such as if she devoted as much energy to finding a husband as she is to selling books, she'd probably be remarried in a year. With her looks and our connections, I know I could come up with some nice, substantial man to take care of her. There still are some unattached widowers and even a few suitable bachelors around, but she'll never get one of them unless she concentrates on it."

"I presume you've told her so."

"Of course I've told her," Margaret said.

"And what did she say?"

"Oh, the usual nonsense about it being too soon to think of things like that. And a lot of garbage about what Sally Cantrell has told her about the scarcity of marriageable men. Silly excuses. Women who *want* to get married *can*. I don't think her idol Sally really wants to marry again. A woman who does has to really make it the focus of her thoughts, practically plan a campaign. If you're set on getting a man you send out thought waves when you meet a bachelor. Not turn him off the way Sheila did at that dinner party last week. Men *know* when a woman is interested and when she's not. And they respond accordingly. That's what's happened to Sally. She doesn't really want another husband and every man she meets senses it."

Terry found the whole discussion distasteful. Not only because his brother had been dead only a little over two months. His wife's attitude was so coldly mercenary. She wasn't giving a thought to Sheila's happiness. Only to her "status" and her bank account.

"Has it occurred to you," he said finally, "that maybe Sheila isn't anxious to marry again either? She's tasting independence for the first time in her life, Margaret. Maybe she likes it. She seems to like her job. Could be it gives her the first real sense of accomplishment she's ever known. I think she's proving something and I admire her for the way she's taken hold."

"Oh, for God's sake, Terry, you too?"

"What do you mean, 'me too'?"

"You sound like Bob Ross! He's singing the same praises about Sheila's 'bravery.' Men! They're basically so damned impractical! Face it, my dear, Sheila's only hope is another husband. And now she says she's too exhausted after a long day at the store to accept any invitations I cook up for her in the evening. I think I'd kill myself if I had her life! Nothing but eat, sleep, and work."

"She has Tommy."

"Terrific. I can hardly think of anything more stimulating than the company of a fifteen-year-old boy."

He felt himself growing angry. "Leave her alone, Margaret! I mean it! Sheila has a right to run her life her own way, without your matchmaking and your opinions about what she ought to do! All this planned manhunting is disgusting! If Sheila meets someone she loves, sometime in the future, I'll be happier than anybody about it. She's a wonderful woman and I hope she finds somebody who can appreciate her. But only if she *wants* it that way. Not because you and your parasitic friends think it's the only answer!"

Margaret was speechless. Terry was usually so mild-mannered and agreeable. It had been hard to believe that he and Sean were brothers, they were so different. And here he was, yelling at her like Sean himself!

"Well!" Margaret was indignant. "I'm very sorry you consider me a parasite!"

He was remorseful. "You know I didn't mean it that way. I just meant that you and all the women you know are so used to the good, easy life that you can't imagine anyone refusing to try to duplicate it. Look, dear. If I died tomorrow I know you'd want to marry again as soon as possible. Not because you don't love me. Because you can't imagine a life that doesn't include a husband and companion." He wanted to add "and provider" but he didn't. "I'd want you to marry again, because security is very important to you."

"And you think it isn't to Sheila?"

Terry pondered that for a moment. "Yes, I think security is important to everyone. Emotional as well as financial security. But I don't think Sheila would miss it as much as you would, because I don't think she ever really had it with Sean."

"He didn't provide for her, but God knows they lived well while he was around. As for his little flings," Margaret shrugged, "personally I wouldn't have stood for them, but Sheila must have felt secure enough, knowing Sean would never take any of them seriously. Her life might not have been ideal, but it was a helluva lot better than the one she's chosen now. She could do worse than look for another man like Sean."

He was weary of this conversation. He'd had a talk with Sheila a couple of weeks after she started work. She admitted it was hard, particularly, she laughed, on her feet. But she was enjoying it. He believed her. It was the first time in years he could remember his sister-in-law looking eager and interested, with a sparkle in her eyes. He hadn't seen that kind of vitality in her for more than twenty years. Sean subjugated her completely, Terry thought. She loved him, but she'd grown used to thinking of herself as an appendage rather than an independent entity. And God knows she was independent. Without mentioning it to Margaret, he'd offered to help her out financially with a little check every month.

"I think I can make it on my own, Terry," she'd said. "And I'd really like to try."

He couldn't imagine Margaret, in similar circumstances, saying the same thing.

Chapter 7

October and half of November disappeared without Sheila knowing exactly where they went. She had fallen quickly and easily into the routine of the job and as the department approached the peak pre-Christmas selling period she began to be caught up in the growing excitement of a retail store at its busiest season. The fall itself had been interesting. Kitty had brought in half-a-dozen authors, eager to push their books by personal appearances and Sheila had actually met a much-admired writer of political books, a cooking expert she'd seen on TV, a Hollywood columnist with a juicy exposé of the film industry, and a woman who'd written a sad, thinly disguised novel about a twenty-two-year-old daughter who'd died of leukemia.

Sandwiched in among the personal appearances were the briefings Kitty gave them on the new books—novels, children's stories, and the big, expensive volumes of art and photography known in the trade as "coffee table books" to be given as gifts to impress the recipient who would leave them unopened and unread on a conspicuous table in the living room.

Once, urged by Dorothy Parker, Sheila had had dinner in town with her coworker and a group of the "amusing people" Dottie claimed to know. Sheila did not find them amusing. They dined at the apartment of Clifford Josephson, an interior decorator whose name was well-known to

Sheila and who had, in fact, decorated two houses in Chagrin Falls where Sean and Sheila had spent several evenings. She didn't mention this fact. It would have seemed out of place, somehow, as though she were "putting on airs," as Rose used to call it.

She and Dottie went straight from the store to the Chesterfield, a big, new, luxury apartment building close to the city's financial hub. Sheila had never been inside the big modern building that overlooked the minipark. It was opulent in a decorator-way with the kind of studied chic that she found impersonal and cold.

"Wouldn't it be terrific to live here?" Dottie was visibly impressed. "Cliff makes tons of money and he's so nice! You'll love his apartment and you'll adore him. Not seriously, of course. He's—you know—one of the boys. But God is he *elegant!*"

Cliff was, indeed, "elegant." He glittered with heavy gold bracelets and wore a black velvet suit and matching slippers with "CJ" woven on the instep in an intricate gold design. He was also extremely hospitable and courteous to Dottie's friend. She and Dottie were the only two women at the dinner party with six young men, all unmistakably friends of Clifford's and all fifteen or twenty years younger than Sheila.

She tried very hard to join in the general conversation, but she was miserable, uncomfortable, and bored. She hoped it didn't show. It was kind of Dottie to try to "get her out of herself" and the young men were attentive and well-mannered. But she felt "square"—a word she remembered, with amusement, people didn't use any more. She only knew she felt out of place, the way one felt when there was an "inside joke" among a group of which one was not a part. She didn't dislike these people, she simply could not relate to them. How on earth could I? Sheila wondered. This is a world as foreign to me as anything could be. I must be something of an oddity to them, too: a suburban matron with children as old as they are. She couldn't wait to leave.

"You're a smash," Dottie whispered happily to her halfway through the evening. "Cliff just told me he thinks you have style—and that's the highest compliment he can pay *anybody!* Are you having fun?"

"Yes," Sheila lied.

"Isn't the apartment divine?"

Another lie. "It's superchic." Super-Freudian is what I really mean, Sheila thought. I've never seen so many chairs made out of tusks, so many obelisks and horns. I've got to get out of here, away from these exotic young males and this overeager woman who's substituting superficiality for loneliness. Even Dottie is too old and too "square" for this. Doesn't it make her feel as unfeminine as it does me? There are so many women like her, Sheila thought sadly. They pretend that any company is desirable as long as it wears pants. She had nothing against these men. For the most part they were amusing, considerate, attractive, and "safe." She

51

could imagine going to the theater with someone like Cliff Josephson or having dinner with him, but this total world was something she was determined not to get involved in. It was a trap into which widows, divorcées, and single women fell all too easily. Sally was right. "Real" men were scarce, so single women of their age settled for this or affairs with married men. Or put up with those impossibly spoiled widowers or confirmed bachelors Margaret was eternally trying to get her to meet. She'd tried *that* once, too, and in a totally different way it was just as bad as this. Maybe worse. Margaret's candidate had acted as though he was doing her a great favor taking her to a dinner party in Shaker Heights. He'd spent most of the evening talking about how many invitations he received, how much in demand he was. Sheila had nearly expired of boredom and had breathed a sigh of relief when she'd quickly and firmly closed her front door on an aging roué who expected to be asked in for a nightcap. It was a relief to be alone. She'd rather spend every evening by herself than play the coy, you-big-wonderful-man act that Margaret's candidate expected. Just as she'd rather put up with her own company than spend her time in groups like this one.

For some inexplicable reason, Sheila thought, they probably *do* find me stylish. They liked "older women" and especially those they knew had some background. Dottie undoubtedly had built her up as "Shaker Heights Society." It was funny and sad and depressing.

At ten o'clock she rose from her chair and charmingly apologized for the fact that she had to leave. Everyone looked surprised and distressed.

"So early?" Cliff said.

"I'm sorry. It's been a lovely evening, but I really must go. I live out at the end of nowhere and I'll be good for nothing tomorrow if I don't get to bed."

"You're sure we can't persuade you to stay?"

"Thanks, Cliff, no. I honestly can't. You were so kind to ask me. I loved it."

He hesitated. "I'll be glad to see you home."

You'd die if I took you up on that, Sheila thought. She shook her head. "No need. I'll take a cab."

His relief was almost laughable. "Well, in that case Jonathan will put you into one, won't you, Jon?"

A young man in a turtle neck, tight pants, and lots of gold chains and bracelets rose nimbly from the floor. "Of course. Glad to."

Dottie followed her as she went to get her coat. "You don't like them, do you?"

"Oh, Dottie, I do! They're charming. But you know I worry about Tommy alone in the house. I never stay out late. Thanks so much, darling, for introducing me to your friends. They're all very nice." She kissed Dottie on the cheek. "See you tomorrow."

She was home in twenty minutes, several precious dollars poorer. She would have taken the train but didn't have the nerve to ask Jon to escort her to the Rapid Transit. Dottie would have "lost face," she thought, amused. It probably wasn't a good idea at that hour anyhow, even though she only had a block to walk when she got off. She did it when she worked late nights at the store, but there were more people about at eight-thirty than at half-past ten.

She went lightly up to the third floor and tapped gently on the door of Tommy's "apartment."

"Come on in, Mom."

He was in bed, reading. "Have a good time?"

She smiled. "Lousy. What about you? Did you heat up the stew? Watch TV?"

"Sure. Both. Sorry you didn't have fun."

"Live and learn," Sheila said. "I find I'm happier at home."

"Didn't you meet anybody interesting?"

Was that anxiety in his voice? Is he afraid I'll meet someone who'll try to take Sean's place?

"Not a blessed soul," Sheila answered lightly. "You're still the best company I can find."

She kissed him on the forehead and went to her own room on the floor below. I won't leave you, Tommy. Someday, too soon, it will work the other way around. You'll "meet someone interesting" and leave me. Like the others did. That's how it will be and that's how it should be. But not yet, thank the Lord. Not quite yet.

Tommy lay awake a long while. It was the first time he'd ever lied to his mother. He hadn't stayed home and watched TV and eaten the stew she'd left for him. It was just luck that he'd gotten home before she did. He hadn't expected her so early.

He wondered what Sheila would have thought if she'd known how he spent his evening. Wondered, hell! He knew what she'd have thought. She'd have been out of her head, but she'd have hidden it under that infuriatingly understanding attitude of hers. She didn't understand him at all. She thought of him as a child and he guessed in a way he was. But physically he was a man, tall, strong, well-developed and, in the last two months, suddenly aware of himself as a young male.

At University, he now realized, they'd all led a sheltered life. That is, there was a lot of cussing and elbow-nudging-suggestions about girls. But they were more interested in sports and school activities. The fifteen- and sixteen-year-olds he'd met at Shaker High had much more advanced ideas. Some of them were on drugs, but more of them had given that up in favor of hard liquor.

It was kind of funny, Tommy reflected, the way parents were always a step behind. He knew the whole damned community was worried about drugs. They didn't know that "the kids" had passed that stage, leaving the joint-smoking and wine-drinking scene to people in their twenties and thirties. Like Maryanne. The teen-agers he had come to know recently were hung up on booze and broads. And tonight Tommy had had his first encounter with both.

He'd almost refused when he'd been asked to the "party," but he hadn't wanted his new friends to know that he'd never had a drink or been with a girl or that he was too "chicken" to try both.

So he'd gone with three other boys to this girl's house, armed with two pints of scotch of which his share had cost two dollars. The girl—Nancy was her name—was someone he knew only by sight at school but he'd been assured that she was "hot stuff." She was only sixteen, but she looked older.

"She digs it," one of the guys had said. "Give her a couple of stiff snorts and stand back!"

"You mean . . . she'll . . . that is . . . all of us?"

His informant looked at him with surprise. "Sure, man. All of us. You never been to a gang bang?"

Tommy tried to bluff his way out. "No. Not exactly. That is, I usually take my women one at a time."

"Penny-ante stuff. Watching's half the kicks. Gets you *really* steamed up."

It had been a disaster. Nancy's parents were out for the evening. The quartet had arrived, the drinks were poured, and there was a lot of dirty talk that everybody but Tommy seemed to enjoy. He hated the taste of the scotch, but he pretended not to and took two big swigs hurriedly, hoping he'd get in the mood. Instead he began to feel sick and when the group moved into Nancy's bedroom, he hung back.

"What's with you, Callahan?" his mentor asked.

"Nothing."

"You wanna go first?"

Tommy shook his head. "No. I wanna get steamed up like you said."

It hadn't worked that way. It was the first time he'd ever seen sex except in dirty books and fuzzy-focus films. He'd never even been to a hard-core porno movie. Already feeling ill, the scene swam before his eyes as Nancy and the first of the four flopped down on the bed together. There was a lot of fumbling and then hard-breathing from the participants and the audience. He knew he couldn't make it. He wanted to try. In a crazy way he was excited and frightened all at the same time. He wondered what it was like to be with a girl. And he knew he couldn't find out this way.

They weren't paying any attention to him as he quietly left the room. Outside, in the bushes, he was actively sick. And then he walked home.

He'd make up some excuse when he saw the gang tomorrow. Like he wasn't feeling well, which was true. Or that it was all adolescent and dopey to a man of his much more sophisticated experience. "I don't lay tarts," he'd say loftily, "when I can get something exclusive any time I want." They'd never believe him, of course. They'd know he'd been scared to death. Probably even guess that he was a virgin.

Lying in his own bed he felt rotten and scornful of himself. He *was* a baby. Even though his parents talked to him like a grown-up, they'd known he wasn't. He wondered what Sean would have said about tonight. Tommy wasn't sure he'd have told his father, but if he had, would Sean have made fun of him? Or been disappointed, maybe pegging him as a "mama's boy"? Tommy staunchly told himself that his father would have had neither reaction. Sean was a lusty man. He could hold his liquor and he liked women. Young as he was, Tommy had known for a long time that the big, handsome Sean Callahan "played around." But his son doubted that he'd go for anything as sordid and sick as that scene tonight, nor would he blame Tommy for rejecting it. Still, he'd probably tell me it was time I got laid, the boy thought. Maybe he'd even have arranged it for me.

No, Sean wouldn't have done that. He'd have expected me to go find my own willing partner, on my own. Provided I'd ever have felt comfortable enough to discuss the problem with him at all. I wonder if I would have. He always scared me. I always felt I never lived up to what he wanted. I probably wouldn't have the guts to tell him about tonight, even if I could. I don't know if I could even discuss it with Pat. Tommy stared into the darkness. I wish we were closer, Pat and I. He's been home so little. Always off at school and then married right away. He liked his older brother, but the age difference had kept them apart in the early years because Tommy was so much younger. Now it kept them apart because Patrick wasn't enough older to be consulted as one would consult a father.

Tommy turned over and punched his pillow. Why can't I be like those other guys? Maybe I'm queer. His own foolishness made him smile. No. I wanted to. A lot. I still want to. But not like that. Not like part of a pack of dogs after a bitch in heat. Mr. Magoo began to snore noisily at the foot of his bed. Lucky you, Tommy thought. It's okay for *you* to be an animal.

Sally Cantrell drove over on Tuesday, Sheila's day off, to pick her up and take her to the Playhouse Club for lunch. Sheila had protested.

"I'd love to," she'd said on the phone, "but you can't imagine how many things I have to do today. I have to do the marketing for the whole week and drop some things off at the cleaner's and go to the hardware store and . . ."

"We'll do all those things after lunch. For God's sake, Sheila, it's your only free day except Sunday and you haven't relaxed one single Tuesday since you went to work! I'll pick you up at noon and we'll go have a 'ladies lunch,' the way we used to. A couple of martinis and a lot of catching up. I've barely seen you in weeks! It'll do us both good."

Sheila didn't put up much of a fight. Sally was right. It would do her good. They used to lunch often at the club where they were both on the board and active in fund-raising for the Playhouse. It was always fun to walk into the noisy, crowded room, through the entranceway lined with photographs of Joel Grey and Paul Newman and dozens of other celebrities who got their start at the Cleveland Repertory Theatre. It was fun now, to perch up at the bar and say hello to a dozen people she hadn't seen in months. I'll never be a "career woman," she thought. I'm much happier dawdling over a two-hour lunch in this ornate Victorian ambiance than grabbing a sandwich on my forty-five-minute lunch break. And then hated herself for her self-pity. She should be damned grateful for any kind of job, and especially one in pleasant surroundings among nice, kind people.

She was sorry that there seemed to be constraint between her and Dottie since the dinner party at Cliff Josephson's. Sheila had tried to thank her, the next day, for including her, but Dottie had been outspoken.

"I know you hated it," she said. "I guess you aren't used to the lower classes."

Sheila had been aghast. "Dottie! Don't be crazy! Anybody who lives in an apartment like that can hardly be called 'lower class.'"

"You know what I mean. They probably make more money than your late husband but they're not your social cup of tea. It's okay, Sheila. I understand. I just thought you'd enjoy an evening out."

What a snob she thinks I am, Sheila realized. Maybe I am. But not the way she thinks.

"All right, Dottie, it's true. I didn't enjoy it. But it had nothing to do with 'social status.' I'm scared of that scene. I've seen too many lonely women get caught up with men like that. It's deluding yourself. At least that's how it seems to me."

"I'm not deluding myself," Dottie said resentfully. "I know there's not what you'd call a 'future' with those boys, but it's a helluva lot more fun than sitting home watching 'All in the Family.' Of course, you probably get invited out to a lot of dinner parties in Shaker Heights, so you don't need it. But in the five years I've been divorced, I haven't been deluged with invitations from old friends. Extra women are a pain in the ass. You'll find that out."

I already have, Sheila thought. In the first few weeks following Sean's death there had been invitations from people feeling sorry for her. She'd gone out a few times and hadn't enjoyed that either. But she needn't have worried about refusing parties. In a very short time the phone stopped ringing. People had "done their duty" to the widow, and unless she began to reciprocate their invitations—which she had not the time, strength, or money to do—she knew she'd be alone as Dottie was. Except I prefer that, she told herself, to the embarrassment of being the "token female."

"Dottie, dear, I'm not critical of how you or anyone else chooses to spend her time. It just isn't for me. That won't keep us from being friends, I hope."

"No. Of course not."

But it had made a difference, nonetheless. They were still friendly, still ate lunch and took coffee breaks together when the timing worked out, but Dottie made no more mention of her "interesting friends" and when Sheila impulsively suggested she might like to come for dinner some Sunday, Dottie refused.

"Thanks, but I don't think I'd fit in."

"What are you talking about, 'fit in'? There'll only be Tommy and me. Not," she added hastily, "that it would matter who was there. All my friends and family would like you. You're a charming, interesting woman."

"But not 'Shaker Heights charming.' East is East and West is West, et cetera, et cetera. I'm strictly from the other side of the river. Strictly West Side Market hamburger, not hummingbird tongues from Tassi's food shop."

"All that nonsense about where you live in Cleveland is as outmoded as the bustle! There are all kinds of people, all incomes, all races living on both sides of the Cuyahoga. You know that, Dottie. You're being silly."

"Maybe. But I'll take a rain check."

Over luncheon, Sheila told Sally about it, beginning with the ill-fated dinner party.

"You're both right, you know," Sally said. "There isn't that much difference any more between East Side and West. At least not on the surface. We both have our country clubs and our 'catered affairs' and our slums and our crime. But honey, the dug-in Clevelanders, our generation, still can't believe that University City—or the Cuyahoga River if you prefer—isn't really the Great Divide. We have our Art Museum and the West Side has its Zoo. *You* know it. Look what a fit you threw when Maryanne moved to the West Side."

"That was different. It wasn't just living in Ohio City. It was . . . it *is* . . . the *way* she lives . . . that terrible musician, the hanging around bars, all of it."

"Sure."

"It's true, Sally. Ohio City isn't that bad. Now if she'd chosen to live in Hough . . ."

Sally looked amused. "My God, what a thought! Our first rioting ghetto! They tell me it's becoming more respectable, of course. Maybe you're right about the West Side, at that. All those Gold Coast apartments aren't chopped liver. Anyway, the hell with all that. Tell me how you are. And how Tommy is."

"I'm tired is how I am. Tommy? I guess he's okay. I don't think he likes Shaker Heights High very much, but he doesn't say anything. In fact, we have a hard time communicating these days. No friction. Just not much conversation. I suppose he's at the age when he needs a man to talk to. For boys, a mother's not for confiding."

"Forgive me, love, but I don't think Sean would have been all that good at the father-to-son stuff. Was he with Patrick?"

"No, but Pat never seemed to need someone the way Tommy does. Maybe just knowing he had a father helped. Anyway, he's never been as introverted as Tommy."

"If you're worried, maybe you could get Pat to spend some time with him."

Sheila shook her head. "Patrick's up to his ears in long hours at the hospital and trying to find some time to spend with his wife. I've hardly seen him, between his schedule and mine. I'll see him at Thanksgiving, of course. Betty's been sweet enough to invite us all there for dinner. Maybe I'll try to talk to Pat about Tommy. But somehow I think he needs the company of a more mature man."

Sally dug into her chef's salad. "Don't we all," she said. "I hope you have luck finding one for Tommy. Then you can concentrate on a couple for you and me."

Chapter 8

Thanksgiving had always been Sheila's favorite holiday. Even this year, though she'd not be at the foot of her own table with an expansive Sean at the head, she looked forward to it. It was dear of Betty to take over the chore of cooking the big family meal. Sheila had protested, but Betty had been firm.

"It's your one day off," her daughter-in-law had said. "You're not going to spend it in the kitchen!"

"But it's *your* one day, too," Sheila answered. "You work just as hard as I do!"

Patrick, smiling, had listened to the affectionate exchange. "Tell you what," he said, "let's all go out for dinner. Then nobody has to cook."

"Thanksgiving dinner in a *restaurant?*" Betty was scornful. "I think you've lost your mind, Doctor! It's a family holiday. Who needs a bunch of strangers around? To say nothing of leathery turkey kept warm on a hot table in a kitchen, and waiters who hate you because they have to work on a holiday. Thanks a lot, but no thanks. We'll all be at our house, counting our blessings. And that's that."

"My God, I think I married an old-fashioned girl!"

Sheila laughed. "And probably too good for you, at that." She was pleased. This year, more than ever, she needed the reassurance of being with those she loved: Tommy, Betty, and Pat. Even, possibly, Maryanne.

Her daughter had only half-promised to come, giving evasive answers to Betty's invitation, saying she never planned her life more than one day in advance. They all knew the real reason. She felt, correctly, that Rick would be out of place, though Betty had cordially included him. Maryanne was torn between her old life and her new, in so many ways.

Betty had no family of her own. She was an only child and both her parents had been killed in a car crash two years before. Her husband's relatives had become her own and she wanted them all there. She'd even written to Rose Price and to the senior Callahans to join them, but all the grandparents had gratefully declined. It was too long a trip from Florida for Sean's parents. And though New York was less than an hour and a half flying time away, Sheila's mother didn't feel up to the hectic undertaking of holiday travel. Sheila had called her after Betty received Rose's regrets.

"I do wish you'd come, Mother. You don't have to be here for just one day. You could come early and stay on."

"And what would I do with myself all day while you're away at work? Could you take the rest of the week off?"

"Darling, I'd love to, but it simply isn't possible. From now on is our busiest time at the store. But there are other people around. I'm sure Sally would take you to lunch and, after all, we'd be together in the evenings."

The familiar sigh came over the wire. "No, I'll stay home. You enjoy yourself."

"What will you do?"

"Me? I haven't thought. Maybe have my usual dinner at Schrafft's."

I'm supposed to say I'm sorry, Sheila thought. Dammit, I won't. She remembered the pledges she'd made to herself when Sean died. I'm not going to feel guilty. I'm not going to apologize. She knows she's welcome. If she wants to play martyr, then that's what she'll have to do.

"We'll miss you," she said instead. "Betty's excited about cooking her first Thanksgiving dinner."

"Who's coming?"

"Besides Tommy and me, she's asked Sally and Maryanne. Unfortunately, Terry and Margaret have promised to go to Margaret's mother's."

Rose gave a little sniff. "It would seem to me your brother-in-law and his wife would be with you this year, above all others."

Sheila didn't answer.

"And is Maryanne bringing that dreadful Polack?"

Sheila counted ten. "I'm not sure Maryanne can make it, but Betty has asked Rick too, of course."

"Well, have a good time."

"Thanks, Mother. You too."

She'd hung up feeling angry and depressed. Almost immediately the phone had rung and it was Betty.

60

"I just figured out we're top-heavy with women," she said. "You, Sally, and me with only Pat and Tommy." (She wasn't counting on Maryanne, Sheila realized. Smart girl.) "So I thought I'd invite another man. There's a very nice doctor Pat knows. Name's Jerry Mancini. He's older—thirty-seven or eight, I'd guess—but he's been helpful to Pat at the hospital. We just found out that he's at loose ends on Thursday, so I asked him here. Okay with you? I mean, he isn't family, but it is the season to take in waifs and strays, don't you think?"

"Of course, darling. It's a lovely idea. Doesn't Dr. Mancini have family?"

"No. That is, not exactly. He and his wife separated six months ago. She has their little girl and they're going to Jerry's in-laws for Thanksgiving."

"Sounds like a good deed," Sheila said. "What can I contribute to the feast?"

"Just your own sparkling presence. And a little prayer that this fiercesome turkey doesn't eat me before we eat him!"

"Face him down," Sheila laughed. "Remember you're bigger than he is."

"Not a helluva lot," Betty said. "He looks old and tough . . . which is more than you can say for me!" She giggled. "The only thing in my favor is that *he's* dead." There was an awkward pause. "I'm sorry, Sheila. What a dumb thing to say."

"Don't be ridiculous. I haven't ruled the word out of my vocabulary."

That certainly was true. The word "dead" was what Sheila felt so much of the time. Dead-tired, deadly bored, deathly afraid of the future. The brief euphoria she'd felt when she first got her job had disappeared as the triumph became monotonous reality. It was economically difficult, socially impossible, emotionally draining to be "starting over" at forty-seven. I'm exactly the wrong age to be a widow, she thought. Too young to resign myself to a life alone; too old to do everything differently. I wish I had the courage to pick up myself and Tommy, sell this house, move out of Cleveland, begin all over again in a new climate. But I'm afraid. Afraid to leave familiar surroundings, to search for new friends and—she was almost embarrassed by the thought—a new love. For that was what she really wanted. She missed having someone to love, some man to talk and dine with, to make herself pretty for and, yes, to go to bed with.

She was a normally healthy, physical woman and she missed an active sex life. In that she'd been spoiled by Sean who'd been a more than satisfactory bedmate, in spite of his outside activities. When they made love, she didn't think about his other women. She was his wife. She was the one he loved beyond the physical act. She'd been able to live with that for more than twenty years. The sensuous part of her nature ached for the delicious feeling of being a woman. It was, she knew, why she'd been so uncomfortable with Dottie Parker's friends. Knowing that a man could not possibly desire her made her feel displaced, neuter. She'd known only one man intimately, but she was always aware of men, frankly liking their eyes on her, enjoying harmless flirtations, taking pleasure in Sean's occasional, unfounded jealousy. He'd been jealous of Bob Ross.

"He'd like to get you in the sack," Sean had said more than once. "My best friend, that sonofabitch! He'd really like to!"

Sheila had laughed. "I'm flattered. Even though you're crazy. Bob Ross has no interest in me, except as a friend."

"The hell he hasn't! That bastard has the hots for you. He damned well better not try anything."

She hadn't turned his own words on him, bitterly suggesting that if anybody recognized "the hots" it would be Sean. She hadn't even believed it then about Bob. But in the past three months she'd become sure she was right. *I could have an affair with him if I chose,* Sheila thought again. *But I don't choose. Not because he isn't attractive. Not even because I care that much about Emily. If I could live with an unfaithful husband, so could she.* It was that she wanted something more. Something called, in the current cliché, a "meaningful relationship." She wasn't sure what that meant. Not marriage, necessarily, but not a hit-and-miss affair with a married man who'd have to sneak an hour or two with her when he could. She wondered whether any of Sean's women had had the same feelings. Was it enough for them that he dropped in for an hour or so in the afternoon or evening? Didn't they care that he was never available on Sundays and holidays, or that "their time" was subject to *Mrs.* Callahan's plans for her and *Mr.* Callahan? Perhaps they were different. Some of them had husbands, so it probably worked out all right for them. It wouldn't for her. A lover—if she found one—had to be free, someone with whom she could be seen in public, with whom she could spend Sundays and Christmas and New Year's Eve.

She tried to convince herself that she'd never find anyone like that. Sally had told her so. So had Dottie. And yet she wouldn't believe it, couldn't believe it. Her body ached for the touch of a man. Shameful. Sean dead only three months and she felt this physical craving. *It's a good thing I never had "the calling"* she thought wryly as she dressed for Betty's dinner. *I'd have made a lousy nun. How did anyone endure a lifetime of celibacy?* She didn't believe that what you'd never had you didn't miss. She didn't even believe (heretical idea!) that spiritual love of God replaced physical love of man. It was a supplement, not a substitution. At least that's how she saw it. But then, she'd never really been a "good Catholic." She gave sincere but token respect to the church, reserving the right to question some of its practices, like that one.

When she and Tommy arrived at Pat and Betty's apartment, her daughter-in-law drew her aside.

62

"Maryanne isn't coming," Betty said quietly. "I'm sorry. She called an hour ago to say they couldn't make it."

Sheila felt letdown, hurt. She hadn't really expected her daughter but she had childishly hoped that Maryanne would understand how important it was to her mother that they all be together on this first Thanksgiving without Sean. Why couldn't she make such a tiny effort? Didn't she owe it to her family? She caught herself. I'm thinking like Rose! Oh, no! Don't let me do that! Don't let me try to make Maryanne feel obligated, duty-bound as I always have. She's an adult, though not a mature one. Please God, give me the wisdom and understanding to accept her as she is.

"I'm sorry, too," Sheila said now. And this time she meant it. "Particularly since she didn't give you much notice."

"That's no problem. Forgive me, dear, but I didn't really expect her."

"I know. Neither did I. Not really."

In spite of the absences, the dinner was a huge success. Betty had been right to invite "outsiders." It made it more of a party and less of a solemn gathering of the clan. Sally was her usual sparkling, witty self, and Dr. Mancini was a charming, good-looking, interesting young man. He's a good model for Pat, Sheila thought approvingly. One sensed that his professional skill did not completely overpower his concern and compassion. She liked his directness, among other things.

"I'm sorry about your husband, Mrs. Callahan," he said to her in a quiet moment during cocktails. "First coronaries usually aren't so massive, but it's an easy way to go. You don't know what hit you. It's harder on those who are left behind."

"Yes. But I'm glad he didn't become an invalid. Sean couldn't have stood that."

"Neither could you," he said matter-of-factly.

For a moment Sheila was startled. The statement seemed inordinately blunt. And then she liked it, because it was true. Sean would have been an impossible cripple. She'd have hated it for him. She repeated the last thought aloud, realizing it for the first time.

"You're right. I'd have hated that to happen to him. He was such a strong, vigorous man. He'd have loathed being restricted."

"Forgive me, but I meant more than that. You'd have hated it for your husband, but I think you'd also have hated it for yourself. People are strange. Or maybe I should say 'human.' They patiently take care of ill ones they love, but in time they come to resent the one who's ill. Particularly younger people, like yourself."

"You don't make me sound like much of a person."

"On the contrary, I think you're a lot of person. You'd have stuck by, been as patient as possible and as miserable as normal. But I haven't met many saints in my lifetime. Resentments grow, even in the best of us."

Sheila wasn't sure whether she was intrigued or offended.

63

"You seem to know a lot about human nature for one so young."

"I'm a doctor. And I'm thirty-two years old. The combination adds up to a lot of experience with people."

"You seem much older than thirty-two!" The words came out involuntarily. Betty had said thirty-seven or eight, and Jerry looked it. Thirty-two! My God, he's only six years older than my Patrick! Biologically I could be his mother! The thought made her feel very old. She tried to make a fumbling recovery. "I don't mean that in an uncomplimentary way. When you're my age, thirty-two seems like a baby. I was married when you were five!"

He had an easy, warm laugh. "And I was married when you were thirty-five. So what? I have a daughter ten years old and you have a son who's fifteen. Does that help make us more contemporary?"

Sheila had to laugh, too. "I don't know. But it isn't really important, is it?"

"If you mean age isn't important, I agree. Minds are. Bodies are. But calendars aren't."

Betty appeared suddenly. "I hate to break up this little tête-à-tête, but the monster is out of the oven. All those ready to take a chance on my cooking signify by saying 'Aye'!"

Dinner was delicious, the atmosphere easy and the talk unstilted. Even when Patrick proposed a toast to his father, it was not sad.

"Here's to Dad who could outeat, outdrink, and outcuss any of us. Here's to a man who had it all and loved every minute of it."

They drank to Sean. Sheila's eyes met Jerry's across the table. She nodded as though to say, You're right. My husband was very human. And so am I.

She was not surprised to get a phone call from Dr. Mancini early the next Sunday morning.

"It's a beautiful day," he said without preamble, "and I wondered whether you'd spend it with me."

He didn't even identify himself. He took it for granted she'd recognize his voice, that she'd even been expecting to hear from him. Sheila hesitated for a moment. Why on earth would this young man want to be with her? There must be a hundred women his own age who'd jump at the chance. And yet she'd known he'd want to see her, just as she wanted to see him. There had been something instantaneous and electric between them last Thursday. He'd been in her mind ever since.

"I'd love to. What time?"

"I'll pick you up around noon, if that's okay. Maybe we could take a little drive and have lunch somewhere. The rest of the day can just evolve, unless you have some commitments."

"No. Tommy's been invited to the football game and then to spend the evening at a friend's house. You're saving me from some idle, boring hours."

It was a half-truth. Her Sundays were never idle. She caught up on her personal laundry, washed her hair, straightened Tommy's room, did all the household and "be-kind-to-yourself" things that a day at home allowed. But bored she'd be. And from that Jerry could save her.

He picked her up promptly, almost before she was ready. She'd spent too long fussing over what she'd wear for such an indefinitely planned day. A drive in the country and lunch certainly called for casual clothes, but what about later? Did he mean to also take her out for dinner or perhaps to drop in on some of his friends? She put on and took off half a dozen outfits. No pants suit, she decided. She didn't really like them. The fact was she was vain about her legs. Sean had always said she had sexy legs. What in hell are you thinking of? she asked herself. Are you trying to be sexy for this *boy*? Yes. No. I don't know. I do know I'm as nervous as though I were going on my first date. More nervous. I don't remember ever being so tense about meeting Sean or, before that, Bill Reardon. But I was young and "in practice" then. I haven't had a "date" in twenty-seven years. Besides, with Bill I wasn't wondering whether I was going to end up in bed. I knew I wasn't and this time, let's face it, I'm not so sure. Sheila, you're crazy, going out with this kid. Sheila, stop "thinking old." He likes you. He doesn't care that there are fifteen years between you. Sheila, for God's sake, relax!

"You look beautiful," he said. "I love women in skirts and sweaters, particularly when they wear them to such advantage."

She knew she was literally blushing. He saw and was amused.

"Don't tell me compliments make you uncomfortable!"

She felt better because she could laugh. "I'm afraid so. I've never learned the art of accepting them gracefully."

"It can't be because you haven't had enough of them."

It was all moving too quickly. "When you're an old widow lady of forty-seven," she said deliberately, "you don't really expect them."

He raised an eyebrow. She was laying it out right off, trying to protect herself, probably scared that she looked like a fool going out with a man so many years her junior.

"I do beg your pardon," Jerry said solemnly. "If you'll tell me where you keep your wheel chair, I'll stow it in the back of the car."

"*Touché.*"

"Now that that nonsense is out of the way, may I repeat that you look beautiful?"

"Yes. Thank you. So do you."

"Naturally. We're a couple of the beautiful people." He helped her into her coat. "How about the Red Fox? Suit you for lunch? I made a reservation at one."

There was, after that initial moment, no awkwardness as Sheila had feared. They talked easily on their leisurely drive and later over lunch. The Red Fox was a charming restaurant, as was the town in which it was situated. Sheila loved Gates Mills which reminded her of a little New England village, quaint and friendly. No wonder Sally didn't want to leave her house on its outskirts. The thought of her friend made her uneasy for a moment. What if Sally should walk in and find Sheila lunching with this very young man? Well, what if she did? What harm was there in that? I'm not an old crone, Sheila told herself. Why do I have this hang-up about going out with a man fifteen years younger than I? Sally would be the last one to be disapproving. Sally would be glad she was enjoying herself. And she was.

Jerry seemed extraordinarily mature for his age. She supposed that being a doctor, and apparently a successful one, made him more understanding than if he'd been in a more "frivolous" profession. He talked, frankly and freely, about his private life. His soon-to-be-ex-wife, Barbara, was a lovely girl from a rich family. ("All struggling doctors are supposed to marry rich girls, aren't they?" he asked, a corner of his mouth turning up in mock cynicism.) They'd married while he was still in school and his in-laws had supported them. He'd been twenty-one and Barbara a year younger. She'd become pregnant immediately and they'd moved (courtesy father-in-law) into a big house in Shaker Heights, only about a mile from Sheila's. The marriage had been as unspectacular as it was ill-fated.

"We just weren't equipped for the whole concept of marriage," Jerry said. "I loved Barb and I know she loved me. I think we'll always love each other, if only because we have Joyce in common. She's a nice kid, Sheila. A pretty little girl who's as devoted to me now as she was when I lived at home. Barbara's been good about that. There's no bitterness between us, and certainly Barb hasn't tried to make Joy feel any resentment toward me. I see them both a lot. It's friendly and sensible. We have a legal separation and eventually there'll be a divorce, but neither of us has found anyone else, so there's no need to rush."

"Maybe you'll get back together," Sheila said.

"No. We gave it ten years before we admitted to each other that there was devotion but no communication. It was better to split while Barb still has a chance to start over."

"Barb? What about you?"

"Me too, I hope. But I'll pick differently next time. I hate using that cliché about how we were too young to know what we wanted, but of course we were. Barbara shouldn't be married to a doctor. She's a spoiled girl. That's not her fault, of course. She grew up with lots of money and social life and travel. Even when I could give her money, I couldn't give her the undivided attention she wanted. I can't take long holidays or go

66

to parties every night when I know I have to be on call and alert at eight the next morning. She was bored. That's understandable. She's still young. She should be married to a broker or a banker. I hope she will be. I hope she finds a nice guy. Not one who wants her for her money."

Sheila was silent.

"What are you thinking, pretty lady? That I married her for her money? I didn't, Sheila. Believe it or not, I didn't think about it. Maybe I'm something of a rat, but it didn't even bother me that her family supported us for so many years. Money's not that big a deal to me. I like it. Who doesn't? But I never had any macho thing about having to be the breadwinner. If I had the entire practice of Cleveland, I couldn't make as much in a lifetime as Barbara's father has coming in every month. I knew that. It wasn't important. Other things meant more to me. They still do."

"What other things?"

"Being a good doctor," he said quickly. And then he hesitated. "And now, someday I hope, finding a woman, not a girl. Someone with serenity and understanding and intelligence. I'm complex as hell. I know it. I don't know if there's anybody in the world who could put up with my moods and my single-mindedness. Barb didn't know how to cope with my interests, any more than I could really understand hers." Jerry smiled. "She conforms to the pattern of a well-brought-up WASP. I'm inclined more often to act like an Italian tenor."

"I'm sorry," Sheila said.

"Don't be. Sure, it would have been nice if the marriage had worked, but it didn't. Not really after the first year. You'll probably find this shocking, but I'm actually enjoying my freedom. I'm trying to make up for all the years when other men were living it up as bachelors. Not that I'm doing such a hot job of it," he admitted. "Women are supposed to be swooning at my feet. To tell you the truth, most of them I've been out with in the past six months bore me to death."

He's lonely, Sheila realized incredulously. He's as lonely as I. That's what our instant communication is all about. We're both reaching out for comfort, for someone to cling to, even temporarily. The idea did not deflate her ego. If anything, it relieved her mind. She hadn't been able to understand why this attractive young man had wanted to be with her, why he'd been interested in his friend's mother. Now she knew. She was a safe haven, a respite from the stormy emotions he denied. She felt great tenderness for him. At that moment he seemed no older than Tommy. But her reactions were not maternal. Not by a damned sight. He wanted solace. So did she. In that moment she made up her mind to have an affair with him. There was no future in it, she told herself, but it might make them both feel alive and desirable again.

He was smiling at her now, that crooked, appealing smile. "I am one helluva bore," Jerry said, "and you're the soul of patience to let me rattle on about myself. Tell me about you, Sheila. Did you have a very happy marriage? You started young, too. Did you miss the 'wild oats' period?"

The phrase amused her, as though he was intentionally using the jargon of her generation.

"A happy marriage?" she repeated. "I suppose so. As happy as most. Maybe happier than most. Sean was an exciting man. We did lots of things together." (And some alone, she thought.) "We produced three kids, had a nice home, a pleasant social life. Yes, I guess you could say I had a good marriage, Jerry. It had its bad spots. What marriage doesn't? But I never thought of life without him."

"You miss him a great deal, don't you?"

The question brought Sheila up short. Yes, she missed Sean. It was a different house, a different world without him. The comfort was gone, even the financial worries she used to have seemed nothing in comparison to the precarious way she lived now. But what she really missed was the feeling of womanliness he gave her. Not only in bed—though that was a great part of it—but in the sense of simply being around a man. She'd never been one for the company of women. She had a few good friends, like Sally, but a constant female environment had always bored her. It was why she'd never gone in for afternoon bridge or long shopping expeditions or any of the things that so many wives did. Men stimulated her. Her husband had stimulated her. That's what she missed most. This new feeling of being wanted only as a mother or an employee or a friend was not enough.

"I miss him," she said honestly. "But I don't intend to stop living because he's gone."

It was an unsubtle, unmistakable invitation.

"What about the 'wild oats'?"

She didn't smile. "I missed those too."

Without discussion they went back to Sheila's after lunch. At three o'clock on a sunny November afternoon they undressed each other tenderly and made love. It was a glorious, fully-satisfying experience.

"You really *are* beautiful," Jerry said. "Inside and out, you're a beautiful woman."

Looking at the strong young body, comparing it, with a pang of conscience, to Sean's middle-aged, heavier one, Sheila was happy about what she'd done. She couldn't hold Jerry. There was no way in the world that this union would last. They were using each other. But for now she felt complete, satiated, even young herself. She was glad she'd kept her own figure trim and firm, glad there were no wrinkles on her bottom, no 'spare tire' at her waist. Glad her breasts were still firm and upright, that the nipples grew hard at his touch. Glad she could please this lusty young man as he did her. When it ends I won't be sorry, she told herself. A week, a month, I don't care. He has restored me and I love him for it. I won't weep when he leaves for a day or forever.

68

Chapter 9

When she thought back on that winter, Sheila wondered how she survived it, it was so unlike any she'd ever known, so full of intense highs and lows, like a fever chart gone mad.

In December the store was pure frenzy, to the point that Kitty Rawlings, normally cool and in control, was given to outbursts of nervous, irrational anger. She reduced her little clerk Natalie to tears at least once a day and even snapped at her "ladies," the saleswomen to whom, at other times, she was the soul of kindness. The whole department was on edge, exhausted from the steady stream of gift-book shoppers quite different from the "regulars" who bought at other seasons. It took mental discipline and physical stamina to cope with the Christmas trade and there were many days when Sheila was sure she'd never make it to closing time without giving in to a fit of hysterics or collapsing with fatigue.

"You think *this* is bad?" Dottie Parker asked over a hasty lunch. "Wait until the day after Christmas when the exchanges start. Selling is a positive pleasure compared to writing credit slips and putting up with little old ladies who want to exchange *The Joy of Cooking* for *The Joy of Sex*."

Dottie had gradually become more friendly again. They had not seen each other socially since the ill-fated dinner party, but she and Sheila were once more on comfortable terms, united in the misery of the season.

"I could have wished for Our Saviour to have been born in better weather," Sheila said. "Even getting here in the morning isn't an ideal way to start the day."

It wasn't. They were having a bitter winter with snow piling upon snow. In the morning, Sheila was numb with cold and breathless from the biting wind by the time she got to the little covered platform on Shaker Boulevard to wait for the train. Thank God it arrived in the station right under the store and that she left from there in the evening. But the trains were always crowded with ill-tempered people, frustrated shoppers, harassed workers, men and women, like herself. In spite of how tired she was, she almost ran back to her house in the December blackness. It seemed to her she never saw daylight. It was dark when she awakened and barely light when she left for the store and it was pitch black when she got to Shaker Heights again. Quite often, these days, she regretted not having gone along with Tommy's idea that she try to get a job in the area where she lived. It would have been much easier to drive a few miles to a local store instead of fighting this daily battle to downtown Cleveland. Even the pace of work would have been less hectic in a suburban branch. Foolish-pride-Sheila, that's me, she thought. If she'd known then what she knew now, she'd gladly have waited on her friends instead of facing a howling mob of strangers every day.

In spite of this, the job problems were only temporary. Regardless of Kitty's dire predictions of the days to come, Sheila knew that in a month the department would settle down again, Rawlings would be her calm, pleasant self and the routine would return to normal. Even though months of winter lay ahead, with all the horrors of commuting, spring was inevitable, a certainty to be anticipated, making it possible to endure these days.

Much more serious was the situation at home. She felt Tommy drifting away from her, becoming almost a stranger. He went out almost every evening, God knows where, and when he was home he was withdrawn and quiet. She blamed herself for the change in him. She was gone from morning until night and though this was something she couldn't help, she worried about the boy being so much on his own, without parental supervision. All fall he'd been conscientious about his schoolwork and was keeping up his grades, but he'd lost the gentle, loving personality that had always been Tommy. When she tried to talk to him, he fell silent. Only once had they had a serious argument, and that was not really an argument. It was more a one-sided tirade of accusations against her. It had started innocently enough on one of the rare evenings they were both at home, just before Christmas.

"Darling," Sheila had said, "is everything all right at school?"

"Sure. You know that. You got my grades."

"I didn't mean scholastically. I meant are you happy?" How stupid it sounded, how ridiculous. Sheila blundered on. "I used to know your friends at University. You'd have the boys here at the house and their parents were our friends. I knew you were having fun. I don't know anyone you see now."

There was a slight change of expression, a trace of cynicism. "How do you think we could work that out, Mom? You're not around during the day like you used to be. I know you can't help that, but it's still true." Tommy's voice hardened. "As for the evenings, you either go to bed right after dinner or you see Dr. Mancini."

She tried to ignore the last part of the sentence. "Honey, I know I'm not good company these days. The store is brutal right now. I can hardly hold my head up at night, I'm so tired."

"Not too tired for that doctor." It was a flat statement, strangely mature and bitter. "You don't seen too pooped when he calls."

She was quiet for a moment. "You don't like Jerry do you?"

"I don't care about him one way or the other."

"You're not a very good liar, Tommy. Has someone been talking to you about Jerry and me? Have you heard something against him?"

Suddenly he was furious. "For Christ's sake, stop treating me like a goddamn baby!"

"Tommy! Your language!"

It was as though he hadn't heard her. For a moment he reminded her of Sean in one of his irrational rages.

"I can't stand seeing you make a damned fool of yourself!" Tommy screamed. "Playing around with a guy who could practically be your son and pretending I don't know what's going on! You never see anybody you and Dad used to see. All you want to do is get home, stuff some dinner down me, and hope that horny creep will call you! And if he doesn't, you go to bed. No wonder I get the hell out of here at night! What am I supposed to do? Sit around and watch you moon over each other? Or go to my room so you can have the house to yourself? Or would you like me to invite my friends over to meet my mother's little boy friend?"

Sheila's pain was literally physical. She could feel it around her heart and in the tightening of her stomach muscles. It was the way she used to feel when Sean used his anger and sarcasm on her like a whip. Crack. You're a lousy mother. Crack. You're a silly woman. Crack. You're driving me out of the house. The lashes from Tommy's tongue were as real as though he'd struck her. For a moment she wanted to strike back, just as she had sometimes answered Sean's Irish temper with her own. Then she remembered that Tommy was just a boy, needing attention and reassurance. For all his adult words and ways, he was a teen-ager who felt lost and rejected. If I'm not careful, she thought, he'll *really* go away. The world was full of runaway kids of his age, youngsters who felt unloved and unwanted at home. And yet, he couldn't be allowed to direct her life.

71

His jealousy—and that was most of it—mustn't be permitted to deprive her of the only moments of joy she had these days.

"Tommy," she said finally, almost in a whisper, "please try to understand. I love you more than anything in the world. I want to be a good mother to you. It's what I've always wanted. But, darling, I'm a woman, too. I need adult companionship and, yes, admiration. Don't you think I know how people are talking about the 'unsuitability' of my going out with a man fifteen years younger than I?" She shook her head. "I'm aware of the gossip but I didn't realize you thought anything of it. I thought you wanted to be with your friends in the evening. I didn't know I was driving you out of the house. I'd never do that." She looked straight at him. "Tom, I enjoy being with Jerry Mancini, but I'm never going to marry him. I know one day he'll get tired of me. He'll meet someone his own age. I'm prepared for that. But meantime, dear, can you understand how it feels for me to be alone after so many years of marriage? Can you understand how much my ego needs this flattery, superficial and transient as it may be? I never meant to neglect you. I didn't know you felt neglected. I suppose I just thought you had your own life, your own world, and not very much need of me."

He was quiet now, looking at her with love, like the "old Tommy." "I'm sorry, Mom. I guess I never thought about your feelings. But couldn't you meet somebody more your type? I mean, I can understand how lonesome you are, but does it have to be Jerry?"

She ached for him, but she stood firm. "Yes, darling, for now it has to be Jerry. I'm sorry if it embarrasses you. Perhaps it won't so much if you understand that I'm not being a fatuous old fool."

He didn't answer.

"No, I see it won't change," Sheila said wistfully, "so I expect the only answer is some kind of compromise. *I'll* try to be more available to you, and *you* let me a little more into your present life. How about that?"

Tommy shook his head. "Forget it, Mom. You wouldn't have anything in common with the kids in Shaker Heights High. I mean, you'd never know *their* parents. And as for being with me more, how can you? Like you said, you need adult companionship and when you don't have Jerry you need your sleep."

She felt very sad and helpless. "When the Christmas rush is over, I won't be so tired. We can have lots of evenings together. Go to the movies. Visit Pat and Betty. Anything you like."

"Great." He didn't even try to make it sound like the truth. "I better go up and crack the books now."

"It's your Christmas vacation!"

"Yeah. Well, there's a lot of reading I need to do. Good night, Mom."

She kissed him. "Good night, Tommy."

72

Her "romance," indeed her whole life, was the topic of conversation in other households as well. It was no secret that she was "dating" Jerry Mancini, a fact of considerable interest and some concern to those nearest to her. The reactions ranged from approval to dismay, from surprise to envy.

Emily Ross was one who was secretly envious and overtly outraged. In the midst of wrapping Christmas packages while Bob worked at his desk in the study, Emily gave a vicious yank to a red satin bow and said, "I'd like to pull Sheila Callahan's hair that way!"

Her husband looked up. "What brought *that* on?"

"The way she's behaving. The way she's been behaving practically ever since poor Sean died! It's shocking. Talk about the Merry Widow!"

Bob went back to his papers.

"I really think you should speak to her about it," Emily said. "She's making an ass of herself over that young doctor. Everybody in town is talking about her. Not five months since her husband died and she's having an affair! And with a *boy* at that!" Emily stopped long enough to write "Warmest Love and Christmas greetings" on a gift tag and then put down the pen. "Bob, you're not paying attention."

"To you or the gossip?"

"Neither, I gather!"

He swiveled around in his chair and looked at her. "All right, Em. That's true. I'm not paying attention to either. Sheila's behavior is not your business or mine or the neighborhood's."

"That's some attitude for a man who was supposed to be Sean Callahan's best friend!"

He felt himself getting angry, but he managed to control himself. They'd been fighting more and more lately over everything, anything. Since summer Emily had been in a strange, unhappy mood. He wondered whether she was starting change of life. She was his age, fifty-three. Certainly time for it. At best she'd never been easy to live with. If she was going to start the snappishness and distress of menopause, he wasn't sure he could cope.

"I was Sean's friend," he said now, "and also his lawyer. I'm now Sheila's lawyer and friend. But I don't think those facts give me the right to meddle in her life. Besides, honestly, I don't see what she's doing that's so terrible. Good God, the woman's gone to work at a tough job. She's still making a nice home for Tommy. She never whines about what a dirty deal she got from Sean—dead or alive." He stopped. He hadn't meant to say the last three words. Certainly not the final one. The world knew how her husband had humiliated Sheila. He wondered whether the world suspected that Emily had been one of the women Sean had used as a tool of that humiliation. Bob had been almost certain of it for months

73

before Sean's death, months in which Emily had been euphoric and Sean nervous. He'd said nothing to either of them, not certain why he kept his mouth shut and then realizing, incredibly, that even if it was true, he didn't care. He hadn't been in love with Emily for years. He hadn't slept with her as man and wife for months, even before he suspected she was going to bed with Sean Callahan. When he did suspect, he hadn't said anything at the time or since. Maybe, he thought now, I didn't really want to believe it. Or maybe I hoped Sheila would find out and divorce Sean. If so, I was being stupid. She had to know about his constant infidelities. But maybe she didn't know about Emily. The idea struck him that Emily had not only been unfaithful, she'd really been in love with Sean. Of course! How dense could he be? Her terrible change of mood coincided with the death of her lover. Maybe Emily had entertained the same wild idea Bob had: that Sheila would let Sean go. And when death interrupted her dreams, she took her anger and frustration out on her husband. And now on Sheila. Emily was looking at him with hatred, her eyes blazing.

"That's right," she said bitterly, "defend her. The poor, brave little widow. Going to work, keeping up the house for her son, never complaining about anything. That's how you see her, don't you? Well, let me tell you something. She's heartless. Always has been. Always will be. Why do you think Sean . . ." She stopped abruptly, suddenly aware that her hatred had nearly betrayed her.

"Why do I think Sean *what?*" Bob's voice was cold.

He knows, Emily thought. He knows about Sean and me. Nonsense. He'd never have kept quiet about it. She decided to brazen it out. "Why do you think Sean ran around with women? That's *what!* Happily married people don't cheat. If Sheila hadn't been such a selfish, domineering, frigid bitch, Sean wouldn't have had to look outside for someone who understood him! Sheila Callahan's fooled everybody in this town for years. But she never fooled me."

He wanted to kill her. Not for her adultery, but for thinking she could make a fool of him by accusing Sheila of being the rotten one in the Callahan marriage. Most of all by trying to pull off this bluff about "other women," as though she were not one of them. He was amazed by the calmness with which he could answer her.

"So Sheila never fooled you. But *you* fooled *her*, didn't you?"

"I don't know what you're talking about."

"Come off it, Emily. I know about you and Sean. I also know that you were one of a long list of that 'misunderstood man's' conquests. Sheila didn't drive him to other beds. Cleopatra and Madame DuBarry rolled into one couldn't have made Sean Callahan monogamous. He was a born tomcat. But he only *loved* one woman: Sheila."

The color drained out of Emily's face.

"That really kills you, doesn't it? You honestly thought that Sean was in love with you. What a fool you are, Emily. Worse than that, what a vicious, small-minded woman. It wasn't enough you tried to take Sheila's husband. Now you want to punish her for having had him all those years."

"You're crazy! You're twisting this whole thing around because you've always been in love with your best friend's wife and a 'gentleman' doesn't admit such a breach of conduct! You're deliberately trying to put me on the defensive to cover your own guilt feelings!"

He laughed, and his laughter was the last straw. Emily ran across the room and began to hit him with her fists. He caught her wrists and held her as she struggled. She was crying now, hysterical.

"I hate you!" Emily screamed. "I hate you because *you're* alive!"

He felt pity for her and loathing for Sean. And something else. Emily was wrong when she accused him of twisting the story, for his accusations were true. But she was right about one thing. He'd always felt desire for Sheila and refused to admit it even to himself. He'd not wanted to think of himself as a Sean, lusting after other men's wives, but he now faced what he'd tried to deny. He loved Sheila Callahan. Loved her completely and hopelessly. Loved her enough to hope she'd find happiness with this young doctor or any other man who appreciated her. Slowly he released his wife.

"Don't ever criticize Sheila again," he said flatly. "And don't ever get out of line again, Emily. Because next time I won't stand for it."

At Sean's brother's house, it was Terry who brought up the subject of Sheila's unorthodox behavior.

"Maggie," he said, "you picked up any rumblings about Sheila and some young doctor?"

"Jerry Mancini," she said. "He's a friend of Patrick's. Separated from his wife. He and Sheila met on Thanksgiving at Pat and Betty's. I understand Sheila's been seeing him for nearly a month."

"You knew and didn't tell me?"

"I figured you'd be upset, which you obviously are."

Terry looked indignant. "That's a helluva poor excuse for not letting me in on what's going on with my brother's widow! I have a responsibility for her, after all. If she's getting herself involved with some fellow half her age, it's my duty to have a talk with her."

Margaret was sarcastic. "He isn't half her age. Only about fifteen years younger. And what do you think you'd accomplish by this fraternal advice? You know I've tried to introduce her to suitable men and she wants no part of them. Carl Dougherty told me she practically slammed her front door in his face that night he took her home after the dinner party here."

"Carl Dougherty is a dirty old man."

"Probably. But he's a widower and in Sheila's age bracket, more or less. There aren't too many of those around, but I've decided Sheila doesn't care. Apparently she likes dirty *young* men."

"You think she's having an affair with this Mancini?"

"My dear, I haven't been under the bed, but she's a grown woman and I daresay . . ."

Terry frowned. "I don't like it. She'll get hurt. And it's no good for Tommy, seeing his mother carry on with his brother's friend. He's at an impressionable age. Besides, it's all too soon, no matter *who* the man is. There should be a decent period of mourning. It seemed to me that Sheila never handled the whole thing properly from the beginning. Too fast. Too cold. That closed casket and not even wearing a veil to the funeral."

"You're a few months late with all those objections, if you don't mind my saying so. Where were all those strong convictions last summer?"

"I was too stunned. Too concerned about Sean's wife and children. And about our parents. They'd be very upset now if they knew Sheila was seeing some thirty-year-old and Sean was only a few months in his grave. You don't think they know, do you?"

"I would doubt the news has reached Sarasota unless some 'good-hearted soul' like Emily Ross has written."

Terry let that pass. "What about Patrick? Does he know?"

"I'm sure he must. He works with Jerry Mancini."

"Maybe I should discuss this with Pat before I talk to Sheila."

"Good idea," Margaret said. "Except, of course, it was Pat and Betty who got them together in the first place."

"Well I'm sure they didn't intend it to work out this way! I'm going to call Patrick right now."

Margaret didn't answer. You are really a dull-witted man, she thought. How lucky you are to have a strong wife who knows how to handle you.

Patrick put down the phone and shook his head.

"Don't tell me," Betty said; "let me guess. Uncle Terry has just caught up with the romance of the century."

Pat nodded. "And pretty hot under the collar about it. Lots of pompous goings-on about 'suitable mourning periods' and injuries to Tommy's psyche."

"What does he want you to do about it?"

"Talk to Jerry."

"You're kidding!"

"I wish I were. The giant brain of my Uncle Terry has concluded that Mom won't listen to reason so I should advise Jerry to get out of her life."

Betty sighed. "So she can eventually take up with one of Margaret's more appropriate candidates, no doubt."

"I imagine so. He hinted as much."

"I see dear Maggie's fine, devious hand in all this, somehow. Things haven't worked out as she planned and she's probably irritated to death. What are you going to do, Pat?"

"You're the psychologist in the family. What would you suggest?"

"Quick answer? Butt out."

"Honey, you know I can't get away with that. It's too easy. Besides, there is one thing Uncle Terry said that halfway made sense. He's afraid Mom's going to get hurt. The age difference. I worry about that, too. Jerry's a terrific guy, but I can't believe he's serious about Mother."

"Whoever said he was? I'd be surprised if even Sheila thought it was going anywhere. Pat, darling, she's having fun. For the first time in a long time. Why should anybody want to take the joy out of her life? Hasn't she had enough problems? Hasn't she still?"

Betty made sense and Pat knew he'd feel like a damned fool going up to Jerry Mancini and asking him in effect what his intentions were. Still, now that the family had wind of it, there'd be no peace until he did something. But he couldn't talk to Jerry. It was absurd.

"Maybe I'll have a talk with Mom," he said.

"I have a better idea," Betty said. "Let *me* talk with her. Emotional problems are my line of work, remember? Not that I think Sheila has any. I'd feel like I was doing a helluva lot more good if I could get at Maryanne. She's the woman in this family who needs help."

"Tackle one that might be solvable," Pat said. "I'd appreciate your talking to Mom, baby. You'd be wasting your time on my sister."

"Maybe. Anyway, first things first. I'll call Sheila tomorrow."

"You're a love."

"I know," Betty said. "I'm adorable. Me and Dr. Joyce Brothers."

Chapter 10

Life had always been easy for Giovanni Mancini. Easy to accept, unquestioningly, the twelve-hour days his Italian immigrant parents had put in at their little delicatessen so that there'd be money to educate their only child. Easy to bask in their adoration when he was named "Most likely to succeed" in his high-school yearbook, when he was top of his class in college and med school, when his good looks and inherent Latin charm caused him to be "taken up" by the sons and daughters of Cleveland's richest and most socially prominent families. Even his "pursuit" of Barbara had been no pursuit at all. She'd fallen blindly in love with him the first night they'd met at a party, had called him the next day to boldly suggest a date, had married him six months later. Her parents had gently opposed this match. Not that they didn't like Jerry. Everybody did. But they had understandable reservations about the youth of the pair and conservative doubts about the wisdom of a young man just starting medical school taking on the responsibilities of marriage. Privately, they also were less than happy about the merging of such disparate backgrounds. The Newtons were "old Cleveland" with position as well as money. They'd hoped for a different sort of husband for their beautiful Barbara, someone of her own "class," someone substantial and established by birth in the circle Barbara had been brought up in.

But they gave in to what she wanted, as they always had. Jerry and

78

Barbara had a big wedding and a brief but lavish honeymoon in Hawaii. They settled into the house bought and paid for by the Newtons and lived on the generous allowance provided by Barbara's parents. When Joyce was born a year later the Newtons were ecstatic about their granddaughter. And in time, when Jerry developed a lucrative private practice, they began to think that they'd been overly apprehensive. True, they'd made a sizable investment before Jerry "got on his feet." But once he did, he almost immediately acquired an impressive reputation, not undeserved. He was a good and dedicated doctor, confidence-inspiring because he never lacked confidence in himself. To him, medicine was easy, as school and social acceptance and marriage had been easy. He'd never, for one moment, questioned his eventual success in his profession or, when he thought about it, which was rarely, his satisfactory qualities as a husband.

So he was genuinely shocked when Barbara quietly announced one evening, ten years after their marriage, that she wanted a divorce.

"A *divorce?* What are you talking about?"

"I mean it, Jerry. I haven't been happy for a long time. You've just been too busy to notice."

He stared at her, dumbfounded. "I don't understand. You've never said anything about being unhappy. My God, we don't even fight!"

"Exactly. I don't see enough of you to indulge in that healthy outlet."

He tried to reason with her. "Barb, this is crazy. People don't get divorced without warning."

"There have been warnings, Jerry. You've just ignored them. You're too wrapped up in yourself and your work to think about me or anybody else. I'm lonely. I'm bored." She looked sad. "It's not your fault, not really. I'm not cut out to be a doctor's wife, I guess. I want to have some fun before I sink into middle age. I hate never being able to go away on a holiday or even out for an evening without your checking your answering service every fifteen minutes and half the time leaving me alone at a party while you rush off to deliver a baby. I want a full-time husband, not an extension of a delivery room."

"You're not making any sense," Jerry said. "I'm an obstetrician and gynecologist. You knew that's what I planned to be when we got married. Delivering babies is my job, and they don't time their arrival to avoid interrupting dinner parties!" He was angry now. "This is unreal! You have a home, a child, even, strangely enough, a *faithful* husband. And out of the blue you want to chuck it because you're *bored!* After ten years, without so much as a preliminary discussion, you decide you want out. What about Joy? Have you thought of her in all this? Have you thought of me? I love you, you know. Wouldn't it have been only decent to give me some hint of what you were feeling?"

"I told you I tried. I begged you to stop working so hard, to spend more time at home, to take a vacation now and then. You thought I was only nagging. Maybe I was too passive about it. Maybe I should have yelled and screamed and thrown dishes to get your attention, to make you see how I was stagnating while you were enjoying life. I'm sorry, Jerry, but you're a selfish, self-centered man, rotten spoiled by your parents and mine. I'm sure you can't help it. It's all been so effortless. You've come to take everything for granted—success, popularity, money, and position. Not to mention *me*."

"Spoiled!" he echoed. "Listen who's talking about spoiled! You've never done a day's work in your life. You don't know how damned lucky you are! You should be like Betty Callahan. She's working in a slum clinic to put her husband through his internship, coming home and cleaning a crummy little apartment and cooking meals at any hour Pat gets off duty!"

Barbara's expression hadn't changed. "It's too bad she didn't have rich parents to support her and her husband through these difficult years."

Jerry was furious. "So now you're going to throw that in my face, too —the fact that Pa Newton paid the bills here for so many years!"

"Well, my dear, you *did* let him."

"I suppose you'd rather we'd done it the way the Callahans are!"

"I don't know," Barbara said. "Nobody ever asked me."

He'd moved to a hotel next day and after a couple of weeks he and Barbara had seen each other and talked quietly. They'd agreed to stay on friendly terms. He could see Joyce whenever he liked and though Barbara insisted on a legal separation she promised not to rush into a divorce.

"I have no reason to," she said. "I'm not leaving you for another man."

"How is your family taking it?"

"They're sorry, but I think they understand. Yours?"

He gave a humorless laugh. "You'd think it was the end of the world. Mamma hasn't stopped sobbing into the spaghetti and Papa just shakes his head like he can't believe it."

"They must hate me."

"Strangely enough, no. For the first time they see a flaw in *my* character. They're not sure what I've done wrong, but they know it must have been something terrible to make a wonderful young woman like you decide she didn't want to be married to me any more."

"Didn't you tell them the simple truth—that we just aren't right for each other? That it really isn't anybody's fault?"

"I tried, Barb, but they're of the old till-death-us-do-part school. In their world people don't separate because they're incompatible. In fact, people don't separate at all."

"I'm sorry, Jerry. I really like your parents."

He hesitated. "Barb, are you sure this is the right thing we're doing?"

"Yes, I'm sure. I've had time to think these past couple of weeks. I said some nasty things to you. Unfair things, really. I guess I've never really grown up, Jerry. I *am* spoiled, I suppose. Childishly spoiled. Not that you aren't, too. But perhaps a more mature woman would understand you better, make you happier."

"I was happy."

"No you weren't. You were just busy."

He'd had to settle for that. He found himself a small, well-furnished apartment. His work occupied most of his time and after a few weeks, when the news of his separation got out, he began to accept invitations from friends who always had "a darling girl" they wanted him to meet. The darling girls were a bore. Most of them were in their late twenties, still single, or divorced and man-hungry. They were perfectly willing to go to bed with him and if he took any of them out more than twice he saw the telltale look of possession begin to come into their eyes. He'd move off quickly, then, to the next repetitious encounter. It was still all too easy.

Sheila was the first woman he met in the six months of his separation who really interested him. He supposed, in a way, that beginning an affair with her had been easy, too. They'd made love the first time he took her out, but somehow it was different. He had no feeling that she expected anything to come of it, sensed that he was free to disappear from her life whenever he chose. She almost overdid the emphasis on their age difference, as though to reassure him that she knew it was a temporary thing, something they both needed, but something that had no possible future. He didn't know exactly how he felt about Sheila. Sometimes, particularly in bed, he thought he was in love with her and that she couldn't possibly fail to be in love with him. But she refused to say "I love you" except in a lighthearted, almost casual way, the way people said the words to dear friends or even chance acquaintances who'd done something nice for them.

He remembered Barbara saying something about a mature woman, someone who would understand him. Maybe she'd been right. Maybe Sheila with her wisdom and experience, her undemanding acceptance of him was what he needed. Fifteen years wasn't all that terrible. He'd always felt old for his age. Right now it didn't matter that she was so much his senior. It was only when he thought about the future that he felt uneasy. When I'm forty-five she'll be sixty. When I'm fifty-five and still in my prime she'll be an old lady of seventy.

To hell with it. Right now he was enjoying Sheila and doing her more good than harm. Besides, she wasn't taking him seriously. He was positive of that.

Jerry couldn't have been more mistaken. Sheila did tell herself that her affair with the young doctor never could go anywhere, that there was no hope of anything permanent for them, that it was one of those fortunate interludes that had come along at the right time for a widowed woman and a separated man. And yet, knowing, intellectually, that it was stupid, she could not suppress the idea that maybe it *was* more than a momentary thing. There was no doubt that Jerry was devoted to her, but she forced herself to believe that he was not in love with her, even though he said it often. She told herself, over and over, that his was a temporary infatuation, that she represented something intriguingly different from the young, spoiled wife who, he admitted with appealing candor, had rejected him.

But to her dismay, she sometimes found herself fantasizing about life with Jerry, even half-planning what marriage to him would be. Her uncontrollable thoughts, so at odds with her good sense, frightened her. I'm in love with him, Sheila thought. If he walks out on me, no, dammit, *when* he does, I'm going to suffer. She thought sometimes of ending the relationship before she became even more attached to him. There were evenings when she decided that this would be the night she'd break it off. And then he'd arrive, full of warmth and kisses and funny presents with loving cards, and she'd melt under the flattery that was so satisfying, the passion that made her feel so young and desirable.

She was aware that everyone knew she was seeing Jerry. They'd made no secret of going out in public, and Shaker Heights, big and sprawling as it was, was still a small town interlaced with a village grapevine. She was sure that Bob and Emily Ross and Terry and Margaret knew what was going on. But she discussed it with no one. Except for the disturbing conversation with Tommy and a brief mention to Sally Cantrell, she acted as though there was nothing in her life but her family, her home, and her job.

Tommy's resentment of Jerry concerned her, but she clung stubbornly to the idea that he was a child who could not truly understand. Sally's reaction was something else. She didn't know why she told Sally about the affair. Wrong. Sheila knew very well why she'd told her. She had to tell someone, perhaps to test "public opinion." More likely, she thought, ashamed of the pettiness, she wanted someone to know that she could attract a lover. She'd been so long an accepted part of one man's life, as familiar as a piece of furniture. She was wise enough to recognize the motivation that made her confide in her best friend. In effect she was saying, "Look at me! I'm forty-seven. I have grown, married children. And a young, successful man has picked me over any of the twenty-year-olds he could have! I'm not over the hill. I have maturity and experience and I'm *wanted*." It was disgusting, Sheila's reason told her. She was going to end up looking like an idiot. But she couldn't make her emotions believe what her intellect told her was true.

I love him, she thought. God help me, I do.

She did not say all these things to Sally, but she did volunteer the information, trying to sound casual about it, that she was going out with Jerry Mancini.

"I know," Sally said. "Hell, Sheila, *everybody* knows."

"I suppose they think I'm making a fool of myself."

Sally didn't pull any punches. "I guess you could say that's the popular opinion. You didn't think it would be otherwise, did you? Sweetie, you're doing everything to scandalize people. You started going with a man only three months or so after your husband died. And as if that weren't enough, you picked one quite a few years younger than yourself and one who's married, to boot! Now *that* combination of goodies has got to offend the tender sensibilities of the local squares."

"He's not married," Sheila said inanely. "He has a legal separation."

"Terrific."

"I know it's unorthodox. Tasteless, I suppose. But is it so terrible that I'm finding a little pleasure? Do you agree with everybody, Sally?"

"No, I don't agree. I know you've mourned Sean in a realistic way. I know his death was a shock and a shame, but I'm glad you haven't gone around wringing your hands and saying your life is over, like some of our more hypocritical widow friends. You have too much class for that. I see nothing wrong with your going out with a man. In fact," Sally laughed, "I'm a teeny bit envious of the fact that you found one so fast. And finally, I don't think his age matters a bit at this point. In fact, in a way it's good for you to find out after twenty-seven years with one man that other men find you attractive, especially young, virile ones."

"But," Sheila said. "Go on, Sally, I know there's a 'but' at the end of this."

"But," Sally said, "I hope you're keeping it in some kind of perspective. Not that I don't think Jerry Mancini wouldn't be the luckiest kid on the block to get you. You have everything to offer. But these things usually don't last, Sheila. I'm sure you know that. I'm positive you've considered that Jerry could meet someone tomorrow and the whole wonderful dream would be over. Maybe it won't happen that way. There've been good marriages where the woman is older, but they're still rare. I'd feel a lot better, if I were sure you're braced for the day you might find the good doctor letting you down. I don't want to see you hurt. I know what that kind of rejection could do to you, especially after all you've been through. I'm not saying it will happen. I just don't want to see you go into a tailspin if it does. And I hope you're smart enough to consider that it might. Have fun with him, Sheila, but for God's sake don't fall in love with him."

"Thank you for understanding," Sheila said. "I knew you would. And you needn't worry. I've told myself those same things a hundred times in the past month." But I can't make myself truly believe them, she added silently. I know I should. I must face reality. And I don't want to.

It was almost funny that she'd be having a conversation along some-what similar lines with her daughter-in-law a few days after she'd discussed Jerry with her best friend. Betty rang up on Sunday morning and asked whether she could come over, ostensibly to discuss Christmas.

"Pat's working," she said, "and I thought if you were free we might spend a couple of hours together."

"Of course," Sheila said. "I'd be delighted."

"I'm not interrupting any plans you have?"

"None at all." It was true. This was Jerry's day with Joyce. He was going to take her to the Cleveland Zoo and to a "grown-up lunch." Later he'd come to take Sheila out to dinner. He'd suggested, the night before, that Tommy join them, but the boy had almost rudely refused, and his churlishness had angered Sheila.

"Tommy, why not? We'll go to some nice place, just the three of us. You're really being very ungracious!"

"It's okay," Jerry had said. "Tom would probably rather watch TV than hang around with the old folks."

The boy had given him a withering look. "Yeah, that's right. It's more fun to be with people your own age." And then, with exaggerated polite-ness, "Thanks anyway, Dr. Mancini. It's nice of you to include me, but I'll call up one of the guys and go get a pizza."

"You'll do no such thing," Sheila had said. "If you won't go with us, I'll feed you before we leave."

"Don't bother, Mom. The other way's easier."

"What am I going to do about him?" Sheila asked when Tommy left the room. "He's such a changed child these days."

"Darling, the first thing you'd better do is get it into your head that he's not a child any longer. They grow up fast these days, Sheila. Look, he resents me. Classic, at his age, and especially in his new situation. Be patient with him. He's a good kid with good instincts. He'll grow out of this." Jerry grinned. "Hell, in time he may even come to accept me."

It was the kind of little offhand statement that foolishly set Sheila's heart pounding. It hinted that Jerry would be around a long time, maybe forever. Stop it! she told herself. Don't blind yourself to the real facts. Don't let your wishful thinking cloud your common sense.

She was thinking that now as she waited for Betty to arrive. She had a strong hunch that this was a contrived visit. They knew they were com-ing to her for Christmas. It was all set. Even Rose was coming from New York. And Maryanne had said she'd be there if she could bring Rick. Sheila was less than thrilled with that idea, but she'd rather have her daughter come with her lover than not show up at all. Could be, Sheila thought ruefully, I'm a little more tolerant of her behavior since I'm guilty of it myself. The comparison, of course, was ridiculous. Sheila was a grown woman, having an affair with a respectable man. Maryanne was throwing her life away on a sordid, futureless relationship with a low-class dropout. Maryanne's life was ahead of her; her mother's was more than half over. And yet they were both adults, presumably capable of making their choices without censure from others.

Jerry was coming for Christmas dinner, too. He'd spend the morning with Barbara and Joyce, to be with his child when she opened her gifts. Then he'd come to Sheila's about four o'clock. "Provided," he said, laughing, "that none of my ladies chooses that day to produce a Baby Jesus."

She wondered what they'd all think of Jerry. It was possible that Maryanne didn't know he existed, and Rose certainly had no clue, but she soon would. She was coming two days ahead and Sheila would have to tell her about the man she was seeing. She shuddered to think of her mother's reaction to that.

Terry and Margaret always spent holidays with Margaret's family, but they'd drop in later. So would the Rosses. Sean's parents couldn't be there, but they'd all talk to them on the phone. She'd asked Sally but her friend had decided to go away for the holidays.

"It's the one time of year I can't stand to be home," she said. "At least you have family, Sheila, but I feel like Orphan Annie. I'm going to New York to stay with Liz Mayberry. It'll all be very chic and cynical and phony, with gold and white Christmas decorations on her penthouse terrace and lots of lonely people all pretending they hate the season. It'll be unreal, but there won't be memories. I'm not surprised that the psychiatrists say the period between Thanksgiving and New Year's is a heyday for suicides. Everybody gets childishly depressed. Everybody who's alone, that is. I keep telling myself that December 25 is just another goddamn day, but I still come unglued remembering happy Christmases. Or at least they seem happy in retrospect. I'm not sure they were, even then."

Sheila's mind wandered over many things as she fixed a light lunch for Betty and herself. She was glad her daughter-in-law was coming, and a little curious as to why. Like herself, Betty always had a thousand chores to do on her day off. It was unusual for her to come calling. Sheila hoped there was nothing wrong between Pat and Betty. It seemed such a good marriage. Her son had chosen well, a generous, understanding, feet-on-the-ground girl, a perfect complement to his inherited fey Irish nature. No, she was sure there was nothing wrong with those two. But there was something wrong somewhere. Sheila sensed it and waited impatiently to find out what.

She didn't have to wait long.

"I didn't pop over to discuss Christmas," Betty said almost as soon as she sat down.

"I figured. What, then?"

85

"You."

Sheila raised her eyebrows. "Me? In what aspect?"

"You and Jerry. Your family's having a fit and I'm the designated spokesman. I wasn't drafted. I volunteered."

"You mean Patrick's upset?"

"No. Well, not really. He's glad you're happy if you don't get hurt."

"Tommy," Sheila said. "Tommy's been talking to you and Pat."

Betty shook her head. "Not a word out of that one. It's Sean's family. Uncle Terry, to be exact. Aided and abetted, I'm sure, by dear Aunt Margaret."

"Of course." Sheila half-smiled. "I should have known." She had little love for Sean's brother and less for his wife, small-minded people, both, given to pronouncements. Not bad people. Simply unable to understand anything outside the norm. "Strange," Sheila said, "I was just thinking of them, wondering how they'll react to Jerry when they meet him late on Christmas Day. We haven't had much contact lately. Not since I proved so unco-operative about Margaret's matchmaking efforts. So they've heard about my 'cradle snatching,' have they? And they're horrified. Terry wouldn't have courage to face me himself, so he called you and Pat, right? You're supposed to read me the riot act, make me 'come to my senses,' as Margaret would say. Okay, Betty, my love. I doubt there's much you can say that I haven't already mulled over in my own mind. I'm behaving stupidly. My finger is on the self-destruct button. That's the gist of it, isn't it?"

Her daughter-in-law's heart went out to her. She understood Sheila better than any of them, not only because it was her job to understand people but because she felt close to Pat's mother. Betty saw her not as a replacement for her own mother, but as someone she admired as a woman and a friend. She had integrity and honesty, qualities Betty admired above all others. Sheila had never fooled herself about Sean or Maryanne, never tried to pretend they had no faults, as some wives and mothers would have. Yet she'd never made a public display of her problems with either. She kept her 'dirty linen' to herself, never playing the martyr or asking for help. Just as, now, she obviously was trying to come to terms with her own feelings about Jerry.

"I'm not here as the family spokesman," Betty said now. "Pat thinks I am, but I'm not. I'm here as a friend. I'm not putting down my husband or even the aunt and uncle, Sheila, but I don't think they have a right to mess in your life. I'm sure they're doing it out of concern for you, at least I know Pat is, but I think they underrate your intelligence. Not to mention your courage."

Sheila looked surprised. "You don't think I'm wrong to see Jerry?"

"Wrong? Who made up rules about right and wrong? 'Society' says its wrong for a woman to enjoy the company of a man younger than herself, even though it's all right for any old duffer to take out a girl young enough to be his daughter. Nobody thinks *that's* disgraceful, in fact it's almost expected. Nobody gets all hung up about *his* sensibilities if the girl drops him for whatever reason. I suppose they think he can replace her without blinking an eye or shedding a tear. It seems to presume that the male is the stronger sex emotionally as well as physically, and I have my doubts about *that.* You know I'm no big Libber, Sheila, but this is one double standard I can't swallow. Why should people condemn you for seeing a man who's not your age? What the hell's wrong with that? I know a lot of guys who like more mature, experienced women, 'real' fellas in their thirties who're bored to death with the aimless chatter of dames my age. And, lately, young women are so competitive, so hell-bent on being 'equal' that more and more young guys are realizing that it's exciting to be with a really feminine female. One like you who isn't out to castrate them. One who knows how to make a man feel strong and protective. That kind of knowledge comes with experience, and you don't get that experience—socially and sexually— when you're two years out of college. The whole damn system is cockeyed!" Betty had become more vehement as she went along. "Dammit, Sheila, if you and Jerry are finding something you need in each other, who's to say that isn't 'the thing to do'? And if it doesn't last, why shouldn't you be expected to handle the consequences? You know the pitfalls, but you also know the pleasures, and I, for one, am not worried about society going 'tsk, tsk,' any more than I'm worried that you'll come unglued if the whole romance goes up in smoke!"

The long, impassioned speech brought tears of gratitude to Sheila's eyes. Even Sally hadn't been so fiercely loyal, so completely sensible. It was because Betty was of a new generation, Sheila thought. A much freer, more understanding one, not brainwashed by conventional rules. But it was also, she realized, because Betty had faith in her and loved her. Her daughter-in-law, so young yet so wise, would defend her unorthodox behavior now, and be around to help pick up the pieces, if that was called for later. Sheila swallowed hard and tried to sound lighthearted.

"You're a traitor to the family, darling, and God bless you for it. You're the only one who understands."

"I know *you,*" Betty said quietly. "You've taken a lot without whimpering. You can take criticism now and disappointment later, if you must."

"Yes," Sheila said thoughtfully, "I think I can. Jerry's done something for me that I needed. I don't know where we're headed, if anywhere. I try to tell myself that we're creatures of the moment, though I don't want to believe it, even while I know I should. I suppose I just want to live for now and not think about the future. I know I haven't felt as alive in years."

"Then enjoy it, and don't let the Terrys and Margarets of this world spoil one second of it." Betty smiled. "And hold that thought when Grandma Rose gets here, too."

Sheila returned the smile. "That's when I'll need it for sure. You may have to come back and give me another fight talk about 'women's rights.'"

"Any time," Betty said. "Any time at all."

Chapter 11

She was determined to make Christmas special. Normally, she didn't like this holiday. Even as a child, Sheila thought, I never really liked it. Most people's early memories were of tingling excitement, the joyous anticipation of waiting for Santa Claus and, later, the delicious expectation of gifts and glittering trees and a feeling of warmth and lovingness among friend and family, even a momentary softening of strangers' faces on the street. Her recollections were not like that. Rose had considered Christmas a burden and a chore, and had not had the good grace to keep that fact even from her child. Sheila could remember her mother's martyred expression as she returned from her shopping expeditions, complaining that the crowds were enough to kill you, the merchandise shoddy and overpriced and the whole sacred season turned into a commercial carnival. Sheila could not remember her mother ever being pleased with a gift she received or ever giving one with pleasure. She'd gone through all the motions, but disapprovingly, even resentfully.

Sheila's father had tried his best to offset the depressing tone his wife set. He and Sheila had shopped for the tree and, when she was old enough, decorated it together on Christmas Eve. He'd always picked out wonderful gifts for his daughter and for Rose, expensive, lovely things which brought a flush of happiness to Sheila and a reprimand from Rose for his extravagance. He'd tried to laugh off the latter.

"Is there anyone I'd rather spend money on than my two best girls? Come on, Rosie. It's Christmas! Time to be joyful!"

Lord knows he had little enough joy, Sheila thought. Rose was a rigid woman, not given to frivolous things. She took her "duties" as a Christian wife and mother seriously, finding little humor in any of them, and, Sheila supposed, little happiness as well. How had Frank Price stood it for thirty-eight years? His daughter never heard him complain, rarely saw him even slightly angry. The only time she could remember him sounding annoyed was at this time of year. Rose infuriatingly insisted upon referring to it as "Christ's birthday" rather than Christmas. It gave the whole thing a kind of pretentious solemnity. Not that the term could be disputed, but for some strange reason it came out sounding like an accusation against enjoyment.

Later, when Sheila was married, Christmas was better. Sean adored it, from the round of parties to the elaborate gifts he gave and expected in return. When Patrick and Maryanne were toddlers, Sheila liked the spirit of it, too. Christmas was for children and she threw herself wholeheartedly into making it the kind of spectacular time she had missed. Even later, when Tommy came along, there was a feeling of excitement for weeks ahead as she and the two older ones conspired to sustain his belief in Santa Claus. In those days she'd almost been able to forget the mercenary aspects of it all, the exchange of dollar-for-dollar gifts with their friends, the petty counting of Christmas cards and that stupid assessment of "who didn't send us one" this year. She'd forced herself not to be upset by the display of holiday decorations which went up earlier and earlier every year until the stores were strung with Yuletide ornaments even before Thanksgiving. In those days, with her family around her, she'd felt something of the goodness of Christmas, had almost forgotten how far away it all was from the real meaning of love and gratitude. Not Rose's *somber* kind of gratitude, but thankfulness for a feeling of hope and peace to men of good will.

Since the children were grown, she'd gone back to feeling that Thanksgiving was the only "honest," undemanding celebration. Christmas was false gaiety. She'd kept up the traditions, the big family gathering, the selection of cards, and the exchange of gifts. Even this year, except for sending cards, which she (thankfully) thought might seem inappropriate for a recent widow, she'd gone through the same preparations. There was a tree and gifts and a big dinner planned. The senior Callahans had not returned to Cleveland for several Christmases, but Rose was coming, as she had for so many years. Only Sean would be missing. It was still strangely hard to believe. Even though she was having an affair with Jerry, she sometimes had to remind herself that she was not married, that Sean would not be around to carve the Christmas turkey and make the traditional eggnog that everybody hated but which had to be there because it was part of the performance. It was hard to imagine Midnight Mass or Christmas Day without Sean. She allowed herself a cynical thought: At least at those times I knew where he was. Shame, Sheila, for such disrespectful thoughts of the dead! Still, it was true.

She hoped Christmas would go as well as Thanksgiving had, and simultaneously doubted it. Rose was bound to be maudlin about her "beloved" son-in-law, certain to cast an air of gloom over the occasion. Sean had never permitted Rose to be gloomy. He simply wouldn't tolerate it and told her so. Sheila was incapable of that. She felt guilty about dreading her mother's arrival, hating the idea of it and hating herself for hating it. She was still more than a little worried about Jerry's presence, too. Not that she didn't want him there. But there was Rose to think of. And Maryanne. And the others.

The hell with it, Sheila told herself. I've been all over that in my mind. *I* want Jerry here. It's my house and be damned to those who don't approve of my guests. But inside she was terrified. What if they drove Jerry away from her? What if Rose or Terry or Margaret or Emily made him so uncomfortable he'd never come back? What if he found Maryanne ridiculous and Rick vulgar and distasteful? Again, she scolded herself. If such things could put Jerry off, then he couldn't feel very deeply about her. And he did. Every day she felt more sure he did. He was so mature, so tender, so unfailingly devoted. It would take more than disapproving family and friends or hostile children to ruin their relationship. Look how he was handling Tommy's open resentment, with understanding and infinite patience.

I have so much to be thankful for, Sheila thought. I'm keeping my head above water financially. My children are healthy. I have a job I like and friends I care about. She refused to add, even to herself, that she had a lover she adored. The knowledge almost superstitiously frightened her. It was too good. The old unreasonable feeling of inadequacy came back. Widows were supposed to be miserable, lonely, and bereft. Why have I escaped? Do I deserve to? Will God punish me for not feeling more deeply grieved? How had she come by this inexplicable feeling of somehow being unworthy or undeserving of happiness? It was utter nonsense and she'd have no more of it. I was the best daughter, wife, and mother I knew how to be, Sheila told herself. Why do I always feel that people expect more of me than I'm able to deliver? An analyst would have a field day with my deep-seated sense of inferiority. I'm masochistic to blame myself for Maryanne's defection, for Tommy's withdrawal, for the censure I know I'll get from Mother. I've even blamed myself for Sean's unfaithfulness, she realized. I felt that somehow I failed him.

Well, no more! She had a sudden sense of well-being. No one can hurt

91

me. Most of all, I'm going to stop hurting myself. Feeling purged, she went ahead with the preparations for Christmas. For the first time in many years, she felt good about them.

Christmas was on a Tuesday and Rose Price arrived in Cleveland on the preceding Sunday. Sheila and Tommy met her. Jerry had offered to drive them, but Sheila had made a lame excuse about it being silly for him to waste his precious time when she was perfectly capable of driving the station wagon to the airport.

"It's never a waste of time when I can be with you," he'd said. "Besides, the weather's lousy and I know you hate driving in snow and ice."

"It's sweet of you, darling, but it really isn't necessary."

She hadn't fooled him.

"You're nervous about my meeting your mother, aren't you?"

"No. Of course not."

He'd looked at her reproachfully.

"All right," Sheila said. "Yes, I'm nervous about it. God knows why. It's ludicrous. I'm a grown woman and she makes me feel like a wayward child."

"She always will," Jerry said. "Some mothers are like that. To them, their children never become adults."

"Spare me! God, I hope I'm not like that about my own!"

She thought about that as she and Tommy drove toward the airport. She supposed her generation still had that hang-up, as her mother's did. It was only the new breed of mothers who seemed to treat their children in a relaxed, easy, companionable fashion. Almost casually, judging from the few things Jerry said about Barbara and Joyce. Not that these young women in their twenties and early thirties didn't care about their kids. They simply seemed less intense about them. Sheila faced the fact that she couldn't manage that, even now. Didn't she worry, quite unnecessarily, about Patrick's marriage? Didn't she fret over Maryanne's stupid squandering of her life? Wasn't she troubled over Tommy's change of personality? They were all adults. Even Tommy was no longer a little boy. And yet she felt as much responsibility for their happiness and well-being as she had when they were children. She vowed to let them go. To let them make their own mistakes, if they had to. The older ones certainly. Even Tommy could handle himself better than she gave him credit for, she supposed, if she'd stop thinking of him as a baby.

She glanced at her big, strapping young son in the seat beside her. In a few months he'd be eligible for a driver's license of his own. In a couple of years he'd be in college. And before she knew it he'd be married and having a family of his own. She wondered whether he'd ever been with a girl. She couldn't imagine her Tommy in the sex act, but he was old enough for such things. Certainly he knew the facts of life. Not that she'd ever discussed them with him and she doubted that Sean had, but he was well aware. He'd proved that in his one angry outburst and his crude references to her "horny doctor." Still, she was not aware that he was "dating," much less showing interest in any one girl. But then, so much of the time she had no idea where he was or with whom. And the things one read about teen-agers these days! She found herself suddenly anxious about her youngest. She'd been so determined not to fuss over him that she'd neglected him. No, that wasn't true. She'd been so involved in her own life, particularly with Jerry, that, beyond the daily necessities, she hadn't paid enough attention to Tommy. Not demanding, accusatory attention, such as Rose had focused on her, but genuine interest in him as a person. She tried to sound relaxed.

"We haven't talked much lately, pal," she said now. "What goes on in your life these days?"

She felt him stiffen. Had she somehow heard about that night at Nancy's? No. Impossible. Any more than she knew about the booze he'd now learned to drink without getting sick. Or the porno flicks he and his friends sneaked into. She was just trying to be A Mother.

"Nothing special," he lied in answer to her question. "I just kind of hang around, listen to a lot of discs at somebody's house, cruise, once in a while, in one of the older guys' cars."

"How about girls? Met any nice ones?"

"No, they're a drag. Either all het up about Women's Lib or talking about how they want to have houses and families, like their own folks." Well, that's true, at least, Tommy thought. The "nice girls" *were* like that. They had no interest in anything important, like social causes or politics. But neither did the guys. Including himself. His generation of teen-agers was disenchanted, apathetic, and pessimistic about the world. When Maryanne and Pat were growing up in the sixties they were protestors and zealots, from what he'd read. Much good it did them! The government stank, the economy was going to hell, and the racial thing was bunk. At school the blacks and whites sat on different sides of the cafeteria and you could feel the hatred between them. The world was a crock, and all Sheila was interested in was whether he'd met any "nice girls." He knew what she was really after. She was dying to know whether he'd screwed anybody. Damned if he'd tell her that he hadn't. There were plenty of "un-nice" girls he could have tried to make on his own, not in one of those jerky group things like Nancy's, but he lacked courage. He was terribly afraid of failure. And not only sexually. He didn't know why, really. He supposed it was some kind of hangover from Sean who'd seemed to be such a success while he was living and turned out to be nothing much of a man after all.

Sheila didn't know how to pursue the conversation. He must think I couldn't possibly understand anything he might choose to confide. She didn't believe he was uninterested in girls. It had been so different with Patrick who was always having groups of kids at the house, always up to his eyebrows in activities and excitement. This boy was a loner and she didn't know how to reach him. Feeling like a coward, she fell back on clichés.

"Well, darling, you're still growing up. Plenty of time for falling in love. I just hope you're happy with your friends. I still wish I could meet some of them. Wouldn't you like to plan a party at the house after school starts? There must be a lot of attractive boys and girls you could invite. Pat and Maryanne did that when they were your age."

Goddammit, he wanted to say, I'm not Pat or Maryanne! I'm *me*. With a dead father who wasn't any good and a mother who's trying to act like a teeny-bopper! I'm a private-school kid trying to fit into a public-school world. And I don't belong in either place. Attitudes among the young had changed since his brother and sister were his age. His world was grim and cynical. And so was he. Parties were of another time. His gang would hoot at the idea. But he said none of this to Sheila.

"We'll see," he said instead. "Right now, let's get through the holidays. Including Grandma."

Sheila smiled, willing to be reassured that he was only "going through a phase," pleased by his companionable, shared concern about the difficult Rose. He'll be all right, she told herself. He's always been an intelligent, sensitive boy. I'm foolish to have this gnawing anxiety. I suppose it's because I'm entirely responsible for him.

"Fasten your *mental* seat belt," she said lightly. "Grandma's just about unfastening hers now."

"You're looking well, Mother."

Rose looked up from her chair (Sean's chair). "*I'm* looking well? Don't try to fool me, Sheila. I've aged twenty years since August, worrying about you." She shook her head. "It seems it was needless worry. *You're* the one who looks well. In fact, you're positively blooming. I don't understand it, with all you've been through. Not that I'm not delighted, of course."

For a moment, Sheila didn't answer. This was the first moment they'd been alone since Rose's arrival. In the car, coming home from the airport, there'd been a three-way, general conversation about the difficulties of travel, the run-down of family information—Tommy's new school, Patrick's job, a brief reference to Maryanne's unchanged situation. The rest of the drive had been devoted to Rose's usual diatribe about the "spectacle" of Christ's birthday. Now, relaxing over a cup of tea in Sheila's living room, with Tommy up in his own quarters, they were about to have the mother-daughter conversation Sheila dreaded.

You're not really delighted that I'm looking well, Sheila thought. Consciously, you think you are. But actually you're disappointed not to find me wan and tearful. No, that wasn't fair. She knew her mother really wanted her to be happy, but she expected Sheila to fall into the more familiar "widow's role," the one that Rose herself had maintained for months, years after Frank Price's death. She wants to identify with me. She wants me to react to things the way she does. She'd like to forget that there are twenty-six years between us. Probably she thinks that for the first time ever we have a mutual bond: bereavement.

"I'm doing all right, Mother," Sheila said gently. "There have been a lot of adjustments, but I haven't had time to sit around feeling sorry for myself. In a way I suppose it was good that I had to go to work. It's kept me occupied. And people have been very kind, seeing to it that I'm not lonely."

"You're fortunate that Sean was so popular. I'm glad his friends haven't forgotten you."

For a moment Sheila was angry. It was the kind of "put down" that Rose had done to her all her life, assuming that whatever admiration Sheila enjoyed was somehow accidental. The anger quickly passed, but not the resentment of her mother's belief that she was incapable of being accepted for herself.

"It isn't so much Sean's friends." Sheila was calm. "It's more my own. Like Sally Cantrell and people I've met since Sean died." She decided it was the moment to plunge on. "I've even been seeing a very nice man. A doctor. You'll meet him Christmas Day. He's joining us for dinner."

Rose looked at her in disbelief. "You're going out? So soon? Sheila! What on earth must people be saying?"

You'd be surprised what they're saying, Sheila thought. But she didn't voice what was in her mind. "I'm sure there are those who think it's 'disrespectful,' Mother, but I really can't worry about that. If they're fond of me, they can only be glad that I've met someone nice."

"But it's only a little over four months!"

"What difference does that make—four months or four years? My sitting home weeping won't bring Sean back."

"I don't understand you, Sheila. How can you even be *interested* in another man when you're still in mourning?"

"I'm not 'in mourning' in your sense of the word. I do grieve for Sean. I think about him a lot and I'm sorry he died. But I think it's macabre for women to figuratively jump into their husbands' graves for a proscribed, conventional period. It does the dead no good, and it does the living a lot of harm."

Rose was outraged. "There *is* something known as respect! I assume *that* hasn't gone out of fashion."

"No," Sheila said, "but there are different ways of showing it. I try to encourage Sean's children to have pleasant memories of him. Tommy especially. I try to remember the good things about my husband and not dwell on the bad. I'm grateful for having had a relatively satisfactory

95

marriage. But if respect means living like a nun, then, yes, as far as I'm concerned, it's an outmoded, superficial bit of play-acting for the benefit of the world."

"You sound as though emotions can be controlled at will. You make it all sound so cut and dried, Sheila."

"I don't mean to. I'm just trying to be realistic."

Rose couldn't resist. "Realistic or selfish? Who is this man? Where did you meet him?"

"His name is Jerry Mancini. As I told you, he's a doctor. And I met him through Pat and Betty, on Thanksgiving."

"Is he married?"

"Not exactly. He and his wife are separated. They're planning a divorce."

"A divorce! Sheila, your religion forbids you to marry a divorced man!"

Sheila couldn't help laughing. "Mother, you're amazing! A minute ago you couldn't believe I was going out with a man and now you're assuming I'm going to marry him! Dear, I've only known Jerry a month. Believe me, there's been no talk of marriage." She sobered. "But I have to tell you this. If it ever comes to that, I won't let religion stop me. To be perfectly honest, it's one of the things I can't accept about the Church."

"I don't know where I failed with you. You were brought up to be a good, God-fearing girl."

"I hope I still am."

The remark was met with silence.

Might as well get it over, Sheila decided. "There's a much more real problem than religion, as far as Jerry and I are concerned. That is, I don't think it really is a problem, because I don't think marriage is in the cards, but Jerry's younger than I. And I'd worry more about that than I would about God's forgiveness."

"Younger? How much younger."

Sheila swallowed hard. "Fifteen years."

Rose stared at her in horror. "Fifteen years! You're not telling me you're running around with a *boy!*"

"Hardly a *boy*, Mother. He's thirty-two. I'm forty-seven, remember?" It was a deliberate piece of nastiness. Rose hated to be reminded of Sheila's age. It forced her to recognize her own. Sheila was ashamed of her pettiness, but dammit, Rose deserved it.

"And what," Rose said coldly, "do you a think a young man like that could possibly see in a woman of your age?"

There it was again. The disparagement, the rivalry, even the jealousy that Rose felt. Poor Mother, Sheila thought. I never realized it before, but she's always been in competition with me without being aware of it. She'd be shocked if anyone suggested such a thing. Shocked and hurt. But I'm sure she subconsciously resented my closeness to Daddy. She was nasty about Sean because he was all the glamorous things her husband was not. And now, when she thought I finally was as manless and unworshiped as she, I come up with a lover, and a young one at that. It must be bitter for her.

"I don't know what Jerry sees in me," Sheila answered. "You'd have to ask *him*. All I know is that we enjoy each other very much. I don't feel old when I'm with him."

"Does he know how old you *are?*"

Suddenly Sheila was impatient. "Of course he knows! I told you he's Patrick's friend and it doesn't take a mathematical genius to figure out that the mother of a twenty-six-year-old man can't very well be thirty! Why are you being so beastly about this? Don't you think it's possible that I could attract someone, even at my 'advanced age'?"

"How hard you've become, Sheila! And how cruel!"

"I'm not hard and cruel! Mother, please try to understand, I'm having a good time. Do you begrudge me that? I'm not hurting anyone."

"Yes, you are. You're hurting yourself. I'm sure your children are ashamed of you, too. People must think you're a fool, running around with a friend of your son's. I suppose you've been to bed with him."

Sheila lost control. "Not that it's any of your damned business, but yes, I have! And enjoyed every minute of it!" She was sorry immediately, angry with herself for letting Rose goad her into such infantile behavior. She broke the self-imposed vow she'd made that summer. "I'm sorry, Mother. That did sound hard and cruel. But I'm a grown woman. I know what I'm doing."

"Do you, indeed? I wonder."

Sheila took a deep breath. "Look, dear, let's not let this get blown up all out of proportion. I told you I don't intend to marry Jerry. I'm sure he doesn't wish to marry me. But suppose we both came to feel differently? What would be so terrible? There are a great many good marriages between older women and younger men." She tried to laugh. "I read somewhere the other day that there are two thousand women over fifty-five in this country married to men under twenty-five. It's not a social stigma any more, Mother. I told you, it won't happen, but if it did it wouldn't be the end of the world!"

"That depends upon whose world you're talking about. It would be the end of mine. I'd die of shame."

Sheila gave up. "I wish you didn't feel that way, but I can see you won't change. Just promise me one thing. Be pleasant to Jerry on Tuesday. I'd like him to see what a charming woman you are. He's heard a lot about you."

Rose's face was a frozen mask. "I'm sure he has. I hate to think what."

"Mother!"

"Don't worry. I'll be polite. *I* won't shame *you.*"

"Thanks," Sheila said bitterly. "That's good of you."

Chapter 12

       As she let herself in the front door of her house late on the afternoon of Christmas Eve, Sheila wondered where she was going to get the physical stamina to see her through the next twenty-four hours. She'd liked to have crawled into bed and stayed there until Wednesday morning. Instead, she had to cook dinner for Tommy and Rose tonight and go with them to Midnight Mass. Tomorrow morning she'd be up at dawn to set the table, prepare the Christmas dinner, and brace herself for the emotion-charged gathering of the clan. Somewhere in between, she still had to wrap packages, trim a tree, and make that damned eggnog. It was too much to contemplate. Other years, she'd had plenty of time. Other years she hadn't been dragged through the nightmare of Christmas Eve in Higbee's book department, with frantic, last-minute, short-tempered shoppers making impossible demands on her time and patience. Other years she hadn't been faced with the prospect of presenting a young lover to largely disapproving family and friends.

       All day she'd been wishing that she hadn't asked Jerry to join them tomorrow. If she'd kept him out of sight during Rose's visit, she'd never have gotten into that wrenching conversation with her mother yesterday. She could have avoided introducing him to Terry and Margaret and the Rosses. He wouldn't have had a chance to be confronted by an unpredictable Maryanne and a startling Rick Jawolsky. Why was she making it unnecessarily hard on herself? Because I have nothing to be ashamed of, she thought. And because I want to be with Jerry on Christmas.

There was, at least, a pleasant surprise as she walked into the front hall: the smell of cooking. Rose came bustling cheerfully out of the kitchen, a different Rose from the one of the night before. Her mother had still been in her room when Sheila went off to work Monday morning. Sometime during the night, or the day, she must have had a change of heart or an attack of conscience. Temporary, without doubt. But Sheila was thankful for any blessing.

"You must be exhausted," Rose said. "I've fixed a nice pot roast for dinner. Tommy drove me into the village to shop for it."

"Tommy drove you? Mother, he's not allowed to drive! He knows how, but he doesn't have a license and he's not permitted to take the car."

"My goodness, Sheila, there's no need to be so upset! I know he doesn't have his license, but it's only a short distance. I didn't think you'd mind." She sounded almost wistful. "I hoped you'd be pleased not to have to cook dinner. There's so little I can do for you."

Sheila was remorseful. It was horrid of her to snap at Rose who obviously was making a peace overture. More than a peace overture, Sheila thought. It must give her pleasure to feel useful in even the smallest way. This was what people like her mother missed most, the sense of being necessary. Even when she was at her most complaining during Sheila's early years, Rose still knew the Price household could not operate without her. Now she had no one, not a husband or a child to make her feel that she contributed something.

Impulsively, Sheila gave her a kiss on the cheek. They were not "kissers," she and Rose. Frank had always been the openly affectionate one, cuddling and teasing his daughter while Rose stood by, aloof, cool to such demonstrative behavior. She looked surprised now by Sheila's display of affection. Surprised and pleased.

"I'm sorry, Mother," Sheila said, and this time she was sincere. "You're an angel to have done dinner. I can't tell you how much I appreciate it. My God, it's been a killing day! And there are a thousand things to do between now and tomorrow. Where's Tommy?"

"I don't know. He went out after lunch but he said he'd be home by dinnertime. By the way, Dr. Mancini called a few minutes ago. He asked you to call him when you came in."

"Oh?" For a moment Sheila again found herself half-hoping that Jerry had decided not to come for Christmas. "Did you and he have a chat?"

"Only a short one. He said he was looking forward to meeting me tomorrow." The note of disapproval crept back into Rose's voice. "I said I was anxious to meet him, too."

So he was coming. Good. It was better that way. It was cowardly of her to want him out of sight, as though she was ashamed of him, or of herself, or of them. "I'll ring up and see what's on his mind," she said.

"Speaking of phoning, aren't you going to call Sean's parents?"

"Tomorrow," Sheila said. "So they can talk to Pat and Maryanne as well."

Jerry sounded concerned and loving on the phone. "I didn't call you yesterday, darling, because I figured you and your mother would be catching up. How's it going?"

"Just fine! Everything's wonderful! How are *you?*"

"If ever I heard fake enthusiasm! I take it Mom's within earshot."

"That's right."

"You're getting the naughty child treatment, aren't you? Because of me?"

"Partly."

"Sheila, would it be easier if I stayed out of the family picture tomorrow? I want to be with you, you know that, but I don't want to put a damper on your Christmas."

It was always like that. As though he could read her mind. "I wouldn't hear of such a thing. See you about four."

"I miss you."

"Yes."

He laughed. "All right, love, since you can't say it, I'll say it for you. 'I miss you, Jerry. I need you, too.'"

Sheila returned his laughter. "Right, Doctor!" She was still smiling when she put down the phone.

"Why do we have to go to Sheila's tomorrow evening?" Emily Ross sat at her dressing table, creaming makeup off her face.

Bob, halfway into his pajamas, turned and looked at her. "What kind of a question is that? We've always gone to the Callahans on Christmas and it never bothered you before."

"It'll be a bore." Emily made a face. "Those terrible children. And Rose Price. God!"

"You seemed to like it well enough when Sean was there."

Emily was furious. "And now I suppose you'll like it even better because he *isn't*. Don't you see enough of Sheila? You come up with enough flimsy excuses to have meetings with her about her 'financial affairs.' Or are they more than financial? Maybe she's perfectly capable of handling both you *and* her young doctor."

Bob climbed into his twin bed. "Emily, I'm not going to get into a stupid argument with you. We're going to Sheila's tomorrow evening."

"Why? Because *you* want to?"

"Precisely. Because *I* want to."

Margaret Callahan climbed into the car beside her husband. "Are we picking up Sheila on the way to church?"

"No. She and Tommy and Rose are coming on their own."

"What about Patrick and Betty?"

"I'm not sure they'll go to Midnight Mass. They sometimes don't."

Margaret shivered. "Doesn't the damned heater in this car work?"

"The engine has to warm up, honey. I've told you that a hundred times."

They drove for a few moments in silence.

"Sheila's invited that young doctor tomorrow," Margaret said. "Just like he was one of the family. Apparently Patrick's talk with her didn't do much good."

"Pat didn't talk with her," Terry said. "Betty did."

Margaret began to laugh. "Oh, won-derful! I can imagine *that* conversation!" She imitated Betty. " 'You're an adult, liberated woman, Sheila dear. If you choose to be a cradle snatcher, it's nobody's business. You're entitled to live your own life.' God preserve me from smart-ass young psychology majors! I'll bet you ten dollars Betty's encouraging her in this ridiculous romance. Why on earth did you let Pat get out of talking to his mother? Really, Terry, sometimes you're so spineless! You should have talked to Sheila yourself, for that matter."

"All right, I was wrong. That doesn't mean I still can't talk to her. I will. As soon as the holiday is over."

"What holiday? Fourth of July?"

"Shut up, Maggie. For Christ's sake, it's Christmas Eve!"

Rick rolled over on his back. He'd just made love to Maryanne and they'd enjoyed it. Sometimes lately it wasn't so good. She still drove him wild, but for the last few months she hadn't been as crazy for him as she was at the beginning. They had lots of sex, but most times it wasn't as terrific as it used to be. Maybe she's smoking too much grass, Rick thought. They say that can decrease the urge after a while. She'd been less interested for months. Ever since her father died and she spent those few days at home. He wondered if something had happened out in Shaker Heights. Had her mother gotten to her somehow? No. No way. If that was true, Maryanne wouldn't have come back to Ohio City. Maybe she was just getting tired of him. Rick rejected that idea, too. He had what she wanted. And plenty of it. More than any of those college jerks she used to run around with. I hate those snobs, Rick thought. I hate all those goddam people, including her family. He nudged her. "Hey, babe, do we really have to go to your old lady's tomorrow?"

Maryanne, satiated and sleepy, didn't open her eyes. "Yep. We have to."

"Why?"

"Because there'd be hell to pay if we didn't."

"You mean if *you* didn't."

"All right. If *I* didn't."

Rick thought for a moment. "Listen, I think I'll cut out of that scene. You go by yourself."

She finally looked at him. Rick couldn't read her expression. Was it relief? Anger? Defiance?

"It'll be a helluva lot better all around if I don't go," he persisted. "You know damn well your family thinks I'm dirt. And I think they're pains in the ass. So what's the point? Let's do your mother a favor. We'll give her a big Christmas present: my nonappearance."

"No."

"For Christ's sake, Mare, why not?"

"Because I want you there."

"What for? So you can show them what a big, free spirit you are, living with a spaced-out musician? Big deal. They already know that. You don't have to keep pounding it into their heads that you hate them. They know that, too."

"I don't hate them. I pity them. Anyway, you're my old man and I'm entitled to bring you to Christmas dinner."

Rick got out of bed. "And I'm entitled not to go, okay?"

She sat up. "Where are you going?"

He was getting into his clothes. "Out. Have a good time tomorrow. See you when I see you."

"Rick! Wait! Don't leave! I won't go tomorrow, either. I don't know what's the matter with me. I don't even *want* to go."

He pulled on his jacket. "Sure you do, babe. That's really where you belong."

"No! This is where I belong!"

"Maybe. But I don't think you're sure any more. I think something's changed, lover, but I don't know what. Why don't you go back to Mama till you figure it out?"

She said nothing as the door closed behind him. For all his lack of background and education, he had uncanny instinct. Rick was right. Like an animal, he smelled fear. Maryanne didn't know what she wanted, hadn't known for a long while. She just knew she was desperately afraid. There had to be something more than the kind of life her parents had lived. But there also had to be something more than the one she'd been into for the past two years. She was terrified of both extremes. And almost suicidally despondent.

They didn't get around to trimming the tree until after they got home from Midnight Mass. Sheila insisted Rose go to bed.

"It's late, Mother, and you're worn out. Tommy and I can get it done in no time. Everything's laid out and it won't take us more than an hour. Please get some rest. You'll be exhausted tomorrow."

The older woman put up only token resistance. "Well, all right. If you're sure. But you must be dead-tired yourself. You worked hard all day."

"I feel fine," Sheila lied. "I've got my second wind. Besides, I'll make Tommy do all the hard work, like climbing up and down the ladder. I'll just hand him things."

Rose surveyed the tree which nearly touched the ceiling. "I don't know why you had to get such a big one this year. So much work!"

"It's the kind we always have. I detest those scrawny little table-top things. Now, shoo!"

They worked methodically in silence for a little while. First the lights, tested and, as usual, refusing to work until they found the one devilish bulb that had to be replaced before the whole string went on.

"The annual sabotage," Sheila muttered. "Happens every time. And it's always the last bulb you try. I never can figure out how you can put away a working set of Christmas lights and find one has expired during the year. Why on earth don't they hibernate, like bears?"

"They're okay now, Mom." Tommy began to drape them through the branches. "Hand me the star for the top, will you?"

Sheila fingered the ornament lovingly before she gave it to him. It was beginning to look terribly battered, its gold surface dull and tarnished, but it still had the place of honor, as it had for twenty-seven years.

"Your dad and I bought this for our first Christmas tree," she said.

The boy didn't answer.

"Do you miss him, Tommy?"

"Sure. Toss up that tinsel, will you?"

Sheila gave him one end of the long, golden string. "You don't really like to talk about your father, do you?"

"Not especially."

"Why not, Tommy? You loved him. I remember your face the day he died. I've never seen anyone so sad."

"People get over things."

She felt the implied accusation. "You're still angry with me, aren't you? It bothers you that I see Jerry."

"Nope, it's okay if that's what you want. Can you start handing up those balls now, please?"

"Why can't we talk, Tommy? What's happened between us? We were always so close. It isn't just Jerry or my working that's made us like strangers. You know everything about my life, but I feel as though I know nothing about yours."

Perched on the ladder, he turned and looked down at her. "You wouldn't understand."

That hurt. At the same time, she realized it probably was true. At least in Tommy's mind. She assumed that Rose wouldn't understand her. Why shouldn't Tommy feel the same about this next-generation gap?

"Try me."

"Mom, don't get all worked up over nothing. I'm not a baby you have to worry about all the time. I can handle myself. You act like I'm turning into a juvenile delinquent."

"It's not that, darling. I do worry that there's no man you can turn to with a boy's problems. If your father were here . . ."

She saw him tense up.

"He wouldn't have understood any more than you can," Tommy said roughly. "He'd have been too busy being Mr. Wonderful."

She pretended not to understand. It was an automatic, protective reflex. "Of course he'd have understood! When Patrick was your age . . ."

"Jesus, Mother, will you stop pretending? Maybe Pat wasn't too bright. Maybe he *still* thinks Dad was a great man. I don't. And I haven't for a long time. He was a phony. You kept pretending everything was peachy, but I knew better. What do you think drove Maryanne away? Watching that make-believe life you and Dad lived, that's what. It just took her a little longer to catch on than it did me. And she picked a dumb way to rebel. That weird-o world she ran to was supposed to punish you and Dad. Well, maybe it hurt *you*, but I doubt that *he* gave it much thought."

Sheila stood frozen. He really hated his father. Maybe he even hates me. He was discussing Maryanne but he was really talking about himself, too. What form would Tommy's rebellion ultimately take? Would it continue to be this withdrawal or something more active and terrifying? And was it true that Maryanne wanted to punish them for not being honest? Had she and Sean somehow failed the girl? She didn't understand it, any of it. She felt utterly helpless and confused. This was a Tommy so drastically changed in the last few months. No longer tender and loving, no longer even as understanding as he'd seemed when they'd had their talk about Jerry. He was a different boy. He took his cue from his companions now, she supposed. And who were those companions?

"I'm sorry we let you down, Tommy." Inadequate words, but somehow they seemed to reach him. Suddenly he was a boy again, her boy.

"*You* didn't, Mom. I mean, not really. You thought you were doing the right thing, covering up everything that was lousy in your marriage. But don't ask me to think of Dad as a hero just because he's dead. And don't kid yourself that he'd have been much help to me now, even if he were alive."

"But *I'm* here, Tommy. I don't want to drive you away, the way I did Maryanne."

He came down off the ladder and put his arm around her shoulders. "You won't. I was just making a big speech. Forget what I said about Maryanne. She was always mixed up. Heck, you even managed to get her to a shrink, didn't you? I know Dad thought that was a waste of time."

Sheila's smile was rueful. "Apparently he was right."

Tommy hesitated. "I think she'd like to come home, Mom. Now that Dad's gone."

She looked at him in surprise. "What gives you that idea?"

"I don't know. It's just that when she was here this summer I kind of thought she'd like to have stayed."

"No, you're wrong, dear. I asked her. She was very explicit about wanting her own life."

"Okay. I guess I read her wrong." Tommy shrugged. "Hey, we'd better get on with this tree or we'll never finish."

They said little more until the Christmas tree was decorated. It was beautiful, splendid, and overpowering, yet it had great sentiment. It bore ornaments collected over the years, expensive, handmade decorations triumphantly borne home by Sean, and funny, crooked objects the children made at school. She'd been silly about the tree, always, finding it the best part of Christmas for her. Among the elaborate "store-bought" angels she'd hung Patrick's teething ring, Maryanne's rattle, Tommy's favorite Mickey Mouse toy. These were meaningful representations of her life. Sean had thought they made the tree look tacky. She'd known that they'd given, even for a few days, the semblance of solidarity in a house that really had so little of it.

In bed, she reviewed her talk with her youngest. She realized that she had been (cleverly? deliberately?) diverted from any in-depth discussion of his problems by the introduction of Maryanne's. She still didn't know where Tommy's head was today. He'd only talked about the past. She wondered whether he possibly could be right about Maryanne wanting to come home. Nothing would please Sheila more, but she found it difficult to believe. On the other hand, she didn't really know her daughter. Any more than she really knew Tommy. Perhaps the two of them had talked this summer. Maybe her fifteen-year-old was going on more than a hunch. Maybe—disloyal thought—the removal of Sean would let them be a close family for the first time ever.

I *must* get some sleep, Sheila told herself. She remembered reading about some new school of thought which advised one to pretend there was a brown paper bag by the side of the bed. You were supposed to mentally take your problems and drop them into the bag, leaving your mind clear and quiet. She tried it, visualizing the sack on the floor. Into it went her questions about Maryanne. Thump. In went her anxiety about Tommy. Plop. She tossed in her guilt about Jerry, her annoyance with Rose. Plink, plunk. The whole thing was so absurd it made her smile. And yet, within two minutes she was fast asleep.

In his room, Tommy kicked off his sneakers, dropped his jeans on the floor where he stepped out of them, threw his T-shirt at a chair and missed. Skillfully avoiding a stack of rock records, a clutter of books, and an assortment of soft-drink cans, he was in and out of the bathroom in three minutes. He crawled into his bed where he lay on his back, wide-awake, arms crossed behind his head, staring at the ceiling and thinking.

What he'd said about his father was true, though he'd not admitted, even in his own mind, what a rotten husband and parent Sean Callahan was. Not admitted it until this fall, that is. He guessed he'd known it for years, but it was something he hadn't wanted to think about. It wasn't until Sean died that Tommy allowed himself to be critical of him. More than critical. Scornful was more like it. His father was always putting on an act. In that, he was no different from most adults. They all pretended to be concerned citizens, trying to set a good example for their kids. They actually thought they got away with it. It was insulting to the intelligence.

Mr. Magoo moved restlessly at the foot of the bed, gave a huge sigh and began to snore. Tommy poked him with a toe and the snoring stopped, but the dog slept peacefully on. Lucky beast, Tommy thought. You have nothing on *your* conscience. Not so with me. I hate it when Mother starts trying to find out what makes me tick. I love her. She's trying to do her best. But she's another generation. She doesn't know how things have changed. Even the prep-school kids, the ones at University, aren't the same as they were in Pat's day, much less Dad's. And the friends at Shaker Heights High, the ones she was always so anxious to meet, have even less use for Mother's world.

He wondered what Sheila would say if he ever *did* bring his new buddies home: Artie Connolly, who drove the souped-up heap they cruised around in most every night; Paul Bellows, who'd been picked up on a shoplifting charge and was on probation; Sam Johnson, the black guy in the group who thought it was funny how scared "The Man" was of the influx of Negroes into Shaker Heights. Sheila would be bewildered by his companions. He wasn't quite sure why he'd chosen to become part of this particular crowd. There were lots of other guys more like himself, from the same kind of "respectable" homes, whom he could have decided to hang out with. He supposed he'd taken up with this wild bunch because it was so totally different from anything he'd ever been exposed to. He was bright enough to realize that it was a kind of rebellion. And dangerous. They'd already stolen two cars for joy-riding. They'd been lucky enough to get them back before the owners discovered they were gone. But one day they might get caught. Just as they might get caught for lifting things from the drugstore counter or buying booze from a liquor store that wasn't too particular about ID's. It was crazy to take such chances, but it was exciting. Like accepting a dare. It was the kind of thing his father or Patrick would never have dreamed of doing. Maybe that was the best part of it.

Tommy turned over and thumped his pillow. He could see Sheila's concerned face, the way she looked tonight when they talked. He'd been ashamed of himself, making her unhappy. That's why he'd made up that stuff about Maryanne maybe wanting to come home. There'd been no talk of that this summer. His crazy sister was on a defiance trip, just the way he was. He'd only lied to give Sheila something to hope for. It was a jerky thing to do; she'd soon be disappointed. Like tomorrow. But I had to get Mom off my back, he reasoned. He'd known that talking about Maryanne's imaginary change of heart would be a sure-fire way to do it. And it had worked. She'd stopped questioning him about his activities and his feelings. Damn. He couldn't explain the anger he felt about everything. He didn't know it was typical teen-age rebellion mixed, in his case, with disillusion and an irrational sense of loss. He would have snorted with disdain if anyone had told him he really did miss his father, frailties and all. He'd have said they were crazy if they'd suggested that he was going through a unique period somewhere between childhood with all its parental dependence and adulthood with its props of clear-thinking and experience. Fifteen was an age in which one hung suspended between the familiar and the unexplored. But Tommy didn't know that was usually the case. He felt unique and misunderstood, and not very happy with himself.

Chapter 13

It had all the ingredients of a storybook Christmas. A layer of new snow covered the ground and trees, even curved itself into the corners of the windowpanes, as precise as if it had been put there by a department store display man. Inside the Callahan house, the "greeting-card setting" continued. A huge fire was set on the hearth; the smell of pumpkin pie slithered out of the kitchen; mounds of gifts, cheerfully wrapped, waited under the glittering tree. All the inanimate objects were in perfect order, all the trappings of tradition and outward signs of peace and plenty. Only the living things injected a jarring note.

Sheila had been up at dawn, wrapping her gifts, setting the table for seven (such an odd number it seemed) and preparing food for cocktails and dinner. At eight, Rose appeared, offering to help. Sheila gently refused.

"I appreciate it, Mother, but you know how it is when someone isn't familiar with a kitchen. You just sit down and have your breakfast. I really can do it faster than I could if I had to tell you where things are."

Rose's feelings were hurt. She sniffed loudly as she poured a cup of coffee. "I suppose I'm capable of making myself a piece of toast?"

Sheila tried not to be exasperated. "Darling, I didn't mean you weren't capable. I just meant you don't know where I keep the good china and the special things for the table. That kind of thing."

"Naturally not. And I couldn't be expected to *find* them in my own daughter's house. I'm much too senile for *that*."

Oh, shut up! Sheila said silently. Can't you see I'm a bundle of nerves? But she didn't answer. Rose made toast and stood behind Sheila, plate in hand, watching her daughter dress the turkey. Every time Sheila moved she stepped on her mother until finally she couldn't stand it.

"Mother, why don't you sit down at the breakfast table and relax? The morning paper's there."

Rose dripped dignity. "Of course. I apologize for being in your way. Perhaps you'd prefer I went back to my room?"

Sheila bit her lip. "No, dear, of course not. It's just that I keep falling over you! Now go on and sit down over there. Keep me company. Tell me what's in the news."

"I can tell you without reading it. Murder. Rape. Robbery. Watergate. Juvenile delinquency. What's always in the news these days? Do you ever see anything good in the paper any more?"

"Sure. Sometimes a nice human interest story. Even a Woman's Page story. Try skipping the news and the stock market and go to the entertainment section."

The attempt at lightness fell flat. "I don't know how you can be so frivolous with all your problems," Rose said.

"There are worse ones. Some people have no family, no money, no Christmas except at the Salvation Army. People are starving in Africa and dying of cancer in Cleveland and committing suicide in Kansas City."

Rose looked at her in astonishment. "What kind of talk is that?"

Sheila laughed. "Okay. Truce? You started it, you know, with all that gloom about what's in the paper."

"I did nothing of the kind! Really, Sheila, I don't understand you."

"I know, Mother. That makes two of us."

Rose was temporarily vanquished. "Where's Tommy? Is that child going to sleep all day?"

"It's only eight-thirty, Mother. He and I were up until God knows when doing the tree."

"I thought you said you could do it in no time."

Sheila permitted herself a sigh. "It took a little longer than we expected. Let him sleep. There's nothing for him to do."

"Seems to me *somebody* should be helping you. I'd have thought Maryanne might have come early. Or Betty. Thoughtless, all these young people. Selfish. Is Maryanne bringing that dreadful young man?"

My God, I forgot all about him, Sheila thought. Talk about your mental blocks! No wonder I had an odd feeling that seven was a strange number at table. I wasn't counting Rick. "I presume she is," Sheila said in answer to Rose's question. "He was invited."

She slipped out and quickly rearranged the table for eight. When she came back into the kitchen Rose was reading the paper.

"Did you see this item about your friend Bob Ross?"

"No. What?"

"The Mayor's appointed him. Some new civic project."

Sheila scanned the item. "Why, that's marvelous! I didn't know Bob was involved in the water-pollution thing. It's a big problem here, Mother. We voted in a hundred-million-dollar-bond issue to fight it and Cleveland has one of the country's toughest antipollution codes now." She smiled. "I must confess it wasn't a moment too soon. We have the only river I know of that actually caught fire. It's true. The Cuyahoga was so polluted it literally burned. I'm delighted Bob's been named. We'll have something extraspecial to celebrate tonight."

"I suppose your friend Emily will be more unbearable than ever."

"Mother, why *do* you have this thing about Emily? I know you never really heard anything about her and Sean, now did you? All that was a big bluff."

"Call it a bluff if you like. I believe in my instincts. That's an unfriendly woman. Tell me, Sheila, has she spent much time with you these past months?"

"Well, no. But that doesn't mean anything. After all, I'm at work during the day. Bob comes over once in a while in the evening to help me with business things, but it's not a social call."

"Do tell," Rose said smugly.

"It's true! And Emily knows it. What's more, I'm sure she knows about Jer . . ." Sheila's voice dwindled off.

"All the more reason for her to be jealous. She's probably laughing at you, too."

The ringing of the phone interrupted what was threatening to turn into a full-scale quarrel. Sheila reached for it gratefully. It was a strangely subdued-sounding Maryanne.

"Mother? I'm afraid I can't come out today. Sorry. I hope it doesn't inconvenience you."

"Can't come out?" Sheila echoed. "Why not? What's wrong, Maryanne? Are you sick?"

"Yes, sort of. That is, not really. I, well, I just don't feel like coming. I mean, actually I don't have any way to get there."

"I thought Rick would be driving you."

There was a pause. "Rick can't make it. He has another appointment and he's taken the car."

They had a fight about coming here, Sheila realized, and that horrid young man has taken off. What a rotten trick, walking out and leaving that girl alone on Christmas!

"Sweetheart, there's no reason to let a transportation problem spoil our day. Get a cab. I'll be glad to pay for it."

"No, it's too expensive. Besides they're practically impossible to get on a holiday. It's okay, Mother. I don't feel very full of Christmas spirit anyway. I'd probably be a killjoy."

"Honey, I don't want to be sloppy, but this is one day I really want all the family together. Especially this year. Look, it's simple. I'll have Pat come and get you. I'll call him now and he can pick you up around three. Now don't argue! Just be ready when Pat comes."

Maryanne wavered. She really did want to be there. Shaker Heights suddenly represented unquestioning love and security and in the frame of mind she was in, she was almost afraid to be left alone. Maybe Rick was right. Maybe that's where she *did* belong. She needed a refuge, even a temporary one. A few days at home would do her good and teach Rick a lesson. She didn't want to admit how shallow their relationship was, how unsatisfactory, lately, it was to both of them.

"All right," she said quietly, "if you're sure Pat won't mind."

"He won't mind," Sheila said firmly. "I'll call him now."

But Pat wasn't at home when she called. He'd be at the hospital until late in the afternoon, Betty explained. In fact, chances were they'd be a little late getting to Sheila's. It all depended upon what time Pat could get away.

Conscious of Rose's rapt attention to the conversation, Sheila tried to sound unworried. "It's just bloody inconvenient that Rick has this job today," she said. "I was expecting both of them."

"No problem. We're a two-car family. I'll go get Maryanne and meet Pat at your house."

"I hate to put you through that long drive."

"It's a cinch. I do it every day. The clinic's close by Maryanne's apartment."

"Thanks, Betty, dear. I appreciate it. So will she."

"I take it we're to be deprived of the uplifting company of Maryanne's paramour," Rose said tartly when Sheila hung up.

"He has to work," Sheila lied. "And Maryanne doesn't have a car. anyway, the problem is solved. She felt terrible that she might miss Christmas with us, poor child."

"Poor child, indeed! She's my own granddaughter but I still say she behaves abominably. Twenty-four years old and nothing to show for her life. When you were her age, Sheila, you were married and had two children."

"Times have changed, Mother. Marriage isn't the ultimate goal for young women any more."

"Even if I accepted that, which I don't, I'd think they'd have *some* goal. Something other than living in sin. I know I'm old-fashioned. I read what goes on these days but I still think it's disgraceful. I don't understand why you put up with it. You should make her come home, Sheila. She should live in this house, get herself a job and help you. At least until she finds a decent husband!"

Sheila looked at her helplessly. "Mother, Maryanne is an adult. I can't order her to do anything. I don't like what she's doing any better than you do. But I can't make her do what she doesn't want to. I can only hope that one day she'll get whatever is bothering her out of her system. She knows I'm here if she wants me."

"I thought you had more spunk! If Sean were alive he wouldn't put up with this!"

That did it. Sheila flew into a rage. "It was going on for the last two years of Sean's life! He didn't do anything about it because he couldn't, any more than I can now! What in God's name do you want from me, Mother?"

"I want you to take your responsibilities more seriously," Rose said. "And Maryanne is your biggest."

Sheila was aghast. "Take my responsibilities seriously! What do you think I've been doing all my life? What do you think I've been doing these past four months?"

"I think you can answer that better than I," Rose said. "Maryanne's totally out of control, Tommy is completely unsupervised, and you're having a high old time with some young doctor. If that adds up to responsibility to *you*, it certainly doesn't to *me!*"

It was so unfair, so cruel, that Sheila couldn't answer. Her mother chose to ignore the circumstances of Sheila's widowhood, the efforts she'd truly tried to make. She continued to endow the son-in-law she once detested with qualities he never had. Realization came slowly. She's angry because I didn't ask her to come and live with me. She's furious that I've found Jerry and some kind of independent life. She's punishing me for those things by trying to make me feel guilty about my children. Sheila felt her anger ebbing. Poor lady, she thought. She needs to have power over someone, and she's trying to have it over me, as though I were still a child myself.

"I'm sorry you have such a poor opinion of me, Mother. I know I'm far from perfect, but I'm doing the best I can. You're right, Maryanne *is* beyond me, but I haven't given up hope." She started to repeat what Tommy had said last night, but decided against it. She had no idea whether there was any basis for his conjecture. "My children know I love them and they'll always come first. But they're not babies. I can't spank them and lock them in their rooms."

"Who's getting locked in their room?" Tommy asked from the doorway.

The two women turned, startled. "*You*, you lazy thing," Sheila said, managing to laugh, "unless you get your tail feathers moving! Good morning, love. Sleep okay? How about getting yourself some breakfast and then doing a few chores for me? I need wood brought up from the basement and we still haven't put the wreath on the front door."

Half-expecting Rick to come back, Maryanne dawdled around the apartment all morning. He hadn't returned last night and by two o'clock on Christmas Day there'd been no word from him. Okay, the hell with him. Let him miss me for a while. She packed a small bag and started to write a note, saying she'd decided to stay at her mother's for a few days. Then she tore it up. He'd know where she was. It would be interesting to see how long it took him to come after her. If he came at all.

A little after three, there was a knock on the door. Patrick, come to fetch her. But it was Betty, looking cheerful.

"Your car awaits, Madam, complete with chauffeur. Me."

"I thought Pat was coming."

"Busy with labor pains. Fortunately not his own. I'm the replacement." Betty looked at the suitcase. "Going to stay a while?"

"I thought I might."

Betty hid her surprise. "Great! Sheila will be thrilled. So am I. Maybe we can have a chance to talk."

"About what?"

"You, mostly."

"Betty, don't practice your two-bit psychology on me. I've been rejected by experts."

"Okay, you don't want to talk now. But maybe you might feel like it sometime in the next few days. I'm on holiday until after New Year's. Sisters-in-law or not, we *are* contemporaries. At least we understand our own generation. Different life styles, maybe, but we have a lot in common."

"Do we?" Maryanne asked. "I'd never have thought so."

Betty refused to be turned away. "I think so," she said. "Anyway, let's go. The clan will be gathering and Sheila wants to call Florida before the 'non-family' arrives, if possible. I hope Pat makes it in time."

"Non-family? You mean the Rosses? Aren't they coming after dinner, as usual?"

"Yes." Damn, Betty thought. Of course she doesn't know who I mean. I'm sure she's never heard of Jerry Mancini. "Yes," Betty repeated, "the Rosses are coming later and so are Terry and Margaret after they have dinner at Margaret's family. But we do have a non-family guest coming early. Dr. Mancini. He's a friend of Pat's and mine . . . and Sheila's." She hesitated. "He's separated from his wife. At loose ends for Christmas. Sheila thought it would be kind to ask him. No, that's not really true,

Maryanne. Why should I lie to you? Sheila's been going out with him for the past month."

Maryanne looked amazed. "Mother's going out? You mean she's found a man? Well, how about that? Good for her!"

"Yeah. Most of us think so."

"Most of us?" Maryanne repeated. "Oh, I get it. Grandma Rose is uptight about it, I suppose. Too soon after Dad and all that Victorian garbage."

"That's part of it. The suitable-mourning-period stuff. The rest of the criticism, shared, I might add, by your aunt and uncle and a few others, is based on the fact that Jerry Mancini's a good bit younger than your mother."

They were in the car now, driving rapidly toward Sheila's.

"How much younger?"

"About fifteen years."

Maryanne did some rapid calculation. "Then he's like thirty-two."

Betty nodded. "Does that bother you?"

"Me?" Maryanne laughed. "You must be kidding! Listen, if Mother's found a guy who digs her, I think that's terrific. God knows she's paid her dues. I hope she's having fun. It makes me feel like she's human."

"She's human, all right," Betty said. "Very much so."

Sheila didn't comment when she saw the small suitcase Maryanne brought in, but she felt a small surge of hope. Perhaps Tommy had known something after all.

"I'm so glad you're here, darling," she said.

"Me, too." Maryanne hesitated. "In fact, I thought you might take me in for a few days, if it's convenient."

"I'd *adore* to! For as long as you like."

Over Maryanne's shoulder, Betty gave her mother-in-law a conspiratorial nod and wink. How wonderful it would be if she'd stay, Sheila thought. For a moment she knew how Rose felt. Being with your daughter was like seeing your youth happen all over again. But she wouldn't make demands, ever.

Patrick arrived soon after and they were able to make the "family call" to Bill and Jean Callahan. Rose and each of the children said a few words to Sean's parents, and then Sheila, who'd been first on the phone, took the receiver again.

"I wish you were both here," she said. "I never stop missing you." She tried to sound gay. "Not that I'd wish you here in this terrible weather! It must be lovely in Sarasota."

"We're moving this week, Sheila," Bill said. "We've taken an apartment in Palm Beach. So many of our friends have moved there lately. Jean and I like Sarasota, but the east coast might be a little more lively,

114

even for us old duffers. Here's the new address and phone number. Maybe you could come down for a visit when we're settled?"

She scribbled it down. "I'd love to, if I can. Probably not this winter, but maybe next. Have you found a nice place?"

"Yes," Bill said, "a two-bedroom garden apartment on Australian Avenue. Just a couple of blocks from Worth, where all the shopping is. Jean will like that, even if she only looks but doesn't buy!"

"I'm sure it will be nice."

"Yes, nice." Jean was on the extension. "But it will never really be our home." She paused. "I'm glad you've stayed in yours, Sheila dear. We both are. It seems to keep Sean alive, somehow. We think you're marvelous, dear. You've been so brave, so strong."

Sheila swallowed hard. They'd never know how frightened, how lost she'd been. Sometimes she felt as though she was still in shock, still going on her nerves. She might one day just get hysterical and come apart. You did what was required of you. You tried to put the pieces together and make things function as near normally as possible. But you had moments, many of them, when you wondered whether it was worth the effort.

"Sean would have wanted us to go on as we always have," she said now. "That's why Christmas is as near like the old days as we could make it. I do wish you were here," she said again, and meant it. She loved the Callahans. *They* were the strong, brave ones, quietly and sincerely mourning a son they thought was almost perfect. No one, thank God, would disabuse them of that idea.

"We wish so, too," Bill said. "But you're in our hearts, all of you."

"Our hearts and our prayers, Sheila darling," Jean added.

"And you're in ours. Take care of yourselves. And Merry Christmas."

"Nice people," Pat said when Sheila hung up.

She smiled at him, and then at Rose who was looking left out. "Yes, Patrick, you're all lucky. You have good genes on *both* sides. The Prices aren't too bad either."

Moments later Jerry arrived, his arms full of gifts. Sheila introduced him first to Rose, wondering nervously how they'd react to each other. Rose was polite but restrained, using what the family called her "company manners." Jerry pretended not to notice the lack of warmth.

"I'm so glad to meet you, Mrs. Price. Did you have a good trip from New York?"

"Yes, thank you."

"I wanted to come with Sheila and Tommy to the airport. I thought you might not get a porter. But your independent daughter said she could manage."

Rose glanced at Sheila. "Independence has always been one of Sheila's strong points."

Sheila quickly took his arm. "Come meet the most beautiful member of the family, the only one you haven't met, my daughter, Maryanne."

They shook hands cordially. "You're just as advertised," Jerry said, smiling.

Maryanne looked at him steadily. "So are you." There was no bitchiness in her tone, no condemnation. There was, instead, almost a note of approval. Sheila breathed a sigh of relief. It had not occurred to her until a couple of hours ago that Maryanne didn't know about Jerry. When she realized it, she also realized it was too late to explain him before they met. How stupid of me! I should have told Maryanne about him, prepared her. But apparently Betty had done that on the way over, and done it well. Maryanne was smiling and at ease, her manner in marked contrast to Rose's chilly acknowledgment. "I'm glad you're here, Jerry," she said. There was something in her tone that made Sheila look at her sharply. The words, simple and mannerly enough, had an almost seductive ring. Ridiculous! Sheila told herself. My God, am I going to get uptight every time a pretty young girl speaks to Jerry? Even when that girl is my own daughter?

Jerry seemed not to notice anything unusual. "I can't tell you how happy I am to be with Sheila's family. You're a handsome bunch, and generous to take me in today."

"How about a drink, Mother?" Patrick asked. "I'll tend bar. Grandma, what for you?"

"Just a little sherry, if you have it, please."

"Uh huh, I know you," Patrick teased. " 'Just a little sherry' she says. Watch her, everybody. You know about those proper matrons who get bombed on their 'little sips of sherry'!"

"Patrick!" Rose was indignant, as the others laughed.

"White wine for me, please," Maryanne said.

Jerry glanced at her. Pot, no doubt. People who smoked grass never drank liquor. She gave him a knowing smile.

"Right," Patrick said. "Wine for Maryanne. Scotch for the rest of us." He turned to Tommy. "What about you, Squirt? A double martini?"

His condescension made Tommy want to hit him. As a matter of fact, he'd have liked to have a drink, but he didn't dare, of course. "I'll get myself a Coke," he said.

"What about a little wine, darling?" Sheila asked. "It couldn't hurt you. And this is a special occasion."

"No, thanks."

Drinks in hand, they opened packages. There was nothing elaborate or expensive exchanged, but there were small, thoughtful gifts for everyone. Sheila unobtrusively set aside the sweater she'd bought for Rick. It was his only package. Maryanne had brought none. "I'm sorry," she said. "I didn't get around to shopping."

Jerry received two presents, a book from Betty and Pat and a scarf from Sheila. He had something equally unpretentious for everyone in the room. As soon as she could, Sheila motioned him to join her in the kitchen.

"Darling, I have a real present for you," she said, "but it didn't seem wise to bring it out at this point. I'll save it until we're alone."

He pulled her to him and kissed her. "Witch! That's *my* line! I have a goodie for you, too, for private presentation. You didn't think that silly little bookmark was your real Christmas present, did you?"

"No. Any more than you thought the scarf was what I'd give you." She backed away from him nervously. "We'd better join the others."

Jerry looked amused. "You think we're kidding anybody in that room?"

She smiled. "Probably not, but one must keep up appearances, mustn't one?"

He made a solemn face. "Yes, indeed, dear Mrs. Callahan. One must not shock the proper people. Especially the one whose initials are Rose Price."

"You hate her."

"Honey, of course not. I understand her. She's exactly what I expected."

"And Maryanne?"

He thought a moment. "No, she's not exactly what I expected. Much nicer, in fact. A charming girl. Very like her mother. Give her a few years and she'll be another Sheila. She's going to be all right, baby. You'll see. Take the doctor's word for it."

She felt wonderful. It was going to be a good Christmas after all.

Chapter 14

Bob Ross called Sheila at the store two days after Christmas saying they should meet to discuss her taxes.

"It's important," he said, "and I wondered whether you know how to go about gathering the information for filing."

"You know damned well I don't."

"Well, why don't we have a drink and talk about it? I could meet you after work tomorrow, if you're free. That bar in The Sheraton Cleveland, what's it called? The Bunch of Grapes. How about meeting there around six?"

"Fine. I don't even have to go outdoors. I can get there from the store right through the arcade."

When she hung up, it struck her there was something odd about Bob's invitation. If he wanted to talk business, why didn't he come to the house in the evening as he often had since Sean's death? Why a dark, crowded bar with a vocalist so loud that conversation of *any* kind was almost impossible? It was hardly the place to discuss taxes. She'd met Jerry there once or twice. It was a place—she grimaced at the thought—to meet somebody else's husband, not to consult your lawyer.

There could be any number of reasons why Bob had suggested a cocktail bar. It might be as simple as the fact that he'd be in the neighborhood. His office was nearby, or he might be staying in town Friday evening for

118

a meeting on the water-pollution thing. Perhaps he had an hour to kill. It could be as insignificant as that. But she felt it wasn't. She knew Bob wanted to talk to her alone. Maybe, for some reason, without Emily's knowledge. Or without the possible distraction of Tommy's presence or Maryanne's.

Maryanne. They'd had no opportunity to talk, between the frenzy of Christmas and the ubiquitous presence of Rose. "The Price tag," as Pat irreverently and secretly called his grandmother, had left the day of Bob's call, and though Sheila felt a stab of sadness and guilt seeing her return to her solitary apartment in New York, she also recognized a sense of relief. She loved her mother but she could never get over this constricting feeling of having to be "on her best behavior" when Rose was in the house. It was inexplicable. She should have felt more at ease with her mother than with anyone in the world and yet this guarded, unnatural relationship was always there. Always had been. It bothered Sheila terribly. Not only for the constraint between herself and Rose, but even more because she felt something of the same thing between her and Maryanne. It was a kind of wariness she couldn't define. As though she were afraid to talk to her daughter, and as though Maryanne was unable to confide in her. So far, the girl had said nothing about staying or leaving. She simply remained in the house, a pleasant, non-participating member of the menage. What were her plans? Was the thing with Rick over and done with? Did she intend to stay in Shaker Heights? She hadn't brought all her clothes and belongings on Christmas and yet she showed no signs of returning to Ohio City. Tonight, Sheila decided. Tonight we'll talk.

Right after dinner, Tommy went out. Almost apologetically, Sheila asked where he was going.

"Just to meet some of the gang," he said. "Maybe go to a movie."

"Honey, I hate you wandering around at all hours." She couldn't restrain herself. "Don't be late, will you?"

"Okay." It was a grudging agreement as the door slammed behind him. Sheila turned to Maryanne. "I sound like a nag, don't I?"

"Minor variety. You can't help it. You still think of him as a child."

"But he *is*, Maryanne. He won't be sixteen for another six months."

"That's juvenile only where the law's concerned, Mother. Kids are different these days. They do all the adult things from the age of twelve on. I'll bet Shaker Heights, like all the high schools in America, has its share of pregnant fifteen-year-olds, or aborted ones." She shrugged. "I know you can't imagine Tommy doing any of the things you read about. Maybe he doesn't. But I don't think he goes out every evening to play tiddlywinks."

Sheila sighed. "I feel so helpless."

"You are, Mother. All parents are these days."

It was the opening Sheila had been looking for. "What about you, darling?"

"I'm not fifteen."

"I'm not talking about age and you know it. What's happening with you, Maryanne? What about Rick? Are you going back to him?"

"Do you think I should?"

Sheila felt angry. Maryanne wasn't really looking for answers, she was baiting her mother, and the knowledge made Sheila's reply sound cold and sarcastic.

"You're not really asking my *advice*, are you?" She expected her daughter to laugh in that hostile way Sheila had come to know. But, instead, Maryanne looked at her pleadingly.

"Yes, believe it or not, I am. Mother, I don't know what to do. I don't feel I belong anywhere. I don't know where I'm going. I envy you. Good times or bad, you know who you are, how you want to live. You still have those 'values' we once talked about. I have nothing. Nothing at all."

Sheila melted. There was no doubting the girl's sincerity. "Maryanne, that's not true. You have everything to look forward to. You're young, beautiful, intelligent. You can be anything you want. It's all ahead of you, dear. Envy *me*? That's ludicrous! My life is half over. *More* than half over."

"At least it's been productive. Marriage, kids, a world you could count on, even if it wasn't absolutely perfect." She gave a little laugh. "Funny. All the things I've spat on for years suddenly seem to have some kind of orderliness that I want. It's crazy, but I even liked Christmas, with all the sentimental family goo. Two years ago I'd have called it middle-class crap. Now I wish it were my way of life."

Sheila couldn't believe what she was hearing and yet she had no reason to think it wasn't true. She spoke cautiously.

"It *can* be your way of life. Don't you see what's happened? You thought you despised your background because you had nothing to compare it to. For two years you've lived in a totally different world. Now you can balance the two. You've been both places, Maryanne. Neither is idyllic, but if there's a choice, a girl with your good sense has to come down on the side of decency and consideration for others."

There was no answer. Sheila pushed her advantage.

"Honey, do you love Rick?"

"What's love?"

Sheila smiled. "You're going to hate my answer because it's going to come out in clichés. I wish I could be poetic and inspiring, spouting lofty phrases, but I'm too simple for that. For me, love between a man and a woman is physical compatibility, mutual support and respect, shared interests and a sense of growing together. It's being your own person, but knowing you're part of someone else. It's fights and arguments and less than one thousand per cent adoration or agreement, but it's also knowing that you miss him when he's not there, that you'd rather be with him than anyone in the world, that you can count on him when things are too much to cope with alone. It's *liking* him, Maryanne. Not all the time, because no man or woman is flawless, but loving is liking the person and being realistic about his weaknesses because you know you have just as many of your own."

"Is that the way you felt about Dad?"

"Yes," Sheila said slowly. "For all our imperfections, I loved him. I liked him."

"And Jerry?"

Sheila was deliberately evasive. "What about him?"

"Are you in love with Jerry?"

Sheila was silent for a few seconds. "I think I am, Maryanne, but it's too soon to be sure. We've only known each other a little over a month. I haven't really begun to find out about Jerry, nor he about me. Not *really* find out. Besides, as you know, there are obstacles. A number of them."

"You mean the age difference? Who cares?"

"Lots of people. Maybe even me. Maybe, in time, Jerry. But there's more than that. He should have more children and I'm too old to give them to him. Even if he took on mine, my youngest, at least, it would be difficult. Tommy dislikes him intensely."

"Tommy's jealous."

"Perhaps. But in any case, this is all speculation. Jerry's not even divorced, you know."

"But he will be. What then?"

"I honestly don't know, Maryanne. I just know he's been a blessing for me these past weeks. I'm grateful for him. That's enough for now." She looked at her daughter. "You're a sly one. This all started because I asked you whether you were in love with Rick and you turned the conversation around to the subject of love in general and me in particular. Now, how about an answer to my specific question?"

"No. I'm not in love with Rick. He was part of that other world. Sex. Pot. Dropping out. If I accept your definition of love, I'll have to go looking for someone like Jerry. And maybe that's what I'll eventually do, Mother."

Sheila's eyes filled with tears. "Oh, sweetheart, I'm so glad! Doubly glad because you came to the decision yourself. You've grown up, my dear. And that's lovely to see."

"I hope I have. Maybe I've just made a start. When I left Rick at Christmas I did it to punish him, to make him come after me. I feel differently now. But who knows? I might change tomorrow."

"You won't. I know you won't."

"But I still don't know what I want."

"Stay here. For a while, at least. We'll get the rest of your things from the apartment. Give yourself a few weeks to be peaceful and think things through. Then you can decide where you want to live and what you want to do."

"I can't impose on you, Mother. I know how tight things are, even with only Tommy to support."

"Don't be silly. The house is here, your room is here, and one more mouth to feed isn't going to wreck the budget. Anyway, I know it won't be forever. But let's don't put a time limit on it."

"If you're sure . . ."

"I've never been more sure of anything in my life. Oh, Maryanne, I'm so happy!" Sheila wiped her eyes. "Damn! I must be getting old, weeping for joy!"

Maryanne gave a little laugh. "If that's so, I must have aged a lot in the last hour."

Sheila looked at her. Tears were streaming down her daughter's face.

When she woke the next morning, Sheila had a moment of panic, wondering whether Maryanne had changed her mind overnight. But obviously she hadn't because she got up for breakfast with Sheila and asked if she could borrow the keys to the station wagon.

"I thought I'd go down to the apartment and get my things. I'll wait until late in the evening. Hopefully Rick won't be there."

Sheila thought of her cocktail date with Bob. She could easily break it. "Want to pick me up at the store and I'll go along to help?"

Maryanne shook her head. "No thanks. Besides, aren't you meeting Bob Ross for a drink?"

"Yes, but that's not important."

"I don't mind going alone, Mother. In fact, I'd rather."

She doesn't want me to see where she's been living, Sheila realized. I was never invited there and I never intruded. Pointless to start now. "All right," she said. "If you're sure you can manage."

"I don't have that much stuff. I can handle it."

Sheila still felt uncomfortable. "What if Rick *is* there? What if he makes trouble? I don't think you should go alone."

"Mother, I can take care of myself." She sounded irritated. "Look, we'd better get something straight if I'm going to move back in. I've been on my own. Don't start treating me like a child or it won't work."

Sheila nodded. "You're right. It's a habit I'll try not to fall back into." She thought back to her discussion with Jerry. He was quite right. No matter how old your child was, it was hard to remember that she was no longer a little girl. Maryanne needed a long leash. She'd have to give her one if there was any hope of keeping her at home. Sheila got up from the table. "Well, I'm off. See you when I see you."

Bob Ross was waiting for her when she walked into the cocktail lounge that evening. He kissed her lightly on the cheek, ordered a scotch and water for her, and then sat back in his chair and looked at her intently.

"You're looking wonderful, Sheila. I didn't have a chance to tell you so on Tuesday. It was a nice evening, by the way. Emily and I enjoyed it."

"I'm glad. It wouldn't have been Christmas without you." She smiled. "I can't really say I'm sorry it's over, though. It's always been a trying time for me, and this year, of course, it was even more difficult."

"Without Sean, you mean."

"Yes, that, mostly. But other things, too."

"Rose?"

"She's one of them. You know I've always had ridiculous guilts about her, Bob. And now, knowing we're both husbandless, I felt selfish not asking her to move to Cleveland."

"For God's sake, Sheila, don't ever do that! Emotionally, you might think it's the thing to do, but intellectually you know that mothers and daughters can't live under the same roof once they've had their own homes."

Sheila didn't answer for a minute. Then she said, "I hope you're wrong."

"Don't tell me Rose is coming to live with you!"

"No. Maryanne is. She's decided to come home. Oh, Bob, I'm so glad about it! I can't begin to tell you how I've worried about her these past few years. Just to get her away from that terrible atmosphere and that awful man is such a relief. And the best part is, I didn't urge her. She just miraculously seems to have come to her senses."

He frowned. "Miraculously, indeed. Sounds like an overnight transformation. What do you think brought it on?"

"I'm not sure," Sheila said. "Maybe she's been thinking about it for a long time and was too proud to admit she's been wrong. Maybe it was, indeed, the 'miracle of Christmas.' Or," she hesitated, "maybe she thought she couldn't come home while her father was there."

"Could be any one of those things."

"You don't sound convinced."

"Well, Sheila, it *is* sudden. Even you'll admit that. You've hardly seen her, except at the funeral, for two years. Now all of a sudden she decides she'd like to come home."

"People grow up. They change their minds." She was annoyed, disappointed that he didn't share her joy. "Good Lord, must you always have such a lawyer's mind? Can't you believe that sometimes there's no real 'motive in the case'? She's had it with that Bohemian life, that's all. She's tried it and gotten tired of it. It's as simple as that."

"Okay, okay! Don't attack me! You know I'm glad about anything that gives you peace of mind. And I like Maryanne. I always have. So what's she going to do, now that she's back in the land of respectability? Get a job? Look for a husband?"

Sheila relaxed. "Both, I hope. But I'm not going to rush her. She needs to recharge her batteries, as it were."

"Maybe I can help with the job situation. This environmental thing I'm on is always in need of people. She can type, can't she? I'll make inquiries, if you want me to. It's the kind of project that young people can identify with. She might like it."

"That would be wonderful! Yes, she types. Probably rusty, but she could get her skills back, I'm sure. Bob, that's marvelous of you! I'm so appreciative."

"Well, don't mention it to her just yet. I have to find out if there are openings. I'll let you know in a few days." He paused. "What about you, Sheila? Things going all right?"

"Yes. Fine." She wasn't going to get into her vague anxieties about Tommy. One child's problems at a time, she thought. Sheila gave him a look of mock fright. "Fine, that is, unless you're the bearer of some awful tidings about taxes. You *did* say that's what you wanted to talk to me about, didn't you?"

"Partly. I do want you to gather all your bills and receipts together soon so we have them in order when I do your taxes. And it will be more complicated this year because of Sean's estate, what there was of it. Next year won't be as complex. Fortunately—or unfortunately—you have so little income that you'll hardly owe anything. Are you really managing, dear? Do you need any help?"

"So far, so good. But thank you, anyway."

"That job must be a horror."

"No, it isn't. Not at all. Christmas was rough and the 'return season' isn't particularly fun, but all in all I like it. The people are nice and I've gotten over being nervous. It's good that I'm occupied during the day. Working has made these last months easier in many ways. I know I'm not cut out for a big career in business. Selling books is enough satisfaction for me."

"Selling books and seeing Jerry Mancini, you mean."

Sheila shot him a surprised look.

"I'm sorry," Bob said. "I guess I'm out of line. But I . . . that is, we all care about you. We don't want to see you hurt."

"What makes everybody so damned sure I'm going to be hurt?" Sheila snapped. "My God, everybody I know is giving me unasked-for advice! All right, I'm seeing a man. A younger man. A married man. All of you act as though I'm dimwitted. What am I doing that's so terrible? I wish everybody would stop clucking long enough to tell me *that!*"

Her vehemence only confirmed his suspicions. She was in love with Jerry. He felt a very personal kind of despair. What did he expect? That she'd be there for him to love? An impossible, unattainable dream? That was it, of course. He didn't want her to belong to anyone. He'd never even wanted her to belong to Sean. It was insanity. He couldn't have her and he couldn't bear the idea that someone else could.

"Sheila, you'll have to forgive us. All of us who love you. We're only concerned for your future and your well-being. We don't want some irresponsible young guy to break your heart. You're too vulnerable at this particular time."

She was really angry. "Well, I *don't* forgive you! Dammit, I find all this 'concern' insulting! It implies that I'm stupid. And it's just another way of saying that I'm too old and unattractive for any man under seventy-five!"

"Don't be crazy! Nobody thinks you're stupid. And God knows nobody thinks you're old or unattractive! We want you to be happy, Sheila. You've been through a traumatic time. It's easy for any man or woman who's suddenly alone to fall into a situation that offers escape. As long as you know that it might not be permanent, there's no reason why you shouldn't see Jerry or anybody else you want."

"Well, thanks a lot! I'm so glad my friends are willing to give their conditional approval to my conduct! It's really big of all of you!"

"Don't take it that way, dear. Please. Nobody's giving 'conditional approval.' Nobody would presume to mention any of this if we weren't devoted to you and anxious that you don't put yourself in a spot where you could be disillusioned."

She calmed down. "It's strange that everybody's so sure I'm going to get kicked in the teeth. Why is that, Bob?"

"Because it usually happens that way, I guess," he said reluctantly. "Even to women as beautiful and desirable as you. This is a disoriented period for you, Sheila. That's all I meant."

"I see. I'm sorry I flared up. But I have only one thing to say to you and all my dear friends."

"What's that?"

"I love you all and I wish you'd mind your own damned business."

Sheila was disgusted with herself as Bob drove her home after their meeting in The Bunch of Grapes. Sitting in the car beside him, she tried to think of a way to apologize for being so nasty about his genuine concern. And that's really all it was. Good lord, was she turning into one of those ridiculous women who thought every man was interested in her, just because he showed some small consideration for her well-being? She hated women like that. Women who read some kind of sexual significance into every polite compliment, every perfectly normal meeting. She'd seen a lot of them, particularly man-hungry, middle-aged widows and divorcées, and she'd found their self-delusion unattractive, almost indecent. Had she been reading the same kind of ego-building innuendoes into Bob Ross's many kindnesses over the past months? Probably. Undoubtedly. It was ridiculous. And yet when they reached her door he said, "Do you really have to go home? Couldn't we go somewhere for a bite of dinner?"

"I'm sorry. I really can't. For one thing, I'm anxious to see whether Maryanne had any problem getting her things out of the apartment. She's always said Rick was 'non-violent,' personally and politically, but it makes me uneasy to think of her going back there alone, after she walked out on him."

"Nothing will happen to her, Sheila. She's well able to take care of herself. Probably better than you are."

"Maybe so. But I can't help worrying. Besides," Sheila said lightly, "isn't Emily expecting you?"

"I'm a big boy. I can stay out for dinner. In fact, I often do. It beats hell out of listening to Em's complaints."

She didn't want to get into that. "All wives complain, Robert. It goes with the territory."

"Did *you?* I can't imagine you nagging Sean, and God knows you had a right to. We don't have to kid each other about him, Sheila. We've both had firsthand experience with his Don Juan complex."

She ignored the implication about Emily. "I don't want to talk about the past, Bob. And I don't think you should, either."

"All right, then let's talk about the present and the future. Sheila, you must know how I feel about you."

She opened the car door. "Don't, Bob. Don't spoil a very precious friendship. I'm flattered, but I can't play those games." Impulsively, she gave him a little kiss on the cheek. "Thanks for everything, dear. Including the tax advice. I'll get to work on it right away. Bless you. Good night."

He hadn't answered or tried to stop her. He watched her safely inside and then drove off.

Switching on lights inside the dark house, she thought about the past two hours, not with any great surprise, but with a kind of unhappiness that Bob finally had declared himself. Thank God it had been passed over so quickly, without any real embarrassment for either of them. Still, it was bound to change their relationship, erect a barrier of constraint that would never again allow her to feel easy and relaxed with him. She'd feel less comfortable now, even when they were legitimately struggling with the mess that was Sean's "estate." And though she was innocent and Emily guilty, she'd even be self-conscious around Bob's wife. Damn. It was all too sordid. She didn't want to speculate about Sean and Emily.

She certainly didn't want to know that Emily's husband cared for her as more than a friend. She didn't need these complications in her life.

Her mind leaped, automatically, to her children. Neither of them was home. As usual, she didn't know where Tommy was. She hoped Maryanne hadn't run into any problems. I should have gone with her, Sheila thought. It would have been better for many reasons, including the fact that I'd not have had that unsettling conversation with Bob.

The house was so quiet, and she needed the sound of a cheerful voice. She dialed Jerry and the answering service nasally reported that the doctor wasn't in. She left her name. Probably he'd been called out on some emergency, a "post-Jesus baby" perhaps, Sheila thought, smiling. This was what it was like to be in love with a doctor; your greatest rival was Nature. She went to her room, restlessly switched on the TV set and then turned off "Sanford and Son." It was getting late, but she wasn't hungry. Besides, she hoped that any minute the children would appear and they'd eat together. It was nine o'clock when she heard the front door open. She called downstairs.

"Tommy? Maryanne?"

Her daughter answered. "It's me."

Sheila came down to find Maryanne surrounded by battered suitcases and shopping bags. "Good grief! I thought you said you didn't have much!"

"Junk mostly, but I managed with the aid of the itinerant Super who fortunately wasn't too drunk to help."

"Everything go okay? Was Rick there?"

"Yes, he was there. We talked a little."

"And?"

Maryanne shrugged. "Rick doesn't take things too seriously."

"Does he want you to come back?"

"I suppose so."

Sheila's heart quickened. "What about you?"

The old resentment at being questioned came across the girl's face. "I'm *here*, am I not? With all my worldly goods."

Sheila knew better than to pursue it. Just as she knew, for all her hopes, that Maryanne could have another impulsive change of mind. But for the moment she *was* here. She had brought her belongings. That, at least, was a good sign. "Hungry?" Sheila asked. "I've been waiting for you and Tommy, though he hasn't surfaced yet." She frowned. "I'm worried about him."

Maryanne didn't answer. Instead she said, "I'm really too bushed for dinner, Mother. Think I'll stow this stuff away and maybe have a glass of milk later. Do you mind? I figured you'd be out with Jerry tonight."

"I haven't heard from him. He'll probably call later. You go ahead, dear. I'm glad it all went well."

She watched Maryanne's slim young figure disappear up the stairs. Had it gone well? Or was she even now wishing she was back with Rick? Just as I'm wishing I were with Jerry.

As though in response, the phone rang. "I've just slapped something seven pounds and three ounces into life," the familiar voice said, "and the exertion has made me ravenous! Had dinner yet?"

"No. I just got in a while ago."

"Good. I'll be over in twenty minutes. I haven't given you your real Christmas present yet, you know. We haven't been alone for almost a week."

"I know. I've missed you."

"I hope you have two presents for me," Jerry said.

"Two?"

"Sure. The real one and the one money can't buy."

She couldn't help laughing. "You're incorrigible."

"I'm also on my way."

She went back upstairs to change, suddenly realizing she was edgy. It hadn't troubled her to make love in her own house with Tommy securely locked away on the floor above. But with Maryanne only two rooms away? She couldn't. We'll have to go to Jerry's, she thought. Suddenly she began to giggle. She felt like a nervous virgin. Forty-seven years old and I've never made love to a man in his apartment. Hell, I've never even been to a man's apartment alone! Everything is certainly changing, Sheila, she told herself. Everything.

Jerry tucked her Christmas present into his pocket, thinking how much she'd like it and how much significance she'd see in the little gold charm. It was a tiny gold turkey with a diamond eye, a reminder that they'd met at Thanksgiving. It was sentimental and special. Sheila would like that. He was sure she had something equally personal for him. He looked forward to the exchange of gifts and the lovemaking that would follow. He was crazy about her. He might even marry her, once he was sure he was over Barbara.

Damn. That was the trouble. He wasn't sure he really did have her out of his system. He'd thought so until Christmas Day. She'd seemed different that morning when they were with Joy, watching her opening her gifts, hearing the child's delighted squeals and receiving her kisses. Barbara had seemed affected by it, too. "Like old times," she'd said. "Yes," he'd answered, remembering happier Christmases, remembering how much in love they'd been, how proud he'd been to have captured this desirable, socially superior creature. And then he'd felt the old bitterness. She'd sent him away. Nobody had ever done that before. He'd been unable to believe it was happening at the time, wasn't sure he believed it now. Maybe she regretted it. Maybe she wanted him back. For the first time there were indications she did.

She'd unexpectedly asked him, that morning, if he'd like to go with her and Joy to his in-laws for Christmas dinner. He'd said he was sorry, he couldn't.

"Would you like to have dinner another time?" Jerry added.

"Yes," she'd said like a polite schoolgirl, "that would be very nice."

"How about tomorrow night?"

"Fine."

They'd had dinner, trying to behave naturally, making guarded, polite conversation. But something remained between them, a flicker of the old desire, a hint of unforgotten passion and, for Jerry, the excitement of having seen Barbara make the first tentative overture. Nothing had happened, but the feeling lingered. He told himself it was pure nostalgia. She couldn't compare to Sheila who loved him unselfishly. Sheila would never reject him. She understood what that did to a man.

Chapter 15

Tradition, to those who cherish it, comes before personal preference or even, as in the case of Emily Ross, outright hostility. Emily thought of herself as a "good woman," basically respectable, with a sense of the fitness of things. True, she had broken her marriage vows, but only with one man, Sean. Aside from that single, uncharacteristic lapse, she clung to the conventions of her group and her environment, including the tradition of spending New Year's Eve at the country club.

The Rosses and both Callahan brothers and their wives had "seen in" every New Year together at the same table in the same festooned, balloon-filled ballroom for more than twenty years. This time, there'd be no Sean to greet 1974, but it did not occur to Emily that there'd be no Sheila. Not that she welcomed the idea. Her dislike of Sheila—a resentment made up of envy for her beauty and jealousy of her marriage—had been latent until these past few months. Since Sean's death and Sheila's unconscionable behavior she'd developed an actual hatred for her, heightened in no small degree by Bob's continued devotion to "the widow."

Still, like her or not, it was accepted that people would be together on this presumably gala night. Emily checked Margaret Callahan to be sure Maggie had reserved the same table at the edge of the dance floor. Maggie had.

"Who's Sheila bringing?" Emily asked. "That doctor?"

"Sheila's not coming," Margaret said. "I've asked the Weatherbees to join us this year."

Emily's relief was only slightly less than her surprise. "Not coming! Why on earth not?"

"I don't know. I called to confirm it with her and she said she thought she'd beg off this year. Something about her membership expiring." Maggie's voice clearly said she didn't believe a word of that invalid excuse.

"That's ridiculous! What does one thing have to do with the other?"

"I really don't know, Em. All I know is that she won't be there."

"I suppose she's embarrassed to show up with that young man. Or maybe we're all too old and dowdy for her, now that she's joined the swingers. I just don't understand your sister-in-law. Chasing after her son's friend, bringing that lazy Maryanne home to lie around all day, neglecting Tommy, who I hear is running wild! I really think you and Terry should have a talk with her."

Although she was completely in accord with Emily's views, there was enough family loyalty in Margaret not to openly concur. All she said was, "She's a grown woman. Neither Terry nor I can dictate her actions."

"But I know you don't condone them."

Margaret didn't answer.

"Well, it's too bad she won't be with us," Emily said, "but I presume we'll survive. The Weatherbees are fun." She changed the subject. "What are you wearing?"

"My black lace. It's two years old, but I can't find anything I like better. I've shopped everywhere. You?"

"I picked up a Halston. Divine but outrageously expensive. Bob had a fit when he saw the price." She laughed. "You know, I think men secretly *like* it when we're extravagant. They yell, but it does something for their egos to know they can afford us. Sheila was always foolish that way. Too careful with Sean's money. She made too few demands. No wonder he had to keep proving his virility."

What the hell was Emily talking about? She probably was spouting something she'd read somewhere and getting it all mixed up, at that. Anything to put down Sheila, Margaret thought. I wonder why she hates her so? Anyway, it was a pointless conversation. Margaret didn't think much of Sheila these days, either, but she couldn't fault her for the wife she'd been.

"Well, if Sheila didn't spend Sean's money, it didn't do her much good," Maggie said. "He sure didn't leave her much."

"She seems to be managing," Emily snapped, "with a good deal of help from my husband."

So that's it, Margaret thought. She's angry about Bob's concern for

Sheila. Silly woman. Bob Ross wouldn't stray far from the reservation. He'd be afraid Emily would kill him.

"I don't think you have to worry about Bob."

Emily laughed again. "Believe me, my dear, that's the furthest thing from my mind!"

Margaret was frowning when she hung up. *I wonder what Sheila* is *doing New Year's Eve. The story I told Emily was true, insofar as it's what Sheila told* me. *I don't believe it, of course. No one would. Undoubtedly Sheila plans to be with Jerry Mancini, possibly at a party with* his *friends, or more likely spending a "romantic evening" alone with him. It was all terribly unattractive, but there wasn't a damned thing any of them could do about it. Sheila was making her own bed. She could lie in it,* wherever *it was.*

At lunch on Sunday, Sheila cheerfully asked her son and daughter what their plans were for New Year's Eve.

"What are *yours?*" Tommy asked defensively.

Sheila looked at him, curiously. "I don't know, dear. I imagine I'll be with Jerry, but we really haven't discussed it. I was kind of waiting to see what you were up to."

"If you're worried about staying home on my account, don't. I'll probably be with the gang."

"Somebody having a party?" Sheila asked.

"Yeah," Tommy said. "Sam Johnson."

Maryanne glanced at him. "That's your black friend, isn't it? The one you and Paul Bellows and Artie Connolly run around with?"

Tommy's mouth flew open. "How did you know about them?"

"I've been looking up some of my old chums the past couple of days. They have kid brothers, too. Everybody in Shaker Heights knows the gang you hang out with, Tommy." Maryanne was calm. "Not a very savory group, chum."

"Listen who's talking!" Tommy was red with rage.

Maryanne calmly buttered a roll. "*Touché.*"

Sheila was bewildered. "Who are these boys, Tommy? I've asked you before and you never tell me. I think it's time you did."

He didn't answer.

"Tommy! Answer me! I've tried to pay you the compliment of respecting your privacy. I've trusted your good instincts and your maturity. But you're still only fifteen years old. If you've gotten yourself mixed up with a bad crowd, I want to know it. And I want it stopped before you get in trouble! Now tell me who these boys are!"

He glared at his sister. "They're just kids from school, that's all."

Maryanne was expressionless.

"I'm sorry," Sheila said, "that's not enough. If the whole neighborhood knows about your friends, it will be easy enough for me to find out. But frankly, I'd prefer to hear it from you."

"Okay! Sam Johnson is black. And Artie Connolly is a big, dumb jock who drives a souped-up car. And Paul—"

"Yes?" Sheila's voice was quiet. "Paul?"

"He's a helluva nice guy. All right, he got in a little trouble once a couple of years ago. Picked up for shoplifting. But he's clear of that now. He was on probation but he's never done anything like it since. Jesus! They're nothing compared to that crowd of junkies Maryanne's been hanging around with!" He scowled at his sister. "Thanks a lot! We needed you here, making trouble. Why didn't you stay where you belong?"

"Tommy! Stop it!" Sheila's voice was a command. "We're not discussing your sister, we're talking about you. This may all be very harmless. I can't judge that. But I want to meet your friends. Until I do, I'm afraid I can't let you go out with them. Not New Year's Eve or any other night until you bring them here."

He couldn't believe it. "You're treating me like a damned baby!"

"If you act like one, I'll treat you like one."

"Well, I won't do it!"

"Why not? Are you ashamed of them?"

"No. But I don't have to have my friends screened. What are you, the FBI?"

Sheila spoke gently. "I'm not screening them, Tommy. Not in that way. I just want to meet them. Probably they're very nice boys. But don't you see? I'm responsible for you. You're not Maryanne's age. Not that I'm happy about her friends, either. But she's grown up. You're not."

He shook his head stubbornly. "I'd look like a jerk, telling my friends they have to come around and meet my mother."

"It's your choice, dear. And I don't see what's so terrible about it. You always brought your friends here when you went to University. This is no different."

"Sure it is. Everything's different."

There was a long silence. "Invite them over for supper this evening, Tommy," Sheila said gently. "Please."

"No."

She sighed. "Then I'm afraid you're grounded, son. Indefinitely."

He looked at her. "And what will that do to *your* social life, Mother? Are you going to stay home every night and play watchdog? Assign Maryanne to make sure I come home right after school in the afternoon? Why don't you just lock me in my room and be done with it?"

Sheila tried once more. "We're letting this get out of hand, don't you think? It could be so easily resolved."

"Sure. By my being a good little kid who does what Mama tells him. I told you a long time ago you wouldn't understand my friends. They're not *your* friends' children, so they'll automatically be dirt. Bringing them here is a waste of time."

"That's what it's all about, isn't it? You really *are* ashamed of them. It's not the 'humiliation' of bringing them home for me to meet; it's your certain knowledge that they're not the kind of boys you should be spending your time with."

Tommy rose. "May I be excused?"

"Certainly."

When he left the room, Maryanne looked at her mother. "I could kill myself! I never meant to start all this. I thought you knew who his friends were. God, I'm sorry!"

"Don't be. I should have looked into it long ago. I've had a hunch that he's in a bad crowd. He's such a changed boy. But I tried to think it was just adjustment to a different way of life. Kidding myself, as usual."

"But maybe that's all it really is," Maryanne said. "All kids are a little wild these days. He hasn't gotten into trouble. No reason to think he will."

Sheila shook her head. "I've been too preoccupied with everything but him. It's not fair to him. He needs his parents—or one of them—right now. He's crying out for discipline as a sign I care. And instead I've given him freedom that he's interpreted as indifference. He's still a boy, wanting to be noticed, wanting rules to live by."

"And what about you, Mother? Are you supposed to devote your life to him?"

"I don't know. I just know I've been doing things wrong. I'm going to call Jerry and tell him I can't go out Monday night. I lied. We *did* have plans. He was taking me to a party at one of his friend's." She smiled. "No big deal. He can go without me."

"You're being silly! Silly and a bit of a martyr! It's really not very becoming."

"Don't *you* start! I've had enough for one day!" She patted Maryanne's hand. "It'll work out. All of it. By the way, you never said what you're doing tomorrow night."

"Donna and Ted Harris are having some people in. I'm invited, but I'm not sure I want to go. She was Donna Werber, remember? My best friend in school. Got married about a year ago. They live over on Chalfant. I called her yesterday, just to catch up, and she asked me to come by and see the old gang."

"I always liked the Werbers. And Donna. Why don't you go?"

"For one thing, I'm not sure I'm ready for all that reunion business with the young marrieds. For another, I don't have a date." Maryanne made a face. "I'll see. I'll probably end up going. Damn. I wish I'd gone skiing with Pat and Betty. I really *hate* the holidays!"

Sheila smiled. "You come by it naturally."

Jerry sounded upset when she reached him that evening. "Can't go to-morrow night?" he repeated. "What's this all about? It's New Year's Eve! Don't you want to meet my friends?"

"Darling, you know better than that! I was looking forward to it so much!" She explained about Tommy. "He's under 'house arrest' for the moment, so I have to stay in."

"Do you plan to play warden until he's twenty-one?"

"Of course not. But I have to make him understand that I mean what I say, that he's still subject to discipline. He needs that, Jerry. He's just a kid."

"So he stays in tomorrow night. Does that mean you have to baby-sit? I don't get it. He's been alone plenty of evenings in the past few weeks. Why tonight?"

"Because until today I didn't know the kind of boys he was running with. I assumed they were the same sort of decent kids he's always known. Now I'm afraid. If I leave him after the confrontation we had, it'll be a sure sign that I don't really give a damn what he does."

"I'm having a hard time following your thinking, Sheila."

"I know. It's hard to explain. Call it maternal instinct. But I've got to get him back on the track, even if it means sacrificing a wonderful night with you."

She waited. She fully expected him to laugh, call her a crazy lady and say okay, to hell with the party, he'd come over and they'd have cham-pagne in front of her fireplace. But he didn't. Instead, there was a long pause.

"Jerry, dear," she said, "I'm sorry. It seems silly and martyrish, I sup-pose. Maryanne thinks so. But I can't back down on this. It's a crucial moment for Tommy. And for me."

"Seems pretty clear where I rate on your priority list." He sounded petulant, jealous.

"They're two very different lists," Sheila said quietly. "You have a child. You should know."

"I know I wouldn't let her run my life!"

That's exactly what I've been telling myself these past weeks, Sheila thought. And it's been blindly selfish. I don't intend to sacrifice my life for Tommy, but I must face the fact that he has needs, too. Just as I have a need for Jerry.

His voice changed suddenly, became mature and gentle. "I'm sorry, darling," he said. "I'm behaving like a fifteen-year-old myself! Look, who cares about a party? I'll come over tomorrow night and we'll have our own. I assume Maryanne's going out."

"I think so. She's invited to some old friends', Donna and Ted Harris." Sheila hesitated. "Jerry, you know how much I want to be with you, but I think you should go to the party you'd planned to take me to. I *hoped* you'd say you'd come and stay with me, and I love you for offering, but

I'd feel guilty about spoiling your fun. You should be with your friends. I'd feel terrible all evening, knowing I was keeping you here because of my obligations. I don't want to do that. I'd probably spend half the night apologizing. Please go to the party, love. I'll feel much better if you do. We can have plenty of other nights alone."

"No way. This isn't just any night we're talking about. I want to greet 1974 in the company of my girl."

Girl, Sheila thought. If only I were, with all the youth and lack of responsibilities of a girl.

"Sweetheart, go to the party," she repeated. "You have little enough time for such things. Whether we're physically together when the horns blow isn't what counts. It's what we feel for each other every day. I *want* you to go, Jerry. And I won't feel sorry for myself, because I know you'd rather be with me."

"You're sure that's what you want?"

"Absolutely sure."

"Well, okay. But it won't be any fun without you. Damn that kid! I could kick his behind!"

Sheila tried to sound gay. "Believe me, if he doesn't straighten out pretty quick I'll gladly give you that privilege."

"I'll talk to you tomorrow evening when you get home from work. Probably call you at midnight, too."

"I'd like that. Jerry, I'm really sorry," she said again. "I hope you understand."

"Of course I do, baby. There's nothing else you can do. It's just that I'm so damned disappointed!"

"Not half as much as I."

Monday was a terrible day. The store was practically deserted. Most business offices had closed for the long weekend and even the "regular customers" whom Sheila had come to know were not in the mood to buy books. The weather was as glum as Sheila's spirits. It's a gray, depressing world, she thought, watching the minutes crawl by as she waited for closing time. There was no joy even in the thought of going home. Tommy had not spoken to her since the argument. Maryanne had said this morning that she'd decided to go to her party, but she seemed to regard it more as a necessary evil than a pleasure outing. Sheila could hardly blame her. It wouldn't be much fun turning up with no escort. For a moment Sheila had almost taken her up on her breakfast-hour offer.

"I'd honestly just as soon stay home tonight," Maryanne had said. "Then you and Jerry can go to your party. At least *you'll* have fun."

"Nonsense. Jerry understands why I have to be here. Besides, I'm delighted you're re-establishing your contacts with old friends. That was the point of coming home, wasn't it? To get back into a normal life? This is the best possible chance for you to see a lot of people you know."

"They probably haven't changed. They'll be as boring as ever."

"Maybe they'll have grown up, too," Sheila teased.

Maryanne was on the phone when Sheila came in. "Oh, wait a minute," she said. "Mother's just walked in." She handed the phone to Sheila. "It's Jerry."

"How did it go today, honey?" His voice was sweet and concerned.

"I could have 'phoned it in.' I don't think there were two customers all day. Even the trains were empty. What about you?"

"Quiet in the female-complaint department, too. All my ladies are at the hairdresser. Too preoccupied with one end to worry about the other, I guess. And nobody's in labor, thank God! I never envy the obstetrician who has the dubious honor of slapping the fanny of the first baby of the year."

It was the first time she'd laughed all day. "Let's hope your luck holds through the evening."

He sounded strange. "I feel like an insensitive clod."

"Jerry, not one more word about that! You have fun. And call me if you feel like it."

"I will. Call you. *And* feel like it."

She felt more cheerful when she hung up. Jerry always did that for her. She changed her clothes, tapped on Tommy's door, and said, "I'm home!" and was rewarded with a grunt of acknowledgment.

"Tommy been in all day?" she asked Maryanne.

"Yep. Sulking in his tent." The girl watched as Sheila began to prepare dinner. "Mother, what good is all this going to do?"

"I'm not sure. Maybe it'll just make him realize that I care whom he sees and where he goes."

Maryanne shook her head. "You're wrong, you know. It's only going to make him more rebellious."

The idea was disturbing. "I'd welcome any suggestions, dear. I don't know how to handle him. I've tried giving him his head, asking no questions, and that seems to be leading him in the wrong direction. So what else is there but a show of discipline which he knows is love?"

"You're not facing up to the real problem," Maryanne said. "You know he's jealous of Jerry. He was always jealous of Dad. This kind of discipline isn't going to work any better than the loose rein you gave him this fall. Tommy has a real hang-up about you, Mother. He always has had."

Sheila stopped what she was doing. "I know some of that," she said slowly. "We had some talks before you came home. I never realized how much he disliked his father. And of course I know he resents Jerry. But what am I to do, Maryanne? Send him to a psychiatrist? Devote my whole life to him? I can't afford the first and it's unrealistic to consider the second. If you're right—and you may be—what's the answer? I couldn't afford to keep him in University, so I certainly can't afford to send him *away* to school. I'm not sure it would be wise, even if I could. It would only confirm his idea that I don't want to be around him. That he's in the way."

"Mother, what if he *could* go away for a few months, not at your instigation but at somebody else's?"

"What do you mean?"

"Look. I'll bet Grandma and Grandpa Callahan would love to have him. He could go to school in Florida for a while. He's crazy about them."

"It wouldn't work," Sheila said. "It's no different from sending him away to school. He'd still feel rejected."

"No! That's the whole point. *You* wouldn't suggest it; *they* would. You could fill them in on the problem and have them write and invite him. You could even pretend to resist it. Make him beg you to let him go. Mother, he needs to get away from you, much more than he needs to be near you. He's too attached to you. It's what everything's all about."

Sheila was unconvinced. "I don't know. I'm not sure."

"You'll be sure if you see your darling son turn into a flaming queen."

"Maryanne!"

"It could happen. A boy who never liked his father. A kid who thought that at last he had his mother all to himself, only to find she's taken up with a new 'rival.' Right now he's trying to punish you by worrying you so that you'll keep your eye on him. You're playing right into his hands."

"You don't know what you're talking about," Sheila said angrily. "Tommy turn homosexual? Impossible. That's the least of my worries. I'm much more concerned that he'll get into trouble, associating with bad company."

"You just can't see it, can you? If he gets in trouble that's just more punishment for your having loved a couple of men. Okay, I'm no trained psychologist, like Betty. Why don't you discuss it with her? I think you'll find the situation is classic. Every first-year college student learns about this pattern."

After dinner, Maryanne took off in the station wagon and Tommy went to his room.

"Aren't you going to see the New Year in with me?" Sheila asked. "How about some gin rummy?"

"No, thanks. I'm going up and play some tapes."

"Tommy, I know you're angry with me, but couldn't we declare a truce for tonight? What's the point in both of us sitting alone on New Year's Eve?"

"It was your idea. Not mine."

138

Staring into the fire, Sheila almost had to laugh. *This* boy in love with his mother? How crazy could Maryanne get? He doesn't love me, Sheila thought. He hates me. And I don't know what to do about it. She dismissed the idea of cooking up something with Jean and Bill Callahan. Even if it worked, it wouldn't be fair to them. They'd raised their own sons. Why should they be expected to take on a problem child at their time of life? No, the answer had to be somewhere else. When all was said and done, there probably was only one real solution: time. It was a phase he'd grow out of. Especially when he met a girl he liked. But what will happen to him in the meantime? And what, Sheila thought with healthy selfishness, will happen to me?

Chapter 16

Sheila awoke with a start, aware that the telephone was ringing. She glanced at the mantel clock. Eleven-thirty. The book she'd been trying to read lay open in her lap, the fireplace logs had become embers while she dozed. Eleven-thirty. Too early for Jerry to be calling to wish her a Happy New Year. Her mother, maybe. Or Sally, from New York. But the voice on the other end was briskly male.

"Mrs. Sean Callahan?"

"Yes."

"Sergeant Brockton here. Eleventh precinct. We have your son in custody. I think you'd better come down to the station."

It took Sheila a minute to find her voice. "My son? Patrick Callahan?"

"No, ma'am, he says his name is Thomas. You *do* have a son named Thomas Callahan, don't you? Fifteen years old?"

"Yes, but he's at home. He's been here all evening. There must be some mistake."

The policeman verified the address and description. "Sounds like your son, Mrs. Callahan. You sure he's there?"

"Of course I'm sure! He's in his room!"

"Why don't you go and look, ma'am?" The officer sounded sympathetic. "I'll hold on."

She raced up to the third floor and burst into Tommy's room. It was

140

empty. So was the bathroom. So was the hook on which Tommy's sheepskin-lined jacket always hung. He'd slipped out sometime during the evening, defying her, creeping out of the house quietly, like a thief. She was disbelieving, frightened. Sergeant Brockton was waiting. She picked up the phone.

"He's not here," she said. "What has he done, Sergeant? What are you holding him for?"

"He and some other boys tried to steal a few bottles from a liquor store about ten-thirty tonight. The other kids got away, but the owner managed to hang on to your son until we got there."

"Oh, no! Oh, God, no!"

Brockton was kind. "It isn't too bad, Mrs. Callahan. Not like they'd tried armed robbery. More like shoplifting. I'm pretty sure it will go easy with him, especially if he tells us the names of the other kids."

Not too bad! Sheila thought. It's a nightmare!

"I'll be there as soon as I can. Is he—is he all right? I mean, he wasn't hurt, was he?"

"No ma'am. He's pretty scared, but he's okay."

"Thank you, Sergeant," Sheila managed to say. "Please tell him I'm on my way, will you?"

"Yes, ma'am. I'll do that."

She felt frozen, but her mind was racing in all directions. How could she get to the police station? Maryanne had the car and it would be impossible to get a cab on New Year's Eve. Besides, she couldn't face this alone. Jerry. Of course. Jerry will come and get me. She realized she didn't know the name of his friends, but his answering service would know where he could be reached. Fingers shaking, she dialed and got the number. She could hear the sound of a party in the background when a woman answered.

"May I speak with Dr. Mancini, please? This is a friend of his."

"I'm sorry, but Jerry isn't here. He called to say he couldn't make it. He said he'd check us later for messages. Would you like to leave one?"

Sheila was too frantic at that moment to be surprised. "No. I don't suppose you know where I could find him now."

"I have no idea. Sorry."

Sheila tried to think sensibly. Pat was skiing, unreachable or at least too far away to be any help. Maryanne. Hastily she dialed information for the number of Ted Harris on Chalfant. It seemed an endless wait before the operator returned and gave it to her.

"That number is listed in your telephone directory," the robotlike voice reported. "Please make a note of it for the future."

There were the same party sounds when she reached the Harris house.

"This is Sheila Callahan," she said. "May I please speak to Maryanne?"

"Mrs. Callahan? This is Donna. Donna Werber. How are you?"

"Not too well, Donna. There's an emergency. Could you put Maryanne on, please?"

"She's not here, Mrs. Callahan. We expected her, but she never showed up."

It *is* a nightmare, Sheila thought. It's a terrible dream in which something has happened to Tommy and I can't find anyone to help me. It's like being trapped in a maze.

"If I hear from her, shall I have her call home?"

"Yes. No. That is, never mind, Donna. Thank you."

There was only one thing left to do. She rang up the country club and asked them to call Mr. Robert Ross to the phone. As she waited, it crossed her mind that she should have asked for Terry. After all, he was Tommy's uncle. It simply hadn't occurred to her. Or perhaps, subconsciously, she couldn't bear the thought of his pompous moralizing. Not now. Not when she felt so much at fault.

Bob was calm, reassuring when she told him what had happened. "I'll be there in ten minutes. Stay cool, Sheila. These cases are never . . ."

The sound of singing and horn-blowing drowned him out.

"What? I can't hear you, Bob! There's so much noise!"

"Never mind!" He was shouting into the phone. "It's midnight. That's what the racket's all about! See you shortly!"

Midnight. Tommy was in jail. She was alone. Jerry was God knows where. Maryanne was missing and Sean was dead. Happy New Year, Sheila, she said to herself. Happy, happy New Year.

They brought a pale, frightened Tommy from some room in the back of the police station. Sheila ran to him and hugged him. "It's all right," she said. "Don't be afraid. We'll have you out of here in a few minutes." She held him close to her, protectively, feeling his heart beating as rapidly as her own.

"Mom, I didn't mean . . . That is . . ."

"Hush," Sheila said. "We'll talk about it later." Out of the corner of her eye she saw Bob in discussion with the desk sergeant. At one point they were interrupted by the arrival of a policeman with a belligerent drunk in tow. Bob stepped aside until the man was booked and taken away, then went back to his earnest conversation with the police officer. Finally he beckoned her and Tommy to come to the desk.

"Sergeant Brockton, this is Tommy's mother, Mrs. Callahan. She'll take full responsibility for her son if you release him in her custody. I'll also give you my personal assurance that there'll be no more trouble." He looked at Tommy. "I think this young man has learned his lesson."

"What about it, Tommy?" Sergeant Brockton asked not unkindly. "Have you learned your lesson?"

"Yes, sir." Grudgingly.

"And you'll give us the names of the other boys?"

Tommy was silent.

"I'd advise you to do that, Tommy," Bob said. "It's not a question of ratting on your friends. We know *you* haven't been in trouble before, but they'll have to check out the others. Fortunately, you haven't committed a serious crime. Still, the police have a duty to see whether any of the other boys are previous offenders."

"What will happen to them?" Tommy asked.

"Probably nothing. But they'll be questioned and their records checked." Bob put his arm across Tommy's shoulders. "Come on, Tom. Let's have it. You and your mother have been through enough tonight."

Sheila remained quiet. She knew who the others were. The same names Maryanne had mentioned. She didn't remember them, but she could bluff it through. "You might as well tell the sergeant, Tommy," she said. "Otherwise, we'll just have to find out in a different way."

He knew what she meant. He, too, remembered the conversation earlier in the day. In a voice that was hardly more than a mumble, he recited the three names.

"Addresses?" Sergeant Brockton was busily writing.

Reluctantly, Tommy gave them.

"Okay," the officer said, "we'll pick them up for questioning. Don't worry, son. I'm sure it'll be just routine."

"What happens now?" Sheila asked.

"Well, ma'am, first thing is you can take him home. He'll see a probation officer within seventy-two hours. It'll be up to the officer whether he adjusts the case himself or sends it to court."

"To court! You don't mean Tommy could go to court!"

"He *could*, Mrs. Callahan, but I don't think there's much chance of that. You see, it's a first offense, the kid seems sorry and I know he comes from a good home. He probably even has a good school record, right?"

Sheila nodded.

"All that's in his favor. So's the nature of the crime, and it *was* a crime, even though Tommy might have thought of it as an adventure. Still, nothing was taken, and from talking to the liquor store owner I think he can be persuaded not to press charges." Brockton shook his head. "It all sounds too easy. Well, in your son's case, I think it was just a dumb prank, though he's old enough to know that stealing is illegal. It's the system I worry about. Any kid under sixteen knows that under our laws he's a juvenile. We can't fingerprint him or photograph him. And no matter what he does, he can't get more than eighteen months in a house of correction. The bad kids—the violent ones—rob and rape and even kill and know they'll only be sent up for 'rehabilitation' and out on the streets again in no time, to threaten society. Most of them don't even feel remorse. We're breeding a generation of child-criminals, Mrs. Callahan. You make sure your boy doesn't become one of them."

Sheila felt sick at her stomach. These were babies he was talking about. Not old enough to be entrusted with a driver's license, but old enough to commit the most hideous crimes and smart enough to know that they were free from the threat of severe punishment.

Driving home in Bob's car, the three of them were silent for a long while. Sheila looked at her son. *Was* he sorry? Frightened, yes. But remorseful? She admitted she didn't know. Any more than she knew what she'd say to him when it came time to talk. I can't handle it, Sheila thought wildly. I can't watch him every minute. I can't even reach him any more. Maybe Maryanne was right. Maybe I am the worst person for him. It was a wrenching thought that two people who loved each other so much were the instruments of each other's destruction. It was Bob who spoke first.

"You had a close call, buddy. That was a pretty dumb thing to do. You're lucky. The probation officer will probably adjust the case himself. But God help you if you get in trouble again." He kept his eyes on the road. "Any of those other boys been arrested before?"

"Yeah. One of them." Tommy sounded sullen. "That's one reason I didn't want to tell. But I had to. Mom would have, if I hadn't."

"Yes," Sheila said, "I would have. I'd have done anything to get you out of there." She was surprised by her ability to speak calmly. Inside, her stomach was churning to the point of nausea. "What kind of misguided loyalty would make you consider holding back information like that? You weren't in this alone. Those other boys are as guilty as you."

"As guilty maybe," Tommy said, "but not as dumb. *They* didn't get caught."

She was shocked. "Is that what matters? Not that you tried to steal but that you got caught?"

He didn't answer.

Bob gave her a little signal that meant "not now." She knew he was right. It would be better to wait and talk in the morning when they were less emotional, but she couldn't stop herself.

"Tommy, those other boys have to be questioned, too. Their families deserve to know they could be headed for serious trouble! It was the only right thing to do. Can't you see that?"

"No, I can't!" His voice was loud and angry. "Can't *you* see that I'm a fink? Just because I was too clumsy to get away? Do you think I can ever go back to school and face those guys now? Why couldn't you both have left it alone? They'd have let me out of there without my having to tell! Hell, it's penny-ante stuff! The cops are too busy with those rapists

144

and murderers Brockton was talking about to spend time worrying about kids who try to lift a couple of bottles of booze on New Year's Eve!"

"All right, that's enough for tonight!" Bob commanded. "Knock it off. *Both* of you. Neither one of you is in fit condition to talk now. Save it for the light of day!"

His take-charge attitude did the trick. Sheila and Tommy lapsed into silence, seething with rage and frustration. At the Callahans' door, Tommy leaped out of the car, and using his own key, disappeared into the house. Sheila sat for a moment.

"I'm sorry about pulling you away from the club tonight," she said, "but I honestly didn't know what else to do."

"Don't be ridiculous. You did the right thing. That's the least of your problems, Sheila. That kid upstairs is what you have to worry about."

"I know. Bob, what am I going to do?"

"Right now you're going in and go to bed. Take a sleeping pill. Face it tomorrow, when you'll have a better perspective. Try to talk calmly and understandingly to Tommy. If you want me to come over, I will."

"Thank you. I don't know what I'd have done without your help tonight. Or, for that matter, without your help all these months."

"That's what friends and lawyers are for. Now promise me you'll get some rest."

"Yes. Good night, Bob."

"Good night . . . darling."

She dragged herself wearily upstairs to her room, passing Maryanne's. It was half-past one. Perhaps Maryanne was home and they could talk for a few minutes. If she was in, the girl would be wondering where Tommy and her mother were. She tapped lightly and then opened the door. The room was empty. For a moment Sheila felt anxious, remembering that Maryanne had not gone to the Harris party. Where could she be? What if she'd had an accident? No, I can't start thinking about that. For two years I never knew where she was. Besides, if, God forbid, anything had happened, the police would let her know. Just as they'd let her know about Tommy.

I must go to bed, Sheila thought. It's still early for New Year's Eve. No reason to expect Maryanne home yet. She pulled off her clothes and crawled between the covers. It felt so safe and warm there, but she wasn't sleepy, and she wasn't going to follow Bob's advice and take a pill. I mustn't be drugged, she thought. What if Tommy needs me? What if he's also lying awake, miserable about everything?

She heard the hall clock strike two and three and four. A few minutes later she heard footsteps on the stairs and the sound of Maryanne's door opening and closing. Where has she been? Sheila wondered. Did she drive home alone at this ungodly hour? Stop it! You're beginning to sound like

Rose! Your daughter is a grown woman. She's free to come and go as she pleases.

Suddenly, exhaustion overcame her. She drifted into restless sleep and the next thing she knew light was pouring in her windows and the bedside clock confirmed that it was ten o'clock on the morning of a brand-new year.

At noon, Maryanne wandered downstairs, yawning. She found a pale, drawn Sheila staring at the makings of breakfast as though she didn't know what to do with them.

"Hey, what's with you? For somebody who spent a quiet New Year's Eve at home, you look terrible!"

"It wasn't what you'd call a quiet New Year's Eve, by any stretch of the imagination." She told Maryanne what had happened, tears coming into her eyes as she described the cold, antiseptic atmosphere of the police station and Tommy looking like a terrified child.

"Where is he now?"

"Still asleep," Sheila said. "I looked in his room about half an hour ago and he was dead to the world."

"Jesus," Maryanne said. "What a mess! Thank God Bob Ross was with you."

The mention of Bob rekindled Sheila's questions about her daughter's change of plan.

"I tried to call you at Donna's when it happened, but she said you hadn't shown up."

Maryanne looked uncomfortable. "I decided at the last minute not to go. I told you I knew it would be a drag, all those same, dreary people I used to know." She waited for Sheila's obvious question, but it didn't come. "I went to a different party instead," Maryanne volunteered. "Some people I met last year were giving a bash. It lasted pretty late. Must have been after three when I got in."

"After four," Sheila corrected. "I was only worried about your driving home alone at that hour. It isn't safe, these days."

"Oh, I wasn't alone," Maryanne said. "That is, not exactly. I had to get your car back so a friend followed me in his."

"Rick?"

Maryanne looked away. "Forgive me, Mother, but I don't think I have to account to you any more. I got home safely, that's all that matters, isn't it?"

"Yes," Sheila said. "I suppose so."

"I *am* sorry you couldn't reach me." Maryanne sounded sincere. "Naturally, I had no idea you'd need to."

Sheila looked grim. "Apparently nobody was where he was supposed to be last night. I couldn't find Jerry, either. Strange. Even his answering service had the wrong number. That's not like him. He's fanatic about always being reachable."

Her daughter didn't answer. Instead she said, "What are you going to do about Tommy?"

"I wish to God I knew. He'll have to see a probation officer sometime in the next three days. It will be up to him to decide whether Tommy has to go to court. Bob thinks its unlikely they'll do anything to him. I gathered the police were of the same opinion. Anyway, he's still on vacation the rest of this week, and I won't go into the store. Miss Rawlings will understand when I tell her I'm having family problems."

Maryanne looked at her sympathetically. "That's fine for the rest of this week, but what then? When Tommy does go back to school, what happens? Does he fall right in with the same old gang and get in even worse trouble?"

Sheila half-smiled, humorlessly. "He certainly won't be part of the same gang. He doesn't even want to go back to the same school. He had to give names to the police and we know one of his group is a second offender. But whether Tommy will pick up with other kids just like these or worse, I really can't tell you. I'm afraid to think."

"Have you talked to Jerry today?"

"No. He didn't call me at midnight. And I haven't been able to gather my thoughts this morning. I imagine he'll be in touch soon."

"Mother, remember what we talked about? About sending Tommy to Florida for a while? Maybe that's the answer, at least for now. Get him away from this school and those kids and all the unpleasant reminders of these past months."

Sheila knew what she really meant. "Get him away from *me* is what you're saying, isn't it?"

There was no reply.

"Maryanne, I can't dispute the sense of some of the things you've said. I did a lot of thinking last night and I'm inclined to agree that separation from me might be a good thing for Tommy. But I can't do that to Bill and Jean. They're not young. They haven't been around young boys in forty years, and they've *never* been around one as confused and rebellious as Tommy. No, it would be unfair to them. I can't ask them to take such a responsibility."

"It could be the best thing in the world for them," Maryanne said. "They're both hale and hearty, but they have no purpose in life any more. It's good for people to feel indispensable, especially older people. They might welcome the responsibility."

There was a great deal of insight in what Maryanne was saying. Sheila thought about Rose, wanting so much to feel someone needed her and so unhappy because no one did. But that didn't mean that Jean and Bill Callahan felt the same. They had each other and that made all the difference. Or did it? Sheila hesitated.

"I don't know," she said. "They've just moved, but I know they wouldn't refuse if I asked them. How would Tommy feel about it? Wouldn't he feel I was pushing him out of the way, especially now when he's gotten into trouble?"

"Maybe. But maybe it would also help him grow up."

Sheila put her head in her hands. "God, I wish I knew what was right." A thought struck her. "I don't even know whether he'd be permitted to leave here, assuming the probation officer doesn't take him to court. He's free in my custody until that decision is made. They might not let him go live in another household, not to mention another state."

"I don't know all the technicalities," Maryanne said, "but I know enough about juvenile delinquency to know that in minor cases the probation officer can handle things just to cut the judges' work load. Good Lord, Mother, Tommy isn't a criminal! But say the worst happened. Even in court he wouldn't be treated as a criminal. Kids under sixteen aren't even called 'defendants,' they're called 'respondents.' They're not 'indicted,' they 'respond to a petition' drawn up by the complainant, and you say in this case the liquor store owner probably won't press charges. But even if he did, there's no such word as 'guilty' where juveniles are concerned. The judge rules whether the complaint is true. Then he makes a 'finding.' He doesn't reach a 'verdict'; he decides where the kid should be 'placed,' not 'sentenced.' It's a great break for innocents like Tommy who don't even think they're doing wrong. But it's a bad system for society, because what applies to stealing a bottle of liquor also goes for those little public enemies who rape women and shoot people and terrorize the community."

Sheila stared at her, openmouthed. "You sound like a lawyer! How on earth do you know so much about all this? I've never heard some of the things you're telling me!"

"There's been an awful lot about it in the papers lately," Maryanne said. "You just haven't been reading. She shrugged. "No, that's not fair. I haven't been reading, either. I know all this because Rick explained it to me. He was picked up once for stealing a car when he was a kid. And down in Ohio City, it goes on all the time. Half the people I know have kid brothers, or sisters, who've been in trouble with the police. We've spent a lot of time talking about the system. Ask Bob Ross. He'll tell you that what I've said is the absolute truth. Tommy won't go to court. I'm sure of that."

"Maryanne, I'm so glad you're out of all that. You are, aren't you? For keeps?"

"Mother, nothing is for keeps. I think I should tell you . . ."

The phone rang.

"Let it ring," Sheila said. "Go on. *What* should you tell me?"

"Nothing. Just more of my half-baked philosophy. Not important. Get the phone. It's probably Jerry. I'll throw on some clothes while you're talking and then we'll have breakfast. Hurry up, will you? That damned thing's never going to stop."

It wasn't Jerry. It was Sally Cantrell calling to say she'd be home next day.

"Happy New Year," Sally said. "Everything okay with you? How were the festivities in Cleveland?"

Sheila was relieved to hear her dearest friend. No time to go into all that happened, not on a long-distance call, but she realized how much she needed a woman to confide in, and how happy she was that Sally would be back the next day.

"Everything's fine here," she lied. "How's New York?"

"It's just Cleveland with a Bergdorf Goodman. Bor-ing! I'll be glad to get home."

"I'll be glad to see you. I'm taking the rest of the week off, Sally. Call me when you get in."

"What's the matter? You sick?"

"No. Just need a little rest. Tell you all about it later."

There was suspicion in Sally's voice. "How's Jerry?"

"Working hard. Otherwise fine."

"And the kids?"

"Everything's in good shape. Would you believe Maryanne's moved back home? Pat and Betty went skiing over New Year's."

"And Tommy?"

Sheila hoped she sounded natural. "Still behaving like a fifteen-year-old. Listen, I'll bring you up to date tomorrow. This call will cost a fortune! Stop behaving like a rich lady!"

Sally laughed. "Are you kidding? I *am* a rich lady. See you tomorrow. We'll dish."

That we will, Sheila thought as she hung up. You have no idea how much we have to dish about.

The irony was that Sheila herself didn't know how much.

Chapter 17

In midafternoon, Jerry called. "Hello, luv," he said. "Happy New Year!"

"Same to you," Sheila answered.

"Oh-oh. The lady sounds very frosty. I know. I'm about fifteen hours late with that greeting, right? I'm sorry, Sheil. I really meant to call you at midnight, but things got a little hectic."

"How was the party?" She waited for him to say he hadn't gone.

"Not bad. Sorry you couldn't make it."

She felt surprise and then anger. He was lying to her. Of all offenses, lying was the one Sheila found almost impossible to forgive. It destroyed her faith in the liar and, perhaps even more important, it insulted her intelligence. People who lied to her assumed she was so stupid she didn't know the difference. Sean's lies had killed her respect for him, had made her marriage a superficial thing rather than the deep, honest alliance she had hoped for. And now Jerry was lying. She felt a kind of terrible, fatalistic disappointment.

"Sheila? Hello? Are you there?"

"Yes, I'm here, Jerry."

"You sound funny."

"I had a few problems last night and I have a strange feeling that I'm about to have a few more. Jerry, you didn't go to that party. I tried to

150

call you there. They said you canceled early in the day. Why did you feel you had to lie about it?"

He wanted to ask in turn why she'd tricked him into lying, but he didn't. It was not the kind of thing you could go into on the telephone. He had to face her.

"Look, how about dinner tonight? We'll talk about everything then. What kind of problems did you have? Anything dire?"

"Yes. Quite. That's why I tried to find you. Tommy was picked up for attempted robbery."

"My God! You're not serious! Where is he now?"

"Home. And so am I until we get things straight with the probation officer. So I can't go out to dinner tonight, Jerry." She hesitated. She longed to see him. There was some reason why he hadn't told the truth about last night. There had to be some simple explanation. She wanted to believe there was. "Why don't you come over here this evening? I'll feed Tommy early and you and I can have a quiet dinner after that."

There was just a fraction of hesitation. "What about Maryanne? Will she be home?"

"I don't know. I haven't asked her. Why? Does it matter? If she doesn't have a date, she can eat with us. I know she'll be discreet enough to leave us alone later to talk."

"Are you sure you can't go out? If Maryanne's there, there's no reason why you both have to baby-sit."

"I told you, Jerry. I don't *know* her plans. Anyway, I honestly don't feel like having dinner out tonight." She tried to relax. "What's the matter with you?" she teased. "I've never known you to turn down a home-cooked meal. What do you think I'm going to do—poison you for not calling me at midnight?"

He sounded relieved and yet the trace of reluctance was unmistakable. "You're on. What time shall I be there? About seven?"

"Yes. Fine."

"Anything you need?"

"Not a thing. The house is well-stocked. I even have an unused bottle of champagne." Damn, Sheila thought. That sounds like more recrimination. "See you then."

Maryanne was reading in the living room. Tommy, having finally appeared for breakfast, had returned to his own quarters. Sheila had tried to talk to him while he ate, but he answered her questions in almost inaudible monosyllables. She'd finally lost her patience.

"Young man, we'd better talk about last night and a lot of other things! I want to know what's changed you. We have to be open with each other. The probation officer will be here this week. Your future and mine can be affected by that interview. Dammit, Tommy, if I've somehow failed you, tell me!"

He'd finally relented, but only slightly. "Do we have to talk today, Mom? Can't it wait? I feel so lousy about everything."

It was not what she wanted, but he was so pathetic she couldn't press him. He'd had a traumatic experience. He needed a little time. "Okay, we won't talk about it today. I want you to stay in the house until this thing is settled. I'm taking the rest of the week off, too. We'll have plenty of time to talk."

"You're not going to work tomorrow?"

"No." She tried to smile. "I'm feeling a little lousy about everything myself."

"I'm sorry, Mom."

"I know you are. But we'll get things straightened out."

"Will they send me away, do you think? Like to reform school?"

She wanted to hold him and comfort him. Poor baby. That's what he was, for all his misbehavior, just a baby. "No, Tommy, I don't think they'll send you away. In fact, I'm sure they won't. But you'll have to shape up, buddy. Nothing like this must ever happen again."

He'd nodded and gone quietly to his room. She and Maryanne had sat in silence until Jerry's call. Now Sheila returned to the living room.

"What are your plans for the evening, Maryanne?"

"I'm not sure. Why?"

"Just wondered. Jerry's coming over for dinner. You're welcome to join us, of course."

A peculiar look came over Maryanne's face. "I think I'll be going out. I'm sure Jerry would like to be alone with you."

"We can be alone after dinner, honey. There's no need for you to make yourself scarce just because Jerry's coming." She stopped, appalled by a horrifying, ridiculous suspicion. She began to add up a series of events. Maryanne had been on the phone with Jerry when Sheila came home yesterday afternoon. She hadn't been at the party she'd said she was going to. And neither had Jerry. She was acting strangely now, when she heard Jerry was coming. Just as he had seemed reluctant to come over when Maryanne might be there. Sheila hadn't been able to find either of them last night. They were together, she thought. My daughter and my lover. Oh, God, no! I can't stand it! I don't want to know about it. I don't want it to be true. It can't be true. I'm putting a few stupid coincidences together and creating a monstrous accusation!

She looked at Maryanne who seemed to be avoiding her eyes. I can't ask, Sheila thought. I won't. They'll have to tell me themselves.

Maryanne stood up. "May I borrow the car again, since you're not going to use it?"

"Of course." And who will follow you home tonight? Sheila wanted to ask. Who'll see that you get safely to your mother's house?

152

"I won't be late," Maryanne said. "Not like last night, so don't worry."
"I won't," Sheila said bitterly. "I know you can take care of yourself."

The awful certainty of betrayal was a bitter taste in Sheila's mouth as she fed Tommy, prepared a steak and salad for herself and Jerry, and then bathed and dressed carefully in her most becoming housecoat. She found wry amusement in the fact that she was taking extra pains with her appearance. Almost as though she was saying "I may not be twenty-four years old, Doctor, but I'm not over the hill. Not just yet!" It wasn't that she was hoping to seduce him or even that she hoped to keep him. By now she was certain that her flash of intuition about Jerry and Maryanne was right and nothing would be uglier or more demeaning than competing with her own daughter. She prayed desperately she'd find out all this was her imagination, and all the while grew more convinced that it was not. If it's true, what am I going to do? Sheila thought wildly. I'll lose both of them. There is no way, no way ever, that I can see them again. She wanted to hate and could not summon up hatred, not for the man she loved nor the woman she'd borne. The momentary bravado left her. All she felt was a terrible sense of loss and futility and a feeling of having been a blind fool. A blind old fool.

She was composed by the time Jerry arrived. He came in, smiling, and gave her a big kiss. A Judas kiss, Sheila thought. She did not return it with her usual fervor but Jerry didn't comment.

"Tell me about Tommy," he said as soon as he'd made drinks for them.

She told him the whole story, leaving out only the fact that Maryanne hadn't been reachable either. She swore to herself that whatever happened she'd keep her dignity, that she'd not become an accusatory shrew.

Jerry whistled. "That's a tough scene, honey. I'm sorry you had to go through it. It's a good thing you got hold of Bob Ross."

Sheila sipped her drink, not answering.

Jerry got up from his chair and began to pace the living room. "All right," he said, "we might as well get to it. Maybe it's just as well you found out I wasn't at that party last night. It forces me to tell you something I've known since Christmas and haven't had the guts to say. Sheila, I love you. These past weeks have been terrific. *You're* terrific. I tried to tell myself you were the right woman for me. I *wanted* you to be. But it doesn't work because there's someone else."

Here it comes, Sheila thought. Maryanne. She felt icy-cold and when she spoke her voice trembled.

"I knew that's what it was, but I couldn't believe that you and Maryanne . . ."

He interrupted her. "Me and Maryanne? Sheila, what are you talking about?" He came over and knelt in front of her chair. "I have no interest in Maryanne! She's an attractive young woman, but that's all. My God, you can't think I'd make a pass at your daughter or that she'd encourage me! What kind of people do you think we are?" He took her hand. "Sheila, darling, it's Barbara. My wife. I'm going back to her. We both realize we made a mistake. That's where I was last night, talking it out."

Shock made her forget her determination to be dignified. "Talking it out! In bed, I suppose!"

"Yes," Jerry said quietly, "part of the time. But it isn't just physical attraction with us. We lived together for a lot of years, Sheila. We have a child. The separation has made both of us see how selfish and stupid we were. We think we can make a go of it this time. She wants me back."

"And you want to go."

"Yes. I don't know whether I'd have made the overture. Barbara did, at Christmas. But in this past week I've found out that I need to go home."

He was still on his knees. Sheila rose and pushed past him. "Then go!" she said. "Get the hell out of here! Leave me alone!"

He stood up. "Sheila, please. Don't let it end this way. I never meant to hurt you. We never had a commitment. You know that."

She turned a furious face toward him. "I know a lot of things! That you're a liar and a damned good actor, among others! Good luck, Jerry. And good night!"

"I'm sorry. You're a very special woman."

"What would you know about a woman?" Sheila lashed out. "All you want is a young, selfish, spoiled, rich girl! Well, you've got her back, so go to her!"

He picked up his coat in the hallway and then came back to the living room door.

"I thought you'd understand," he said.

"Did you? Well, isn't that nice! Like your mother would have understood, I suppose. Like everyone has 'understood' and forgiven you all your life."

He shook his head. "Good-by, Sheila. Take care of yourself."

She didn't answer, but when she heard the front door close she threw herself onto the sofa and cried hysterically, sobbing with disappointment and loneliness and self-pity. It seemed hours before she could control herself. And then she turned her anger inward. Where were all those high-flown attitudes she'd had? Where was "sensible Sheila" who'd told herself and Sally that this romance had no future, that it would end and she'd not be hurt? Had she ever really believed it? No, you damned idiot, she told herself. You never did. You wouldn't admit, even to yourself, that it was impossible. Maybe, at the very beginning, you thought you could handle it. But for a long time you've deluded yourself. You even allowed thoughts of marriage to Jerry to come into your head. You're a middle-aged romantic who's conned herself into believing she's still young and desirable. And it's your own fault, Sheila Callahan. You can't blame anybody except yourself.

Mechanically, she put the uncooked dinner food in the refrigerator, straightened up the living room, and went to bed. She didn't want to see Maryanne that night. She was ashamed of what she'd been sure her daughter had done. How could I have been so hideously suspicious of her? Sheila wondered. What a terrible person I must be, jumping to such disgusting conclusions. Still, she couldn't help wondering where Maryanne had been on New Year's Eve. If not with Jerry, then with whom?

I must get some rest, Sheila thought. Nothing is making any sense. Not Tommy. Not Jerry. Not Maryanne. And certainly not me. She went into the bathroom and took a sleeping pill. I can't be too desperate, she thought inanely. At least, I'm only taking *one.*

Kitty Rawlings was more than understanding when Sheila called her next morning to ask for the rest of the week off. The others in the book department were always having family problems with their children or grandchildren. That's the way it was with the grown women she preferred. Better that, the buyer often thought, than a staff of youngsters who were too hung-over to come to work, or too distraught over their love lives to be efficient, or who got pregnant or married, in either order.

"Anything serious, Sheila?" she asked. "Anything I can do to help?"

"Thank you. That's kind of you, but it'll be all right. My young son got in a bit of trouble. Nothing that can't be straightened out, but it may take a few days. I'm sorry to ask for the time. I appreciate your being so understanding, and I'll be there Monday. Maybe before, depending on how things go."

"Take your time. It'll be a slow week. And let me know if there's anything you need."

What I need, you can't give me, Sheila thought. I need a sense of being desirable, of being loved, of feeling that my whole life hasn't been spent trying to please other people and not making a notable success of it. Thank you, Miss Rawlings. I'd appreciate your telling me how to be thick-skinned and self-indulgent, sure of myself and uncaring that I don't understand the motivations of my children or of the man I thought loved me. Offer me those things, Kitty, and I'll bless you forever.

The thought of Jerry, the realization that she'd never see him again had an unreal quality. It was almost impossible to grasp the idea that he was going back to his wife. She'd heard enough from him about Barbara to make it seem unbelievable that he wanted to return to her. Not that Jerry had been nasty or vicious about the beautiful young "Jewish princess" he'd married. He'd always spoken of her as a good person, but unbearably spoiled and demanding, unable to adjust to the inevitable inconveniences of being a doctor's wife. He'd never mentioned love. Not even now. It was not, Sheila thought, even a longing for his daughter that had sent him home. He loved Joyce, but he'd seemed perfectly content with his "visiting privileges," had promised that one day soon the three of them would have a Sunday outing.

"I want you and Joy to know each other," he'd said. It had been a tacit indication that his attachment to Sheila was growing. Only one of many little hints that he planned to become a permanent part of her life and that he meant her to share the most important parts of his. And then, without warning, this sudden reversal. Where did I fail? Sheila wondered. Wasn't I exciting enough in bed? Did I become too possessive? Was I too little of a challenge? Should I have been less understanding, more demanding of him, as Barbara was? Perhaps that's what he needs, an independent woman more interested in her happiness than in his. Apparently. At least that's what he'd gone back to.

Her desolation was all the worse for feeling that somehow she'd handled everything wrong. This morning she wished she'd had more control last night. She should have talked with him, tried to find out what really happened, what made him so suddenly change his mind about his marriage. Instead, she'd reacted like a wounded animal, ordering him out of the house instead of talking calmly about his abrupt change of heart. Perhaps she could have made him see things differently. Perhaps she'd have him still.

She reached for the phone to call him and then stopped. It was too late. She'd sound like a groveling, sniveling, pleading woman. It was not a role she fancied. Nor, she sensed, was it one to which Jerry would respond. It was only a little after ten o'clock, too early for Sally to have gotten home from New York. Sheila longed to see her. She needed to talk about Jerry with someone she could trust and, even more important, someone who could identify with the mental state of a middle-aged woman who'd made an idiot of herself. Hopefully she'd see her later in the day.

She heard the back door open and close. For a moment she was frightened until she realized it was Annie Winchester coming to "shovel them out," as Sheila thought of it. She went into the kitchen and startled the black cleaning woman who was changing into a housedress.

"Mrs. Callahan! What you doing home?"

"I have this week off. How are you, Annie? Did you have a good holiday?"

"So-so. You enjoy yourself?"

Sheila smiled. "It was all right. I never like holidays. You know that. And this year wasn't the best."

The woman's face softened. "I know. It must be a bad time for you without Mr. Callahan." Annie sighed. "Sometimes it's mighty hard to understand the Lord. Well, I'll just get at my work."

"Annie, you'll find a few changes this week." Sheila hoped she sounded unconcerned. "Tommy's home from school. He's up in his room."

"He sick?"

"No. School's still closed." She debated whether to tell the truth and decided to. Annie had been with them since Tommy was a baby. She was devoted to all the Callahan children. Sheila explained the events of New Year's Eve. "I expect the probation officer this week. That's why we're both home."

Annie looked stricken. "I just can't believe it, Mrs. Callahan! Not our Tommy! He's always been such a good boy!"

"I know. But these are strange times, Annie. He's been moved to a different school, met the wrong boys. And," Sheila hesitated, "I suppose some of it is a sense of loss of his father and even of me, since I'm not around during the day. For that matter," she added gently, "neither are you, worse luck. He looked on you as a second mother, Annie. He's at a vulnerable age. I'm worried sick about it. I can't deny that. But I hope he's learned his lesson."

"Tommy stealing!" Annie shook her head. "I can't get over it. Those must be some terrible boys he's taken up with. They oughta be horse-whipped, those bad kids!"

"I can't blame it all on them. They didn't force Tommy to do what he did. Anyway, we'll get it settled this week. Mr. Ross thinks there's no need to worry. There's some other news, too. Better news. Maryanne has moved back home. I'm so happy about that. And Dr. Patrick and his wife are well. So *everything* isn't gloom and doom." (No need to mention the other doctor. Annie didn't know he existed.) "Well, I'll let you get on with your work. I just didn't want you to be surprised when you found Tommy in his room and Maryanne still asleep in her bed."

Sheila went back into the living room and tried to concentrate on the morning paper. Thank God there was nothing in it about the boys' escapade. It was too trifling an item to merit space, not when the pages were full of Watergate and international rumblings, to say nothing of local homicides, suicides, and "juicy" news stories far more titillating than four boys trying to steal whiskey from Lew Wiseman's liquor store.

Soon after eleven, a pleasant-sounding woman called and identified herself as Frances Sandman, the juvenile probation officer. "I've been assigned to your son's case and I'd like to see both of you today, Mrs. Callahan."

"Of course. Where would you like us to appear?"

"Can you both be at home about one o'clock? I could drive over to see you."

Sheila was surprised. "I'd be glad to bring Tommy. . . ."

"No need. I'll be in that area anyway. Lots of work there, these days. One o'clock, then?"

"Yes. Certainly. Thank you, Mrs. Sandman."

There was a little laugh. *"Miss* Sandman, Mrs. Callahan. And I won't even compromise on Ms."

Dialing Bob Ross, Sheila found herself smiling. At least the woman had a sense of humor. Or so it seemed. Maybe things wouldn't go too hard for Tommy.

Bob reassured her. "Miss Sandman wants to look over the home environment, no doubt. Nothing to it, once she meets you and Tommy and sees the way you live. You want me to be there?"

"No, thanks. I think it will look less 'official' if my lawyer isn't present."

"I agree. Tommy doesn't need a lawyer unless he's charged with an offense that could deprive him of his freedom. And this little dust-up is a far cry from that. Let me know what happens, will you?"

Sheila went to tell Tommy who looked frightened by the prospect.

"There's nothing to worry about," Sheila said. "Miss Sandman sounds very nice, and if you're contrite—as I know you are—I'm certain this will be the end of it."

"What about the other guys?"

Sheila stared at him. "I haven't the faintest idea. And frankly, Tommy, to quote Rhett Butler, I don't give a damn!"

"I was the one who ratted on them." It was a scared, small-boy voice.

"You did what you had to do."

"Mom, I don't want to go back to school."

"We'll talk about that later. And *not* in front of Miss Sandman. Now you get yourself neatly dressed and out of this room. I want Annie to clean it up. Miss Sandman may want to see it and the rest of the house."

Her own words reminded her of Maryanne who'd also have to be rousted out of bed and alerted to be on her good behavior. It was important that they present a picture of a nice, "normal" family. Maryanne should be up by now anyway. Sheila hadn't heard her come in last night. The sleeping pill had done the trick. She opened the door to her daughter's room. It was empty and the bed hadn't been slept in.

The visit with Frances Sandman went well. She was a young, attractive woman, businesslike but kind. She asked Tommy questions about the New Year's Eve incident and Sheila was relieved to hear her son sound polite and truly remorseful. The probation officer did not ask to see the house. Apparently the well-kept, expensively furnished living room satisfied her, as did the calm, cordial outward manner of Sheila who was quivering inside.

"Tommy, I'm empowered to adjust this case and recommend we not go to court," Frances Sandman said. "And since this is a first offense and you have an exceptionally good school record, a lovely home, and you seem honestly sorry for what you did, I'm prepared to do just that."

Sheila could not suppress the sigh of relief and Tommy brightened visibly.

"But," the officer went on, "don't overlook how fortunate you are. Mr. Wiseman chose not to press charges which is lucky for you. And remember that if you commit another offense, it will be a different story. I don't think you'd like a correctional institution. I don't like them myself. We like to think that juveniles who go to such places can be rehabilitated with psychiatric help, but I'm afraid that all too often they just learn how to be hardened criminals. You're an intelligent boy, Tommy, blessed with a good background and an enviable environment. Don't become one of our growing numbers of violent children. I see too many ten- and eleven-year-old thieves, junkies, and murderers. By the time they're your age they know all about prison life—even if we don't care to call it that when we commit someone under sixteen." She stood up. "I have faith in you and confidence in your mother. Don't let me down or I'll land on you like the biggest ton of bricks you've ever seen! Don't let the fact that you got off so easy fool you, young man. As I said, you were stupid and lucky this time, but it won't ever be a piece of cake again. I promise you that."

Sheila looked at her son. "It won't happen again, Miss Sandman. Tommy?"

"No, ma'am. Never again."

Frances Sandman smiled. "I'm sure it won't. Good luck and good-by. I hope forever."

Sheila walked her to the door. "Thank you," she said fervently.

"Mrs. Callahan, I bend over backward to go easy on kids who make one crazy mistake. But you watch your son. He's basically a good boy, but you have no idea what our system is like today. We're surrounded by child-monsters. And they're not all from underprivileged families. Not by a damn sight. You can't keep Tommy away from his peers and you can't play watchdog, but I urge you to be alert, because what I told him in there was true. Second offenders don't get this gentle slap on the wrist, as a rule. Not even rich ones with good lawyers. You're a nice lady and he's a nice kid. I know you lost your husband recently and things have been difficult, I'm sure. But give Tommy as much sense of security and normalcy as you can. I know you give him love."

For a moment, Sheila wanted to ask this sensible, sympathetic woman what to do. Should she send Tommy to his grandparents? Try somehow to afford University School for him again? But those weren't Miss Sandman's problems. They were hers. Along with all the others she had.

Chapter 18

Patrick felt wonderful. The few days off had restored him and Betty. Neither of them had realized, until they got to the ski lodge, how much they needed a break in their tough schedules. He thought affectionately of his young wife, and of how lucky he was to have a marriage and a career that suited him. It was a damned shame that Maryanne couldn't seem to get her life together. He hoped being at home again would help. Maybe being needed was the answer for his sister, and perhaps she realized that Sheila needed her even more than she needed Sheila.

Walking down the hospital corridor, he frowned, thinking of his mother. It bothered him that he couldn't help her financially and he felt angry that Sean Callahan had been so extravagantly unconcerned with his family's future. Damned selfish fool. What had he thought—that he was immortal? Sheila was to be admired for the way she'd taken hold. And it was good that Jerry Mancini was making her happy. Nice guy, Jerry, though it seemed unlikely that his "romance" with Sheila would be a permanent thing. It wasn't just the age difference. Around the hospital, Dr. Mancini was known as something of a swinger. Since his separation, the word was that he'd been busy in the hay. Pat hoped Sheila wasn't just another episode to him. He'd discussed it with Betty over the holiday.

"I'd hate to see Mother hurt," Pat had said. "You don't think she's taking Jerry too seriously, do you?"

"I don't know. She's been worried about 'what people will think,' but when we had that talk just before Christmas, I had the feeling she could handle it if 'Dr. Darling' drifted on to other adventures, as long as he brought her some happiness and confidence *now*. It depends upon how emotionally involved she is, Pat. And how stable she is under all that outward ability to cope. We don't know that. Maybe she doesn't, either. Anyway, honey, it's not for us or *any* of the family to move in on Sheila's life. If the thing with Jerry works, fine. If it doesn't, we'll be there to help if she needs us."

"What do you think of Maryanne coming home?"

Betty shook her head. "Not a helluva lot. It's too abrupt a changeabout. She's still a girl in search of something, that sister of yours. I wish I could believe she'd find her answers by Going Home to Mother, but I'm afraid it's a selfish, spur-of-the-moment impulse, like everything else Maryanne does." Betty sighed. "You know, my worry is that she could be more of a heartbreak for Sheila than Jerry could be."

The recent conversation was in Patrick's mind as he went about his duties. He hadn't called Sheila since he and Betty got home late last night. He'd call this evening, find out how things were with her and Maryanne and Tommy. And, perhaps, with Jerry.

As though the thought of the man conjured up his presence, Dr. Mancini came around a corner of the hospital and almost bumped into Pat.

Jerry looked startled, almost embarrassed by the sight of Patrick, and then he smiled.

"Hi," he said. "How was the skiing?"

"Terrific. Nothing like being around people with nothing worse than broken legs and collarbones to give a doctor a good rest. How was *your* New Year?"

Jerry seemed suddenly uneasy. "It was all right."

"How's Mom?"

"You haven't talked to her?"

"Not yet. We got in too late to call and I don't like to bother her at work." Pat was suddenly suspicious. "Why? Is something wrong?"

"I'm afraid so. Tommy got into a little trouble with the police New Year's Eve." Jerry hesitated. "And then I—well I guess I kind of upset her, too. I'm back with Barbara, Pat. We decided to patch it up. Sheila took it pretty hard. Jesus, I feel terrible about it, even though we never had any kind of 'permanent agreement.' Your mother's a terrific woman. We had some great times. But you know how those things are. I don't mean to sound egotistical, for Christ's sake, but I didn't realize how hung-up on me she was. Right now, in her book I'm the world's champion ring-tailed sonofabitch."

In mine, too, you bastard, Pat thought. But I'll never let you know you were that important to any of us. You *aren't* that important, except in terms of depriving Mother of the little pleasure she's had. The Tommy thing sounded much more serious, even though Jerry had dismissed it in one sentence. Tommy in trouble with the police? That nice, model kid? What in hell could have happened? Pat would have been much less surprised if it had been his sister picked up on a pot charge or something worse. Jerry was waiting for him to say something, to reassure him, man-to-man, that he "understood these things." Instead, Pat turned away abruptly.

"Got some things to do, Jerry. See you."

He glanced at his watch. A little past two. Sheila should be back from lunch. He dialed Higbee's from a phone booth and was told that Mrs. Callahan would not be in for the rest of the week. Really alarmed now, he called the house and his mother answered.

"Mom? I called you at the store. You okay?"

She tried, but couldn't conceal her distress. The strain was evident in her voice, though the words were normal. "Patrick, dear! Yes, of course I'm all right. How are you and Betty? Did you have a good time?"

"Perfect. But I hear *you* didn't."

There was a pause. "I suppose you've seen Jerry."

"Just a minute ago. He told me where you and he stood. I'm sorry. I really am, though I must admit I'm even more concerned about Tommy. What in God's name happened?"

She told him quickly about his brother. "But it's all right, at least for now. The probation officer just left. She's adjusting the case and there won't be court action. As long as Tommy behaves himself, he'll be fine."

"That crazy brat! I'll beat his ears off!"

"I don't think that's the answer," Sheila said. "He's unhappy, Patrick. He needs understanding, and probably a man to talk to. That's where you could help."

"You know I'll try. How about if Betty and I come over after dinner? A little family powwow. Will Maryanne be there?"

"I don't know," Sheila answered truthfully. "But you and Betty come anyway. I'm sorry not to ask you for dinner, but honestly I'm too beat to do much cooking."

"Not to worry. It would be tough for me to give you a specific time anyway, my first day back after four whole days away from this madhouse! We'll see you later. You're sure you're okay?"

"I'm better now that I've talked to you."

He hung up wondering whether he should have said more about Jerry, but dammit he didn't know what to say. He'd leave that to Betty. Women are better at such things.

At the other end of the line, Sheila was glad she hadn't told him about her new worry: Maryanne's absence. My God, I'm beginning to sound like "Portia Faces Life," she thought. One disaster after another! It struck her as odd that she assumed Maryanne's overnight absence was another disaster, but somehow she knew it was. Trouble comes in threes, so they said. Tommy. Jerry. And now Maryanne. No word from her all day. Sheila's impulse was to call the apartment in Ohio City. Perhaps Maryanne was there. Or if not, maybe Rick would know where she was. Wait, Sheila, she told herself. Maybe she'll come home soon. Don't panic. For God's sake, don't panic!

She'd barely hung up after talking with Patrick when the phone rang again. The warm, reassuring voice of Sally Cantrell rushed at her across the wire.

"Ta-rah! I'm home! Where the hell are the drums and bugles? Where was the red carpet at the airport? How are you, Sheil? What's new in this bustling metropolis?"

"Oh, Sally, I'm so glad you're back! Lord, you don't *know* how I've needed to talk to you!" She knew she sounded too intense, too emotional, but she couldn't help it. It was as though someone had thrown her a lifeline as she was going under for the third time.

"Hey," Sally said quietly, "you sound hysterical. What's wrong?"

"Lots of things. *Everything.*"

"You'd better get your fanny in the car and get out here."

"Yes." Then she remembered. "Damn. I can't. Maryanne has the car." Wherever she is, Sheila added silently. "Are you too tired to drive over here?"

"Of course not. Get out the martini mixin's."

"At *this* hour?"

"The way you sound, at *any* hour."

Sally was there in less than half an hour, looking sensational. She'd had her hair done a new way at Arden's and she was wearing a great pants suit from the Givenchy Nouvelle Boutique at Bergdorf's. She hugged Sheila warmly and then collapsed in a chair. "All right," she said, "start talking."

"Want your martini first?"

"Not quite yet. I'll let you know when I need it. From the look on your face, I'd estimate that'll be about eight and a half minutes from now. Come on. Give. What's been happening since my back was turned?"

Sheila poured out the whole story of the past two days—the nightmare incident with Tommy, the disappearance of Maryanne and, of course, the shock of Jerry's leaving. Sally sat quietly until her friend stopped for breath. She tried not to let Sheila see how upset she was by what she heard.

"Wow! You sound like a walking soap opera!"

For the first time, Sheila smiled. "My thought exactly. My God, Sally, what's going to happen next?"

"I can't think of anything that *could*. Sounds like you've had the book thrown at you. Let's have that drink and take your problems in order of priority. Or have you also achieved the ultimate disaster—running out of vodka?"

"No. There's plenty of booze. Sean had enough in the house to last a year. A good thing, too. I sure can't afford to buy it."

There was an unaccustomed note of self-pity in Sheila's voice. Sally frowned. The one thing her friend must not be allowed was the indulgence of whining. It turned attractive, popular women into boring burdens whose problems most people didn't care to hear. That wasn't going to happen to Sheila; Sally wouldn't allow it. It was healthy for Sheila to talk to her best friend, to get it all out of her system. She remembered how patient Sheila had been when Fred Cantrell had done his disappearing act, how many hours she'd sat with Sally, letting her cry and rage and try to find her way through her frustration, consoling and sympathizing, acting as a sounding board and making Sally see that her personal tragedy wasn't the end of life. Now the tables were turned. Sheila, sensible and understanding, had helped Sally get her mental processes in order, and the experience had made them closer than sisters. Now it was Sally's turn and she was determined to do as much for Sheila. She hoped she'd be as good at it. That's what friends were all about. You could count on the fingers of one hand those who cared enough to help you work out your problems. And even those, Sally thought realistically, run out of patience, hearing the same story told over and over, examined and dissected for months and years. Again, that would not be the case with Sheila. She was much too intelligent to go on endlessly about her tragedies, even with her dearest friend. But for a little while to come, she'd need the kind of ear and advice that only a "fellow sufferer" could provide. Sally looked at her thoughtfully over the rim of her glass.

"Let's take the horrors one at a time, Sheil. Have you tried to find Maryanne?"

"No. I thought of calling the apartment but I hate to sound like a frantic mother. Maryanne's twenty-four. She's not a baby and I refuse to treat her like one."

"Well, I think you should call," Sally said. "Eight to five that's where she is, with that electric guitarist or whatever he is. You know nothing's happened to her. You'd have heard." Sally considered her words. "Look, dear, I know it's not trivial, but we must give Maryanne lowest priority in your pack of troubles. Not because you don't love her or care what happens to her, but because you really can't do anything for her. Coming home wasn't her answer. She's going to have to find her way. You'll be hurt and disappointed if you discover she's once again renounced the 'conventional life,' but I'm sure that's what happened and you're just going to have to live with it."

"But *why?*" Sheila's voice was almost a wail. "I thought when she came home she was through with all that. Bob Ross was going to help get her a job. I thought she'd outgrown all that rebellion business."

"I'm no psychiatrist. I have no idea what influenced her. I don't know what influences *any* young people these days. Especially young women. I have a big nerve talking about children when I have none of my own, but just looking at them as people, not as flesh and blood, I have to conclude that in many ways they have more courage than you and I did when we were their age. They're not hemmed in by the expected things—marriage and home and children. They want to be free. And they know they can be."

"But I'm frightened for her," Sheila said. "It's not as though she were off on her own, making a career, getting somewhere. She's drifting aimlessly. So unhappy. There must be *something* I can do, some way I can make up to her for whatever Sean and I did that set her off on this defiance trip! I can't just abandon her, Sally!"

"You'd never abandon her and she knows it. Every time she gets terribly unhappy she'll come home, just as she did this time. But you've got to face it: she probably won't stay. And I don't believe you have anything to make up to her for, Sheila. She had everything from you and Sean, including love."

Sheila sighed. "Everything except maybe a feeling of security. We led such a crazy, erratic life. She must have felt the repercussions."

"Maybe. But so did Patrick. And look how well he's turned out. No, my dear, you can't blame yourself, or even Sean, for Maryanne's endless discontent. You can just be here when she needs you. That's the best you can do." Sally paused. "Now let's talk about Tommy. He's *not* an adult. What are you going to do about him?"

"I don't know. I've been trying to figure how I can send him back to University School, get him away from this new crowd."

"You think that's the answer?"

"It's all I can come up with at the moment. He began to change as soon as he went to the new school, so I assume he's reacting to different influences."

Sally got up and refilled her glass. "Other things changed for him, too," she said. "He lost a man in the house. He probably felt he'd lost you, between your job and Jerry. Maybe he just wanted your attention, Sheila, and would do anything to get it, including a dumb thing like trying to heist a few bottles of booze. He's too attached to you, too possessive of you, even if he doesn't show it."

Sheila looked at her with surprise. "That's almost what Maryanne said. In fact, she thought it would be a good idea if I'd send Tommy to Jean and Bill Callahan for a while, to get him away from me."

"It's a thought. He loves his grandparents and they're crazy about him. Would they take him?"

"I'm sure they would, and love it. But I don't know if it's right. I'm afraid if he feels rejected now he'll feel even more so if I ship him off to Florida. Besides, he's all I have." The sorry-for-herself tone crept back into Sheila's voice. Toughness was the only way to fight that, Sally thought. Maybe even a little cruelty.

"You're really thinking of yourself, aren't you? You're more concerned with hanging on to Tommy than with doing what's best for him. All that stuff about 'more rejection' is just a convenient excuse to keep your 'baby' with you, especially now that Jerry's gone." She hated herself for the hurt look that came over Sheila's face, but she plowed on. "For once I think Maryanne's right. A change of scene, a man around the house, a feeling of someone there waiting for him when he comes home from school—those things might be the best therapy Tommy could have. I don't see an alternative, Sheila. You must work and you can't lock yourself in the house every night to be a companion to a fifteen-year-old. You'll go stark, raving mad. And Tommy will become more dependent than ever. You want his happiness more than your own, but dedicating your life to him is wrong for both of you. He's got to get away. And you've got to become a whole person again."

Sheila understood what Sally was trying to do for her, why the shock treatment that, seconds before, had been like an unexpected stab in the back. They must both be right, Sheila thought. Both Sally and Maryanne. I'll smother Tommy if he stays here. And, God help us, he'll strangle me.

"It seems unfair to burden Jean and Bill with a teen-ager at their time of life," she said, uncertainly.

"If you really think so, then send him away to prep school. I can easily lend you the money, but *not* for University. He should live away from you, Sheila. Really away."

"You're so generous. I'm grateful for the offer, but I can't accept it. All right. I'll talk to the Callahans and to Tommy. Maybe I *am* hanging on to him in a kind of desperation now that Jerry's gone. I know it's important that he not build his life around me."

"It's also important that you analyze your feelings about Jerry. Or, rather, about losing him," Sally said. "What happened to that woman who could take a little fun and romance and not buckle at the knees when it ended? Are you really in love with Jerry? Or does his leaving seem to you a confirmation that you're getting older? You swore to me that you *knew* nothing could come of this. And now it's over and you're destroyed. I don't think you're heartbroken over Jerry, my dear Sheila. I think you're frightened of middle age. It's a goddamn shame that this had to happen just at this time, just when you were coming to believe that after all the years of belonging to one man you could be attractive to others. Jerry's leaving is a loss. I don't underrate the extent of it. He was fun and gay and flattering and sexy, and you needed all those things. But you allowed yourself to forget what you knew in the beginning: that it was a futureless relationship. Your ego's been badly bruised, my friend. Your confidence is shaken. But when the pain of rejection goes away, you'll be okay. You'll meet other people. Hopefully someone right for you. You're a beautiful, gracious, healthily physical lady and you have a damned good mind. Don't let a quixotic young guy make you think you're anything but desirable. Jerry has his own problems, it seems to me. And lack of emotional stability is one of them." Sally watched her friend carefully. "You had one unpredictable man in your life. Maybe that's the kind you're drawn to, but I hope not."

"It's not!" Sheila said vehemently. "God knows I've had enough see-sawing! But Jerry wasn't like Sean. He was a dedicated professional, a gentle, considerate man. I let myself fall in love with him, Sally, almost without realizing it. And I'm lost without him. I wouldn't say this to any-one in the world but you, but I'm grieving more over the loss of Jerry than I did over Sean. Isn't that shocking and terrible?"

"No. But it isn't true. You're grieving for the few months of feeling young and desirable, after all the years of being taken for granted. You feel cast aside by the living instead of abandoned by the dead. You're hurt that another woman could take your lover away from you, as all your husband's women were never able to do. It's rotten luck, it really is. I hoped Jerry would hang around long enough for you to get tired of him. It would have happened, you know. He wasn't grown-up enough for you." Sally smiled. "Rely on God's two greatest creations—time and Valium. Both of them will help you get over Jerry Mancini."

"I hope you're right."

"I *know* I'm right about this part of your troubled life. I've been around the same course once or twice since my divorce. You think you'll die from it, but you don't. The good doctor will probably come back, but don't mope around waiting for him. And for Christ's sake kick his behind out the door when he *does* come!"

Sheila shook her head. "He won't be back."

"Don't be too sure. I know his type. Just don't make the same mistake twice. And above all, don't take this as some kind of sign that you're in-adequate or aging. You have everything going for you, Sheila. *Every-thing.*"

Sure I do, Sheila thought when she was alone. I've got everything going for me except youth and money and even the vaguest idea how to hold a man. She envied Barbara Mancini her age, her wealth and, most of all, her obvious ability to intrigue through selfishness. I wish I could be like that, Sheila thought. Catering to a man doesn't pay. You must be de-manding, elusive, even irritating. Will I ever learn? Probably not. It's too late for me to change.

Though it solved nothing, really, the talk with Sally had helped. Sheila wasn't sure about the analysis of her grief over Jerry's leaving, whether or not it was basically more her ego than her heart that was smashed. Nor could she be sure that if Jerry had another change of heart she wouldn't welcome his return. The world suddenly seemed so drab and lonely, so futureless. He'd brought youth and laughter back into her life. He'd made her feel beautiful and tingling with anticipation when she knew they would be together. He'd fulfilled her sexually in a way that even Sean had not managed for many years. She loved all those things. Loved them so much she'd begun to delude herself they'd go on, maybe forever. But did she love Jerry? Really, deeply adore him? She couldn't answer that. The pain of loss was still too strong to separate the excitement from the man himself, for the two were inseparable.

She felt a lump in her throat, a warning of tears about to come again. She willed herself to stop indulging in memories of her own desires. Instead, she thought about Tommy and Maryanne. Sally made sense on both scores. She had to let her children go, for their own sakes. They were not children any more, not even Tommy. She had to stop thinking of him that way.

Before she could change her mind, she went to the telephone and made two calls. One to Ohio City and the other to Palm Beach.

Chapter 19

"We haven't seen anything of your sister-in-law lately," Margaret Callahan pronounced one evening in mid-January. "You'd think that now that she's gotten rid of all her kids and been jilted by her boyfriend she might have some time for the rest of us."

Terry winced. Margaret had a way of making everything sound ugly. Despite his disapproval of the affair with Mancini and the resigned attitude Sheila had taken about her daughter's return to that terrible musician, Terry had felt sorry for her when she'd come over soon after New Year's to tell them, straightforwardly, what had happened. She'd been so brave and yet unwittingly pathetic about it all. As though she hurt terribly, deep inside. He remembered the look of sadness on her face when she said that Maryanne had decided she'd be happier back in Ohio City. And the terrible uncertainty in her voice when she announced that Tommy was going to Terry's parents for a while. He'd seen her bracing herself as she said, trying to sound offhand, "Oh, by the way, I've stopped seeing Dr. Mancini. He's reconciled with his wife."

Terry Callahan was not a sensitive man, but the suffering Sheila was going through did not escape him. He'd have handled the problems with the children differently, but they weren't his to solve. At least he had enough respect for Sheila to defer to her views even if he couldn't go along with them. Not so Margaret. There didn't seem to be an ounce of sympathy in her. He wondered why she was so antagonistic toward his brother's widow. Sheila had never done anything to Maggie, except politely but firmly refuse to attend the matchmaking dinner parties Maggie had tried to set up last fall. Can't say I blame her, Terry thought. Those stuffy "extra men" would bore anybody as vivacious and bright as Sheila. She wasn't one of the middle-aged, lonely women who'd grab at anything in pants. True, he hadn't liked what she finally *had* grabbed, but he had to admit that Mancini was attractive, even though he was unsuitable.

"What's gotten you so down on Sheila?" he asked. "I always thought you liked her."

"I always thought she had some sense. Obviously, she hasn't. Allowing her daughter to live in sin with that dreadful hippie! Making a fool of herself over a man years younger than herself! And now burdening your mother and father with a child who's too much for *her* to handle! Really, Terry, I think Sheila is totally irresponsible!"

There was no use arguing with her. Indeed, he quite agreed with most of what she said. All except the part about Tommy. He approved the idea of his parents taking the boy. It would be good for him to live a normal, organized life. And having talked with them on the phone after Sheila's visit, he knew that Jean and Bill Callahan were thrilled to have Tom.

"It will be a new lease on life for us, Terry," his mother had said. "You can't imagine how we miss young people! Florida's wonderful, but it does attract older souls like your father and me. Imagine having a boy in the house again! Why, it'll almost be like having you and Sean back."

"You're sure it won't be too much for you, Mother?"

She'd laughed. "You and Sheila, both afraid this is an imposition when it's like a belated Christmas present! Darling, your father and I are hale and hearty and slightly bored. We couldn't have *imagined* such good fortune!"

Terry hesitated. "You do know Tommy got into trouble, don't you? I mean, Sheila told you about that New Year's thing."

"Of course she told us. One little mistake, Terry. I'm certainly not expecting a hardened criminal. Kids get into scrapes. You and your brother did. Not this serious, I admit, but when you were growing up, breaking a neighbor's window with a baseball or playing hookey from school was the forty-year-ago equivalent of what Tommy did."

"I hardly think the comparison is valid."

Jean sounded merrier than she had in years. "I know it isn't dear, but times change. Tommy's always been a darling. It's been a hard period for him, as well as for Sheila. I think she's doing a wise thing sending him to us. Sunshine, new friends, the companionship of his grandfather—we're counting on those things to heal him. All he has to do is survive my cooking!"

170

Terry had been reassured. There was no mistaking his parents' enthusiasm for the plan. "It's good of you and Dad to do this for him. And for Sheila."

"Nonsense! We're doing it for ourselves. We're grateful to Sheila for letting us borrow him! I just pray he'll be happy here."

"It would never occur to me that he wouldn't be."

"Well, we'll see. The only thing that worries me is that he'll miss his mother." There was a little catch in her voice. "I'm sure he misses his father, as we all do, Terry."

Her son was ashamed. He didn't really miss Sean, "the golden boy." Terry had been the pedantic, plodding one, the untroublesome one. Yet it had been Sean, with his inconsiderate ways and his undeniable charm, whom people had loved. Even Mother and Dad, Terry thought. He gave them nothing but trouble and still they loved him more than they did me. I suppose I was always jealous of him, envious of his "glamour," his friends, his beautiful wife. Maybe I was even impressed by his unfaithfulness, awed that he had enough confidence and courage to cheat on his vows. I never could. I never could do anything Sean could. But dammit, if something happened to me I wouldn't leave my wife unprovided for. With a rare flash of insight, Terry saw that his devout Catholicism, his professional standing, even his rigid marital and social life were all gestures of defiance toward his brother. It was as though he'd been saying, "You may excel at *some* things, but I outshine you at *others*." Not that Sean would have given a damn, even if he'd been aware of Terry's little ego-building accomplishments. He'd have been amused, condescending, as he always had been. No, Terry admitted to himself, I don't miss Sean, God rest his soul. I'm sorry he's dead but I'm glad to be free of him. His own realization horrified him. I'm thinking sinfully. He wondered what Father Reilly would say when he heard such things in Terry's next confession.

Emily Ross, for other reasons, was even more bitter about Sheila than Margaret was. Her reasons, kept to herself, had nothing to do with irresponsibility or the children. To hell with them. Emily's hatred was a mixture of envy and fear. Envy because Sheila had so easily attracted a virile young man like Jerry Mancini, even though, she thought with satisfaction, she couldn't hang on to him for long. Even more violent was Emily's fear of Bob's affection for Sean Callahan's widow. As each day went by, she became more convinced that Sheila and Bob were having an affair. She wanted to face him with her certainty, but fear of losing him held her back. The one talk they'd had shortly after Sean's death had made her less confident of her hold on her husband. She hadn't dreamed he was aware of her indiscretion, her feeling for Sean. Accusing him now might just be the excuse he was looking for to leave her. Damned if she was going to end up another Sally Cantrell! So she stayed quiet and watched and waited. And her hatred of Sheila became an all-consuming thing. She believed that the survival of her marriage lay in the hands of another woman, one who was free, predatory, and possibly even vengeful. For if Bob knew about Emily's affair with Sean, then by now Sheila might know, too. And what sweeter justice than to take Emily's husband, as Emily had tried to take hers!

Not, Emily told herself, that she ever really meant to break up the Callahans' marriage. The "little flirtation," as she now thought of her afternoons in motel rooms with Sean, was meaningless diversion for a couple of bored, long-married people. Still, if Sean had ever given any sign of "getting serious," she wondered what she would have done. Probably nothing, she thought, almost believing it. She'd been crazy about Sean and hungry for the physical satisfaction that Bob rarely supplied. But leave her security as Mrs. Robert Ross for the fly-by-night existence of Mrs. Sean Callahan? Not likely. Still, she'd been devastated by her lover's death and she'd been stupid enough to blurt out the fact she wished it had been Bob. He'd never forgive her for that. It was the kind of thing Sheila never would have done.

She wondered what that composed, competent woman would do now that she was entirely alone. Would she really go after Bob? God knows they spent enough time together these days. Never secretly, as far as Emily knew. Bob always told her when he was going to Sheila's after dinner "to discuss the estate." He never stayed long, but how did she know that they didn't meet at other times? Lunch-hour trysts, perhaps. No, Sheila only had forty-five minutes for lunch. But perhaps Bob picked her up after work and spent the time with her until he got home at seven? Or maybe they met on Sheila's day off? Emily tortured herself with the fantasy of the two of them in bed. She'd die of humiliation if they decided they wanted each other.

Emily wished now that Dr. Mancini hadn't disappeared from Sheila's life. At least while she had him she was occupied. Now she was footloose and Bob was susceptible. Goddamn her! With her kids all gone why didn't she move back to New York where she came from? Why was she rattling around in that big house, working at that stupid job, never seeing any of her old friends? Emily knew that Margaret and Terry rarely saw Sheila these days. Nobody in the old crowd did except, probably, Sally, that superior bitch. Sally would be the first one to put ideas in her head. After all, somebody had taken *her* husband. Why doesn't Sheila go away? Because of Bob, Emily answered herself. What else would keep her in Cleveland?

In point of fact, the idea of moving back to New York had occurred to Sheila in the past couple of weeks. She still missed her home town, even after all these years, and the house was too big and lonely for her, too "remote from civilization." In New York she probably could get a job as good as the one she had, could look up some of her old friends, could give up the tiring commuting and find a midtown apartment where at least she could walk to Schrafft's for dinner or see a movie now and then.

But there were things emotional and financial that kept her from taking such a step. Financially, she knew she'd have a hard time selling the house, and she'd have to have a two-bedroom apartment in New York, a place for Tommy when he came home. Or Maryanne, if she ever did. New York apartment rentals were astronomical; she undoubtedly couldn't afford what she'd be willing to live in. Emotionally, she was even more torn. It would be good to be in a different city from Jerry. The "time and Valium" Sally prescribed hadn't yet worked their magic. She was often tempted to call Jerry at the hospital, to ask him to see her on any terms. So far she hadn't, but if she lived in New York the temptation would be removed and it might be easier to forget him. Her unhappiness was taking its toll. She'd lost weight and she knew the sparkle had disappeared from her eyes, leaving them dull and uninterested. Perhaps all the things Sally had said were true. It was possible that she simply felt rejected and even a little foolish, but God how she missed him! She was wise enough to realize, though, that running away from Cleveland because of Jerry was an immature thing to do. Not reason enough, certainly, for such a big move. She'd have to live with the fact that he was near but unavailable.

There were other emotional reasons not to leave. Her best friend was here. Sally was a tower of strength, an endless source of wisdom and comfort. And Bob Ross. Sheila had known from the start that he cared for her, but she couldn't, wouldn't use him as a substitute. She was enormously fond of him. Perhaps in a different time, a different setting, she could learn to love him. But she didn't. And though Emily probably surmised that something was going on between Sheila and her husband—he spent so much time at the Callahans'—nothing "improper" had happened or even been hinted at again. But if she moved away she'd miss Bob. She depended on him, felt secure in his presence, turned to him with every bewildering detail of her new "single" life.

Other emotions entered into her decision to stay, too. New York meant Rose. And though Sheila loved her mother it would be impossible to be where Rose was. With the best will in the world, she'd move into Sheila's life again, and it was far too late for that. Rose might even think they should take an apartment together, "the two widows," sharing expenses and company. Sheila couldn't handle that either. She couldn't share living quarters with *any* woman, but Rose would not understand.

Even if she overcame all these hurdles, the most important thing of all was that Maryanne and Tommy know their childhood home was there to return to. It was the only security they had and Sheila sensed it was important to them, more important than they realized, even though Maryanne had left by choice. When Sheila found her—as Sally predicted —back in the apartment with Rick, Maryanne had been apologetic but firm.

"I still can't cut it in Shaker Heights, Mom," she'd said on the phone. "I tried. I really wanted to. I'm sorry to split again, especially with Tommy in trouble, but you have your friends and Jerry. You'll be all right, won't you?"

She didn't know there was no more Jerry. No point in telling her. It would only sound like a trumped-up excuse to get her home. Instead, she told Maryanne about the successful visit with the probation officer and heard the girl's sigh of relief.

"I know you need your car back," Maryanne said. "Will tomorrow be okay?"

"Yes. I'm taking this week off from work, but I do need the car, Maryanne."

"You'll have it tomorrow. I promise."

She'd kept her word, arriving the next day.

"I decided to take your suggestion and send Tommy to Florida," Sheila said. "The grandparents are thrilled."

"What about Tommy? He willing to go?"

"I haven't told him yet, but I think he'll be agreeable, if only because he can't bear the idea of going back to Shaker Heights High and seeing those boys." She looked at her daughter. "What about you, dear? What will you do?"

Maryanne shrugged. "There's talk of Rick's group going on tour. He told me New Year's Eve. Their agent thinks he's got them booked for some one-nighters. I'll go along. Maybe try to do a number or two. They don't have a girl vocalist."

Sheila tried to hide her worry. The girl was still drifting, might go on this way until she was old and worn-out and discarded. It made Sheila feel helpless and unhappy. Another failure, she thought. I seem to specialize in them. She couldn't think of anything to say. If I were a proper mother, I'd urge her not to do this, beg her to get out of that scene. But it would be pointless to try. There was nothing she could do except pray for the day when Maryanne would meet a good man. It was her only answer. The girl was unqualified for a career. My fault again, Sheila thought. I should have insisted on her going to business college instead of those ridiculous, high flown girls' schools where she learned nothing useful. Where would she ever meet the kind of man who would cherish her? Not running around with those indifferent musicians who had no use for the establishment.

Losing Maryanne a second time was almost harder than the first. She'd had such hopes when the girl came home at Christmas. But at Christmas she'd had hopes about a lot of things. She felt she should fight harder for everything, but there was this terrible feeling of inferiority that had been difficult enough to live with when Sean was around and which had become reinforced in her mind since his death. I can't seem to handle anything, Sheila thought. Not my children or my love life or even this house. It was too big for a once-a-week cleaning, thorough as Annie Winchester was. It would be even worse when Tommy went to Palm Beach. There'd be nothing but silence when she came home at night. Deep, dreary, dark silence. And yet she couldn't leave it. The roots were too deep.

Maybe I could get involved in something, she thought wildly. Charity work? Night courses? Don't be ridiculous, she told herself. You're too tired after a day at the store to concentrate on anything demanding. She supposed she should look up the people she and Sean used to see. She rarely called Terry and Margaret, not that she cared for them, but they *were* family. She excused herself on the grounds that she'd been too busy with Jerry. And she couldn't afford to return any invitations she accepted. Excuses. Nothing but excuses. She really wanted to crawl into a hole. I probably need therapy, she thought. I'm too old for psychiatry; it would be too painful. I can't afford a shrink anyway. And I don't really want one. This must be the lowest point of my life. I've hit bottom. There can't be any way to go except up.

The low point really came that week when she told Tommy she thought it would be a good idea for him to spend the next school term in Florida.

"Think how marvelous it will be!" She tried to sound enthusiastic. "That beautiful weather! You can swim and play tennis every day! You'll meet some interesting new young people and," shamelessly putting out the irresistible bait, "you won't have to see those awful kids here. Grandma and Grandpa Callahan called and suggested you come," she lied, "and it struck me as a marvelous idea for all of you. They miss your dad so much, Tommy. You'd make them feel as though they had another son." What a horror she was, playing on his sense of obligation, almost implying it was his *duty* to go! She was dying inside at the idea of losing him, but it was best. The cord had to be cut before Tommy was tangled up in it forever.

He'd just stood there looking at her with those big, surprised eyes, uncomprehending, trying not to feel hurt.

"I don't want to go, Mom," he'd said at last. "I want to stay here with you. You'll be all alone."

"Just for a little while, darling. You'll come back in June, when school ends. I know we're going to miss each other terribly, Tommy. I love you so much. But until things are more settled, my mind will be easier knowing you're happy and having good care." She made up another lie. "I'm going to look for a new job. I like Higbee's, but I'm going to try to find something closer to home so I can be with you more. You'll see. By summer I'll be pulled together."

He didn't answer, but she read his thoughts in his eyes. He did think she wanted to get rid of him, to have more time with Jerry, probably. Or he thought she was sending him off because she was afraid he'd get in trouble again. It was as though he was being punished for being alive.

"Okay," he said finally. "I don't want to be in the way. When am I leaving?"

Her frantically beating heart seemed about to burst out of her body. "Sweetheart, you're not in the way! You never could be! That's not the reason!"

"You don't need me," he said. "You have Dr. Mancini."

"That's not true! I do need you! And I don't have Jerry. That's over, Tommy." She hadn't meant to tell him. It had just slipped out. Maybe it was all for the best. At least he wouldn't think he was being shoved aside to make room for her lover.

He seemed strangely mature. "I'm sorry, Mom. I never liked the guy, but I know you did."

"It's not important. It has nothing to do with us. You've had a tough few months, honey. So have I. The change will do us both good. My mind will be at ease and you'll have a new experience. It's just a holiday, love. Everything will be the same, even better, when you come home."

He nodded, not believing a word of it. "When do I go?" he asked again.

"I made a plane reservation for you for Saturday. I know it is short notice, but you have to get into school and I have to go back to work." Impulsively, she hugged him. "You're glad to be going, aren't you, Tommy? Please tell me you're glad."

"Sure, Mom. It's a good idea. It was just kind of a shock at first."

She tried to make herself believe it. At the airport she'd smiled cheerfully and told him to call when he got to his grandparents. She didn't know whether to kiss him. He might think it was too babyish. But he threw his arms around her and kissed her.

"So long," he said. "You're terrific."

She blinked back the tears. "You're not bad yourself, old boy."

And then he was gone, not looking back. In a few hours, Jean called to assure her of his safe arrival and to repeat how happy they were to have him.

"Is he there?" Sheila asked. "May I speak to him?"

176

"Darling, he and Bill rushed right off to the club. Do you want me to have him call you?"

"No. It's nothing important. I'll call you in a couple of days. Thanks again, Mother Callahan."

"Oh, Sheila dear, thank *you!* We're delighted!"

And so, for the first time ever, she was alone in the big, cold house. She could have called someone, she supposed, but she didn't want to. She had a long bath, washed and set her hair, gave herself a manicure and pedicure, and made ready to go back to the store on Monday. In a way she looked forward to it. At least her mind would be occupied, if indeed there still was a mind functioning inside a body that was only a shell.

Chapter 20

"Four spades," Rose Price said.

Her partner across the bridge table stared at her in amazement. It was an insane bid and Rose knew it the instant the words were out of her mouth, but it was too late. At the end of the disastrous hand, she apologized to "the girls," all elderly widows like herself, who met every Wednesday for a regular game.

"I'm sorry. I really shouldn't have played today. My mind just isn't on the cards."

Her oldest friend, Paula Timmons, looked sympathetic. "What's wrong, dear? Worried about Sheila?"

Rose hesitated. She wouldn't have minded confiding in Paula alone, but the other two women, long-standing friends though they were, would just love to have some new "dirt" to pass along in their endless telephone conversations. There'd be something disloyal about airing Sheila's problems this way, even though Rose was dying to talk about them. It was also a matter of pride. Her cronies were always bragging about the successful marriages their daughters had made, the accomplishments of sons who were doctors or lawyers, the grandchildren who, to hear them tell it, were absolute paragons. Rose didn't like to admit that her only child was practically penniless, that her grandchildren, with the exception of Patrick, were not perfect. It seemed somehow a reflection on her own maternal accomplishments. She wouldn't tell them about Sheila's long letter, the long-delayed one she'd received on Monday. She was annoyed with Sheila. Here it was mid-February and Rose had been kept uninformed for more than a month about the terrible things that had been going on in Cleveland. The more she thought about it, the angrier and more hurt she became. Mother and daughter talked on the phone once a week, and for six weeks Sheila had said only that "things were fine." Rose hadn't known until two days ago that Tommy had gotten in trouble and was in Florida, Maryanne was touring with some dreadful dance band, and Sheila had stopped seeing that silly young doctor. Rose looked at the openly curious faces around the card table. I can't tell them, she thought. I'm too ashamed.

"No," she said now. "Sheila's fine. The whole family's wonderful. I just haven't been feeling well. I think it's my colitis again."

They clucked and related their own ailments and gave advice based on their own experience with "nervous stomachs" or the "tummy troubles" of close friends.

"You must watch your diet, Rose. No roughage."

"And rest. That's very important. Are you sleeping all right?"

"Exercise is good, but it shouldn't be too strenuous."

"Be careful about regularity. You know what they say on TV."

She smiled and nodded and promised she'd be all right by next Wednesday. "It's my turn, right? You'll be at my apartment about eleven-thirty? A light lunch and a game. Sorry about today, girls. I'll be in better form next week."

"Of course you will, dear," Marie-Louise Dancer said. "Thank God it's nothing serious."

"That's the truth," Erica Fitzpatrick chimed in. "It's getting so I hate to pick up the *Times* in the morning. Every day there's an obituary of somebody I know. Even some of my children's friends." She stopped. "Forgive me, Rose. I shouldn't remind you of Sheila's loss. What a wonderful thing Sean left her and the children so well provided for. At least you don't have to worry about her. Fretting is the worst thing in the world for the colon."

Rose's face was impassive. They suspected something but they weren't going to get anything out of her.

"Sheila's never given me a day's worry in my life," she said. "I'm blessed. I only wish Frank could have lived to see how strong his daughter is and how successfully she's raised her family."

"She's like her mother," Paula said. "Good and dependable." Paula was childless. "It must be such a comfort," she said sadly, "to know that if you ever need anything your daughter would be here in an instant. And your grandchildren, too."

Rose looked at her suspiciously. Was her best friend also baiting her?

No, Paula meant it. The others might take secret satisfaction in the Callahans' troubles, but Paula would be genuinely distressed. She knew nothing of Sheila's situation, financial or otherwise. Even to Paula, Rose had not been able to admit what a failure Sean had been. Nor had she confided anything of Sheila's "romance" nor Maryanne's shameful behavior—things she'd known about for months. She certainly wasn't going to go into it now, adding the disgrace of Tommy's arrest.

She went home and reread Sheila's long letter. It told her all that had happened since the first of the year. Nearly all that is. The one thing her daughter did not fully explain was the suddenly terminated romance with the doctor. That she threw away in a single line, almost as an after-thought. "I'm not seeing Jerry Mancini these days," Sheila had written, "but I'm meeting some amusing new people."

There was more in that than met the eye. Sheila had been able to go into the sordid details of Tommy's troubles and the disappointment of Maryanne's leaving with touching honesty. But it was obvious that she didn't want to talk about the doctor. Rose surmised that she was broken up about it and she also correctly guessed that the "new people" were in-ventions.

"I thought it better to wait until Tommy was safely settled and things in good order to tell you all this, Mother," the letter went on. "There was no point in worrying you about it, and it's too long and involved to go into on the phone. I know you'll understand that I didn't mean to keep secrets, but what was the point of both of us being upset? I'm fine now and Tommy seems to be adjusting well to Florida. Jean and Bill give me good reports and I'm sure his little flurry of defiance, or attention-getting, or whatever it was won't be repeated. I feel bad about Maryanne, but there's nothing I can do about the way a twenty-four-year-old chooses to run her life."

Sensitive to every nuance, Rose stopped and thought about that last sentence. Was it Sheila's subtle way of telling her own mother not to in-terfere? As if I ever would! Rose thought indignantly. As if I ever have! I didn't even stop her from marrying Sean Callahan, though I hoped it would be Bill Reardon she'd marry and settle down right here in New York. Rose went back to the letter.

"At least," Sheila concluded, "I can end this melodramatic recital on a happy note. Pat and Betty are going to have a baby in September! Isn't that marvelous news? They've just told me. Wanted to wait until they were absolutely certain. They're overjoyed, though it will be hard on them, financially. As for me, I'm filled with mixed emotions. Pleased be-yond anything for them but not yet used to the idea of being a grand-mother! How about you, dear? Can you fancy yourself a *great*-grand-mother? Young and lively as you are, you'll probably be a great-great! It's really wonderful, isn't it? You must come visit as soon as the weather's decent. It's been a miserable winter, but in another month or so it will be over and things will be green and new-born and beautiful. Everything will be blossoming—including Betty!

"Stay well, dear. And my love to you,

"Sheila"

Rose folded the pages and sighed heavily. The thought of Sheila alone in that desolated suburb depressed her almost as much as the greater tragedies. She should have come back to New York and brought Tommy with her. They'd have gotten a big apartment and put the boy in private school. Lord knows what he was up to, running around loose in Florida with those crazy Callahans who, in Rose's opinion, were no better than their son. If only there was something she could do! But the very tone of Sheila's letter, warm yet independent, told her to keep hands off. Rose was no good at letter writing. She'd wait a few days and then call. Perhaps she could subtly suggest that the sensible thing to do was to gather what was left of the family under one roof. Not, she thought realistically, that Sheila would buy it. Children. You sacrifice your life for them, and they repay you by keeping you at arm's length. And in the dark, at that.

Sheila was grateful to be busy at the store. At least her days were active and interesting. These past weeks had been the loneliest she'd ever known. Except for seeing Sally on her day off, Sheila had virtually no contact with people except in the book department. Pat and Betty checked in with her almost every evening by phone, but she seldom saw them. They were absorbed with their own work and their own friends, and filled with anticipation about the baby. Sheila smiled at the thought of the forthcoming event, admiring the cool way Betty was handling her pregnancy. Girls were so different these days. Betty planned to keep on working until her seventh month. Then she'd take three or four months off, find a good dependable woman to stay with her child, and return to her job. She was organized and calm. And healthy. What a contrast with *my* first pregnancy, Sheila thought. I had all the classic symptoms: morning sickness, cravings for strange foods, a feeling of anxiety that the baby wouldn't be perfect or that I'd die giving birth to it. I suppose I went through all those things because we took it for granted, nearly thirty years ago, that that was how pregnant women acted. Rose conditioned me to expect the worst. Just as she told me when I had my first period that I'd have cramps and I did. Girls don't seem to go through that any more, either. They know that menstrual pain is usually psychosomatic. Like most things, Sheila thought ruefully. I know damn well that these headaches I've had lately are nothing but nerves and boredom and loneliness.

Well, what else did she expect? It had been a fluke that she'd met an attractive man so soon after she was widowed. Many women never found anyone. Not even for a brief period. Look at Rose. It was doubtful that she'd ever even had a "date" after her husband died. I may never meet anyone "meaningful" again, Sheila told herself. I'd better get used to the idea. Sally was right. In their age bracket, amusing, eligible men were almost nonexistent. Better to count your blessings, be thankful you could earn a living, that you had your health. I'm creeping toward fifty, Sheila mused. The men who are right for me are all married. Or if they're getting divorced they already have the next wife picked out. Which is usually why they're getting divorced. The hell with it. I must settle down. If only I could stop thinking about Jerry.

There'd been no word from him since New Year's Day. Despite Sally's predictions, Sheila felt he'd never return. Once, shyly, she asked Patrick whether he ever saw Jerry.

"Sure. I see him around the hospital."

"How . . . How is he?"

"Okay, I guess. Not that I give much of a damn. Our conversation is purely professional these days." Pat's resentment was obvious and it distressed Sheila.

"Darling, you mustn't hold a grudge against Jerry. You always admired him so much. What happened between us was inevitable. I mean, I never really expected . . ."

Pat looked understanding. "I know. But he handled it so badly. Bloody egotist! I don't think he even wanted to go back to his wife. If you ask me, he just couldn't stand being thrown out!"

Sheila sighed. "It's past, Pat. And I have no regrets. Truly. Jerry came along when I needed him most, in those first lonely months. I'll always thank him for that."

"Mother, darling, do me a favor. Don't be so damned noble! The guy is rotten. He hurt you, and I can't forgive him for that."

Betty, who'd been listening silently to this exchange, finally spoke up. "Sheila's right, Pat. It isn't your battle. It was messy and unfortunate, I agree. But I also agree with Sheila that it's over, and the sooner *all* of us forget it, the better." She looked meaningfully at Sheila. "Your mother handled herself beautifully. She has dignity and understanding. *That*, my boy, is maturity."

"Stop it, both of you," Sheila said. "You're making me blush, Betty. I can't live up to that image. As for you, Patrick, I love you for being my Galahad, but you have more important things to fight for. So have I."

They'd changed the subject, but when Pat and Betty went home, Sheila couldn't forget her son's analysis of Jerry's return to his wife. Nor could she accept it. Jerry was no shrinking violet, that was true. But surely he was not so ego-ridden that he'd go back to a bad marriage just to prove something. No, he really wanted Barbara and Joyce. He pretended that being without them didn't matter, but it did. Sheila could understand that. Through all the turbulent years with Sean she'd never considered life without him and her children.

I hope Jerry's happy, she thought. Now that I'm over the shock, I wish him well. Sure, I miss him, but I've become reconciled. Well, nearly. At least the longing gets a little less every day. Sometime in the future I won't even be able to remember his face, or his body, or even his name.

Toward the end of February, Kitty Rawlings gathered her staff in her office one morning before the store opened and announced the upcoming promotional events for March.

"It's going to be a busy month, children," she said briskly. "We've lined up four, count 'em four, visiting authors next month. The publishers will work with us, of course, helping to set up publicity, interviews, local TV shows, all of that. But most of it is up to us." She consulted her list. "Let's see. First we have Virginia Harris who's written that really nifty novel about a department store. Everybody read it? It's called *Lady in Charge*."

Almost all hands went up.

"Good. Did you like it?"

Heads nodded.

"Great. Then you can recommend it enthusiastically. Call your regular list and say that Miss Harris will be in the store on Tuesday, March fifth, from 10 A.M. to noon to autograph her book. Same with all the others. Every Tuesday morning next month there'll be a visiting fireman at the table in the front of the department. On the twelfth we have Jean Yancey's quick-to-fix cookbook. Good and *very* amusing. It's called *Frozen with Joy*. The nineteenth will be a double-header, Drs. Lizst and Lehmann, the sex therapists with their *Fearless Love*. And on the twenty-sixth, one I'm really looking forward to. A non-fiction, highly sensitive account of the troubles in Ireland. It's called *The Innocent Ones*. Got great reviews and I hear the author is a charmer. His name is William Reardon. Used to be a reporter and a writer for *Time*."

Sheila's eyes widened. Of course! She'd skimmed the reviews of *The Innocent Ones* but until this moment it hadn't occurred to her that the author was her old friend, her first beau, Bill Reardon. Kitty noticed the change of expression on her saleswoman's face.

"What's the matter, Sheila? Didn't you like Reardon's book? You looked startled."

Sheila reddened. "I haven't read it. Just glanced at the reviews."

"Then why the double take?"

Her coworkers were looking at her curiously.

Sheila gave a little laugh. "It's nothing. I'm just surprised. I hadn't realized it's the Bill Reardon I grew up with in New York. At least, I *guess* it's the same one. I haven't seen or heard of him in more than twenty-five years and the name didn't ring a bell until now."

Kitty smiled. "Well, take a look at the jacket. The book just came in and there's a very handsome photograph on the back. It's his first and I think it's going to do well. If he's an old friend of yours, maybe you can give me a hand with some of the personal appearances. God knows I'm going to be up to my neck with all these people! Book-and-author luncheons, evening seminars, and the works, in addition to the regular advertising and press coverage. We're going to be busy, girls. I'll need help from *all* of you. Okay. Meeting over, unless there are any questions." There were none. "Fine. I know you'll do your usual great job for all Higbee's guests."

As they left the office, Dottie Parker grabbed Sheila. "What's with Reardon? An old beau?"

Sheila grinned. "My very first. Kid stuff. It was never serious, though I think my mother was secretly planning a wedding. Bill's folks and mine were friends, but I met Sean and that was the end of that."

A dreamy look came into Dottie's eyes. "Hey, maybe it's fate. Your meeting again after all these years. Wouldn't it be sensational if you and he . . ."

"Don't be crazy," Sheila said. "We probably won't even recognize each other. Or if we do we'll both be horrified by what the years have done."

"Listen, stranger things have happened."

"Only in novels, you romantic idiot. Besides, Bill Reardon's probably married with six kids. Or he'll be a boring, middle-aged man. Or both." Sheila shrugged. "It'll be fun to see him again, I admit. But miracles are something else."

"I don't know," Dottie insisted. "I have a feeling about it." She picked up a copy of *The Innocent Ones*. "Look at that face. He's gorgeous!"

Sheila had to admit that Reardon's picture made him look handsome. And not that different from the Bill she remembered. Older, but with the same pixie Irish smile, the same clear, compassionate eyes. Probably they retouched hell out of this portrait, she thought. He couldn't look *that* good. He was her age, a year or two older. Feeling foolish, she read the "blurb" about the author on the inside flap of the jacket. It mentioned his journalistic career, an interest in photography, and the fact that this was his first book. Only when she got to the last sentence did a little chill run down her spine. "William Reardon," it said, "lives in Manhattan where he shares an apartment with two Irish Setters and a tankful of rare tropical fish."

She borrowed the book that evening and started reading it the minute she got home. It was quite a thick book, interspersed with photographs

Bill had taken of frightened little children in Ireland, of bombed buildings, and sad women with grief permanently etched on their faces. The text was even more gripping than Kitty Rawlings had indicated. It was indeed "sensitive," but more. It was sentimental in the most deeply caring way, perceptive and tender without being mawkish. Sheila found herself crying softly several times. She read most of the night and even when she finished the book she was wide awake, full of respect and memories. Bill had always had gentleness, a delicate touch. She remembered his first visit to Ireland, right after World War II, while they were still seeing each other. He'd written letters to her that summer. She still had them somewhere, had saved them because they were so beautiful.

Not caring that it was three in the morning she got out of bed and climbed up on a ladder. Hidden way in the back on the top shelf of her closet was what she called her "memory box." She got it down and opened it on the bed. It had been years since she'd looked into it. On top were photographs of herself and Sean, souvenirs of some of their trips, a newspaper clipping of Maryanne when she sang the lead in some operetta at school, Patrick's candid wedding pictures, Tommy's birth certificate—a mishmash of these and dozens of other important moments of her life. And at the very bottom of the box, a slim package of letters. She riffled through them until she found the special one she was looking for. Bill Reardon had written it to her from Ireland in 1946. His first trip. Just a kid, but already so full of poetry. Sheila opened it carefully and began to read.

Ireland, May 22. A Wednesday in a sleepy town with a nice park and sun, and they serve tea, and children play and mothers knit, and it's about 100 miles from London.

Last night I watched the beautiful sea reflecting the sunset and the wiggling wake . . . the gliding gulls and Dublin disappearing, fading out from reality . . . and how lovely Ireland treated me . . . for a rest, for work, whatever. Some day I hope to return . . . to the slight drizzly days, the memories of sloshing wet-legged through old cemeteries, reading "Under this slab lies the mortal remains of . . . 1826 . . ." and climbing old belfry stairs in a dozen of the ruins I visited, exploding into the sunlight after the dingy, musty and bird-smelling stairs, winding their stone circle up four or five floors or through walls heavily fortified. And the view of Eire . . . to stir the heart, if climbing the stairs didn't do it. . . . The rolling fields and hills crossed and recrossed with stone fences, and lazy animals shining yellow and gold. And green and green and green and then green . . . and sliding on moss and seepy stone on the wet days, mounting the parapets and throwing burning oil and rock on the storming knights below, of fighting and sleeping in damp cells. Castles and cathedrals still cast their little-boy spell of olden times on me, and Eire is filled with history and the natives never let you forget it, toasting to Desmond and O'Brien . . . and down with Cromwell.

I'm sure my big, heavy shoes never expected to have such a work-out and my little car such demanding handling! But mainly I rested, had the quiet of being by myself, and it was the best medicine . . . and I read and saw *Oklahoma!* by the local Light Opera Society of Tralee . . . and in Dublin the Abbey Players . . . and kissed the Blarney Stone, just to keep in touch.

Saw Gypsies on the road and looked at the young girls with their bold, possessive eyes and felt I had better keep moving if I really wanted the rest . . . and spent nights by the sea and lake, went to fetes, with jigging and boat racing and listened to old music, and loved the lace-curtained, whitewashed stone cottages, open door and welcome. And the pubs, whose inhabitants never let you buy a drink or leave before everything's gone, or the bartender throws them out. I stopped at a service station for petrol, to move my legs, to check my map, and there were three little children, red-haired and grimy, and one named Rita was "ten come June" and her birthday was one before mine and when I told her that made her one day older than I, she giggled and hid her face in her hands, and I suggested we have a party there, and since she couldn't speak any more, her little sister offered to get the ice cream. So we all sang, except Rita, who was red and happy, and I waved good-by and it was the nicest party I ever had.

And I combed antique shops as ever, shaking loose the dirt accumulated forever, and, black of hand, I pulled and peeked and found a few things. . . . I danced, or tried to follow, and keep out of the counterclockwise circle, like a swift current that sweeps you along . . . dancing under sexy colored lights in St. John's Parish Hall, with signs in red protesting that "Jitterbugging is not permitted" . . . and had orange squash and apple juice and Double Lager . . . brown homemade bread with strawberry preserves and tea never weak, even after precise instructions, served proudly, certain of achievement, and saw mottoed walls with such undying sentiments as:

> Sleep sweetly in this quiet room
> O thou, whoe'er thou art,
> And let no mournful yesterdays
> Disturb thy quiet heart.
> Forget thyself and all the world,
> Put out each glaring light.
> The stars are watching overhead,
> Sleep sweetly then. Good night.

I've taken a few snaps for fun, to remember the cloisters and some of the faces I loved . . . to remember the women gossiping, the lakes of Killarney and Dingle Bay . . . and the brave, daredevil road-sitting birds who were never hit but forced me to clench my teeth a hundred or two times. And the blind curves that you are certain will reveal a herd of cattle or sheep on the road, a dozen bicycles or a donkey cart . . . and they do. Filled churches, a brown-shawled, colored-kerchief sea . . . teas in homes with cookies and buttered bread and crocheted tea cosies and talk of butchers and grocerymen . . . freckles and the good luck I was sure to get when two of us heard the cuckoo sing . . . and parks with grazing sheep and prancing dogs, heel-snapping and herding . . . little boys running and laughing down hills with wild flowers, throwing stones and chasing the new lambs despite their bleating protests.

I'll remember Confirmation day and veils, and beaming, white-dressed little girls, out making calls on other girls. . . . Reading by flashlight in a rustic inn . . . the smell of spilled whiskey in the car and for days it smelled like a pub itself. . . . Two little boys who begged for a ride and when I said okay and started the engine they both cried and wanted to get out, and never did take that ride. . . . Nuns and priests on bicycles, and flocks of schoolgirls uniformed and medaled. Conversations with everyone asking if I knew their brother who was a priest in Brooklyn. And it was as if we had another state, so closely allied are we. All these things I shall think of when Eire is mentioned . . . and more, and more.

Sheila lay back gently on her pillows. The clock crept past four, but there was no sleep in her. "The stars are watching overhead," she said aloud. "Sleep sweetly, then. Good night." But not this night. She wondered about Bill Reardon and the Ireland he'd written about last year, as opposed to this fairyland he'd first seen so many years ago. How sad he must be and yet how fortunate to have the earlier images imprinted on his soul.

She wondered what her life would have been if she'd married Bill Reardon. And, even more, what his had been, all these long, silent years.

Chapter 21

William Fletcher Reardon was not exactly delirious with joy over the idea of spending three days in Cleveland. It had nothing to do with Cleveland. He felt the same way about any city in which he had to make a "personal appearance" to promote the book. The whole thing was new to him, this business of "author promotion" as the publisher called it. Bill realized it was necessary and, having compared notes with other writers, also knew he was fortunate to have the publicity department get behind a "first book." Usually they devoted their efforts to established writers—the Elia Kazans, Harold Robbinses, Jacqueline Susannes who were sure-fire candidates for talk shows and newspaper interviews. He supposed he should be grateful, and he was. But he hated it. Hated the role-playing, the probing questions most interviewers asked, the sickly feeling of sitting at a desk in a book department, fearful that nobody would come in for an autographed copy of *The Innocent Ones* and that he'd be stuck there for two hours, trying to smile bravely, as though he didn't care. Nobody would believe he was so shy. Few people knew that behind the big, expansive grin and the air of self-assurance lay an insecure soul, scared to death. Nobody would believe him if he told them the veneer of sophistication was a defensive facade, acquired over years of tough training on newspapers and magazines.

But, Bill thought as the airplane droned monotonously toward Ohio on this late March day, if one gave credence to astrology, despite his insecurity he was a true Gemini. People born under his sign were supposed to be full of intellectual energy and a craving for "perfect expression." Once they attained it, they were not content to rest on their oars, but kept seeking understanding and more achievement. They sometimes seemed erratic, hating drudgery and routine. It amused Bill to know that in an ancient list of creatures supposedly ruled by this sign were the house sparrow and the flea, things that understood the advantages of unexpected attack and quick retreat. It was all nonsense, of course, this stargazing, but he'd become fascinated by it years ago when he'd had a magazine assignment for a piece on astrology. He learned, but didn't believe, even though some of the qualities were his. How could you equate such diverse Geminians as John Kennedy, the Duchess of Windsor, Bob Dylan, Lawrence Olivier, Ian Fleming, Marilyn Monroe—and Bill Reardon? Unless you accepted the better-known theory that those under this sign were "split personalities," living examples of their sign, the Twins. *That* far I'll go, Bill thought. God knows there's a public, confident me and a private, thin-skinned one.

Here you go, he told himself as the seat-belt sign flashed on for the landing in Cleveland. Trot out the romantic, adventuresome, professional-Irishman side of Reardon. The other one stayed home with the setters and the tropical fish. And the memories.

A tall, attractive woman approached him as he came through the gate.

"Mr. Reardon? I'm Catherine Rawlings, book buyer for Higbee's. Welcome to Cleveland. Your first visit?"

They shook hands. Nice lady, Bill thought. Cordial. She had a big reputation in "the trade" as a top-notch merchandiser. He'd bet she was really going to put him through his paces these next few days.

"Yes, first visit," he said. "It was kind of you to meet me. Wasn't necessary. I could have taken a cab to the hotel, but I appreciate it."

"No problem. Part of our standard service for literary VIPs." They began the long walk to the baggage area. "I'll tell you, though, it's been a hectic month with a different author appearance every week. Not that I mind! Business is terrific. Still, I nearly sent a substitute this morning, a woman who works for me. She tells me you two grew up together. Sheila Callahan. Remember?"

For a moment he didn't. And then his face lit up with pleasure and surprise. "Sheila Price? You're kidding! For a second I forgot her married name. We haven't seen each other for years, but she was my first girl. Sheila! I'll be damned! What's she doing working? Last I heard she had a husband and kids and a big social life in the suburbs. Don't tell me Sheila's gotten the 'liberated woman itch' and decided she must have a career." He stopped, appalled at his gaffe. He obviously was talking to a career woman. "Sorry. I didn't mean that the way it sounded. I love working women. It's just that I didn't figure Sheila's husband would hold still for that. I've never met . . . what's his name? Oh, yes, Sean. I never figured Sean Callahan would dig his wife getting a job. From the little I heard of him through my family, I had him pegged as the original male chauvinist."

"Could be," Kitty said indifferently. "I never knew him."

Bill caught the past tense. "*Knew* him?"

"He died last summer. Very suddenly. A heart attack. Sheila came to work at Higbee's shortly thereafter."

Reardon fell silent. It wouldn't do to gossip about Sheila with her boss. He wondered whether she'd gotten a job just to fill her time. Her kids must be grown by now. Or maybe she needed the money. Was it possible that the big wheeler-dealer had left her with nothing?

"I'm sorry to hear about Callahan," he said finally. "How is Sheila?"

"She's fine, as far as I know. She's an excellent salesperson. The customers love her and the other women in the department are devoted to her. So am I. She'll be glad to see you, I know."

"I'll be glad to see *her*. Personally *and* professionally. To tell you the truth, these in-store appearances scare hell out of me. I have nightmares that nobody will show up. At least Sheila will be around to keep me from slashing my wrists if that happens."

Kitty smiled reassuringly. "No need to worry, Mr. Reardon. You'll be swamped by the ladies. A lot of them have already been in to look at the book and your picture on the jacket. They're waiting till you come before buying it. Did you see the ad in the morning paper?"

"No, not yet."

"I think you'll like it. Your face is big enough for Mount Rushmore."

Bill looked at her sharply. What did she think he was, some conceited ass? "I'm not really concerned about my picture, Miss Rawlings." His voice was chilly. "I'm here to sell the book, not myself."

"You're new at this, Mr. Reardon. I'm not downgrading the quality of your writing. It's superb. But book and author are often inseparable and being a handsome man can't hurt you." The smile broadened. "I sent your publicity picture to the papers and the TV shows. Wait till you see your schedule. You'll faint. And much as I wish it was because of that compassionate, in-depth story of Ireland today, I'm afraid I'm realistic, or cynical, enough to know that at least *some* of the attention you'll get will be based on the public's idea of you as a romantic, swashbuckling ex-newspaperman who's very good-looking."

His annoyance disappeared. She *was* nice. And direct. Pulled no punches. Bill could see why she was successful and well liked. Except maybe by those shallow producers of illiterate junk who fancied themselves "important authors." But Kitty Rawlings probably booked none of them into her department. He suspected she could spot a phony a mile away.

She dropped him off at Hollenden House, the midtown hotel where a reservation had been made for him.

"I'm sure you'd like to freshen up," she said. "Then why don't you come over to see the store and meet everyone? It's only a little after eleven and your first interview isn't until three. I apologize I can't take you to lunch. I have another appointment. But I'll be in my office until twelve-thirty. We can go over your schedule before then, if you like." She paused. "Maybe you'd like to have lunch with Sheila."

"Would it be all right?"

"Of course. Might be a good idea. Company business, so she can take all the time she needs."

"You're very kind, Miss Rawlings."

"Call me Kitty. And I'm not really all that kind. In this case, I'm being practical. Sheila can tell you exactly what to expect. Save me a lot of time."

She wasn't fooling him, but he played it straight. She probably guessed he was eager to see Sheila. So many years! What would she be like at— my God! she must be forty-six or seven! It was hard to believe.

"Thanks. I'll see you soon, then. Will you ask Sheila whether she's free for lunch?"

"I imagine she will be. Can you find your way to the store? Two blocks down that way and turn left. It's a five-minute walk. You can't miss it."

The desk clerk apologized for not having a suite for him. "I'm sorry, Mr. Reardon. Your publishers asked for one, but we're full up. I do have a nice double room on the eighth floor, though. I hope you'll be comfortable."

Bill hid a smile. You should see some of the dumps I've slept in all around the world, he thought. It wasn't easy, getting used to being treated as a celebrity. Celebrity my ass! You're just a reporter who wrote a long, sad story.

He saw her almost the moment he walked into the department, past the "autographing table" which tomorrow would have a sign inviting people to have "William Reardon, noted author," sign their books. He felt the anxiety starting already. It was as though he was the "bargain of the day," like a blue-plate special in a luncheonette. Come off it, he told himself. It was good business. It was the way you built sales for this and future books, the ones he was determined to write. In the midst of these thoughts he saw Sheila and knew her instantly. She looked older (who didn't, for Chrissake?) but still beautiful and gentle, a lady, worthy of respect. It was the way he'd felt about her when she was seventeen years old, as though she was to be protected, never pawed over or treated the way he and the guys treated other girls. Funny. He felt the same way now, thirty years later. The memory of how much in love with her he'd been washed over him, intimidating him so that he didn't even kiss her cheek. When she came toward him, smiling, he felt so boyishly awkward that he took her hand, almost formally, and said, "Sheila, what a surprise! Miss Rawlings told me you were here. I couldn't believe it."

She gave the little, well-remembered laugh. "Sometimes I can't believe it myself. How are you, Bill? You look wonderful."

"I'm fine. And you?"

"Fine."

There was an uncertain pause. "Miss Rawlings is in her office. I'll show you the way."

He followed her through the crowded aisles, past the tables laden with books. Whenever he got into a bookstore he had a feeling that everybody in the world had written something, that the odds for success were staggering. So vast a choice for such a comparatively small percentage of the population! He'd been amazed to learn from his publishers that the sale of five or six thousand copies of a first novel was considered satisfactory, even good. He'd imagined that every book had to sell hundreds of thousands. That, he supposed, came from living in the world of daily newspapers and weekly magazines where one dealt in figures of hundreds of thousands or millions of copies. And also, he realized, in terms of a selling price of fifteen cents or fifty, not seven or eight dollars per copy. He remembered to smile at the other saleswomen as they passed and even found himself pleased to notice two women customers pointing to him and whispering, obviously recognizing him. Maybe I could get to like being "famous," he thought, amused by the idea. It *was* good for the ego.

Kitty Rawlings motioned him to a little straight chair wedged in among stacks of books. (Unsold remnants of last week's "author promotion"? he wondered dismally.) She introduced him to her clerk, Natalie, and as Sheila started to leave, Kitty stopped her.

"Don't go, Sheila. I'd like you to be here while I go over the schedule with Bill. You may have to be his escort to some of the appointments."

Sheila stood obediently by the desk. There was only one extra chair in the tiny office, the one Bill occupied. He started to rise, but Sheila motioned him down. It felt wrong, sitting while she stood, but he stayed put, listening to Kitty.

"Three o'clock interview at your hotel with the *Plain Dealer*," she said. "Feature. Good stuff. Do you have a suite?"

"Sorry. There wasn't one available."

"Damn. Well then, you'd better do it over a drink in the Gazette Lounge. You have a five-minute spot on the local news at six o'clock. Sheila will take you to the TV station. We've already worked that out."

He glanced at Sheila. "I'm at your disposal for the next couple of days," she said, a slight note of mockery in her voice. He smiled. Kitty was too preoccupied to notice.

"Okay. Dinner's free tonight, unless you'd like to go somewhere special. I'll be glad to take you."

"No. Don't trouble yourself, thanks. I'll probably collapse early and try to be bright for my appearance here tomorrow. Ten o'clock, isn't it?"

"Right. After the appearance there's a luncheon at The City Book Club. I'll go to that with you. You knew about that, didn't you? They'll want you to talk for about twenty minutes."

Bill nodded. "I'll do my best."

Kitty ticked off his other appointments: another newspaper interview, two radio guest shots, and a taping for Dorothy Fuldheim's TV show. "That's a biggie," Kitty said. "She's our best-known and best-loved TV personality, has a great show on WEWS. She's been at it for more than twenty-five years. Marvelous woman. The Gallup Poll recently named her among America's Most Admired Women." Kitty smiled. "So you see, we're not such a hick town after all."

"I never thought for a moment you were," Bill said.

"Well, some authors do."

"They must be deaf, dumb, and blind."

Kitty nodded approvingly. "You'll do." She went on to discuss two or three other appointments set up for him, including a meeting with the president of Higbee's and dinner with her his last evening in town. "My thought was you might like to see something of our fabulous suburbs," she said. "I'd planned to drive you out to Shaker Heights, but now that you have a local friend, Sheila probably can give you the tour without me. In fact, you might prefer it."

He hastened to reassure her. "Not at all, maybe the three of us can dine together. I'd like you to be my guests. I really appreciate all the trouble you've taken. I hope it pays off in sales."

"It will," Kitty said confidently. "That Irish charm will bowl 'em over. Never met a newspaperman I didn't like. Take care of him, Sheila. Not that he needs it. Have a nice lunch; set him up for his interviews this afternoon. I'll see you both tomorrow."

Sheila got her coat and joined him at the front door. He linked her arm in his.

"So we have the whole afternoon together," he said. "Does the formidable Miss Rawlings often delegate you to shepherd lost souls?"

"Never. I couldn't be more surprised. She must be frantically busy. Not that I'm not delighted, Bill!"

He smiled down at her. Tall as she was, he towered a good six inches over her head. "Your Miss Rawlings is a really pulled-together businesswoman. But I suspect she's also something of a softie. I think she's deliberately letting us spend time together . . . because we're such old friends. We have a lot to catch up on, Sheila. Will you give me as much of your time as you can, these next few days? I don't want to impose, but if you're free . . ."

"I'm the freest person you'll ever know, and I can't think of anything I'd rather do than spend time with you."

Over lunch, they began the process of becoming "reacquainted." "You first," he said. "Since my parents moved to Arizona, I've lost complete track of you. Your mother and mine used to exchange information, but it's been years. Tell all."

"I don't know where to begin."

"How about at the beginning? I know you married a big, successful real-estate operator and had three children, but I don't know their sexes, sizes, or ages. I didn't know about Sean until Kitty Rawlings told me today. I'm sorry, Sheila."

She nodded her thanks for his sympathy. Then she took a deep breath and began to tell him about her life and her children, leaving out little. It was hard to talk about Sean, whom she had loved and loathed all at the same time, without sounding disloyal, but she was honest about her years with him, the good parts and the bad ones, including her current, almost penniless situation. Bill frowned when he heard that, but he said nothing.

Sheila told him proudly about Patrick and Betty, her face glowing with happiness when she said she was going to be a grandmother. Feeling easier by the moment, she was even able to talk, with sadness, about Maryanne and Tommy. "But it's all going to come out all right," she said confidently at the end. "I know it is. They're good kids. It's a different world than ours was, Bill. A much more complicated world it seems, though I suppose we gave our parents just as many heartaches, in different ways, as children do today."

"What do you do with yourself? Outside of work, I mean? Haven't you met anyone since August?"

Sheila hesitated. The one thing she could not discuss was Jerry. "I've been out a few times," she said, "but nothing serious. I'm not sure I even care. It's enough to work and try to keep that damned big house in some kind of shape. I don't have much energy left over. And I don't really need the complications of a romance at this stage of my life. Maybe never again."

"You don't mean that, and you know it. Sheila, dear, maybe some women don't need a man in their lives, but you do. You always will. You were meant to be loved and cared for."

There was no amusement in her eyes. "Like a pet poodle by its master?"

"No. Like a grown-up woman with an abundance of love to give to the right man. You won't be happy until you find him."

194

She tried to speak frivolously. "The Women's Movement will picket Higbee's if you throw those old-fashioned sentiments into any public statements, so watch it, buddy! Don't you know we're not supposed to need men to have a complete life?"

"I don't know that. Or rather, I don't believe it. Not women like you. You'll always be incomplete without the love of a man, Sheila. And it's nothing to be ashamed of." He paused. "I'm that way without the tenderness and strength of a woman."

She felt guilty. She'd been going on for almost an hour about herself. At his urging, to be sure. But she hadn't asked him anything about his own life.

"I'm sorry. I've really been hogging the mike," Sheila said. "I want to know about you."

"All right." He told her about the jobs, about the assignment in Ireland that had inspired *The Innocent Ones*, about his new career as a freelance writer and, hopefully, an author of future non-fiction books.

"At fifty it's kind of late to be starting a new career," Bill said, "but I've worked for other people all my life. Now I want to work for myself. I have no responsibilities. I can afford to gamble."

She spoke almost timidly. "I thought—that is, it seems to me that Mother told me you married."

"I did. Twenty years ago. A lovely girl. We had one son. A marvelous kid. He wanted to be a newspaperman, too."

Sheila waited. Bill took a deep breath.

"Billy got his driver's license when he was sixteen. He was responsible and utterly dependable. Two months later he and his mother went out to East Hampton where we had a summer place. He was driving. Some maniac, drunk, lost control of his car and smashed into them." Bill looked away. "Billy was killed instantly. Eileene lingered for a week." He cleared his throat. "I sold the house in the Hamptons, and bought a place in Bermuda, gave up the big apartment in town and took a smaller one, strictly as a base. I asked the magazine to give me overseas assignments and the first one they turned up was Ireland. I spent a year there. Hence the book. End of story."

Sheila felt tears come into her eyes. She complained about *her* lot, and here was Bill Reardon with no one, not the wife he'd obviously adored or the son he'd been so proud of. At least I have my children, Sheila thought. Difficult as they may be, they're alive, thank God. She reached over and covered Bill's hand with her own.

"I don't know what to say. You must have loved them so much."

"I did. But we go on, don't we? *You* know that."

"Yes. We go on." But could I? Could I really have survived if I'd lost any of my children or, as in Bill's case, my only child? She knew, to her shame, that her grief for Sean was not comparable to his for Eileene. Just the way he spoke her name told her worlds. As though he read her thoughts, Bill said, "I never felt as though I lived up to what Eileene deserved. Newspapermen are very careless, very thoughtless creatures by nature. She should have had more of me, more time and steadiness. The only thing I can say in my own defense was that she had fidelity. I never looked at another woman for seventeen years." He gave a little laugh. "Believe me, I took plenty of flak from the other guys about that. They used to threaten to spread the word that I was impotent or queer." His face turned serious. "But you know, Sheila, I never wanted anyone else. She was such a complete woman. God knows how she put up with this incorrigible Irish elf! I was always off on some wild assignment, sometimes gone for weeks, sometimes between jobs in the early years. But she'd just laugh and say she loved me in spite of myself. And I knew she meant it." He looked at his watch. "Good Lord, it's past two and we haven't even had coffee. The big reporter from the *Plain Dealer* will arrive in a few minutes. Stay with me during the interview?"

"No. Better for you to handle that alone. I can go back to the store and pick you up here later. We should get to the TV station about five-thirty, I guess."

"Why go back? Kitty doesn't expect you. Listen, you can relax in my room while I'm doing my number in the bar. Give you an hour or so to take it easy. There's TV and a couple of new magazines I brought." He stopped. "Don't give me that look like I'm trying to get you up to my room for immoral purposes. I swear it's not a trick." He grinned. "It's also not exactly Buckingham Palace or even a first-rate massage parlor, but at least you can kick off your shoes and be comfortable. Okay?"

"Okay," Sheila said laughing.

"And dinner after the TV thing?"

She hesitated.

"I'm not trying to rush you off your feet, but I'll only be here a couple of days." Bill frowned. "Maybe you *aren't* all that free. Probably you have plans."

"No. I have no plans. I told you I'm at your disposal and I am."

He handed her his room key. "Don't tell the house dick," he whispered. "Or do they have those any more?"

Sheila looked happy. "What on earth makes you think *I'd* know?"

Chapter 22

When, with obvious reluctance, Bill Reardon went back to New York, Sheila was left with mixed emotions. Until the last evening, it had been a completely lighthearted time. They'd laughed a lot, more than she could remember laughing in a long while, and she'd told him so, gratefully. She did not tell him that these were the first carefree moments she'd had since Jerry left, but it was true. It was also true, as Bill had said early on, that she truly needed a man in her life.

Not that there'd been anything physical between them. There could have been. It could have started that first afternoon as she waited for him in his hotel room. The memory of that ridiculous room brought a smile to her lips. Its very atmosphere seemed designed for seduction, with two double beds, an ice bucket, and glasses set out, a "Do Not Disturb" sign prominently placed on the doorknob. A very ordinary room, really, except for the beds, yet one that somehow looked as though it was used to accepting lovers.

She'd sat primly in a chair, waiting for him to come up from his newspaper interview in the bar. The phone rang twice in the hour she waited, but she didn't answer. He'd teased her about that when he tapped on the door.

"I tried to call you twice from the bar," Bill said, "but there was no answer. Did you fall asleep?"

"No. I heard it, but I thought it might be personal. Maybe somebody who'd wonder why a woman was answering your phone."

"Sheila, I have no one to account to."

"No one? Not in three years?"

He shook his head. "No one," he repeated. "There've been women, of course. But nothing serious. I'm afraid I'm badly spoiled."

He was thinking of Eileene. What a marvelous wife she must have been, how he must have cherished her, and how deeply he still felt her loss. His devotion made Sheila ashamed of her own conduct. In three months she'd thought she'd found a replacement for Sean, but after three years Bill had entertained no such idea. Perhaps he never would. He's much more moral than I, Sheila thought. And much less shallow. Perhaps less physical, for all the outward manifestations of virility. But his next words startled her so much that for an instant she wondered if she'd spoken her thoughts aloud.

"I'm disappointed," he said. "Thought I'd come up and find you reclining on one of those giant playgrounds, breathlessly awaiting my arrival."

He was joking, of course. The tone of his voice and the grin belied the words. Or did they? Sheila decided to go along with the game.

"I thought of it, but I couldn't decide which bed to use."

"You're right. It's a problem." He laughed, looking at the setup. "My God, did you ever see so much sleeping space in one hotel room in your life? What do you go in for here in Cleveland, group sex?"

The moment of tension, real or imagined, passed. They ordered ice and Bill got a bottle of scotch out of his bag.

"I need a drink after that relentless grilling by the press," he said. "It's funny to be on the other side of the fence. I've spent my whole life trying to pry facts out of people who weren't anxious to Tell All. Now I'm doing the same weaving and dodging with reporters who'd like to know my opinions on everything from sleeping in the nude to my attitude toward premarital sex. It makes me wonder what the hell I was like when I was doing their job. Probably just as outrageous."

"You've only just begun," Sheila said. "Wait until the TV and radio interviewers get at you, to say nothing of your adoring public in the store tomorrow morning."

"Maybe I'll have *two* drinks."

"And show up smashed at the TV station? You'll ruin your reputation and mine! Kitty will never let me play guide to another visiting author!"

"Sweetie, I'm a long way from getting bombed. I'm Irish, remember? Besides, I drank coffee with the reporter. I'm no fool. And besides *that*, I'm not sure I want you guiding other authors. They might not all be so disciplined in hotel rooms."

They let it go at that. For the rest of Bill's stay they were like two dear, devoted friends. Only on the last evening did they tentatively explore their feelings. They had dinner with Kitty at Leonello's restaurant in Shaker Heights. Bill was highly impressed.

"It reminds me of Côte Basque, one of my favorites in New York," he'd said. "Has the same kind of attractive dining area in the back, with that nice mural that looks like the South of France, even though this place *is* Italian isn't it?"

"Continental, my friend," Kitty said. "Strictly posh. Get the smoked mirrors and the wine racks. Not bad for the sticks, is it?"

"I've never had better food anywhere," Bill said. "Nor better company."

"Too bad you can't go to the Ladies Room. Any place that uses facial tissue instead of toilet paper can only be ultrachic!"

It had been a relaxed and pleasant evening. Sheila had picked up Bill in her station wagon and Kitty had come in her own car.

"I can drop Bill at his hotel on my way home," Kitty offered. "Save you going back downtown since you're so near home."

He didn't give Sheila time to agree. "It's kind of you, Kitty, but Sheila promised to show me her house before I left Cleveland. I guess this is the last chance."

Sheila's expression didn't change, though it was pure fabrication. They'd discussed no such thing. He wanted to be alone with her this last evening and she was pleased. She'd really hoped Kitty wouldn't join them for dinner, but there was no tactful way out. At least she'd have a couple of final hours alone with Bill, unless her boss decided to stay with them. Lord! I *have* to invite her!

"Would you like to come with us?" Sheila asked. "It's no show place, but you've never been in my house."

Kitty yawned. "Thanks. Another time, maybe. I'm bushed. You must be, too, Bill, with all those appearances. Thanks for being such a good celebrity. It really went well, all the way. Come back when your next book is published, will you?"

"Absolutely. And thank you for everything."

They waved to her from the front of the restaurant as she drove off.

"I hope you didn't mind," Bill said. "I really would like to see your house. I can get a taxi back to the hotel. I wouldn't want you driving alone late at night."

"Don't be silly. I'm delighted. And it's still early."

"It may not be by the time I leave."

She looked at him sharply. Was he going to try to make love to her? She didn't know how she felt about the possibility. He was attractive and no stranger. My first love, Sheila thought again. Platonic though it was. Do I still want it that way? Does he? Her hand shook as she turned the key in the ignition. She was so very lonely for the comfort of a man's arms. But after Jerry, she was afraid. She'd given herself so quickly and completely to him, the only man other than Sean she'd ever been to bed with. And it had left her bereft and stripped of dignity. A "one-night stand," even with this dear and trusted friend, was something she'd not like herself for, maybe couldn't handle. And yet she dreaded his departure, had hoped for these last few hours alone with him. It was so confusing.

She'd gone around quickly switching on lights as they entered the dark, deserted house. "Nightcap?" she asked. "You'll find everything on the bar over there in the corner."

He poured Drambuie for each of them and sat down on the sofa. "Come sit beside me, Sheila."

Obediently, she joined him. He raised his glass.

"What shall we drink to?"

Sheila smiled. "The success of *The Innocent Ones?*"

"The book or us?" He put down his untouched drink and took hers out of her hand. Then he pulled her close to him, holding her gently. "*We've* been innocents," he said. "I loved you so much all those years ago. I thought I'd die when you met Sean Callahan. For years I kept track of you, Sheila, even when I thought I'd lost you forever. I wanted you so much when we were kids and I never dared even come close." He released her. "Goddammit, I don't even dare now!"

She was uncertain, shaken. The feel of his arms was good, the beating of his heart as strong as hers. It would have been so easy. Just one word of encouragement from her. But for what? Tomorrow he'd be on his way back to New York, out of her life again. No, Sheila thought. No more transient relationships. I was born in the wrong generation.

Almost frantically, she tried to turn the conversation away from this serious, personal tone. She picked up her glass and said, "Let's drink to your success and my clairvoyance. I always knew you were going to be a great writer. Do you know I saved a letter you wrote from Ireland on your very first visit? I reread it when I heard you were coming to Cleveland."

He knew what she was trying to do, but he was intrigued nonetheless. "I've never been so flattered," he said. "All these years you saved a letter from me?"

"I couldn't throw it away. It was like a poem. Would you like to see it?"

"I'm not sure. It's probably embarrassing. Good God, it must be thirty years! What did I know about writing? Even less than I do now!"

"You're wrong. It's beautiful. Warm and gentle and perceptive." Like you, she wanted to add. "I'll get it for you."

He read it, smiling. "What a romantic kid I was! But I did feel all those things and if I do say so as shouldn't, it ain't half bad! Such an extraordinary country, Sheila. Have you ever seen it?"

She shook her head.

"You should. I'd like to take you." He paused. "It can't end here, my dear. You know that, don't you?"

"I don't know, Bill. I suppose I thought it would. We live in different cities, have different friends. It's been wonderful, these few days, but I haven't allowed myself to think beyond them. Besides, people can't go back. You know that. We're not children any more."

"No, we're not children. We're grownups, able to understand and appreciate what we didn't then. We've taken our lumps, both of us. We've found out what counts. I'm not going to say I love you and I want to marry you. Not now. But I want to know you again. I want to see if old flames *can* be rekindled. And not just for one night. God, I want to take you to bed so much I can't stand it! But some kind of desire to 'court you' is still with me. Isn't that crazy? I sound like a Victorian novel. But that's how I feel . . . as though I'm a young man with 'serious intentions.' I suppose I don't want you to misunderstand. I care too much to risk having you think I'm only after your body. That's part of it. But not all of it. Can you understand that, Sheila? Does it make any sense to you?"

"Yes," she said, thinking of the heedless, immediate coupling with Jerry. "Yes, I understand. It's the right way, the only way for people like us. It's how I want it, too."

He looked happy, boyish. "People would never believe it. They'd think we were crazy. Maybe we are." He broke into a laugh. "Eight-to-five Kitty Rawlings thinks we're in the sack right now." Then he sobered. "I want us to be. If you do, too, we will be. Very soon."

"But how . . . where? You're leaving tomorrow."

"Darling, it's only New York. And I wouldn't go tomorrow if I didn't have commitments. Leave it to me. I'm not letting you get away again, Sheila. There's too much fate involved in this reunion. Too much meant-to-be. Just be ready to join me, or have me join you, soon and often. I'll work out the details." She started to speak but he hushed her. "I know. You have responsibilities. Children. A job. I'm well aware. But now you have another couple of responsibilities—you and me. We're getting a second chance. Do you realize how rare that is?"

They'd left it that way. He'd insisted on calling a cab to take him back to the hotel. When it arrived he kissed her deeply, passionately, and she responded with a weakness that ran through her whole body. He felt her trembling and held her, caressing her.

"I didn't dare do that until I knew I was on my way *out* the door," Bill said. "I know how much we want each other. I'm probably out of my mind. I'll kick my tail all the way back to New York."

She was suddenly more reckless than he. "You could send the cab away."

He pretended shock. "Why, you hussy!" Then he looked seriously into her eyes. "Shall I tell you the real truth? I don't want to take you in the bed you shared with Sean . . . and that's the God's truth. I wanted you that first afternoon in the hotel, but that wasn't the place for us either. When we make love, my darling, it will be fresh and new and beautiful, not only the act but the place. You see, to me you're still that little virgin and I'm that lovesick, adoring boy. I know I'm behaving as emotionally as the kid who wrote that letter. Tough, seen-it-all Reardon. Who'd believe? But that's the way I feel."

And he was gone. Forty minutes later the phone rang and he said, "I'm in bed. What about you?"

"Me, too. But sleepless."

"Yeah. I hate myself tonight."

Sheila managed to laugh. "Look at it this way, darling. You won't hate yourself in the morning."

As she hung up, she realized it was the first time she'd ever called him "darling."

Maryanne awakened with a start, disoriented, uncertain of where she was. The drab hotel room looked like twenty others she'd seen in the past month since the group had been on tour. Shabby. Cheap. Like all the rooms she'd shared with Rick in Cincinnati and Detroit and Baltimore and God knows how many dreary cities. She hated them. She hated the tour, the second-rate clubs they played, the crude, wisecracking customers who made unsubtle passes at the "girl singer." Rick thought it was amusing, this verbal fencing with men who thought she was an easy lay. Why shouldn't they? She looked like a tart in the overtight sequin pants, a low-cut jersey blouse deliberately revealing most of her breasts. What would a "nice girl" be doing in such a costume, in such places, singing suggestive songs and accompanying the lyrics with provocative movements of her body? Rick knew she went to bed with nobody but him, but why shouldn't these strangers consider her fair game? Rick's amusement angered her, but she deserved it. Nobody had forced her into this unlikely role. What did she expect? That her lover would punch every dirty-talking drunk in the mouth? When she told him how disgusting it was, he'd merely shrugged.

"It comes with the territory, babe. What the hell difference does it make? They're only doing what comes naturally. Christ, a little *talk* never hurt anybody!"

But it did hurt. It made her feel dirty and degraded. Everything about this tour did. It had been different somehow, when she'd been living with Rick in Ohio City. Her life then had been unconventional to people of her mother's age who still couldn't quite accept a liaison without marriage, who still felt ashamed that a well-brought-up, well-educated girl preferred the company of drifters to that of the uptight young men in the "straight world." But even the knowledge of their disapproval hadn't deeply troubled Maryanne. Perhaps it even made it more exciting. Or maybe in the back of her mind she knew she could always go home, that she really wasn't far away from the protection of Shaker Heights and Sheila.

She was glad Sheila didn't know the kind of life she was living. She hadn't heard from her mother in more than a month. She never stayed in one place long enough to get mail, but she'd dropped Sheila a couple of cards from cities the group had played. She always went to the best hotel in town and stole one of their postcards, covering the writing side with lies about how exciting and successful the tour was, how she adored "show business," and how happy she was now that she'd finally found her "career."

"There's hope for me yet, Mom," she'd written on one. "I may turn out to be this generation's Peggy Lee!" She hoped Sheila believed what she read, that her mind was a little more at ease because Maryanne sounded so thrilled. Thrilled! God, she'd never been more miserable in her life. Sometimes she wished she had enough courage to kill herself. What other answer was there? She had no future, no direction, no talent. And no interest in anything. Even Rick's sexual expertise had ceased to be the exciting thing it once was. How could passion survive lumpy beds and unclean sheets and haphazard meals surreptitiously cooked over a hot plate spirited into dingy hotel rooms? All I need now is to get pregnant, Maryanne thought. That would be the final blow. The terrible part was that she suspected she was. She was two weeks late. She refused to believe it. It was all this traveling and tension that had thrown her off schedule. Rick would kill me, she thought. Maybe that wouldn't be such a bad idea, since I can't bring myself to do it.

She looked at the sleeping figure beside her. Where were they? Oh yes, she remembered. New York. The Big Apple. What a laugh! Last night they'd checked into this flea-bitten hotel on the West Side, brushing past the hookers on the sidewalk. Tonight they'd play some crummy bar on Ninth Avenue. Terrific. She knew how it would be. A pitch-black room, heavy with smoke. A tiny raised platform pretending to be a stage. A crowd of unwashed men and girls, talking loudly, paying no attention to the "entertainment." Outside there'd be an amateurishly lettered sign announcing the appearance of "THE POTBOILERS, World-famous Rock Group featuring Vibrant Vocalist Pattie Thomas." That was her "professional name." Maryanne Callahan sounded too "girl-next-door." Besides, she didn't want to use her real name. Instead she'd rechristened herself, deliberately taking the names of her two brothers. It had seemed funny at the time. It wasn't any more. Nothing was.

The "Thomas" whose name Maryanne had used awakened in far different surroundings. The hot, bright sunshine of a Florida morning illuminated his room. A nice room, with everything he needed, from a super stereo to a closetful of sport clothes, swim suits, tennis shorts, and the equipment to match. A clean, cheerful, boring room in which he felt like a stranger.

He lay naked on his bed. In a few minutes his grandmother would knock lightly on his door, making sure he was awake so he'd be on time for school. He wondered why he was unhappy. His grandparents were terrific people. They loved him and did everything they could think of to make his life good. Tommy loved them in return and appreciated how hard they tried. But it just wasn't working. The school was okay and so were most of the kids there, but he hadn't made any real friends. Jean Callahan worried about that, constantly urging him to invite boys and girls to the apartment, looking troubled when he said he didn't like any of them well enough to bother. It was true. The teen-agers here reflected the lethargy of the whole place. Probably it was the endlessly good weather. The monotony of an unchanging climate provided no stimulation, no challenge. That's why Florida was so good for old people, of course. And the kids who'd never known the kick of spring, fall, and winter didn't know how stifling their atmosphere was. They were like miniature editions of their parents and grandparents—slow-moving and contented. It was all too easy, too unexciting. A guy would have a hard time getting into trouble if he wanted to, Tommy thought ruefully. Not that he wanted to. That one experience in jail had been enough. But damn, it was dull here!

He hadn't let Sheila know of his discontent. His letters, like Maryanne's cards, had been masterpieces of deception, describing how great the place was, how swell Grandma and Grandpa Callahan treated him, how well he was doing in school. When he and his mother talked on the phone he managed to sound happy and cheerful, for her sake and the sake of the anxious grandparents who pretended not to listen. Inside, he was crying, "Let me come home, Mom! *Dad's* parents aren't *mine!* They try to do right, but they're old. Too old, Mom. Everything *here* is too old!

But he said none of this, inquiring instead about Pat and Betty and being genuinely pleased that he was going to be an uncle. He pretended to believe, as Sheila pretended, that Maryanne was becoming a big success as a singer. He asked for Mr. Magoo and was reassured that the shaggy dog was fine but that he missed Tommy.

"As I do, sweetheart," Sheila said during the latest call.

"You okay?"

"Of course. Fine."

"I'll be back in a couple of months. When school closes. I am coming home, Mom, aren't I? I mean, that was the plan, wasn't it?"

Sheila hesitated. She wanted him home, but his life there sounded so sane, so normal and secure. Nothing had changed in Cleveland. She had the same job; she was in no position to send him to private school; there was still the fearsome prospect of his being alone all day, maybe getting into trouble again. She missed him terribly and despite his cheerfulness she instinctively sensed that he was lonely in Florida. But was it too soon to bring him back? It had only been three months. Not nearly enough time for him to become independent of her. Even five months wouldn't do the trick. She remembered Maryanne's words of caution. She didn't want to warp Tommy's life by re-establishing this intense attachment to her. At the same time, she couldn't break her promise to him.

"Of course you're coming home for the summer," she said.

"For the summer?"

"Well, I mean, we'll see what fall brings, right? You're doing so well in school there, maybe you'll want to go back next term."

He didn't answer. He couldn't say what he felt, not with his grandparents listening. But he wasn't coming back to Florida. If Sheila didn't want him, he'd go someplace else. Hell, he wasn't some little kid who had to be shunted around to relatives! He was almost sixteen years old. And he was physically, if not emotionally, a man.

Sheila tried to be chatty. "By the way, darling, you'll be interested to know that your old mother has been hobnobbing with celebrities, going to TV stations, all kinds of different things."

"How come?"

She told him about her old friend Bill Reardon. "He's very nice, Tommy. We hadn't seen each other since before I married your father and it was fun to catch up with him after all these years. You'll like him. He had a son just about your age who was killed with his mother in a car crash about three years ago. So sad. It makes me so grateful that you and Pat and Maryanne are all well."

So that's it, Tommy thought. That's why she doesn't want me home. First Jerry Mancini, now this new joker. For a moment he hated her. Why couldn't she act her age?

"You planning to see a lot of Mr. Reardon?"

She laughed. "Of course not, silly. He lives in New York."

"Then how come you say I'll like him?"

Sheila realized what was going through his mind. He was feeling displaced again, as he had when she was involved with Jerry. She had a sense of despair.

"I just meant he'll probably come back sometime. Or maybe this summer you and I will go to New York for a visit with Grandma Price and you'll meet Bill there. That's all. Don't make a big deal of it, honey. I thought it would interest you to meet a successful author, particularly a man who had a son just your age."

"Yeah. Sure. I better hang up now, Mom, before you go broke with this phone call."

"You're all right, Tommy, aren't you? You're sure?"

"Everything's terrific."

"It won't be much longer till you're home."

"Right. That'll be swell. So long, Mom."

"So long, darling. I love you."

He didn't answer. Sure you do, he thought. When it's convenient.

Chapter 23

Only to Sally did Sheila confide her feelings about Bill Reardon, and at that not until nearly two weeks after he'd left Cleveland. She might not have told even her best friend about this rediscovered happiness if it hadn't been for the invitation to Bermuda.

In the first days after he returned to New York, Sheila tried to believe she probably would never see or hear from him again. It was as though she was cushioning herself against possible disappointment, an old habit of hers which was not exactly pessimism but more a self-protective thing, shielding herself from hurt by expecting nothing. He'd not called her, and after three days of silence, she made up her mind that her hope of a beginning romance was wishful thinking. What would a man like Bill Reardon want with a woman like her? He was attractive and undoubtedly sought after. He could have his pick of women younger, richer, and more beautiful than she. It was nonsense to attach any importance to a sentimental reunion. It had been simply that he knew no one in Cleveland. He'd been glad to see a familiar face, even one so long out of the past. Undoubtedly he did have a lingering fondness for her, but all that talk about "second chances" was just so much blarney. It was, she even thought bitterly, Sean all over again: the irresponsible Irishman with a dazzling facade of charm.

She wanted him to love her, even while she refused to entertain the possibility that he might. No, she told herself, Bill didn't need a forty-seven-year-old woman with an unhappy fifteen-year-old son and an endlessly confused and troublesome daughter. Yet she raced home every night and stayed there, waiting for the phone to ring. On the fourth night it did.

"Hello, love. How's my grown-up childhood sweetheart?"

Childish, she wanted to say, but she forced herself to sound sprightly and unconcerned. She would not let him know how letdown she'd felt these past days, how his silence had depressed her. She'd not ask him why he hadn't been in touch. She detested demanding, accusatory women, and God knows she had no right to be either.

"I'm feeling wonderful," she said. "How are *you?*"

"Lonely. Fish and dogs are no substitute for you."

Sheila laughed. "Thanks a *lot!*"

She could imagine him smiling. "I didn't mean that quite the way it sounded," Bill said. "I've been surrounded by people and lonely for you. Ever since I got back I've been trying to catch up with mail and meetings. I've had nothing but business lunches and dinners with my accountants. 'Tis tax time, my darling, and this disorganized friend of yours hasn't even gathered together his deductions! God, I hate money! No, I don't. I love it. I just don't like having to think about it. I resent having every minute taken up with receipts and canceled checks and bank statements."

There must have been a minute somewhere when you could have called, Sheila thought, pettishly. Again, she scolded herself. When would she learn that men didn't think like women? They saw nothing unusual in three days of silence after some pretty heavy protestations of desire. Their minds were occupied with other things. A woman in Bill's place would have made sure she spoke to a man she cared for. She'd have *found* those few precious minutes, knowing how much they'd mean to the waiting one. The male simply did not think that way. She knew it. But like most of her sex, though she'd learned to recognize it, she'd never really accept these unintentional slights, nor ever fully understand the lack of importance most men attached to "little things." It *was* childish of her, Sheila thought again. Childish and insecure, but she couldn't help feeling neglected. All she could do was try hard not to show it.

"Everything squared away now?" she asked.

"At least until IRS examines the Return. But the hell with that. What have you been doing?"

She was tempted to say she'd been out dining and dancing every night, but she was too old for those coy games.

"Nothing," she confessed. "Just working and spending quiet evenings at home." Did that sound self-pitying or reproachful? Lest it did, she said lightly, "Fortunately—or unfortunately—my taxes aren't as complicated as yours must be. Not that I do them myself, thank heavens! Bob Ross takes care of that."

"Who's Bob Ross?"

"He was a good friend of Sean's and mine. Our lawyer in fact. He's a dear man."

"Really? *How* dear?"

Ridiculously, she was pleased. "Very dear. I don't know what I'd do without him." Shame on you, Sheila. You're playing games after all.

"He married?"

"Very much so. His wife is a friend, too."

"Okay. That's more like it."

She couldn't resist. "Bill Reardon, if I didn't know better I'd think you were jealous!"

"I am. Jealous of every man you know. Jealous of every second I spend away from you. I wasn't kidding about what I said that last night in Cleveland. I *did* kick myself all the way back to New York. When am I going to see you again?"

"That's kind of up to you, isn't it? You're the one with the busy schedule. I'm here."

She knew what he was thinking. She was there. But so was Sean's bed and so was that impersonal hotel room.

"How about coming to New York next weekend?" he asked. "Oh, no, dammit. I have to go to Boston. And the week after that to Minneapolis. Bloody damned personal-appearance tours!" Then he laughed. "I shouldn't say that, should I? If it hadn't been for one of those I'd never have found you again. Look, tell you what. The third week in April is clear and I'll keep it that way if you'll go to Bermuda with me."

"Bermuda!"

"Sure. Why not? Have you ever been?"

"No, but . . ."

"You'll love it. It's all clean and beautiful and civilized. My house is leased most of the time, but it's empty now. What do you say, love? We could have a glorious week."

"I don't know. It sounds wonderful, but I'm not sure I could get time off from the job. I had to take that awful week at New Year's. Kitty Rawlings is understanding, but I'm not sure she's *that* understanding."

"Oh, the job. For a minute I forgot about that." He sounded disappointed, then he said, "Maybe you could tell just a little white lie? Like you have a friend who desperately needs you? It wouldn't really be a lie. You do."

He was so appealing and she wanted so much to be with him. "Let me think about it for a couple of days, all right? There are other considerations, too."

He didn't press her. He guessed she'd have to lie to a number of people. To the Callahans, in case they needed to reach her about Tommy. To Pat and Betty, who might not approve of her going off to Bermuda with a man. Maybe she was even worried about Maryanne, though it seemed unlikely, from what he knew, that the girl would try to get directly in touch with her mother. Sheila's life was not as uncomplicated as his. He must remember that.

"Okay, darling. You think it through. But try to come up with a 'yes' answer, will you?"

"I'll try. I want to very much."

He'd been correct in his guesses about her responsibilities. What he didn't know was that she was almost afraid to go with him. I couldn't take another disappointment, she thought. I seem to get so involved, reading more into relationships with men than I should. Just because Bill Reardon had invited her away for a week didn't mean he was offering her eternal devotion and she shouldn't assume anything of the sort. But I'm so dumb that I probably would, Sheila realized. I can't get used to the idea that grown men and women say deep and tender things to each other, that they can be joined in spirit and in body without its being a lifetime commitment. Good God, Sheila, have you no control over your outmoded ideas? Does every physical encounter have to leave an emotional scar? This is 1974 and you're living a hundred years in the past! You're still wounded by Jerry's rejection of you. So wounded you're afraid to dare another. You're afraid of yourself. Afraid of happiness that may or may not last. The fact is, you're afraid of life—or of taking whatever it's kind enough to offer. Even for a little while.

If I were going to a psychiatrist, she thought, maybe I'd find it all stems from my childhood, from my "strict upbringing," or pity for my father who never seemed to be really accepted by his wife. Or maybe it was Sean who flitted in and out of the affairs I only pretended didn't hurt me, and who never gave me any real sense of having someone or something solid to cling to.

Nonsense. All that was a cop-out. She was just timid under that outward appearance of competence. She supposed that inside she'd never really grown up. She wasn't even as tuned in to nuances as Tommy, or as cynical as Maryanne. Certainly not as enlightened and sensible as her daughter-in-law, nor as practical and realistic as Sally. What do I think I am? Sheila wondered. *Who* do I think I am? Eight months widowed and two men have seemed interested in me. I should be strutting with pride instead of wallowing in ridiculous apprehensions about tomorrow.

The next day she asked Kitty Rawlings if she could have a few days off toward the end of the month to visit her son in Florida. Kitty wasn't delighted, but she agreed.

"I know you miss him, Sheila, but he *will* be home in a couple of months."

She hated lying. Surprising how easy it was. "Yes, but when I talked to my in-laws last night I had the feeling I should get down there. Tommy's restless and they're worried."

Her boss accepted that. "How long will you be gone?"

"About five days, I guess. Naturally, I know I won't be paid. I'm not entitled to vacation time yet and you were so dear when I had that trouble with Tommy the first of the year. I really appreciate this."

She didn't wait for Bill to call. She called him that evening.

"You have a house guest in Bermuda."

He didn't disguise his joy. "Darling, that's fantastic! I'll send you your plane ticket to New York and less than two hours later we'll be basking in sunshine. Unless you want to stay over between planes and see Rose."

"God, no! She mustn't even know I've been in the airport!"

He laughed. "All right, little girl, we'll keep your guilty secret from Mama. Probably a good idea. If I remember Rose, she'd be out there waiting for us with a shotgun."

"You remember Rose," Sheila agreed.

They set the exact date of her arrival.

"Of course I'll talk to you a dozen times before," Bill said.

"Will you?"

"Of course I will," he repeated. "Sheila, darling, don't you think I know how insecure you are? God knows why, but I think you find it hard to believe that anybody can love you." He paused. "Isn't it about time you discovered how damned desirable you are?"

"I'm a middle-aged lady with frown lines and brown spots on the back of her hands."

"Knock it off!"

She laughed. "All right. I'm Raquel Welch with overtones of Marlene Dietrich and a touch of Doris Day. Better?"

"Not a helluva lot. You're *you*. That's the best."

The euphoria carried her through the next few days, enabled her to fib to Tommy and the senior Callahans, saying that she was being sent to Boston by the store as their representative at a seminar of booksellers. She told the same story to Rose, knowing that none of them was wise enough about publishing to know that such a thing was pure fiction, nor suspicious enough to wonder why the store would send a new employee if it were true. They accepted her imaginary triumph with pride which only made her feel guiltier.

She knew she couldn't get away with such an outlandish story to Patrick and Betty, so she told them she was exhausted and was going to Bermuda for a few days with a friend from the store.

"I know it's extravagant of me," she said, "but I just *have* to get away."

She had no idea whether they believed this almost equally improbable story, but if they didn't, they at least pretended to, telling her they thought it was great. They even offered to "dog-sit" while she was gone and on behalf of Mr. Magoo she gratefully accepted.

"I don't know how to reach Maryanne," Sheila said. "I have no idea where she is. I get a postcard now and then but she's never in one spot long enough to get mail."

"How's she doing?" Patrick asked, the concerned words underlaid with annoyance at his sister's behavior.

"Very well, according to her cards. Maybe she'll make a real career out of all this."

Pat snorted in response. It was Betty who understood Sheila's worries.

"Maryanne will be all right," Betty said. "You've done everything you can for her, Sheila. She's just taking a long time to grow up."

"A helluva long time," Pat said. "She's as old as you are. When is that dumb girl going to get wise to herself? She's no singer! She's nothing but a—"

"Pat!" Betty interrupted her husband.

He looked at Sheila's stricken face. "I'm sorry, Mom. I didn't mean that. I know how you worry about Maryanne and it makes me mad that she adds to your problems. Tom okay?"

Reality again descended like a black cloud on Sheila. For a couple of days she'd felt as giddy as a girl going off on an adventure. Even the dissembling had been part of the game. She'd been almost wickedly amused by it. But the discussion of her children brought everything back in a wave of unhappiness.

"Tommy seemed all right when I talked with him," she said in answer to Pat's question, "but I don't think he's happy in Florida. He's anxious to come home. I don't know. Maybe I did the wrong thing, sending him away."

Betty tried to reassure her. "It was the right thing. It really was. Don't take kids his age too seriously. I see a lot of them where I work. It's rough being a teen-ager and they make it tough on everybody around them. Especially on the people they love most." She put her arm around Sheila. "You've been through a lot this last year. I'm glad you're going to have a little holiday."

Sally Cantrell said almost the same thing when she heard the truth about the Bermuda trip and what had led up to it.

"Good for you! You deserve a little fun. And don't give me that guilty look. Your Bill Reardon sounds like quite a man. Believe me, I'm impressed! All the lone women we know would give their eyeteeth for a few glamorous days in Bermuda with a real guy! Including me."

"I do feel guilty," Sheila admitted. "Dashing off with a man I've seen only three days in almost thirty years. Lying to everybody except you about what I'm doing. It just isn't me, Sally. I don't know what's come over me."

"My God, Sheila, you're a couple of grown people known, I believe, as 'consenting adults.' Stop acting like you're committing some immortal sin! I have only one regret. I wish that little cock-of-the-walk Jerry Mancini knew how attractive you are to somebody as super as Bill Reardon. I'll bet that damned little egotist thinks you're still carrying a torch as big as the Statue of Liberty." Something in Sheila's face stopped her. "You aren't, are you? Don't tell me you still think about that bastard? I swear Sheila, I'll kill you!"

Sheila denied it. "Of course I don't think of Jerry. That's over and done with. Just one of those foolish things."

More lies. She thought of him often. Wondered whether he and Barbara were happy. Wondered if and how she could have held him. For all her attraction to Bill, Jerry was not yet a painless memory. He'd been excitement when she needed it most, reassurance when she thought bleak, lonely widowhood was all she had to look forward to. He'd made her feel vital, alive, as though she drank of his youth. Sally couldn't understand that. No one could. They saw only a selfish, shallow young man who'd found her momentarily diverting. He'd "toyed with her affections," Rose would have said. Sheila smiled. All of them were right. But for a couple of months, even less, she'd felt like a girl again. Sheila Callahan, soon to be a grandmother, had seen herself through the admiring, demanding eyes of her "unsuitable" lover. It had been an exciting reflection, fleeting but ecstatic. They were wrong to blame Jerry for "abandoning" her. People made mistakes. He wanted his wife and child back. That didn't mean that he'd lost all feeling for Sheila. In a funny way he *did* love me, she thought stubbornly. We needed each other.

Her feeling for Bill was safer, more subject to approval by her peers. There was excitement there, but of a more passive kind. If anything came of her renewed romance—and, realistically, it was a big "if"—it would be based on more than reckless passion. There'd be physical pleasure, hopefully. But there'd be a soothing feeling of serenity and companionship. God, how she hated that word! Companionship was what old people sought when sexual attraction was over and loneliness was the enemy. The young didn't need companionship or mutual interests or suitability of background. They lived on lust. Look at Maryanne and Rick. There never were two more totally disparate people, yet they shared a greedy desire for danger, for life. They're wrong and foolish, Sheila thought. And yet I almost envy their lack of inhibitions, their refusal to conform. I must be going mad, comparing myself to my daughter, half sympathizing with her unreasonable search for stimulation.

She was aware that Sally was talking again and she made herself listen.

"You just don't appreciate how lucky you are, Sheila, running into an attractive, eligible man! It's not the story of most middle-aged widows, I promise you. Nor middle-aged divorcées, either. What do you think about Bill Reardon? Is he serious?"

"I haven't the faintest idea. I can't believe there isn't someone else in his life, though he says not. A man like that doesn't stay unencumbered for three years."

"But if he *is* serious, would you marry him?"

Sheila looked startled. "I don't know," she said slowly. "I haven't really let myself think that far ahead."

"You should. It would be a good thing all around. He could take care of you. From what you told me of his marriage, he seems a faithful, devoted type. Forgive me if I seem tactless, but I don't think you'd go through with Reardon what you went through with Sean."

Sheila tried to be flippant. "What makes you so sure? He's another wild Irishman."

"There are Irish and there are Irish. Look at Terry."

"God spare me!" Sheila laughed. "I'd rather have lived with Sean and his shenanigans than Terry and his middle-class morality!" She sobered. "I'm confused, Sally. Too much has happened too fast. And I can't think only of myself. I still have the children to consider."

"The only one is Tommy and you know Bill would like him. It would be almost like a replacement for the son he lost."

"Maybe. But would Tommy like Bill?" She remembered the resentment in the boy's voice when she'd told him on the phone about running into an "old friend."

Sally couldn't conceal her impatience. "Use your head! You can't let a teen-ager dictate your future! Tommy'd be happy if he had you to himself forever. At least that's the way he feels right now. You're his only security, Sheila. But in a few years that will pass. He'll be on his own and where will you be? Still alone in that big house? Still selling books at Higbee's? Still scratching for every penny? Good Lord, make sense! Stop worrying about your kids. They sure don't worry much about you!"

Sheila bristled. "That's not true! Pat and Betty have been very attentive. And Tommy's first thought when Sean died was what was going to happen to me. Even Maryanne made an effort to come home for a while."

"Terrific. How often have you seen Pat and Betty in the past months? What has Tommy done except sulk around the house, furious that he had to change schools and finally getting into trouble that damned near killed you? As for Maryanne, she might get A for effort, but she had a short career as a dutiful daughter and right now you don't even know where she is! I'm sorry, Sheila, but I could really shake you! You seem to have the idea that you have to live for everybody else. As though *you* don't count. It's ridiculous and unbecoming."

Coming from anyone else, Sheila would have been furious. But she knew the depths of Sally's devotion, how deliberately she was trying to ease her friend's conscience. There was some truth—a lot of it—in what

Sally said. But the real purpose, Sheila knew, was to assuage her guilt, real or imagined, about being a "bad mother."

Sheila smiled gratefully. "You missed your calling. You'd have made a hell of a psychotherapist."

Sally returned the smile. "I'd have been a lousy one. I get too emotionally involved. But there's one thing I do know: I've seen too many self-sacrificing widows let good chances go by because they feel they must 'devote their lives to their children.' They end up sad, lonely old ladies with lavender-blue hair and TV dinners. That's not for you, my girl. You've given almost twenty-eight years to a husband and children who took you for granted. And now you're torturing yourself because you're going to have a small, illicit fling which may or may not lead to a better life for you. So you've told a few lies. Big deal! I wish you hadn't. I wish you'd told everybody exactly where you're going. The shock might have been good for them."

"There's nobody like you, Sally."

"Hooray!"

"No, I mean it. You see everything so clearly."

"Do I? Then how come I didn't see Fred Cantrell getting out his road maps for the Fountain of Youth? It's easy to be smart about everybody else, Sheila. It's practically impossible to be objective about your own life. I can sit here and give you all kinds of advice about what you should do. Like some damned Delphi oracle. But I haven't done well about my own status. Financially, yes. Emotionally, no. Fortunately for me, I'm not like you, dear. I can live very well without a man. I don't think you can. Not that it's anything to be ashamed of. People are just different."

It was the second time in two weeks that someone she respected had said she was a woman who needed a man. Neither of them meant only sex. That was always available if the need was purely therapeutic and the emotions untouched. They meant she was the kind of loving female who needed to belong, to share, to feel complete only as part of someone else.

I must be a very unmodern woman, Sheila thought. Because they're so right.

Chapter 24

Funny how different Bermuda was from the way she'd imagined it. She'd thought it would be full of, well, "tacky" tourists. That is, she'd heard of it as Honeymoon Heaven for the middle-class young, or the day-long stop of a cruise ship. She had visualized it as full of self-conscious young men and their simpering brides, intermingled with paunchy older men in flowered sports shirts and aging women with garish straw handbags purchased in another port of call.

She and Bill stepped off the plane into quite a different atmosphere. There were, to be sure, a great number of couples with "Just Married" clearly etched on their faces, but the passengers who surged toward the immigration and custom stations looked much more chic and well traveled than she'd expected and so did the people waiting to meet them. The Bermudians were mostly attractive young matrons in good-looking sports clothes, their tanned arms and legs indicating hours on golf courses or in swimming pools, their eyes bright under the brims of poplin hats clearly bought on Fifth Avenue. The "cruise crowd" she'd imagined was not to be seen. But then, Sheila realized, they wouldn't be at the airport. They'd be downtown, where the ships docked, buying all the Wedgwood ashtrays and cashmere sweaters in sight.

Reardon seemed to get special treatment. They were whisked through the formalities of arrival with little delay and in a few minutes were in a cab heading toward Tuckerstown.

216

"You seem to be a big man in Bermuda," Sheila said. "I'd guess that was VIP treatment."

"Semi-VIP. They know me, of course, since I own a house here. It's really quite a small island, almost like a small town for people who maintain residences. The cabdrivers and mailmen don't know from street addresses. They identify every house by its name—"The Jungle" or "Fishpond," for instance—and they know who lives where, and what they're up to." Bill glanced at her, amused. "In twenty minutes, everybody who counts will be well aware that I've arrived with a house guest. Do you mind?"

Sheila deliberately didn't answer. Instead, she looked out of the cab window. "It seems strange to be driving on the wrong side of the road," she said irrelevantly.

"Takes a little getting used to at first, but you adjust quickly. I keep a car at the house, by the way. We'll do some sightseeing, if you like."

"I'd love it. The island is so beautiful!" She jumped as a motorcycle swerved in front of them. Its helmeted young driver saluted as he passed, and the young girl hanging on to his waist from behind laughed as she caught a glimpse of Sheila's frightened face.

"Damn fools!" Bill said. "That's the favorite form of transportation—souped-up motorbikes—and the most deadly. More people kill themselves on those things, doing just what that young idiot did! Thank God they're forced to wear helmets or the mortality rate would be even higher." He took her hand. "Relax, honey. We're almost there."

"What's the name of your house?"

"You won't laugh?"

"I promise."

"All right. It's called 'Cat's Corner.' "

Sheila burst out laughing. Bill looked at her reproachfully. "You promised not to laugh."

"I'm sorry. It's such a ridiculous name."

"I know. I agree. But unfortunately it was already named when I bought it. I suppose the original owners could have called it 'The Cat House' which would have been even worse."

"Why the name?" Sheila asked.

"The woods around it are full of wild cats. Not wildcats, like tigers and jaguars, but beautiful little things that multiply like rabbits. The island is overrun with them, poor little beggars. We have to catch as many as we can and take them to the ASPCA before they starve to death. It's one of the things I least enjoy, trapping them and carting them off to the shelter. But we have to try to keep the feline population under control, for their sake as well as ours. It's like the frogs. We're overrun with them, too, but there's nothing to be done. Years and years ago some well-meaning soul imported a pair of frogs to keep the insects in check. Now we have generations of the damned, ugly, croaking things everywhere. It's startling when you drive at night, seeing their eyes suddenly caught in your headlights."

Sheila shuddered. "Any more unattractive things to tell me about Bermuda?"

Bill thought. "No, not really. We have a shortage of good domestic help, occasional problems with electricity and water supply, and some fairly unpredictable weather. But those are transient woes. The wee beasties are the only continuing pain in the derrière." He smiled. "And the marvelous things so far outweigh the minor inconveniences. It's glorious here, Sheila. I hope you'll love it as much as I do. I only wish I could spend more time at Cat's Corner. Some day maybe I will. If I ever become a rich and famous author, I might even move here."

"I," Sheila thought, listening to him. He never intends to marry again. I suppose Sean might have felt the same if I'd died first. Not that Sean worshiped me the way Bill did Eileene, but the Irish are meant to be free. At least, the Irish *men*.

The cab pulled into a little driveway and stopped in front of what appeared to be a graceful but tiny house. Sheila must have looked a little surprised. All the way to Tuckerstown she'd caught glimpses of big, beautiful homes with Olympic-sized swimming pools and elaborate boat docks. Bill's, by contrast, seemed almost ordinary despite its pleasant lines, its perfect paint job, and the profusion of oleanders and hibiscus that surrounded it. Her expression didn't escape him.

"It's an ass-backwards place," he said. "This is officially the front, but I have a surprise for you on the other side." He opened a gate and Sheila stepped into another world. The rear of the house faced a spectacular view of the open sea on one side, a quiet cove on the other. It sat high above both waters, with a green lawn sloping gently down and lush groves of trees punctuating the landscape. Masses of flowers bloomed everywhere, in the ground, in huge stone pots surrounding a clear and beautiful swimming pool, rampaging in exotic profusion over a broad terrace with deep chaises and chairs and an elegant outdoor dining arrangement. Everything danced and glittered, from the sunlight sparkling on the blue-green water far below to the shiny red rubber ball that drifted gaily from one end of the swimming pool to the other. On the horizon she saw the colorful sails of pleasure boats and the white roofs of surrounding houses, all far enough apart to insure privacy for each.

Bill watched her, delighted by her amazement. "Like it?"

"*Like* it? It's fairyland! I never saw anything so beautiful in my life! Oh, Bill, it's heavenly!"

"Come see the rest. You haven't seen the inside of the house yet. It's not enormous, but it's workable."

The house was enchanting. From the terrace they entered a huge beige-and-white living room with a fireplace and windows that offered a view from every side. There was a small but attractive paneled dining room, a first-floor powder room, maid's room, laundry, and the most complete kitchen Sheila had ever seen.

"I can't get over it!" she said. "I didn't know you were an interior decorator as well as a writer."

He hesitated. "I'd like to take credit, but I can't. A friend of mine did it all for me. She has good taste, I think."

Sheila felt a little pang. Of course some woman would have to have decorated this warm, subtle house with all its perfect appointments. Someone, she thought, who probably spent a lot of time here with Bill. Why was she jealous? Hadn't he said there'd been women since Eileene's death? Why not, for heaven's sake?

"She did a beautiful job, Bill. It's perfect."

He led her up a winding stairway and down a small hall to the master bedroom. Again that damned impeccable taste, Sheila thought almost grudgingly. It was a big, comfortable room with a king-sized bed, ample drawer space and closets, and two deep chairs flanking a fireplace. It was neither aggressively masculine nor unsuitably feminine, done in the beige and white of the living room, with touches of dark brown and Bristol blue in simple but elegant appointments. A room any couple would feel at home in. Or any man or woman alone.

Next to it, with its own bath, was a smaller, equally "anonymous" guest room, suitable for either sex. I hate the woman who did this house, Sheila thought. She's too damned bright. Who was she? Sheila was tempted to ask. Or, discouraging thought, who *is* she?

"What do you think?" Bill waited for her reaction.

"Perfection," Sheila said again. "Sheer perfection."

"There's a little guest house on the property. Just one room and bath that we made over out of a gardening cottage, but it works well when there's an overflow of visitors." He seemed suddenly shy. "I could stay out there if you'd feel better about it. I mean . . . oh, hell, Sheila, you know what I mean! Dammit, why do you always do this to me? I had every intention of our sleeping together in my bed and here I am wondering if you'd be more comfortable if I were in a different house! I must be crazy. I feel like a damned schoolboy!"

She was quiet for a moment. "Bill. The woman who decorated this house. Is she still in your life?"

It seemed an abrupt change of topic and yet he understood. "If you mean, am I having an affair with her, the answer is no. I *had* an affair with the woman who did this place. She's a delightful person, and after the shock of Eileene's death, I turned to her. She was generous with her love and her loyalty. And her help. But we were never in love, Sheila. We stayed here together, but it was never 'our' place, it was always *mine*.

219

We both knew that from the start. Just as we knew we weren't suited for marriage to each other. She's married now, to a good friend of mine. I see them both often. I told you in Cleveland that I have no one to account to. I'm sometimes a nut, sometimes a wild Irishman, a dreamer. But a liar I'm *not*, darling. And *that* you can count on." He smiled. "We seem to have gotten off the subject of sleeping arrangements. Or have we?"

She shook her head. "Not really. I didn't come here for a platonic visit, Bill. I came to be with you, fully and without a care. But I saw this house and I wondered. Now I know. And I believe you. I not only want you in the same house. I want you in the same bed."

He pulled her to him and kissed her as he had that last night in Cleveland. But this time there was no taxi at the door. And it was a long time before Sheila remembered that she hadn't even unpacked the suitcase.

From that moment, they were like two perpetually surprised people. They made love not as though it was their first time together but as though each knew from experience exactly how to please the other. For Sheila, it was unlike anything she'd ever known. Her lovemaking with Sean had been strong and passionate, but she was always the giver, as though she'd felt unconsciously that the duty to please was her responsibility. Not that she hadn't enjoyed Sean's lovemaking. But she'd never realized the tenderness, the concern for *her* pleasure that was possible with a sensitive man. Jerry had not had this delicacy of feeling, either. His lovemaking was thrilling, perhaps because his body was so young and beautiful, his confidence as strong as his desire.

With Bill, it was different. There was excitement and complete satisfaction, an animal maleness in his demands, yet with a gentleness that made her want to make him happy and be happy herself. She loved the firmness of his body, the strength of his hands, the feel of his mouth on hers. And she loved the quiet moments after their lovemaking when they lay in the big bed, soaking up the stillness outside, talking in almost awed tones of the coincidence that had brought them together again.

"I can't believe it," Bill said over and over. "I still honest-to-God can't believe it."

Sheila kissed him. "You're repeating yourself, my darling. It's a sure sign of advancing age."

"Nonsense. I'm a mere broth of a boy!" He held her slim body close to his. "And you're still a wee lass."

"Professional Irishman!"

"Yeah. I forgot. Can't get away with that with you, can I?" He caressed her lightly. "I've thought of this so often over the years, Sheila, without the slightest hope that it would ever happen. You are wonderful, my darling. Completely, womanly wonderful." They lay quiet for a moment, content to be close. "Maybe this was the way it was always intended to be," Bill said finally, almost as though he was thinking aloud. "Maybe if we'd made love as kids we'd never have appreciated each other as we do now, after all the years and all the experiences." He looked down at her composed, satisfied face. "Sheila, I love you so much. I'm more capable of love than that boy you knew in New York. More grateful for it coming this late."

Eyes closed, drinking in every word, she didn't answer.

"Sheila?"

"Yes?"

"I thought I never wanted to marry again. I was sure I'd never find anyone right for me. I told myself that any new woman who came into my life would never be able to replace what I'd lost. And I was right. Because you are not a new woman, you are my rediscovered love. You've been there all the time. We've only been separated. Sheila, you will marry me, won't you?"

Her slight pause filled him with panic. "God, don't say no! There's no one else is there? There couldn't be. Not with what I know you've felt these past days and nights!"

"No, darling, there's no one else. But there's something I have to tell you. Something I left out in Cleveland when I told you about my life. I don't know why I think it's important you know, except that I want you to know everything about me, including what a vain and silly woman you're proposing to."

She told him about Jerry, how it started, what composure she felt at first and how she changed later, how disillusioned she was and how disgusted by her own foolishness. "It's over now. All of it. Including the way I felt about him. But I wanted to tell you. I don't want any secrets between us. Not ever."

He held her. "Such a silly girl! But it was merely an experience, darling, and not one to feel apologetic about. Nor guilty. You were desperate for comfort and reassurance. I know that feeling all too well. Your doctor was also your medicine, sweetheart. And when the patient gets well, neither is necessary."

"But I was such a stupid ass! And it happened so soon after Sean! You must think I'm a nymphomaniac."

"Never doubted it for a moment," he teased. "Sheila, I don't give a damn about any of that, as long as you're over it. You *are* over it, aren't you?"

"Of course. If I wasn't before, you've cured me completely. Oh Bill, I've never been so happy!"

He began to kiss her. She felt desire starting in both of them, the wonderful anticipation of their coming together. And then suddenly he stopped and pulled himself up, his face inches from hers.

"You haven't answered me!"

She pulled his head down to hers. "Marry you? Just try to get away and I'll see you never sell another book in Higbee's!"

"What the hell makes you think *you* will?"

She hadn't thought about it. How her life was going to change when she became Mrs. William Reardon. Where would they live? What would the children say? And Sean's parents? Rose would be happy, but . . .

Her body stiffened as these questions came into her mind. Bill sensed it.

"This, my darling, is an emotional moment. Whatever you're thinking, forget it. Forget everything but us and this magic. I know how to make you do that."

It is magic, Sheila thought. All of it. She gave herself, gladly, mindlessly to the mystery and the wonder.

When they were not happily surrendering to their passion, they spent the days at the pool or on the golf course at Mid Ocean, the club to which Bill belonged. He introduced her to his friends and Sheila found them pleasant, rich and understandably curious. Some of the widows, with which Bermuda abounded, probably were none too pleased to see their favorite bachelor so unashamedly devoted to his "friend" Mrs. Callahan, but they politely accepted the lady from Cleveland and speculated in their morning phone calls about the obvious romance and whether Bill Reardon was really "hooked."

From that first afternoon, Bill had had no doubt that he was. Strange. It wasn't simply their physical compatibility which was enormous, it was something more. Something about the way Sheila seemed so right in his house, the way he instinctively knew she'd be right in any house he chose, whether it was this Bermuda haven, an apartment in New York, or even a strange old castle in Ireland that he'd always wanted to buy. She'd adjust anywhere to his environment, his restless way of life. Perhaps he had Sean to thank for that. Sheila was used to living each day, taking it in stride. Almost guiltily, he realized that was the one quality Eileene lacked. Though she'd never complained about his unpredictable actions, had even been lovingly tolerant, she'd wanted solid footing, roots. It was why he'd bought the East Hampton house, to give her a feeling of security. It had been important to her, "owning something substantial." He'd liked it, just as he liked Cat's Corner, but he'd never felt fierce possessiveness about any inanimate thing. He doubted Sheila did either. He imagined she'd clung to the Cleveland house more out of economic necessity than sentimentality. She'd pick up and go with him anywhere, any time. And be joyous about it. She'd understand, as Eileene, despite her protestations, never had. Writers had to be free, to be unconstricted by middle-class rules. He'd never leave her penniless and burdened, as Sean Callahan had. But he could never "settle down" the way most women he met wanted to—in one spot, with one set of friends, one daily, monotonous vista from the same picture window in the same stultifying suburb.

He wondered why he was so sure of this. Sheila had lived that way, in the same house for twenty-seven years, with the same routine and the same social circle. Yet he believed it was not what she really wanted, any more than he did. She did it for her children, for the convenience of a husband who demanded an outwardly conventional home base to which he could return from his wanderings. Bill sensed, in the little things Sheila said, that she felt a prisoner in Cleveland and a captive in her marriage. It probably was why she had broken loose in such a "scandalous" way with that young doctor so soon after Sean's death. Without realizing it, she'd told him about Mancini to unconsciously show that the spirit of adventure, bottled up for more than a quarter of a century, had spilled out when she was free. He loved her for her loyalty to her family, but he applauded the burning desire within her to taste more of life than could be found in Shaker Heights. He'd show her what excitement really was. Not the kind of nervous uncertainty she'd lived through with Sean's wild financial schemes and his flagrant infidelity, but a life-loving kind of enjoyment of every precious day.

He tried to tell her some of this their last night in Bermuda. To his surprise, she looked thoughtful, almost worried.

"Don't tell me I'm wrong about you, love," Bill said. "I've listened very carefully to everything you've said these past five days, watched your face as you discovered a new way of life. You've been like a blossoming flower, a quite different woman from that careful Ohio matron I was lucky enough to find again. I know you haven't had much security, Sheila, in the usual sense of the word, but you're not Rose, caring about the same kind of circumscribed life style she's known for fifty years, fearful that tomorrow will bring something different and frightening. Life with me won't be Sean all over again, but it may be unpredictable. That's what will make it fun."

Sheila searched carefully for the right words. He was right about so much of it. But perhaps not all of it. She'd thought sometimes, in these months since Sean died, that all she wanted was peace, an untroubled existence with some dependable man who'd make her feel safe. Even Jerry had seemed to offer some of that. He was necessarily regimented in his life style by his profession. His income was assured. He'd live in one place, move in proscribed circles. He wasn't another fey Irishman. She'd had one of those.

Not that Bill was anything like Sean. But like Sean, he had a lust for life that was both exhilarating and frightening. She wondered whether she could go through it all again, all the defiance of regimentation that a big expansive man such as Bill Reardon found irresistible. And yet, for all his freedom-worship, Bill would be a good husband. More constant than Sean, more compatible than Jerry, even if she'd been able to have Jerry. What *did* she want? These five days had been bliss. She was sure she loved Bill, that she'd be happy married to him. And yet something inside made her wary. Where was the dull dependability she should be seeking after all the years of turmoil? It could be found with someone like Bob Ross, solid, strong, unimaginative, cautious man that he was. But she didn't want Bob. Probably she didn't really want the kind of life he represented.

Long minutes passed before she answered Bill. He said nothing, simply watching her from his chair on the opposite side of the fireplace. Waiting to be reassured that he read her right; that she wanted the glorious, adventurous years left to both of them. And I do, Sheila told herself. I love this laughing, lusty, unafraid man. I've been hanging on to my old life for the sake of my children, stupidly anxious to maintain a home that none of them really gives a damn about. Suddenly she felt lighthearted and young. She crossed the little space and curled up in Bill's lap smiling.

"You're not wrong about me," Sheila said. "I want what you want. I want you." He started to kiss her but she stopped him. "Still and all, darling, we can't forget that I don't come to you unencumbered. I have my kids, Tommy especially. He's a problem. He may be one for some time to come. Are you sure you want to take on an unfathomable stepdaughter like Maryanne and a possibly resentful teen-ager like Tommy?"

"I'd take on a collection of hooded cobras if it meant having you."

"Cobras can be put in a basket with a lid on. Kids are less controllable."

Bill stroked her hair. "Poor baby. Always looking for trouble."

"I haven't had to look far these past months."

He nodded. "I know. I'm not being unsympathetic, but it doesn't scare me. We'll do what we can for Maryanne, if she'll let us. As for Tommy, there's a little selfishness on my part. Remember I lost a son just about his age. It's like God's gift to find that the woman I love also brings me a replacement. I may turn out to be the best thing that could happen to our boy at this stage of life. God knows I'll try. Maybe it won't be easy at first for any of us. We may be jealous of your love. You may be torn between us. But eventually it'll work, sweetheart, because you and I want it to now, and Tommy will come to want the same thing. I believe that, Sheila. You must, too."

She kissed him. "I do. I truly do."

"Then that's settled. Hallelujah! Let's open a bottle of champagne and have terrible headaches on the flight tomorrow. Damn, I wish we didn't have to go back so soon! Must we?"

"We must. You know you have to be in Atlanta next week for the book. And I have a lot of organizing to do at home."

"Let's get married right away. The week I get back from Atlanta.

Where do you want the wedding to be, Cleveland? New York? Pago-Pago? Calcutta? Very interesting, India. You could come to the altar on a jewel-bedecked elephant."

She was laughing. "Idiot!" Then she sobered. "Darling, take it easy. There's so much to do, so much to decide. And so many people to prepare for this shock."

"To hell with giving Kitty Rawlings two weeks' notice. She'll just have to manage without you."

She slapped him playfully. "*Will* you be serious? How about July?"

"July! That's two months off!"

"You'll survive. Dearest, I must wait until Tommy comes home in June to prepare him for this. We have to decide where we'll live, and . . ."

"Hold it. Not Shaker Heights, okay? Let's set up our first base in New York and take it from there. I need that for headquarters, honey, close to my editor and agent and all my contacts. Cleveland's fine, but I can't operate out of there. We'll go back as often as you like to see our doctor-son and wife and our new grandchild, but my first request is that you put that mausoleum on the market as soon as you get home."

"But Bob Ross says that this isn't a good time to sell."

"Then rent it. Or give it away. To hell with Bob Ross, personally and professionally." He was in earnest. "I don't even buy the Tommy preparation. We could go to Palm Beach week after next and talk to him, or bring him back before the end of the term. But I can tell by your face that that's an even bigger problem than the house, so I'll give in. I know how much you want him to accept this. I won't give you a hard time about the delay, even though there's going to be a helluva lot of commuting in the next few weeks, New York to Cleveland and vice versa. You've spoiled me, lady. I'm the impatient lover."

"You have a right to be," Sheila said softly. "We've waited almost thirty years."

Chapter 25

        She couldn't believe how much mail had piled up in only
five days. The mailbox looked as though she'd been gone a month. Sheila
sorted idly through the pile, discarding the catalogues from obscure gift
shops in Wisconsin (how *did* one get on so many peculiar mailing lists?),
the pleas from strange charities (Sean always swore that most of the
"missionaries" were only mimeograph machines in somebody's basement), the bills which no longer came predictably on the first of the
month but arrived daily, thanks to the computer age and something mys-
terious called "cycle billing." Every envelope she opened was impersonal
or expensive. Like so much of everybody's life. Not that there was anything impersonal about hers any longer. "I'm going to be Mrs. William
Reardon," she said aloud in the empty house. It sounded good to her.
How would it sound to the people whose approval she wanted? There
was no need to advertise her news to the world at large, but those closest
to her had to be told soon that she planned to remarry and leave Cleveland. She wished she knew how to reach Maryanne, had hoped there
might be one of the uninformative but possibly traceable cryptic postcards her daughter occasionally sent. If she knew even what city Maryanne was in, it might be a lead to the whereabouts of that ridiculous rock
group. What was it called? Oh yes, "The Potboilers." And Maryanne
called herself "Pattie Thomas." That much Sheila knew, but nothing of

her whereabouts. I must find her, Sheila thought, to tell her about Bill and me. Will she be pleased? I think so. I hope so. But more likely, if the truth were faced, Maryanne wouldn't care one way or the other, just as she didn't seem to care about anything, including her own life.

There were times, many of them, when Sheila forced herself to approach the idea that Maryanne was hell-bent on self-destruction, perhaps even literally. But she quickly thrust the terrible thought from her mind. It was an idea not to be maintained even momentarily. Whatever her daughter did, she would live. And while she lived, Sheila would never stop trying to help her.

God, how morbid she was! Only a moment ago she'd still been warm in the knowledge of her own sunny future. It was coming back to this house where she'd known so much anguish that plunged her into the old, cold doubts and fears. Bill was right. She'd put it on the market immediately, take whatever she could get for it, and leave behind forever the "green lawns of Shaker Heights."

Meanwhile, there were all the people to tell. She wanted to start with the easiest—Sally Cantrell. Her friend would be happy for her, enthusiastic and approving. But it was right that the family knew first. She called Pat and Betty and the latter answered.

"I'm home," Sheila said. "How are you two?"

"Sheila! Welcome back! Did you have a good time?"

"Marvelous. I have a lot to tell you and Pat. But first, how are you, Betty? Everything okay?"

"Super. I'm beginning to look like the noon balloon! I don't care what the doctors say, I know it's at least twins. If it isn't, I'm carrying an embryonic Totie Fields! Nobody since Mama Dionne could have looked this big at five-and-a-half months unless they had more than one inside!"

Sheila laughed. "How's Pat holding up?"

"He's fine. Skinny as a rail. I hate him. When are we going to see you?"

"As soon as possible. How about tomorrow? Is it Patrick's Sunday off?"

"It is and we have no plans. Come for dinner? I'm dying to hear about Bermuda. Pat's not here now, but he's just as anxious as I."

Sheila hesitated. "You haven't by chance heard anything of Maryanne, have you?"

Betty sounded surprised. "No, but we never do. Why? Anything wrong?"

"No, nothing's wrong. I'd just like to get in touch with her."

"Maybe I can find out something through the clinic next week. A lot of people down there know Rick and his chums. They might have some idea where the group is playing."

"I'd appreciate it, Betty. I'll explain tomorrow when I see you and Pat."

"You *sure* you're okay?"

"Never better. Just tired from the trip. I only got here half an hour ago. Haven't even unpacked."

"Oh. I thought maybe you were upset. I guess you haven't heard the latest gossip. Jerry Mancini and his wife have split again. I was afraid maybe he'd called and gotten you all shook up. He asked Pat about you yesterday and my damn fool husband told him you were getting back from Bermuda today. You know your son. He's so damned mad at the way Jerry behaved that he wanted him to know you were off having a swell vacation. Otherwise, Pat probably wouldn't have spoken to him at all. He hasn't, except professionally, for months."

Sheila felt a sinking sensation in the pit of her stomach. Jerry and Barbara were separated again and Jerry was inquiring about her. Then she was angry. Goddamn his nerve! How dare he? Did he think she'd be there with open arms waiting for him? She remembered Sally predicting that Jerry would be back, and her own positive reply that he wouldn't. Well, he won't, Sheila thought. Once is enough. And besides, now I have Bill.

The anger enabled her to manage a bitter little laugh. "Betty dear, Jerry Mancini could come crawling back on his hands and knees and I'd kick him in the teeth. I couldn't care less what he does with his life!"

She heard a sigh of relief. "That's what I hoped you'd say, Sheila. He's bad news."

"Well, I'm in no mood for bad news. Nothing but good from now on, honey. That's what I want to tell you and Pat tomorrow."

"My curiosity is killing me!"

"I'll tell you everything tomorrow. Love to Pat."

She was surprised to find herself trembling when she replaced the receiver. Idiot! Why are you even thinking about that selfish so-and-so? Yet when the phone rang almost immediately, she was afraid to pick it up. What if it was Jerry wanting to see her? Well, what if it was? She had no intention of ever seeing him again. She was over it. She'd had a lucky escape. God was good to her, sending her a man like Bill Reardon who loved her and who'd never fail her. On the fourth ring, she picked up the phone.

"I'm suffering from a terminal illness," the caller said. "It's called love."

She almost wept with relief. "Bill, darling. Oh, God, I'm so glad to hear your voice!"

"Well, now, that's a very proper attitude for an engaged lady. Suitably lonely, since we've been separated for almost five hours. I'll never live through eight weeks! Pack your bags and let's go back to Bermuda. To hell with Atlanta and Cleveland and houses and all that crap! What we need is another bout of oleander fever!"

She was laughing now, reassured, convinced by his nonsense that what she'd said to Betty was absolutely true: She *didn't* care what happened to Jerry Mancini and she *would* kick him in the teeth if he came near her.

"Darling, I miss you," she said. "I'm terminally ill, too, with the same marvelous disease. Thank God we'll linger with it for years!"

"Thirty or forty, at least."

"At least."

"Everything go okay with you? I felt terrible watching you get on that damned flight to Cleveland. Did you find everything all right?"

"Everything's fine. The only person I've spoken to is Betty who's large with child. I'm seeing them tomorrow night to tell them about us."

"*All* about us?"

"Only the respectable part. They'll guess the rest." She paused. "I'll wait until tomorrow to call Palm Beach. And then I'll call Mother."

"Shall I call her and announce my honorable intentions?"

"Don't bother. *She'll* call *you*. Probably right after she goes to church and lights a candle in front of the patron saint of prodigal daughters, whoever that is. She'll be one happy lady. She always wanted me to marry you, you know."

"Frankly, I didn't," Bill said. "She always scared hell out of me. Sheila, darling, do you know we're as silly as a couple of teen-agers?"

"Yes, and I love it. I almost can't believe it."

"Why not? Aren't good things supposed to happen to you?"

"I just don't want anything to go wrong."

He pretended to be exasperated. "Don't ever accuse *me* of being the professional Irishman! Talk about your superstitious Micks! Darling, nothing's going to go wrong. Nothing could. Now go to bed and dream of us. 'Forget thyself and all the world, put on each glaring light. The stars are watching overhead, sleep sweetly then. Good night.' Remember that?" He waited. "Sheila?"

"I'm having a lovely cry. Good night, darling."

Sally Cantrell called at ten o'clock on Sunday morning and Sheila answered sleepily.

"Did I wake you up?" Sally asked. "If I did, I'll kill myself!"

"No," Sheila lied. "I was awake. What time is it?"

"Ten o'clock. Ungodly hour on Sunday, but I couldn't wait to hear about your trip. How was it? Did you have a fantastic time? Is the Reardon the answer to a maiden's prayer?"

Sheila propped herself up in bed. "The answer to everything is 'yes.' Sally, it was glorious. And he wants me to marry him."

"You're *kidding!* You're *not* kidding! Sheila, I'm so happy for you! God help us, you *did* say yes, didn't you?"

"I did. We're planning on July."

"So far away? Why don't you do it now before he changes his mind?"

Sheila laughed. "You sound like Bill. Not the mind-changing part, but the do-it-right-away idea. I can't possibly marry him before then, Sally. There's too much to do. He insists we live in New York. I've got to quit my job, get rid of this house, pack up the lares and penates. . . . Lord knows how I'll even manage it that quickly! And there are the kids. I'm not going to tell Tommy until he gets home in June. And I don't even know where to find Maryanne. I want her to know my plans. I can't just disappear from her life."

Why not? Sally wanted to ask. It doesn't seem to bother her that she's dropped out of yours. But of course it didn't work that way. Not with mothers. Kids could ignore them, insult them, wound them, and they still hung on, hoping for a miracle. Sheila had done it more than once. She was still doing it.

"Well, maybe we can track her down if we really put our minds to it."

The hope in Sheila's voice was pathetic. "Really? How?"

Sally hadn't the faintest idea. She'd just said that off the top of her head, hoping to soothe Sheila. "Look," she said, "I know I awakened you. Get yourself some coffee and I'll drive over in an hour or so. By then we can have a coherent conversation, okay?"

"I'd love it. I'm so anxious to see you, Sally. You're one of the main reasons I'll hate leaving Cleveland."

"Well, I'll hate to have you go, but it's not as though we won't see each other often. You know I get to New York half a dozen times a year, and you'll be coming here for visits and . . . oh the hell with it! Let's save it all for later."

When she hung up, Sally thought how perfect the timing was. It was a blessing that Sheila had met Bill Reardon at this moment. She wished they were getting married tomorrow. Before Mancini reappeared and muddled Sheila's thinking again. That little snake, Sally muttered half aloud. She'd heard he was on the loose again. Sure as hell he'd be turning up on Sheila's doorstep with some phony, self-serving story. This time, please let her see him for what he really is, Sally prayed. Please let her be so much in love with Bill Reardon that she'll spit in Jerry Mancini's eye. I'll break her neck if she lets that bastard con her out of the best thing that's ever happened to her!

She wondered why she was so dead certain that Jerry would try to come back to Sheila. Easy. She knew the type. She only hoped there'd be no need to explain it to an incredibly naive and trusting Sheila. Damn. New York was too far away. And two months was too long. Maybe she could nudge her friend into pushing the wedding date up. Get her safely married to that old beau before Doctor Darling got his hands on her again. At least if they could find Maryanne, if everybody knew about the engagement to Reardon, if Sheila were "publicly committed," she'd not do something stupid.

Sally wondered again why she had this ominous feeling. Perhaps she wasn't giving Sheila enough credit. I'm worrying unnecessarily, she thought. She knows better than anyone that Jerry Mancini is chopped liver compared to Bill Reardon. Still, she went to the phone and called a New York number. If anybody could find Maryanne, Paul Birmingham could. He was the best damned theatrical agent in the world, and though he'd never bother with a shabby group like The Potboilers, he'd know how to find the guy who *did* book them. It was a long shot, but worth it. If it worked, at least they'd have the hurdle of Maryanne's ignorance out of the way.

The sleazy little bar on Ninth Avenue where The Potboilers had been playing for three weeks seemed hotter, smokier, and more oppressive than ever. Maryanne felt nauseous as she finished the last number before the midnight break. For a few minutes she thought she'd be unable to finish the song, that she'd throw up in the middle of it. But she got through it somehow and slumped down wearily at a side table, holding her head in her hands. Rick had been called to the telephone and he came back now, grinning from ear to ear. He didn't even notice how green she was. She hadn't told him she was two months pregnant.

"Hey, babe, guess who was on the phone!"

Maryanne took a deep breath. "Who?"

"Paul Birmingham, that's who!"

"Who's Paul Birmingham?"

He looked at her in disgust. "Who's Paul Birmingham?" he repeated. "Just the number-one talent agent in the business, that's all. Jesus! You don't know your ass from third base! What the hell's the matter with you, anyhow?"

"I don't feel well."

"Well you better *start* feeling well, kid. Birmingham's coming in tomorrow night to catch the act."

"I don't understand," Maryanne said. "We have an agent."

Rick snorted. "We have a schnook. Christ, if Birmingham would sign us, we'd really be on our way! To hell with Sandy Stein, that jerk. Booking us into rat holes like this! Birmingham's big time." Rick laughed. "If he digs us, we got it made. You can send those damned postcards to your mother from hotels we'll *really* be staying in!"

Maryanne stared at him. The nausea had receded but she felt empty, confused. "If Paul Birmingham's such a big wheel, why is he looking for us?"

"Damned if I know. Somebody must have clued him in. He mentioned a friend of his. Cantwell? Cromwell? Sally somebody."

"Sally Cantrell?"

"Yeah, that sounds right. You know her?"

"She lives in Cleveland. She's a friend of Mother's. Rick, I don't know what this is all about."

"Who cares? He's coming tomorrow night and, baby, we'd better be dynamite!" He looked at her closely. "You look lousy. You think you got the flu? Jesus! You better split and go to bed so you'll be okay tomorrow."

"I won't be okay for about seven months."

"What are you talking about?"

"I'm pregnant."

He stared at her. "Pregnant! Christ, what a bummer! What are you going to do about it?"

She looked back steadily. "What does one usually do about it?"

"Oh, no," Rick said. "No, you don't. I'm not doing the marriage bit."

"Who asked you?"

"You're crazy! You're not telling me you're going to have this kid anyway!"

Maryanne didn't answer.

Rick was in a rage. "How stupid can you get? What the hell are you trying to prove—that you're some enlightened broad who can have a baby and bring it up by herself? You can't even take care of *yourself!*" He snorted. "That's damned obvious."

She didn't answer.

Rick studied her for a moment. Then he said, more quietly, "I get it. It's the old religious background showing through, isn't it? Abortion is a sin. You'll go to hell for taking a human life, right? Boy, that's a laugh! Except for when your father died, you haven't been in a church for years. Your confession would take a weekend!"

It was like talking to a dead woman. Maryanne didn't move or change expression. Except for an involuntary, nervous drumming of her fingers on the table top, she might have been in a trance. Rick tried wheedling.

"Come on, baby. I know how you feel, but having a kid would be punishment for it *and* you. Growing up with no father, finding out he's a bastard, living God-knows-how with a mother who never wanted him? Is *that* Christian? Listen, honey, there was a damned good reason the Supreme Court legalized abortion, over all the hue and cry. Just for women like you. Isn't that what the libbers say—that you have a right to choose what happens to your body? Make sense, Maryanne. In a week this can be all over, right here in New York, safe and legal. Nobody will know."

She spoke for the first time. "*I'll* know. All my life I'll know." She looked haunted. "What if our mothers had done that to us, Rick? We'd never have been born."

"I can think of worse things. I imagine our mothers can too." He stopped. "That's it, isn't it? This is the excuse you've been looking for to go home to Mommy. You have a screwed-up, face-saving reason to run now, don't you? Poor little orphan of the storm, appearing on the doorstep with a fatherless infant in her arms. Maybe it will be snowing. That would make the picture complete!" He was thoughtful. "Yeah. Sure. That's it. It's got everything. You can run home and hide and you get your final revenge at the same time—by making Mama feel guilty as hell! It's a beauty! A real double-barreled zinger! Sheila will spend her life atoning for your sins. Feeling *she* went wrong somewhere. You'll love every minute of it, won't you? All that jazz about hating Shaker Heights and the conventional life! What a crock! You really hate your mother. You're jealous of her. Furious that she wasn't destroyed by the death of your father. You'll fix her, won't you, Maryanne? You'll present her with a nice, neat armful of responsibility that'll be living proof of how she failed you."

Maryanne's face went white under the make-up. "You're insane! What the hell do you think you have, a mail-order degree in psychology? You're a pig! A dirty, rotten, stupid pig! You're scum, Rick. God knows why I ever wanted to be with you. You're nothing!"

He smiled. "I'm something. I'm the father of that kid. At least I guess I am."

She slapped him hard across the face. People at nearby tables turned to stare, vaguely amused at the argument between the leader of the group and his girl singer.

Maryanne got up. "That's it," she said. "Get yourself another dumb broad—in the band and in bed!" She started toward the exit. Rick went after her. In the two-by-four cubicle that served as her "dressing room," he tried to undo the damage.

"Honey, wait! I'm sorry I said all those dumb things. I was just being crazy. We'll work it out, Mare. We'll talk quietly about the baby. About what you want to do. We can't discuss it here. Simmer down. I was wrong. Look, I'm apologizing. What more do you want?"

"Nothing," Maryanne said. "Nothing more."

He misunderstood. "Okay. We'll do the last set and then go home and talk. We'll find a solution."

"I already know the solution. Good-by, Rick."

"Good-by? What do you mean, 'good-by'? You can't walk out on me like this! What about us? What about our big chance? Paul Birmingham's coming tomorrow night. That Cantrell woman probably sent him because of you! What am I supposed to tell him?"

"Tell him I've gone to hell and I only wish I could take you with me."

For a moment Rick stared at the door Maryanne slammed behind her. Damned, neurotic bitch! He didn't believe she'd gone for good. She'd be at the hotel when he got there later. She'd left before and always come back. Have a baby? She had no intention of having a baby. She was just dramatizing the situation, the way she did everything. Unstable, that's what she was. Living with him, leaving, returning. One minute fantasizing about being a top recording star and the next minute picturing herself as a mother. Christ, she was unbelievable! She'd have the abortion. Day after tomorrow. As soon as it could be arranged. She was his entree to Paul Birmingham and the Big Time. He'd put up with enough from her not to let her blow this contact, the first important one he'd ever made.

Savagely, Rick kicked over the wastebasket. Crumpled Kleenex scattered over on the floor, and the remains of a corned-beef-on-rye fell under the rickety chair in front of the make-up table. He looked at it with disgust. No more crappy Ninth Avenue bars and sandwiches from the corner deli. If somebody had enough interest in Maryanne to get the hottest agent in the business over here to see her, she damned well would be here to be seen. He'd make sure of that, if he had to literally beat her into it.

Nothing like a middle-class broad to give you trouble, Rick thought. They never really kick their hang-ups. In spite of his anger, he smiled. Where in hell had he gotten all that shrink talk about religion and mother hatred? He didn't hold with any of that garbage. Surprising, though, how it had seemed to hit the mark. The things you pick up without knowing it, Rick mused. Probably came from reading too many issues of *Playboy*. They ought to stick to pictures.

Maryanne walked slowly across Forty-ninth Street, crossing Broadway, oblivious to the calculating eyes of the pimps in the doorways, ignoring the suggestive remarks of a bunch of sailors lounging outside a seedy bar near Sixth Avenue. She didn't feel afraid. She never had, and tonight she was too preoccupied to think about muggers or rapists or other weirdos who hung out in that area of New York at one o'clock in the morning.

In her mind, she turned over the things Rick had said, surprised, as he had been, at the penetrating analysis of her morals and her motives. It was true. Deny it as she might, her religion was ingrained. She did believe that life began at the moment of conception. She couldn't murder and live with herself ever after. It was a sin, worse than taking one's own life. Strange Rick would recognize that. She also was certain about her feelings toward Sheila. She didn't hate her. She was envious of the way her widowed mother had landed on her feet, how she always had maintained an air—real or not—of peace with herself even when Sean Callahan was giving her a miserable time. Sheila had always wanted to help her. Still did. Maryanne knew that. But Maryanne was beyond help. She'd been nothing but grief for Sheila these past years. She was not, as Rick suggested, going to go home with an illegitimate child, adding two more burdens to her mother's already difficult life.

At Fifth Avenue, she turned north and passed St. Patrick's. She stood for a moment, looking up at the tall spire, thinking she might go in and pray for forgiveness. She didn't even know whether the Cathedral was open at that hour, but surely there'd be someone to listen to her. No, it was too late to repent. Too late in the night. Too late in her life.

She kept walking up Fifth Avenue, past the airline offices and the junky oriental shops with their perennial, yellowing "Going out of business!" signs, past Elizabeth Arden where women frantically sought beauty, and past Gucci and Mark Cross where they searched for status. She scarcely glanced at Bonwit Teller's glamorous windows and Tiffany's imaginative vitrines. She paused for a moment in front of F.A.O. Schwarz, the famous toy store, looking with a kind of detached curiosity at the enchanting playthings for children.

At Fifty-ninth Street she turned right, walking slowly down the narrow, nearly empty street. It was lonely at that hour. A few pedestrians glanced casually at her, probably deciding she was some prostitute on her way to, or from, turning a trick.

She found herself thinking of her mother, that amazingly self-sufficient product of a sheltered girlhood. Sheila could never have imagined that at twenty-four there was nothing to live for, no hope, no future, no desire to exist in a world that defied understanding. Maryanne was sure that Sheila, through Sally Cantrell, had been responsible for Paul Birmingham's unaccountable call. Mother still wants to do things for me, she thought again. She still loves me. I don't deserve it. I don't deserve anything except, perhaps, the degradation of life with Rick. Rick. Would she have married him if he'd agreed to it? Probably not. I really despise him, she thought. Almost as much as I despise myself. What did she really want? She didn't know. Maybe she wanted to take back these last years of fruitless searching for answers that didn't exist. She was so tired. So filled with disillusion and self-hatred. She realized what she wanted: Peace. No more sleazy hotel rooms, no more trashy companions, no more pretending that glamour and glory were just around the corner in this rotten world. Peace for herself. And peace for her family. She'd tried. She'd really tried to go back and find the Maryanne Callahan who'd been a well-brought-up, decent girl. But that creature was dead. Pattie Thomas in her sequined jeans and rayon halter was all that was left.

Rick would expect to find her at the hotel. He needed her. Maryanne laughed aloud. He was the only one who did. Suddenly she'd become his ticket to success, or so he hoped. Sorry, Rick, she said silently. This is an express train. No intermediate stops.

She crossed Second Avenue and walked quietly up the long ramp to the Queensboro Bridge. She had no purse, no identification, not even a label in her clothes. "Forgive me, Father," she said, and made the sign of the cross.

The police had no idea who the good-looking young woman was when they fished her body out of the East River early Monday morning.

"Some hopeless, pregnant hooker," the coroner said after the autopsy. "Jesus, what a waste!"

Chapter 26

At the very moment on Monday morning, when Maryanne was lying unidentified in the City Morgue, an unaware Sheila was feeling exceptionally content. She'd had a wonderful visit with Sally yesterday and had been touched by what her friend was trying to do to find Maryanne.

"No promises," Sally had said, "but if anybody can find them, Paul can. I just told him we're anxious to locate 'Pattie Thomas' and her group. Didn't tell him who she is or why we want to get in touch. When he zeroes in on them, you can take it from there."

Sheila had been deeply grateful. "I don't want to interfere with her life. Her cards have sounded optimistic and happy. I just want her to know where I'll be after July. In case she needs me." Then she'd given a half-apologetic little laugh. "That isn't entirely true. I mean, that's not all of it. *I* need to know where *she* is, Sally."

"Well, maybe we'll get lucky," Sally said. "Paul seemed to think it was no problem, even on a Sunday. He can put his finger on anybody in the entertainment business, anywhere in the world, any hour of the day or night. We'll probably hear something in a day or two. He even said he'd check them out personally if they're in New York. And speaking of New York, tell me *everything* about Bill Reardon!"

Sheila launched into a euphoric description of her five days in Bermuda. There was no need to hold back anything from her worldly contemporary, and yet she felt a certain reticence when she spoke of their sex life. "We—We're physically compatible," she said almost shyly. "In fact, we weren't in the house an hour before we made love."

Sally laughed. "My God, Sheila, you're actually blushing!"

"Well, it isn't easy to talk about, even with you. I'm really terribly old-fashioned, I guess." Her expression changed. "Funny. The only man I ever practically attacked was Jerry. I came near trying to seduce Bill his last night in Cleveland, but he wanted to wait for the right time. And he was right. My feeling for him is so different. He makes me feel safe and cherished and, well, it's a dumb word but I can't think of a better one: *respectable*."

"You *are* in love with him, Sheila, aren't you?"

"What a strange question! Of course I am! I'm going to marry him. Isn't that proof?"

"In your case, I suppose it is. But it's not always proof, not by a long shot! Bill sounds wonderful. Witty and sophisticated and, to use your word, also 'respectable.' Obviously he loves you and can take care of you. And I'm sure you love him."

Sheila looked at her. "It sounds to me as though there's a 'but' coming."

"I don't know. Yes, there is. It's probably the wrong thing to say, but I'll say it anyhow. The 'but' was going to be that in all the description of Bill's virtues, I don't hear the kind of passion I heard when you talked about Jerry. Every instinct tells me Bill Reardon is the right man for you, Sheila. But some little warning bell in my head tells me you don't get goosebumps at the thought of him, the way you did when you were losing your mind over Mancini. I repeat, I'm sure you love Bill. I think you'll be happy with him. And if it's more quiet contentment than illicit excitement, I happen to think that's good. You'd never have anything but anguish with your young doctor. You know that, don't you?"

There was a touch of fond amusement in Sheila's voice when she answered. "You're so dear when you're trying to be subtle, Sally. I've already heard that Jerry and Barbara have separated. No need to worry. What I said to you before still holds: I don't think Jerry will get in touch with me. But even if he does, it won't matter. I know now he never really cared. I was a diversion. Bill is the real thing. And if I haven't sounded like sixteen, it isn't because I'm not filled with excitement. It's just a different kind. More mature, but gay and anticipatory. I certainly didn't mean to make Bill sound dull! My God, he's anything but that! In fact, he's almost too easygoing. He makes me think a little of Sean, with his laughter and his zest for life. It might be the one thing that scares me a little. Bill's another lighthearted Irishman, Sally. He's not irresponsible, the way Sean was. But there's no craving for power and public recognition." She frowned. "In a crazy way, that was one of the things that attracted me to Jerry. I've never known a man so determined to be important in his own sphere. Bill is and doesn't really care. Maybe when I was seeing Jerry I was in need of that kind of self-involved ambition in a man. I don't know." Sheila smiled. "Anyway, what difference does it make now? I've found a wonderful guy. He'll be a real father for Tommy. And the right husband for me. Jerry would never have been either."

"That's a helluva lot of protesting you're doing."

"No, dear friend, that's a helluva lot of clear, grown-up thinking. Sally, I'm so happy! You're happy for me, aren't you?"

"You know damn well I am. And relieved, too."

Patrick and Betty also had shared her joy when she told them that night. Betty had cried a few happy tears and Pat had kissed her.

"I'm really pleased, Mom. To tell you the truth, I didn't ever like the way things were going."

Sheila had nodded, understanding. There was no mention of Jerry. There didn't have to be.

"Have you told Tommy? And Jean and Bill?" Betty asked. "What did they say?"

"I haven't told them," Sheila admitted. "I spoke to them all this afternoon, but somehow I couldn't bring myself to make the announcement. Not that I think the Callahans will be upset. In fact, I know they'll be glad for me. They're not the kind of people who'd expect me to observe a year of mourning, not even for their own son. It just didn't seem to be a piece of news one dropped in a telephone call."

Betty was silent. It was Pat who came to the point. "You aren't worried about Dad's parents," he said. "It's Tommy, isn't it? You're afraid to tell him you're going to get married again. Why, Mom? He's old enough to understand that you have a lot of good years ahead of you. He should be glad you're going to be taken care of and that he is, too! For God's sake, what is Tommy, some kind of fragile flower who has to be watered with every ounce of your blood?"

"Pat, don't!" Betty said. "You don't understand. You didn't lose your father at the wrong age. You didn't feel lonely and in need of comfort, the way Tommy does." She turned to Sheila. "But Pat's right about one thing. Tommy must learn to understand. To be glad for you. When *are* you going to tell him, Sheila?"

"I thought I'd wait until he comes home. It will be easier to explain to him face to face."

Patrick was still irritated. "What's to explain? He's not your father or your lover, he's your child! You don't have to explain anything to Tommy. You just have to tell him this is what you intend to do with your life."

Betty broke in again. "Oh, for heaven's sake, Pat, shut up! Don't you think Sheila knows that? She just wants to handle it right for every-body."

"And how do you think I should handle it?" Sheila asked. "You under-stand psychology, Betty dear. What should I do?"

"Tell him right away. If necessary, fly down to Palm Beach for a day, if you don't want to do it by phone. But it will be too close to the time you're ready to leave if you wait until he comes home. He'll need time to adjust to the idea. You don't want him coming home to something every-body else in the world already knows. That would be the ultimate insult in his eyes."

"I hadn't thought of it that way," Sheila said slowly. "You're right, of course. With any luck I'll have sold the house and everything will be going into packing crates by then. Good Lord, I must have been crazy, thinking I could wait that long to tell Tommy!" She frowned. "I was just putting it off because I'm afraid to face it. I can't forget how violently he reacted to Jerry."

It was the first time Dr. Mancini had been mentioned.

"That wasn't quite the same," Betty said softly. "I don't think Tommy's reaction to Mr. Reardon will be, either."

"I hope not," Sheila said. "I hope they'd find what they need in each other. Bill is thrilled. It's almost like a rebirth to him. But Tommy? I don't know. Anyway," she said cheerfully, "I'm glad we talked it out. You're right. I'll go to Florida. I can wangle a couple of days from the store. What can they do, fire me?" She laughed. "I'm going to quit any-way. And will *that* be a relief! Not that I haven't liked the job. I think I was damned lucky to get such a good one. But I'm not cut out to be a workingwoman. I don't feel in the least 'demeaned' being a housewife and mother."

The air cleared, they'd talked easily and happily about her plans. She'd keep on working for a few weeks. ("I need the money. Let's face it, I *won't* be a kept woman!") and Kitty Rawlings deserved a month's no-tice. "Good grief, *that's* only a month away!" Sheila said. "It's almost May?"

"You'll come back when your first grandchild is born, won't you?" Betty asked.

"Are you kidding? Just try to keep me away!"

She had them laughing hysterically when she told them about her tele-phone conversation with Rose, whom she *had* told. "Mother came sud-enly all-over Irish," Sheila reported. "She kept saying, 'Saints be praised! Saints be praised!' And the crazy coincidence of my 'intended' being Bill Reardon was almost too much for her. She was always crazy about him when I was a kid. Of course, she had to find *something* wrong. I mean, he's Catholic and widowed and all the right things, including well-off and New York-based. The only thing she could think of to chastise me about was that I was remarrying indecently soon. 'Not a year yet, Sheila,' she kept saying. 'What will people say?' I told her that as long as I wasn't pregnant, people weren't likely to say anything. That threw her into such a state of shock that she was speechless. And then, would you believe, she asked me how my trip to Boston was! I mean, she still hasn't connected with the fact that Bill and I didn't make this decision properly in Cleveland. If I'm lucky, she won't figure it out. I'd have to confess I lied about where I was going, plus arousing dark suspicions in her mind that Bill and I might have behaved 'indecently' before marriage."

Her "children" were convulsed. "What's all this about Boston?" Pat said.

Sheila explained it. "I told the Callahans and Tommy the same story. Only you knew I was going to Bermuda. And only Sally knew with whom."

"Why, you wicked creature!" Betty teased. "Pulling the wool over everybody's innocent eyes! We never *dreamed* your 'friend' was male, did we, Patrick?"

"Never," he said solemnly. "Not my nice, respectable mother."

On Monday morning, getting ready for the store to open, Sheila thought what a good day yesterday was. How lucky she was to have dear friends and wonderful children. She even felt optimistic about Tommy's reaction. When she got to Palm Beach, she'd make him understand. It would be a good life. If only Maryanne could share her joy. But Paul Birmingham would find her and Sheila would be in touch again. She clung to that belief.

"That must have been some terrific vacation," Dottie Parker said. "You're grinning like a Cheshire cat this morning."

"It was. Bermuda was glorious," Sheila said unthinkingly.

"Bermuda? I thought you had family problems in Florida."

Damn. She'd always been a terrible liar. Look at her now. She'd blurted out the truth without thinking. She hadn't intended to take anyone in the store into her confidence and even now she wouldn't, fully.

"Keep a secret, Dottie? I was invited to Bermuda. To a house party. I couldn't tell Kitty that, so I fibbed."

"A house party in Bermuda? That's classy! Meet any interesting people?"

"A few. There's lots of social activity there. I saw one beautiful house after another, but mostly with the same crowd in them."

"No great guys?"

Sheila smiled. "None to speak of." Well that, at least, wasn't a lie. She wasn't ready to talk about Bill. "You won't mention Bermuda, will you? I could get in big trouble here."

"Never heard of the place," Dottie said.

It was no problem to change her day off from Tuesday to Monday of the following week. One of the women in the department was willing to swap with her, and Kitty Rawlings was not disturbed as long as "the floor was covered" with the proper number of salespeople. By taking Monday, Sheila figured, she could fly to Palm Beach on Saturday night, spend Sunday and most of Monday with the Callahans and Tommy, and be back on the job Tuesday morning.

That evening she was very busy on the telephone. She called Bob Ross at home, to inform him of her decision to put her house on the market immediately. Emily answered.

"Well, well! Sheila! What a surprise! I thought we were off your list forever."

"I've been terribly busy, Emily." Why was she apologizing? Telephones worked both ways. Emily hadn't called *her* in months. But the impulse to "stay friends" with everybody from her past—even the ones she didn't especially like—was too ingrained a habit to shake. "The job's terribly demanding. I've seen very few people."

"Really? Bob seems up-to-date on your activities."

Sheila felt anger. I'm not trying to steal your precious husband, she wanted to say. But what was the point? Instead, she said calmly, "Bob's been wonderful, helping me get my affairs in order. I don't know how to thank him."

"He's good at affairs."

Bitch. Sheila ignored the implication. "Anyway, Em, I do need to talk to him about something important. Is he there?"

"No, he's working late night tonight. At least that's what he said. Maybe you can reach him on his outside, private wire. I assume you know the number."

"Yes. Thanks."

"Drop over sometime, Sheila, when you have a free moment."

"I'll do that."

She hung up seething and then found it almost amusing. Emily was a master at the art of unmistakable implication, using phrases and words like little daggers of jealousy. In this case they didn't wound or frighten the intended victim. This at least, Sheila thought, is one area in which I don't have to reproach myself.

Bob was surprised and disapproving when she reached him and told him her decision.

"Things are even tighter now than they were last year," he said. "It's a bad time to try to unload a house. I strongly advise against it, Sheila. What brought on the sudden change of heart?"

"I'm moving to New York, dear. In July."

"New York! For God's sake, why? Don't tell me you've decided to share an apartment with Rose!"

"No. Brace yourself, Bob. I'm getting married. His name's Bill Reardon and he's a writer."

There was a stunned silence. Then Bob said, "Bill Reardon? Who's he? How long have you been seeing him?"

She couldn't resist. "Oh, about five or six weeks."

"Five or six weeks! Sheila are you mad? You can't marry somebody you've known five or six weeks!"

"Really?" she teased. "Why not?" She was enjoying Bob's shock. Poor thing. He really did think she'd taken leave of her senses. She was being mean. "All right, I'll stop playing games and tell you the truth."

She explained her reunion with Bill after almost thirty years. "He's a fine person, Bob. You'll like him."

The answer was more like a grunt. He'd never like anybody who took her away. Not even if he couldn't have her himself. "Writers aren't the most financially secure choices as a rule," he said. "Don't you think you've had enough instability in the past—with one improvident husband?"

"Dear, cautious Bob," she said. "But you don't have to worry. He's well able to take care of Tommy and me. He earns good money and there was a substantial inheritance from his late wife. Not that it matters. I love him. I'll be content with him. Wish me well, Bob, and help me get rid of my burdens here. If we can't sell, perhaps we can rent, with an option to buy."

"Are you sure you're doing the right thing, Sheila?"

"Absolutely. And by the way, don't mention it to Emily just yet, will you? I'm flying to Palm Beach next weekend to tell Tommy and the Callahans. And Sally has a friend of hers trying to locate Maryanne. I've told Rose, of course, but I want *all* my family to know before the world hears about it. By next week I should be in a position to make the announcement, but for now I'd as soon 'the girls' didn't hash it over."

He hesitated. "What about me? You know how I feel about you. I've been thinking a lot of things these past weeks, Sheila. The phone's no place to discuss it, but before you go any further, couldn't we talk? I know you're not the type for an affair. I'm not either. But if I were free . . ."

She stopped him. "No. Don't even consider that. Not for me. I'm not in love with you, Bob, dearly as I love you. And even if I were, I wouldn't take a friend's husband. You know me better than that."

"Emily's not a friend to you."

"Perhaps not. But it still applies." She hated to hurt him, but there was no help for it. "Besides, my dear, I'm incurably romantic. I could only marry for love."

"I could make you love me."

"You don't *make* people love you," Sheila said. "Not that way. It can't be forced or even coaxed into existence. I'll always love you, Bob. But not the way I'd have to, to marry you. I'm complimented, but it's a compliment I can't accept."

She did feel flattered but also sad when they hung up. Bob Ross was a good man and his wife was a terror, but he didn't really want to disrupt his life, even though he might think so at this moment. Men don't like change, Sheila thought again. He'd hate the mechanics of divorce, the adjustment to a new way of life. He's really content with Emily, though he doesn't know it. Six months from now he'll have forgotten that he offered to uproot his tidy world for me. Or at least be glad I didn't accept.

Almost as unsettling was her call to Palm Beach. Tommy answered (at least he stays home *there* in the evening, Sheila thought) and she sensed his alarm when he heard her voice for the second time in two days.

"What's the matter, Mom? How come you're calling?"

"Nothing's wrong, darling. I miss you, that's all, and I've wangled Monday off next week. I thought I'd fly down to see you and the grandparents."

He was too smart to accept that. "Fly down just for the weekend? Isn't that pretty expensive, especially when I'm coming home soon?"

"Well, you know your crazy mother. I get these mad, extravagant impulses."

He didn't answer.

"All right, smarty, I do have a reason. Good news. But you're not going to wangle it out of me till I see you."

"Can I guess?"

Sheila laughed. "No."

"It's about that better job you said you were going to try to get, isn't it? I know. You've decided to work nearer home! Maybe in that nifty Burrows Book Shop in Shaker Heights. The one right on Shaker Square. You'd be just minutes from the house. Am I right?"

"Wrong. It doesn't have to do with the job. At least not exactly. Nor with the house."

"I know," Tommy said slowly, "you're going to marry Dr. Mancini."

"Darling, don't be silly. No I'm not going to marry Dr. Mancini. I told you that was over. Now will you be a good kid and stop wasting my money? Let me speak to your grandmother, will you, please? I promise you it's good, Tommy dear."

"Am I going back to University?"

Sheila laughed again. "Better than that. Now will you get off this bloody phone? I'll see you Saturday night if it's agreeable to the Callahans."

It was, of course. They were delighted by the prospect of her visit.

"Can't you stay more than two days?" Jean asked.

"No, dear. But maybe I'll have more time later. I'll tell you all about it when I get there."

Sheila had barely hung up when Bill called from Atlanta. She told him everything that had been happening and he approved. "Don't let that Bob Ross drag his feet on selling the house. Sold or not, you're moving to New York in July!"

"Yes, sir, Master, sir!"

He was delighted by Pat and Betty's reaction and amused by Rose's. When she told him of the search for Maryanne, he tried to sound hopeful but he was cautious. "Don't expect too much, honey," he said.

"I don't."

"Damn. I wish I were in New York this week. Maybe I could help."

"We don't even know if she's there. I'll let you know what's happening as soon as Sally gets back to me."

"I'm glad you're going to Palm Beach," Bill said. "I think Betty's reasoning is sound. How about if I join you there? I'll be through here on Thursday and I could easily fly down."

Sheila hesitated and then decided against it. In a way, it would have been good to introduce Bill to his future stepson. She was sure he could charm even Tommy. But it was better for her to be alone when she told him and Sean's parents about her plans.

"I'd better do this one on my own, darling," she said. "It'll be the last difficult thing I have to face without you."

"Difficult? Will it be?"

"I don't know. I hope not. I can't be sure of Tommy's reaction. He's been a very emotional kid since his father died. But everything will be okay. Now, enough of me! How's it going in Atlanta?"

"So far, except for finding you, I think it's going to be as terrific as Cleveland. Rich's is great. They've lined up a promotional program that won't stop! And the people are marvelous, every one of them. These Southerners do have charm, plus a lot of savvy. The way this tour is going, I may stop being so insular about New York. I'm seeing America and liking it."

"You mean you don't think New York is the best place to be?"

"My love, I probably will always want it as home base, as I told you. But, for me, I know the best place to be."

"And where's that?"

"Anywhere *you* are. Anywhere I'm with the lady I love."

He was right. Cities didn't matter. People did. Cleveland had its Chamber of Commerce slogans: "The Best Location In the Nation" and "The Best Things In Life Are Here." But slogans were meaningless unless the people you cared about were there. Bill knew that. And so, Sheila thought, do I. It doesn't matter where I live. My roots are only as strong as the growth of love they support.

She'd barely bid Bill a lingering good night when the phone rang. She picked it up quickly, hoping it was Sally with some news, but the voice was one she'd hoped not to hear.

"Sheila? Pat told me you were back. How are you?"

"I'm fine, Jerry. How are you?"

"Better than ever."

It seemed a tactless thing to say, somehow, but Sheila was pleased to find that she was cool, in control.

"I'm glad to hear it." She pretended ignorance. "Going back to Barbara *was* the right thing. You knew it, and you were very wise."

"Yes and no. We've separated again, Sheila. This time for good."

Hearing him confirm it, she suddenly panicked. No, I don't want to hear this. He's going to say he wants to see me. I don't want to see him. I'm in love with Bill Reardon. I'm going to marry Bill.

"Jerry, I'm getting married," she said.

She didn't know what she expected. Protestations? Anger? At least, surprise. But Jerry seemed very calm.

"I see. I'm sure he's a good man."

"Of course. Very good. We've known each other for years. He's . . . extremely suitable."

"And you love him."

The words came firmly. "Very much. I'm going to have a sane and orderly life with him, Jerry. I've stopped being a fool."

"You were never that. That was my role." He took a deep breath. "Sheila, I'd like to come over. Just to talk. I've always felt I owed you an explanation."

"You don't owe me anything. That's the truth. What happened was for the best, for me and, apparently, for you. Let's let it go at that, shall we? No need to rehash that whole period of insanity."

"I'd appreciate your seeing me." He sounded almost humble. "I wish you nothing but happiness. Isn't it possible for us to be friends? Or are you so bitter about me that you won't even listen to what I want to say? For my sake, Sheila, won't you let me really explain?" He paused. "I care about you. I want you to think well of me, that's all."

She knew she shouldn't, but he was so unlike the self-confident Jerry she'd known that she weakened. They could never be friends. That was ridiculous after what had happened. But she was secure enough in her own happiness not to be petty. If it would help Jerry to make his explanations, she could be big enough to hear them. Nothing he could say would change the happy course she was on.

"All right, Jerry. Come over, but not for long. I'm tired and I have to get up early."

"Thank you," he said.

She'd taken off her "work clothes" before she made her telephone calls. She was in an old, baggy robe now. Clean but hardly alluring. The make-up she'd put on at seven-thirty that morning was almost gone. For a moment she debated staying just as she was, but it wouldn't do to receive

Jerry in a shabby dressing gown any more than in a seductive one. She ran upstairs and quickly changed into a shirt and skirt, ran a comb through her hair and didn't bother to redo her face. Let him see her tidy, but give him no idea that she was inviting any overtures. Because she wasn't.

He was there in fifteen minutes. How handsome he is! Sheila thought involuntarily as she opened the door. How young and intense. She held out her hand in greeting. He ignored it and gave her a little kiss on the cheek.

"You look like a schoolgirl," he said.

Sheila laughed. "Class of '45."

"No, I mean it. I've never seen you look so young."

"Thanks. I guess it's because I'm happy."

"You may not believe it, but I'm glad to hear that." He sat down in a big chair. "Buy me a drink?"

"Of course. What will it be?"

"Same as usual."

Sheila's expression didn't change as she handed him his glass. She took nothing for herself. Then she seated herself opposite him and said, "All right, Jerry. What do you have to say?"

"Bang. Just like that, huh?"

"You *did* say you wanted to explain. That's the only reason for the visit."

"Stop trying to be tough, Sheila, darling. It isn't your bag."

"Jerry, *I* didn't ask for this meeting. *You* did."

"Okay. Fair enough. I want you to know I've missed you every minute since New Year's Day. I've gone over every second we spent together. Every laughing moment. Every quiet conversation. Every hour we spent making love."

"Jerry, if this is what you've come to say, then you might just as well leave now. I don't want to hear . . ."

"Wait, please. I was so stupid. I didn't know how much you meant to me. How much you still do."

"Jerry, I told you. I'm in love with someone else. I'm getting married in two months. This is absurd. You walked out on me, went back to your wife and child. There was no warning, not even an inkling. And now for some reason you've left them again and you're back here expecting to pick up where you left off with me! I think you're crazy!"

"Listen. You must understand. When Barbara said she wanted a divorce, I was stunned. Confused and hurt. All the time I was seeing you, I wasn't making sense. And when she asked me to come back, I thought it was the right thing to do. For her and me and Joy. But it wasn't the right thing, Sheila. I hadn't been back a month when I knew I didn't love Barbara. I tried to make it work again, but it wouldn't. And then I knew why. Because I love you. I want to be with you. I was too ashamed to face you for a long while, but last week I moved out of the house and I knew that all I wanted to do was come and plead with you to take me back. Please, Sheila. I know you loved me. I think you still do. Age doesn't matter. Nothing matters except the way we felt about each other." He got up to move toward her. "I never said 'I'm in love with you' in those weeks we were together. I'm saying it now."

She put up her hand to ward him off. Three months ago she would have sold her soul to hear those words. Even now, they sent a chill through her, made her head swim with a mixture of victory and desire. Jerry had sunk back into the chair, looking at her with passion and pleading. Fragments of things Sally and Patrick and Betty had said drifted into Sheila's memory. But most of all, the image of Bill Reardon, his tenderness, his understanding came into her mind. Jerry was youth and a denial of her own middle age. He was temptation and recklessness. But Bill was solidity and loyalty and mature selflessness. She'd not trade that for the anxiety and abasing foolishness-to-please she'd had with this self-centered young man who offered her no peace and never would. She hardened her voice.

"You don't love me, Jerry. You never did." He started to speak but she hushed him. "You weren't making sense when you were seeing me. You've just admitted it. All right. I wasn't making sense either. I was lost and frightened of being a lonely widow. I thought I could recapture happiness through you. We were both in a mixed-up period. We've come out of it now. I've found someone who's right for me. You'll find someone, too. It's over with us. It can never be again." She gave a little laugh. "Funny. Even now I don't think the age difference was our biggest problem. It was just that neither of us knew what we really wanted."

"I thought I still wanted Barbara," he said. "I thought I still loved her. But I didn't. It was you."

"No," Sheila said quietly, "it wasn't I. It was you, your ego. Your actions have proved it. You couldn't stand the idea that Barbara wanted to be rid of you. You couldn't rest, Jerry, until you made her invite you back. That was all you wanted. To be asked back so that this time *you* could walk out on *her*. That's the real truth of it. You're satisfied, now. You've had your revenge. Your monumental conceit is restored. You're no longer the rejected, you're the rejector. And that was the only thing that sent you back to Barbara. Not love, Jerry, but inability to live with the idea that someone could possibly send you away. You had to turn that around, didn't you? Just as now you have to prove that you can whistle and I'll come running. Well, I'm sorry. Sorry for you. Because now you're rejected again. It won't matter as much to you this time. You can always think of me as some nice, over-forty lady for whom you did a favor by making her feel desirable and half her age. It's not the same as having your wife throw you out. And after all, *you* threw *me* out the first time, so the score's even."

He was very quiet. "So that's the way it looks to you."

"Yes, that's the way it looks."

He rose slowly. "You're wrong, Sheila. You're not thinking straight."

"On the contrary, I've never been more clearheaded in my life. Good-by, Jerry. And good luck."

"You, too. But we'll see each other again."

"I doubt that very much."

Chapter 27

Paul Birmingham was used to dumps like the dingy one he approached Monday night. He was used to them, but he'd never learn to like them. Paying off the cab just east of Ninth Avenue, he looked with distaste at the run-down bar which was presumptuous enough to call itself an "Off-off Broadway" spot and display a sign that indicated it had "Entertainment." If The Potboilers were entertainment, Paul thought, he was P. T. Barnum. Still, you never knew. Some of the greatest talent had been discovered in offbeat night spots, like *the hungry i* in San Francisco or in one of the Borscht Belt hotels in the Catskills. What difference? He didn't expect to discover a new star here. He was just doing a favor for a friend.

A fastidious man, he picked his way across the littered sidewalk and plunged into the smoke-filled front room. He went straight to the crowded bar and ordered a bottle of beer, wise enough not to trust what might be poured out of a bottle labeled Chivas Regal. As he sipped his drink, he wondered again what interest Sally Cantrell possibly could have in Pattie Thomas, or whatever her real name was. Sally hadn't volunteered much. Just that a friend of hers was looking for the girl and her group. It hadn't been much trouble to find out about The Potboilers and it would have been easier to simply call Sally and give the name of the bar. But he was curious enough to come and see for himself. They had to be terrible, a group represented by that third-rate agent Sandy Stein and booked into a dive like this. The girl had to be terrible, too. It just didn't add up that a classy lady like Sally whom he'd met at the best parties in New York could have any association with this scene.

"Rick Jawolsky around?" he asked the bartender.

With his head, the man indicated the back room. "In there. Through that door. Admission's three dollars."

"I didn't come to see the show. I have a business appointment with Mr. Jawolsky."

"Then invite him up to your office. Seeing him here costs three bucks."

"Your charm is exceeded only by your good breeding," Paul said. "How much for the beer?"

"One twenty-five."

Paul put the exact amount on the bar. "It *should* cost as much here as '21,'" he said sarcastically, "considering the service."

"Up yours, buddy." The bartender threw the money into a drawer. Under his breath he muttered, "Goddamn faggot."

At the door to the back room, Paul paid his admission and sat down at a small table. The group was at its eardrum-splitting height. Jawolsky apparently was the young, good-looking one with the electric guitar, the obvious "leader." There were three other young men, but no girl. He wondered where Pattie Thomas was. Paul ordered another beer and waited for them to finish the set. It took quite a while. Apparently the patrons demanded quantity if not quality for their three bucks plus drinks. When they took a break, Paul got up and went forward, touching Rick on the sweaty shoulder of his denim shirt.

"Jawolsky? I'm Paul Birmingham."

"Hey, Mr. Birmingham, you made it! Crazy, man!" Rick grinned. "That call last night. I thought maybe it was a put on. Glad to see you. Did you catch the group? What do you think?"

"Not bad. Not bad at all," Paul lied. "But I thought you had a girl vocalist. A friend of mine in Cleveland, Mrs. Cantrell, mentioned her, remember? That's how I happened to call."

"Yeah. Well, look, I'm sorry but Maryanne's sick tonight."

"Maryanne? I thought her name was Pattie. Pattie Thomas."

"Stage name." Rick said. "You dig, Mr. Birmingham. Can you imagine a singer called Maryanne Callahan? Sounds like she should be in the St. Patrick's Chowder and Marching Society Glee Club, for Christ's sake."

Paul nodded. "Doesn't matter. I'm sorry she's not here, though. I hear she's good."

"Fair." Rick shrugged. "Frankly, she's a nice kid but she doesn't add all that much to the group. She's okay but I could replace her in twenty minutes with some broad with better looks and a better voice." A peculiar expression came over Birmingham's face. Goddammit, Rick thought,

Maryanne *was* the key to the whole thing. There was something here he couldn't figure out. Something to do with Cleveland and probably with Sheila Callahan. Maryanne had seemed upset last night when he'd told her about Birmingham, even before they got into that hassle about the baby. The baby. Maybe Maryanne had written to her mother about it. Sure, that had to be it. Maryanne had sent one of her usual "no return address" cards to Sheila. The Cantrell broad probably had volunteered to help find Maryanne through this hot-shot agent. What a laugh. And Rick had thought they were going to be "discovered."

"Your friend, Mrs. Cantrell," he said now. "She interested in music?"

"Isn't everybody?"

"Don't give me that, Birmingham," Rick said angrily. "You didn't come here to catch our act, did you? You came to find Maryanne. I suppose old lady Cantrell is a friend of her mother's. They're probably frantic, hearing she got knocked up. That's it, isn't it?"

Paul hid his surprise. Rick caught on fast, you had to say that for him. But he had a big mouth. He had no idea he was giving Paul information. So the girl was pregnant. And her mother was frantic. He hadn't known any of that. He'd been curious about why Sally wanted her located, but he'd had a whole other theory. He'd figured that "friend" story was a cover up, that this girl singer was interfering in Sally's life. Maybe standing between her and some guy she was interested in. It wouldn't have been the first time a woman of Sally's age had been threatened by some sexy young chick. But it wasn't that at all. It was, Paul realized, far more serious.

"All right, Rick," he said reasonably. "You're right. I didn't come here to check out the group. You're good, but you're not my kind of talent. I was asked to find Pattie—or Maryanne—for my friend. I'm sorry to disappoint you. Maybe I can make it up some other way. I know a lot of good agents who specialize in your kind of music. I'll pass the word along, I promise you. This whole thing won't have been a waste of your time. Nor of mine, if you'll tell me where to find the girl."

"You leveling? You'll send somebody around to hear us?"

"I give you my word." Paul smiled. "And that's good enough for some pretty big stars. Just tell me where I can locate Maryanne."

Rick hesitated. "I don't know. She flew out of here last night, mad as hell because I wanted her to have an abortion. She didn't go back to our room and I haven't seen her since."

"Is that usual? Does she often disappear like that?"

"Hell, no. She's scared to go to a diner alone."

"Did she take her clothes?"

"No. Nothing. As far as I know she hasn't got a dime. She even left her handbag here when she split."

Paul was alarmed. "Would she have gone to stay with someone else? Could she be with a friend?"

Rick shook his head. "No way. She doesn't know anybody in this town. Except her grandmother and she'd never go to her."

"What's her grandmother's name?"

"Beats me."

Paul's alarm turned to anger. "For God's sake, are you telling me that that girl's been missing for twenty-four hours, that she doesn't know a soul in New York, that she's penniless and pregnant and you haven't lifted a finger to find her? What are you, a maniac? Don't you know what could happen to that young woman all alone in this town? You punk! She could be lying in a hospital or the morgue!" He shook Rick roughly. "What's the matter with you? Are you some kind of animal? Don't you give a damn about anything but yourself and your cheap little future?"

Rick was younger and stronger and he shook Paul off like a gnat. "Listen, man, don't come in here talking to me like some kind of crazy missionary! This is a rock group, not the Salvation Army! If that dumb broad wants to cut out, what the hell am I supposed to do about it? Call the Missing Persons Bureau? Alert the FBI? She left. She probably picked up some dude in a bar and spent the night with him. How the hell do I know where she went or what she's been doing? She hasn't exactly been Little Mary Sunshine for the past couple of years, you know. You tell your friend in Cleveland that her Shaker Heights debutante is probably shacked up someplace and she'll be back tomorrow. And meantime, Mr. Birmingham, I'll expect that 'star treatment' from you. I damn well better see one of those agents around here and *soon!* You're a man of your word, are you? Well, fine. I'm a man of mine, too. And my word to you right now is 'Blow'!"

"Where do you live?" Paul asked.

"None of your damned business! Just get your butt out of here. I told you what you wanted to know. Now cut out!"

It was futile to argue further with this angry young man. Paul turned and slowly left the bar. There were no cabs in sight and he walked rapidly toward Broadway, anxious to get out of this neighborhood. He thought of the girl he didn't know, a girl alone and frightened on this same street last night. Maybe that monster Jawolsky was right. Maybe nothing had happened to her, nothing more serious (to them) than picking up some stranger and spending the night with him. Yet it didn't sit right. He could smell trouble.

At Broadway he hailed a cab and gave his home address. On the way to his apartment, he wondered what he should do. It was past midnight. Too late to call Sally. Besides, what could she do? He wondered if he should call the hospitals or the police. But how could he? He didn't even know what "Pattie Thomas" looked like. What the hell was he doing in the middle of all this? What had started out as a simple favor to an attractive woman he barely knew was turning into a nightmare. Like any devout

New Yorker, his reaction was not to get involved. But he *was* involved, worse luck. Tomorrow he'd have to call Sally and tell her what he'd found out. Let her or her friend take it from there. They could reach Rick themselves. And, Paul thought cynically, by that time their precious Maryanne would probably be back in the sack with Jawolsky. Or on her way to an abortionist.

At noon on Tuesday, Patrick answered the page at the hospital and heard Sally Cantrell's voice. From the first word, he knew something was wrong. She was trying to control herself, but there was panic even in the way she pronounced his name. Something's happened to Mother, he thought. Why else would Sally call me at work?

Quickly, Sally told him what Paul Birmingham had reported a few minutes before.

"Oh, my God!" Patrick said. "Does Mother know?"

"Not yet. I didn't know what to do, Pat. That's why I called you. This will kill Sheila. She'll blame herself for everything!"

His professional training came through. "Try to stay calm, Sally. We don't know much yet. Maryanne may have turned up by now. Don't say anything to Mother. I'm off duty at three o'clock. I'll go home and start calling. No point in getting Mother all worked up until we know the facts. I wouldn't take that Jawolsky creep's word for anything. Including the pregnancy. This may be nothing but a bunch of crap he's handed your friend Birmingham. Might be his way of getting back at him because he wasn't really there to sign up the group. Stay cool. I'll let you know what I find out."

He wasn't nearly as assured as he sounded. He moved through the next three hours mechanically, his mind on his sister. He wasn't sure where to start, but the obvious place seemed to be with Rick. Bad luck that Birmingham couldn't find out where he and Maryanne were staying. The whole thing might have been solved by one simple call to a New York hotel. This way he'd have to wait until late tonight to reach Rick or, hopefully, Maryanne at work. Thank God, he had the name of the joint where The Potboilers were playing. But he couldn't wait until ten or eleven o'clock at night. He'd call the club as soon as he got home. Surely they'd know where Maryanne and Rick stayed. What if they refused to give out the information? No, they'd tell him. He'd sound official. The "doctor" title always worked when you wanted to cut through bureaucratic red tape. It should work just as well in this case.

It did. He reached the owner and said in his most severe voice, "This is Dr. Callahan from Cleveland. We have an emergency and I must reach Miss Pattie Thomas at once."

"Sorry, Doctor. We don't have her address."

"Then give me the address of Rick Jawolsky."

The man hesitated. "I'm not sure I can do that. We're not supposed to give out . . ."

Patrick cut him short. "You don't seem to understand. This is a matter of life or death! Now, what are you going to do? Give me that information? Or shall I call the police and have them come and get it?"

That did it. Within seconds Patrick was placing a call to Rick's hotel. A sleepy voice in Room 28 finally answered.

"Rick? It's Patrick Callahan. Maryanne's brother. I'd like to speak to her."

"What the hell do you want?"

"I told you. Put Maryanne on."

"Can't. She's not here."

"Where is she?"

Rick was coming awake now. "Like I told your undercover agent, I haven't seen her since Sunday night. All her stuff's here. Even her make-up." Rick suddenly began to sound frightened. "Jesus, I don't know where she is! I thought she'd be back by now."

Patrick was breathing heavily. "It's going on forty-eight hours! You must have some idea. Think, Rick! Where could she be?"

"Christ, man, I don't know. You think she could have gone to your grandmother's?"

"No. We'd have heard. I'm going to call the police. Tell me exactly what she was wearing Sunday night."

"Uh, let's see. Red sequin pants, I think. And some kind of top that showed her boobs. I don't know what else. No coat. And she left her pocketbook behind."

Patrick felt sick. "So she had no money and no identification."

"No." There was a pause. "She said she was pregnant. You think she could have gone somewhere to get rid of it?"

"Not without money or identification."

"No, I guess not. I mean she'd have called me, right?"

Patrick didn't answer.

"Listen, you'll let me know what you find out, won't you? I mean, I'm really worried now. You might not believe it, but I love her, screwy as she is."

"Call me if she turns up," Pat said. "Here's my home number and the hospital's. Got a pencil? Okay. Write 'em down. And be in touch the minute you hear anything."

"Right. Absolutely." Rick repeated the numbers. "And you'll call me if you hear first?"

You bastard, Patrick thought. If I could, I'd let you go to your grave wondering what happened to her, and it still wouldn't be enough punishment. "Yeah," he said. "I'll call you." He thought of telling Rick to notify the police, the Bureau of Missing Persons, whatever you called it.

But he couldn't trust him to follow through. Rick saying he loved Maryanne. Like hell he did! No sign of her for two nights and that no-good junkie was sound asleep in the middle of the afternoon! Maybe Sally's friend Paul Birmingham would be able to follow up. But he'd already done more than could be expected of a stranger. Patrick racked his brain. Bob Ross with his connections? Uncle Terry? No. Pat was the "man of the family." It was up to him.

He called the long-distance operator in New York and asked for the number of the Police Department's Missing Persons Bureau.

"We have no separate listing for that, sir. Would you like the main number for 'Police Business'?"

"Yes, I suppose so."

"Thank you, sir. You may call area code 212. The number is 374-5000."

He sat for a moment, afraid to dial. Perhaps he should call the hospitals first, but there were dozens of them. Besides, he knew that if a girl were brought in with no identification they'd notify the police. Or if Maryanne were able to identify herself she'd call someone. Probably, Pat thought bitterly, Rick.

Slowly, frighteningly certain of what he'd learn, he called the New York number and was put through to Missing Persons. They were matter-of-fact, asking innumerable, endlessly slow questions about the time and place she'd last been seen, her physical description, any identifying marks, her clothes, and on and on. Finally, the anonymous male voice at headquarters asked him to hold on. Minutes that seemed like hours went by and at last the man returned to the phone. There seemed to be—or was he imagining it?—a trace of pity in the unknown voice.

"Dr. Callahan, we have a female Caucasian who seems to answer that description. Can't be sure it's your sister, of course. The body's at the morgue, sir, pending identification."

Patrick was numb. He'd known it, somehow, ever since Sally called. And yet he couldn't accept it. There had to be a mistake. There had to be.

"How . . . when . . ." his voice faltered.

"Suicide, Doctor. Autopsy was performed yesterday. Death by drowning. Guy walking his dog along the East River Drive saw her go off the bridge early Monday morning and called us." The police official was reading from a report. "She was about two months pregnant. That fit?"

"Yes. I'm afraid it does." Patrick tried to pull himself together. "Of course, it still could be another girl who looked like her."

"Yessir, it could. Like I said, nobody's made inquiry until now."

"I'll be there in a few hours."

"Right, Doctor. You know where to come?"

Patrick took down the directions methodically. He called the airline and booked a seat on the next flight to New York. It left in two hours. And finally he called his wife.

Betty Callahan raced home in a state of shock. Pat had given her only the barest details on the phone, but she knew the dead girl was Maryanne. Still, she irrationally clung to the hope that it was not. Like her husband, she prayed it was all a ghastly mistake. There must be thousands of young women in New York who'd fit her sister-in-law's description. Maryanne wouldn't kill herself. Why would she? Unfathomable, unpredictable, confused girl that she was, she must have known that if things got really terrible she could come home to Sheila. Sheila. Dear God, how would Sheila react? There'd be more than grief for the death of her daughter. There'd be unbearable guilt. Betty knew her mother-in-law. Sheila'd always felt, unreasonably, that she'd failed Maryanne. This, in her tortured mind, would be irrefutable proof.

It was so sad, so terribly sad. Not just the wasteful destruction of Maryanne's young life, but the way, Betty knew with terrible certainty, Sheila would respond to it. Poor, poor Sheila. She'd been so happy on Sunday night, so full of confidence about everything. All her plans for a life with Bill Reardon, her hopes for what it would mean to Tommy as well as herself. Maryanne's death—and Betty realized she'd already accepted that fact—should do no more than postpone those plans. But knowing Sheila, it was questionable. I fear for her sanity when she finds out, Betty thought. This child I'm carrying. What would I do if it grew up as unhappy and desperate as Maryanne? Probably blame myself, just as Sheila will.

Pat, his face white and his hands shaking, was throwing a few things into an overnight case when she got to the apartment. She ran to him and they held each other.

"Maybe it isn't true," Betty said. "It might not be Maryanne, darling."

He shook his head. "I feel it in my gut. It's Maryanne. Jesus! How can this be? How could it have come to this?"

There was no answer. Why did people kill themselves? Out of despair, a feeling of worthlessness or guilt, an inability to believe that anything could ever be good again? Those and a hundred other reasons, including a yearning for peace. Oblivion must seem the ultimate happiness, the exquisite release from self-hatred. People had a right to choose the time of their own death, Betty thought, but not at the expense of the suffering and destruction they left behind. For a moment she almost hated Maryanne. But the emotion passed, replaced by sorrow.

"What are you going to do?" Betty asked. "What do you want *me* to do?"

"I've got to make certain it's Maryanne. Then I suppose I go through procedure. Claim the body, have an undertaker ship it home for burial. I'll have to face that animal, that Rick Jawolsky. God, I hope I don't kill him!"

"Must you see him?"

"Maryanne's things are with him. Mother will want them."

"Does Sheila know?"

"Not yet. And I don't want her to until we're positive." Without warning, he began to cry. The sight was almost more than Betty could bear, and there were no words, no pat phrases to comfort him. In a minute he wiped his eyes. "Look, honey, all you can do right now is wait for my call from New York. Oh, I guess you should call Sally." He explained how the whole process of discovery had started. "Tell her not to say anything to Mother or anybody until we know. And phone the hospital for me, will you? Tell them I've been called away for a couple of days on family business. One way or the other," Pat said slowly, "I won't be back at work for a little while."

"All right. Anything else? Where will you stay in New York?"

"I don't know. I'll find a hotel room for tonight. Hopefully I'll be back tomorrow. Or the next day at the latest." As soon as I can get what's left of my sister released and shipped home, he thought. God knows how long that takes.

"Darling, don't you think I should go with you? I can't stand to think of you facing this ordeal all alone."

"No. You're in no condition to go through it, and you'll do more good standing by here. There'll be arrangements to be made. Again. Not a year since Dad, and Mother has to survive another loss. An even worse one. I don't want her to know anything until I get back. I'm the one who has to tell her."

"Are you sure, Pat? Keeping it from her that long, I mean. Maybe she'd want to go with you, or be there to have a say about the—the casket and things. Her own mother is in New York. She might be the one person in the world Sheila could cling to now."

He looked at her in amazement. "Rose? Mother cling to Rose? Are you out of your mind? Grandma Price will be more hysterical than anybody when she finds out! I hope she doesn't even come here for the funeral! Mother doesn't need that. I'm not even going to call her when I'm in New York."

"Pat, you can't do that! I mean, if it's really Maryanne, you must tell her."

"No. First I come home and tell Mother. I'm not going to do that by phone. After Mother knows, we'll notify the rest."

"I think you underestimate your grandmother. My hunch is that in a real crisis, she's a strong lady. I think Sheila's inherited a lot of that strength, but your mother is still somebody's child. I think she'll need Rose."

"Later, maybe. Not now. There's no time to discuss it. I have a plane to catch in forty minutes." He looked like a pathetic little boy. "I'll call you as soon as I know."

Her heart ached for him as she kissed him good-by. Almost as much as it ached for Sheila who was going happily about her job, her mind filled with thoughts of a serene future. What will this do to that future? Betty wondered again. Nothing, she told herself. Why should it? She'll grieve, but she'll survive. She'll see that there's nothing to be gained by changing her plans. She'll eventually marry Bill Reardon and have a good life. None of us will ever forget poor, pathetic, lost Maryanne. But we don't live for the dead. We don't bring them back by forcing ourselves into eternal penance, by rejecting happiness for a hair shirt. And there's nothing any of us could have done to prevent this.

She realized what she was doing. She was rehearsing the things she'd say to Sheila. Let me believe them, Betty prayed. Please let *her* believe them.

Chapter 28

Even cutting through as much red tape as possible, it took Patrick forty-eight hours to get Maryanne's body released, removed to a funeral home, and prepared for the return to Cleveland. He'd never lived through such an experience. From the first sickening moment of identifying the strangely peaceful face of his sister to the signing of dozens of forms and making undertaking and transportation arrangements in a city with which he was not familiar, everything had an unreal quality, a sense of being part of an agonizing dream. There was not only the sadness and confusion, there was also a feeling of intense loneliness and a sense of guilt. The loneliness was checking into a small hotel, eating indifferent meals in coffee shops, waiting, endlessly, for the morticians to let him know when they'd finish their grim job. The guilt was his decision to keep Sheila in the dark about everything until he could tell her, face to face, what had happened to her daughter.

He was filled with doubt about the rightness of his actions. Perhaps he should have notified Sheila immediately, even before they were sure. Or at least he should have let Betty go to her immediately and be there when he called. Maybe his wife had been right. Sheila very well could have wanted a say in the hundred things that had to be done in the immediate aftermath of death. Most of all, Pat worried that what he'd first thought of as "sparing her" could backfire into a terrible shock. It might have been better to prepare his mother. How could he arrive in Cleveland with Maryanne's body, never having even told Sheila that she might be dead?

I was so sure this was the best way to handle it, Patrick thought. Perhaps, subconsciously, I wanted to believe that it was all a hellish mistake; that the girl I'd be shown wasn't Maryanne. And yet I knew. I knew for sure. He'd talked to Betty on Tuesday night, confirming their fears. That's when she'd begged him to let her go to Sheila and wait with her for his call.

"You can't do it this way, Pat! You can't just arrive with no warning, no chance for Sheila to absorb the idea before she faces the real fact! You *must* call her tonight. I'll go and stay with her until you return."

"No." He'd been stubbornly sure he was right. "I have to be there when she finds out. What difference does time make now? There's nothing Mother can do here. There'll be enough torment for her later."

"You're wrong. You're shutting her out."

He'd been angry, an anger compounded of doubt, frustration, and grief. "Damn it, Betty, stop saying that! I'm trying to make it as easy for her as I can!"

"No. You're only postponing. She has a right to share this tragedy all the way. She may resent you for playing God."

It was as close as they'd come to a real quarrel. Betty was as angry as he. "If, God forbid, it was our child, Patrick," she said, "I wouldn't want to be treated like an outsider."

He started to protest and then grew silent. "You know that's not my intent," he said finally.

"No, darling, I know it isn't. But that's the way it's going to come out."

For a long minute, he said nothing. What if Betty were right? What if Sheila never forgave him for keeping her in the dark even for these few days? No. She wouldn't react that way. She'd understand that he only wanted to protect her from all this. He thought of Betty's comments about Rose. Maybe she was right there, too. Sheila might want her mother with her when she heard the unthinkable.

"I still think she can't be told until I get there," Pat said. "But maybe I should call Grandmother Price. Bring her back with me." He hesitated. "I don't know if she'll understand what I've done, either."

"She will," Betty said firmly. "Call her. Go see her tomorrow, Pat. And bring her back with you."

"All right."

"You want me to call Sally?"

"Yes. But nobody else." He sighed. "Tomorrow will be quite a day. Facing Grandmother. And I'll have to go to that goddamn hotel and get Maryanne's things. I don't know how I can look at Jawolsky. I want to murder him."

261

"Sweetheart, there's nothing admirable about Rick, but he didn't trap Maryanne into white slavery. *She* kept running back to *him*, remember?"

"But why? For God's sake, why?"

"I guess we'll never know that, Patrick."

Late Wednesday morning, after he'd heard from the mortician, he called Rose. She was surprised and delighted to hear his voice.

"Patrick! What are you doing in town? Is your mother with you? Why didn't you let me know you were coming?"

"It was an unexpected trip. Mother didn't come."

"Oh, I see. Some kind of medical business?"

"Not exactly. Grandmother, may I come to see you?"

"Something's wrong, isn't it?" Rose asked anxiously. "Betty? She hasn't lost the baby, Pat! No, of course not. You wouldn't be here if that had happened. What is it?"

"I'll tell you when I get there. I need your help."

"It's Sheila! Something's happened to Sheila. Has she broken off with Bill Reardon? Is that why you're in New York?"

"Nothing like that. Look, the sooner I hang up, the sooner I can get there to explain it to you."

"All right, Patrick. I'll be waiting."

He took a cab to the West Side. Strange. He hadn't been here since he was a little kid and only once at that, when his parents had brought him for a visit. He must have been about two years old. Yet he remembered. They'd brought the infant Maryanne, too. Tommy wasn't even born. Why had they come? Patrick couldn't remember that. It must have been some kind of celebration. His grandparents' twenty-fifth wedding anniversary, maybe? It seemed to him he could recall the trip, even remember this big, old-fashioned building facing Central Park where he now left the cab. He'd never been back. Sean and Rose had no love for each other. His father suffered an occasional visit from his disapproving mother-in-law, visits which grew more frequent after Rose became a widow and which tore Sheila apart in her effort to maintain harmony. They'd never gone to New York again, any of them. Except, this last time, Maryanne.

He couldn't possibly remember what happened to him at two. But it seemed he actually knew this big, ugly entrance hall with its "art deco" furnishings (still hideous despite their re-emergence as the "in look" of the 1970s), its unkempt doorman (surely there'd been a full staff years ago, probably in livery and white gloves), and its perennial token to security—the sign that warned "All Visitors Must Be Announced." Pat gave his name to the uninterested attendant at the door who simply said, "Price? 11-B," and waved him toward an ancient elevator.

Even the gloomy hallway seemed familiar to Patrick. Faint cooking odors, the sounds of women's voices on the telephone, the occasional yapping of an interested dog. He rang the doorbell and was embraced by a neatly dressed, worried-looking Rose.

"Come in, Patrick. Can I get you something to eat? A cup of coffee, maybe?"

For the first time in thirty-six hours, Pat smiled. How typical. She must be frantic with curiosity, but the amenities came automatically.

"Nothing, thanks, Grandmother. You're looking well."

She shrugged off the compliment. "Sit down, Patrick, and tell me what's happened."

He didn't know how to tell her. She'd be hysterical, maybe even physically unable to handle such news. She was not a young woman. Damn, Pat thought, why did I come? But he knew. For the same reason he had to face Sheila with his awful news; because he couldn't let them hear it from some disembodied voice on the telephone.

"It's bad news, Grandmother," he said gently. "It's Maryanne. She— she died Sunday night. Here in New York."

At first he thought she didn't grasp what he'd said. She stared at him blankly and then, with a strange irrelevance, she said, "What was Maryanne doing in New York? She never let me know she was here."

For a second Pat was annoyed. What difference did that make? That's Rose, he thought. Always jumping at the imagined slight—in this case the fact that Maryanne hadn't called her. Then he realized she was in shock, involuntarily trying to ignore the terrible part of his news.

"She was performing here with a rock group, a little orchestra. It wasn't very attractive, any of it. I suppose she didn't want you to know."

Rose continued to look uncomprehending.

"She was terribly unhappy, Grandmother. We had no idea how unhappy. The cards she sent Mother sounded as though everything was going well. It wasn't. I don't know too much" (no need to mention the pregnancy) "but she must have been desperate. Maryanne took her life, dear. I identified her in the morgue last night."

He'd been sure she'd begin to scream, to come apart as the meaning of what he was saying began to sink in. But she didn't move. She sat on the big old couch like some small, carved-in-stone statue, only her eyes widening in horror as she forced herself to accept what she heard. She didn't ask for details of the suicide or what the plans were. She simply said, "Sheila. Sheila. Sheila," over and over again, as though she could bear for herself what she could not bear for her daughter.

Patrick took her hand. "Mother doesn't know yet. I wasn't sure it was Maryanne until I got here." Suddenly it was his eyes that filled with tears while his grandmother sat like a robot, softly repeating her child's name. "I couldn't tell her what I was coming to New York to confirm. And," his voice broke, "I can't tell her until I can be with her." He cleared his throat. "I'll be able to take Maryanne home tomorrow. I know Mother will want her next to Dad."

"Yes." Rose got up. "I'll go with you, Patrick."

"Was I wrong? Should I have called Mother last night?" He was pleading for reassurance, clinging to the woman he'd always thought vain and self-centered and silly.

She seemed to see him for the first time, to be aware of his wretchedness.

"No, Patrick, you weren't wrong. Your instincts were right and unselfish. She'll need you there when she hears."

He was weeping openly now. He got to his feet. "I have to go where she lived. Get her things. I can't believe it."

Rose put her arms around him. "You're a good boy, Patrick. A good son. Sheila's lucky to have you. Just as *I'm* lucky to have *her*." Suddenly she lost control. Grandmother and grandson clung together, crying and trying to comfort each other, groping for understanding, devastated by death, filled with compassion for the unaware woman in Cleveland. They stood that way, not speaking, for a few moments, and then Rose released him. She turned her crumpled face to his own.

"Can I do anything, Patrick?"

He shook his head. "No. Everything's being done. Just be ready to go back with me tomorrow, please."

"Yes, I'll be ready." She still didn't ask exactly how it had happened or any of the hundred questions that, Patrick thought, must be in her mind. "Where are you staying?"

He gave her the name of the small hotel.

"Please come here instead," Rose said. "After you've done what you have to do . . . about Maryanne's things. We should be together. We need each other."

Not "I need you," Patrick thought. That was only part of it. What a strong, surprising woman she really was. She knew he needed not to be alone either. He needed the comfort of family, something in his stupidly superior way he'd always dismissed as "soap opera sentimentality." He'd thought he was objective about "flesh and blood." He'd been cynical about Sean, disgusted with Maryanne, annoyed with Tommy, disparaging about "the Price tag." He hadn't changed overnight, he supposed. Not even now. But there was something reassuring in the knowledge that no matter how one intellectually denied it, the bonds of birth were not easily severed by his generation's sharp, pseudosophistication. Betty was right, he thought. Sheila will need her mother. And Rose will know how to handle those needs, selflessly and well.

"I'll be back," Pat said. "I want to come back."

He was revolted by the dirty little hotel in which his sister had lived. The lobby smelled of urine and stale cigars. An indifferent desk clerk gave him Rick Jawolsky's room number and he took the rickety elevator to the second floor and knocked heavily on Number 28. For a few seconds there was no answer. Patrick glanced at his watch. Too early for Jawolsky to be out. He rapped again, harder, and a sleepy voice called, "Yeah? Who is it?"

"Patrick Callahan."

He heard a fumbling at the latch and then the door opened. Rick, bearded and half-awake, stood naked in the doorway. "Callahan. What's up? What did you find out? Where's your sister?"

Patrick's voice was like ice. "May I come in?"

"Yeah, sure." For the first time Rick seemed to realize he had no clothes on. He fumbled for a pair of shorts and put them on as Pat entered the room.

If the hotel lobby and the sight of this dirty, careless young man had repelled him, his first look at Maryanne's last "home" made him almost physically sick. How could she? Patrick wondered. How could she live in this filthy room with its torn window shades and ragged carpeting, its paint peeling from the walls, it sagging double bed with sheets that looked as though they hadn't been changed in a month? How could she stand the clothes strewn all over, hers included, the welter of cosmetics and shaving equipment, old magazines and piles of dirty laundry? How could a sensitive girl from her background live here, make love here, conceive a child in this or some similar, disgusting place? His thoughts must have been mirrored on his face, because Rick gave a little laugh.

"It ain't exactly the Waldorf, is it? But we weren't being paid like Stevie Wonder."

What excuse is that for living like pigs? Patrick thought. Who was Maryanne trying to punish—you, us, or herself? Maybe everybody. Maybe the whole damned world.

He didn't respond to Rick's sarcasm. "I've come for my sister's belongings," he said.

"You find her?"

"Yes, I found her."

"Well, what gives, man?"

Patrick wanted to smash his face in. "Does it matter to you, Jawolsky?"

"Hey, listen, we had a deal, remember? To let each other know. I've got a right. She was my old lady. Where the hell is she?"

Pat's words were like steel. "Right now she's being embalmed."

Rick's face filled with horror. He opened his mouth but no sound came out.

"That's right," Pat said, "Maryanne's dead. She jumped off a bridge Sunday night with your baby inside her." He was amazed by his own cold, cruel description. He did want to kill this creature. No matter what Betty said, Patrick would always blame him for what happened to Maryanne. Not just the pregnancy nor the insistence on abortion. For caring so little about her, for allowing her to have as little pride as he, for making her last years on earth so ugly and degrading that she couldn't stand the idea of living. God knows what had drawn her to this man, this way of life, and what had made her return to it time and again knowing, as she must have, that it was the road to nowhere.

"Dead?" Rick was saying. "Maryanne killed herself? *Why?*"

Patrick did not conceal his contempt. "*You*, of all people, can ask that? You treated her like a slut, dragged her from one rotten little hotel to another, from one crummy bar to the next." Patrick's anger was mounting. "You refused to accept your baby, wanted no part of your responsibility, didn't give a damn for anything *she* might have been feeling! What did she have to live for, Jawolsky?" Patrick looked around the room. "*This? You?*"

"Wait a minute, man. Your sister knew where it was at as far as we were concerned, but she wanted it both ways, the kicks and the square part. One minute she wanted to hang loose and the next she'd have liked to settle down in Shaker Heights with the straights. I didn't promise her a rose garden, Callahan. She knew damned well what she was into. Who the hell do you think sent her home last Christmas? But she didn't stay. She was a screwed-up dame. Okay, it's tough. But don't blame me." Rick's lip curled. "Maybe you good, middle-class folks should take a look at your part in this, you and your damned hypocritical, nasty-nice lives. You think I'm to blame. That's a nice, easy way to clear your own conscience, isn't it? What about her father who screwed everything in sight and her mother who pretended it wasn't happening? What about the way nobody in that family ever tried to find out what made her tick? A few trips to the shrink and they thought it was all solved. For that matter, Callahan, what about you? Did you ever take time to talk to her these last years? Or were you too busy with your big doctor career and your sensible, high-brow wife? Maryanne told me about all of you. She'd say crazy things like, 'We can't communicate, Rick, my family and I.' I'd say, 'Crap, baby. They ain't worth it.' And she knew I was right. She knew where she stood with me: Expect nothing and take your lumps, I said. Grow up. At least I was honest with her. Right up to the end."

Patrick came at him like a tiger and with one hard punch to the face sent Rick sprawling into a corner of the room. Rick just lay there, rubbing his jaw and smiling.

"Feel better now, Big Man?" Rick asked. "Feel like you've avenged your sister's death? That's nice."

"You lousy bastard," Patrick said. "I shouldn't let you live, you slimy creep!"

"Killing isn't your style, Doctor. You're dedicated to sustaining life, aren't you? Too bad you didn't worry a little less about your patients' and more about your sister's."

266

"Get up," Patrick said. "Shut your goddamn mouth and give me the things that belonged to my sister."

Rick didn't move. He just waved his hand. "Help yourself. Anything here that looks like it belongs to a broad is hers."

Angrily, silently, Patrick opened the one closet. There were a few pairs of women's slacks and a couple of shirts, three glittery "costumes," and a jumble of shoes, a cloth coat he remembered, good but old and worn. He slammed the door and turned to the bureau. Maryanne's "good jewelry," what there was of it, lay in a plastic tray on top: the opal ring she'd gotten for her twenty-first birthday, a couple of gold bangles. She'd had many more nice, modest pieces—gifts given to her over the years.

"Where's the rest of her jewelry?" Patrick asked. "Where's her watch and the little diamond pendant she used to wear?"

"Damned if I know. She probably sold them. I didn't keep track of that junk."

Pat wondered whether he was lying. It didn't matter. Maryanne had nothing of great value, but Sheila would want everything for sentimental reasons. He opened the bureau drawers, pushing aside the few pieces of lingerie. In a corner of one he found a cheap, quilted box, the kind you bought in a variety store. Inside was all there was of Maryanne. Some old snapshots of her family, her college ring, an obituary notice about her father from the Cleveland paper, a mediocre review of her singing from *The Village Voice*. Pat put all the pitiful reminders of her into the box and tucked it under his arm. Wordlessly, he turned to the door, not looking at Rick.

"That's it?" the man on the floor asked. "Sure you don't want to search some more? I might be holding out on you."

Patrick turned and stared at him. "You took the only thing we cared about a long time ago," he said.

Chapter 29

Later, Sheila was never again to believe in "a mother's instinct." She had no uneasy feeling, no ESP, if you will, during the time Patrick was coping with his family's latest and greatest tragedy. If anything, she was unusually blithe, preparing for her Palm Beach weekend, thinking how to phrase the news of her marriage, to make Tommy happy about it. She was even proud of the way she'd handled the meeting with Jerry. She'd been able to see him clearly and dispassionately for the first time, could feel a certain mature pity for the insecurity he must feel, the still-childish need to prove that no one could resist him. Bless Bill for that, she thought. Without him, I probably would have closed my eyes to what a selfish little boy Jerry really is. I might even have gone back to him out of loneliness and fear of the future. He was still an attractive man, no denying that. No denying either, the kind of animal magnetism he possessed. But compared to Bill Reardon, Jerry was three feet tall, a passionate playmate who might wander off at any moment to pursue his games in somebody else's back yard.

I'm so lucky, she thought. It's too good to be true. How many widows or divorceés are fortunate enough to have a wonderful man in love with them? How many people, for that matter, get a second chance at what always should have been? Without thinking, she knocked on wood. Then she smiled. Bill would have teased her about her superstitious belief that

268

good things just couldn't happen to her. It was still another of the ridiculous, inbred feelings of "I-don't-deserve" that had plagued her most of her life, feelings that Bill finally had dispelled.

The only thing strange was that she hadn't heard from Sally. Sheila had called Tuesday evening, hoping Sally might have had some word from her friend Paul Birmingham, but there was no answer. Nor had her friend been in touch. By Wednesday, Sheila began to feel uneasy. It was unlike Sally not to check in, to be unreachable, especially when she knew how anxious Sheila was for any word of Maryanne. What if Sally were ill or had had an accident and was lying in her house unable to call for help? No, that was almost impossible. Her maid came every day. She's probably just busy, Sheila decided, and hasn't called because she hasn't anything to report. Maybe Birmingham couldn't find The Potboilers. They were such an obscure, unimportant little group that it might be almost impossible to locate them. In any case, Maryanne would contact her mother again, sooner or later. Sheila only wished the girl could share in her happiness, and that Maryanne could find a feeling of peace approaching her own.

Had she been of a more suspicious nature, she might have found it odd that Sally's silence was in contrast to Betty's unusual attentiveness. Her daughter-in-law called her twice on Wednesday, without, apparently, anything specific to say. On the second call, Sheila did say, lightly, "Not that I don't love hearing from you, sweetheart, but what's this sudden telephonitis? Are you okay? There's nothing wrong about the baby, is there? I mean, everything's okay with you, isn't it?"

Betty had laughed. "I'm fine. Probably just having pregnancy jitters. I guess I need to talk to another woman. Part of my delicate condition."

The explanation had satisfied Sheila. She could understand that, identify with it. Betty had no mother to share this new experience. She remembered when she was carrying Patrick how often she'd phoned Rose. Sean had been disgusted, uncomprehending. "For God's sake," he'd said, "do you have to call your mother all the time? You never did before!" She'd never been quite able to explain it to him, or even to herself. She'd never felt that close to Rose, yet at that particular, frightening time in her life, she felt the need to be in touch with a woman who'd shared the same anxieties. That was how Betty felt now. In a way, Sheila was pleased. Betty was like a daughter to her. I'm closer to her; I understand her better than I do Maryanne. We know each other the way my own child and I never have. She had no idea that Betty, horrified by Patrick's determination to keep Maryanne's death secret until he got home, kept calling Sheila as though the calls would make up for her husband's well-meaning but ill-conceived plan. To Betty, the calls to Sheila eased the bad conscience that Pat had thrust upon his wife. Even though she said nothing about Maryanne, she felt somehow that Sheila would know later what these calls had really meant.

Betty suffered terribly in this conspiracy of compassionate silence. She had told no one except Sally what Patrick had found in New York. It had been the worst twenty-four hours of her life. She'd reacted by wanting to let Sheila hear the voice of one who loved her. Sally's reaction, after the first horrible shock, had been to avoid her friend. It was cowardly, but she simply could not talk to Sheila, knowing what she knew and pretending she'd heard nothing. She knew her voice would give her away. She'd burst into tears and break the promise of secrecy that Pat had imposed through Betty. So she simply didn't answer the phone at night, though she was sure it was Sheila calling. And she gave instructions to her maid to say she was out if anyone called during the day.

After Betty's call, Sally had gotten hysterical, alone in her big, beautiful empty house. She wanted to rush to Sheila, to offer whatever comfort she could, and she was frustrated and angry that this was not allowed. Patrick is crazy! He can't come back to Cleveland with a casket and present Sheila with the most terrible shock of her life! Betty agreed, but she was equally helpless.

"What can I do, Sally?" she'd asked. "I know this is wrong, but Pat's adamant. He doesn't want Sheila rushing to New York and going through all that ugliness."

"He's depriving her of her rights!" Sally said.

"I know. But he can't see it from a mother's point of view. He thinks he's being protective. Making it as easy for Sheila as possible."

"*Easy!*"

"Right now, I mean. He knows what it will be like when he brings Maryanne home. He's trying to save Sheila this preliminary torture. He means well. He just doesn't understand how a woman would feel at a time like this."

"What . . . what happens when he arrives?"

Betty sighed. "God knows."

On Wednesday evening, thinking of her conversations with Betty, Sheila impulsively decided to call Rose. She hadn't told her mother she was going to Palm Beach. Not that it was necessary that she should, but she didn't like to be unreachable, if she could avoid it, in case Rose needed her. The only time she didn't know where I was, Sheila thought with amusement, was when I was in Bermuda, the only time in my whole life, nearly forty-eight years of it, she wouldn't have been able to find me. Even as a kid I was always "checking in," even if I was going to be out later than expected on a date. "You mustn't worry your mother," her father had said. And for the most part, she never had, even when she was grown and married and no longer Rose's responsibility. In her early life, she'd resented those demands. Now she understood them. All the more because one of her own refused to conform. It wasn't so much to ask, Sheila thought almost angrily. Maryanne could let me know where she is. I wouldn't interfere in her life.

She dialed Rose's number in New York and a man's voice, a familiar voice, answered. She knew it instantly and was so stunned that he said "Hello?" three times before she could speak.

"Patrick?" She was incredulous. "Patrick is that you? What on earth are you doing there?"

He was even more dismayed to hear her. Oh, Jesus, why had he automatically picked up this damned telephone while his grandmother was in the kitchen? Why had Sheila chosen this moment to call? Had Betty told her? No. Otherwise she wouldn't have been so genuinely surprised to hear him on the other end of the line. Think fast, he told himself. But he couldn't. He was too numbed by what he'd been through to come up with a glib, believable explanation.

"Patrick!" Sheila was almost shouting now. "What's going on? Has something happened to Mother?"

"No, she's all right," he said finally. And then, because he couldn't stand it any longer, he blurted out, "It's Maryanne. I'm here because of Maryanne."

"You've found her!" There was joy in Sheila's voice. "But how? When? Why didn't you *tell* me?"

There was no way around it now. All his plans for breaking the news to her gently, for holding her as he told her how peaceful Maryanne looked, all the patient, tender things he'd hoped to say to soften her shock and grief—all these had gone up in smoke with one stupidly coincidental phone call.

"Dear," he said, "it's not good news. That's why I didn't call you to say I was coming here. I wanted to be sure first how bad it was."

He sensed Sheila grasping at a last straw. "She's ill, isn't she, Pat? Very ill?"

I can't, Patrick thought. Oh, God, I can't!

"Maryanne's gone, Mother," he said, his voice trembling. "She died Sunday night."

There was an instant of silence and then a sound so terrible and heartbreaking it sounded as though it came from a soul in hell. "No! No, no, no! No, my little girl isn't dead! No! That isn't true. Tell me it isn't true. Patrick, please tell me it isn't true!" She was babbling incoherently, crying, half shrieking, half sobbing the words.

"Darling, hold on to yourself," he said, choked with pity. "Hold on as best you can until Betty gets there. She'll be with you in a few minutes, Mother. Hang on. Be brave; be strong."

"No!" she kept repeating. "No! Not Maryanne!"

271

Rose came out of the kitchen and Patrick beckoned frantically to her. "It's Mother," he said, his hand covering the receiver. "I had to tell her. Help me, Grandmother. Please."

White-faced, Rose took the phone. "Sheila. Sheila, darling, it's Mother. We're coming to you, love. It's terrible. Terrible. But it's what she wanted. It's God's will, Sheila. You must accept it. We all must."

Sheila didn't answer, did not comprehend what Rose meant by "Maryanne's wanting it." She continued to sob and moan like a lost soul. Then she mumbled, "I can't. I can't take this. Why is God punishing me? Why did he take my child? Why am I cursed, always cursed?"

Rose's lips froze into a thin line. This was not like Sean's death when Rose could be dramatic because she was touched only on the surface. This time Rose's grief was so deep that it tapped some inner source of strength. She loved her only granddaughter, just as she loved her daughter. One was gone. The other had to be saved, even with harshness.

"Stop thinking only of yourself," she said sharply. "God hasn't singled you out for punishment, Sheila. There are others as destroyed as you. Your son, for one. He's been through agony for your sake. Don't make it worse for him now. He's had about all he can take."

The stern words seem to take effect. Sheila quieted down a little. "Mother," she said pathetically, "you're coming to be with me? I need you."

"I'm coming tomorrow, darling. We all are. Betty will be there soon. She'll stay with you. Have strength, my dear. Have faith. Pray, Sheila. Pray for your daughter's soul, child. Pray God will forgive her. And thank Him for all the love that's around you."

Her own tears starting to flow, Rose handed the phone back to Patrick. "She'll make it," Rose said.

Betty was there within half an hour. Damn Patrick! she thought as she raced toward the house. If only he'd done as I asked, so I could have been there when Sheila heard. She shuddered, thinking what it would be like to be all alone when you heard such news. She was almost afraid of what she'd find now. Hysteria, at the least. Maybe I should have called Sally or Bob Ross or someone to come with me. But there'd been no time. After Patrick's call, she'd jumped in the car and headed for this poor woman who must be going out of her mind. For a fleeting moment as she rang the doorbell, Betty wondered whether in those first black moments Sheila could possibly have taken Maryanne's way out. It seemed as though the door was never going to be opened. She rang again, harder, more insistently, and finally Sheila appeared. Betty breathed a sigh of relief as she silently took her mother-in-law into her arms. It was like holding a piece of wood, a living but lifeless thing whose arms hung limply at her sides and whose face was vacant, with a glazed, unseeing expression. Betty led her gently into the living room and helped her onto the couch. It was like maneuvering a doll whose joints responded automatically and whose china eyes stared straight ahead. Silence surrounded her like a shroud. She's in deep shock, Betty realized. I must get help.

"Darling, I'm going to call a doctor," she said. "He'll come and give you something to help you rest."

Only then did Sheila respond. She shook her head. "No. I don't want to rest. I want to remember."

Betty protested. "Not now, dear. Later. Right now you need something for the pain."

Sheila finally looked at her. "I deserve the pain. I demand my right to it."

What am I going to do? Betty wondered. She should be sedated but I know she won't accept it. She's already begun to punish herself. How far will she go with it?

"Then let me call Sally."

Sheila stared at her, almost without recognition. "Can she bring Maryanne back?"

Betty was in despair. She'd been prepared for uncontrollable grief, for tears, for breast-beating, but not for this dead, terrifying calm. "All right, dear. Whatever you want. Will you take a little brandy if I get it?"

There was no answer. Then Sheila said, in a strange monotone, "How did it happen? Do you know?"

How can I possibly tell her about the deserted bridge, the cold, dark water? How can I tell her about the desperation of a pregnant young woman who must have felt utterly hopeless and abandoned? How can I explain a daughter who couldn't, or wouldn't, come home?

"She did it to herself, didn't she?" Sheila said. "That's what Mother meant when she said Maryanne wanted it that way."

"Yes." All the sadness Betty felt was in that one word. "She must have been temporarily out of her mind, Sheila. I believe all people who take their lives are. It wasn't Maryanne. It was that other person inside her, the one no one could reach. No one, Sheila," she repeated. "Not even you."

There was no answer.

"It's true," Betty said quietly. "You must believe that. You mustn't blame yourself. You tried. You did everything you could for her." She wasn't sure Sheila even heard her. After that first, involuntary cry of pain, Sheila had retreated into a kind of mindless state. I can't pull her out of it now, Betty thought. I dare not even suggest she go to bed. All I can do is stay with her.

The two women, one awaiting a child, the other unable to accept the loss of one, sat silently, ghostlike, through the long, black night.

As they had less than a year before, they all came, gathering around Sheila in her grief. But it was different, in so many ways, from Sean's death. Not only because the victim was so young, not even because the stupid but unmistakable stigma of suicide hung in the air. It was different because Sheila was different. She'd been shocked and saddened by her husband's sudden death, but she'd been within the limits of reason. She was not now. She's aged twenty years in twenty-four hours, Betty thought late the next night. She's more of a corpse than the young woman who lay in the same Cleveland funeral home that had held her father only months before.

No one could get through to her. Not Sally whom Betty called early Thursday morning and who arrived and took charge the way Margaret had last August. Like Betty, Sally put her arms around Sheila, crying and stammering words of consolation. But Sheila responded only with the same kind of passive acceptance Betty had received. Sally and Betty exchanged worried glances and the younger woman simply shook her head as though to say, There's nothing we can do but wait.

It was Sally who made the awful calls this time, to Terry and Margaret, to the Rosses, and finally to the Callahans in Palm Beach. She went into as few details as possible, but of course they had to know, all these people who were closest to Sheila. The family was devastated. The friends were shocked and almost disbelieving and, in Bob Ross's case, terribly concerned for Sheila. He wanted to come over, but Sally dissuaded him. "Not just yet, Bob. She's talking to no one, not even Betty or me. Patrick and Rose arrive this evening. Give her a day to pull herself together." I wish I believed it would be a day, Sally thought. I don't recognize this mute, far-away person who's my dearest friend.

The call to Florida was the hardest, of course. Fortunately, Bill Callahan answered and after his first horrified gasp, he asked for details. Sally told him what she knew, leaving out the fact that Maryanne was pregnant. Not even Sheila knew that. It would be better if she never did, if she never knew she'd lost a grandchild as well. Bill kept his voice low. "Tommy's out," he said, "and Jean's in the other room. I'll tell them, Sally, as best I can. We'll leave here immediately, of course. What are the arrangements?"

She told him they were waiting for Patrick and Rose to arrive with Maryanne's body. "I talked with Pat early this morning," she said. "He thinks, subject to Sheila's agreement, that it should all be quick. Services on Saturday morning and, if we get dispensation from the Church, burial next to her father."

"Does Sheila agree?"

Sally sighed. "She doesn't talk, Bill. She hasn't even asked how it happened or why she didn't hear about it from Sunday night until Wednesday evening. It's as though she's withdrawn from everything and everybody."

She couldn't mention Bill Reardon, the only one Sheila might listen to.

She couldn't find Bill in New York and when she asked Sheila where he was, she just turned her head away. But Sally imagined he'd be calling here. He did, almost every day. I'm putting a lot of faith in his appearance, she thought. If anybody can snap her out of this, he should be able to. She paused. "I'm sorry. I hate being the one to bring you such news, especially so soon after Sean."

"You can't help that, Sally. Maryanne's death is a terrible blow, but I'm worried about Sheila. What you've told me makes me very apprehensive about her. And there's Tommy. I don't know how he'll take this. Poor kid. He isn't the boy he was before his father died. Jean and I haven't wanted to worry his mother, but we were glad she was coming down here. Tom hasn't given us any real trouble, it's just a kind of don't-give-a-damn attitude that worries us. And now, with Maryanne, well, I don't know. Seems like Sheila has had more than any one person can be expected to bear."

"Yes. And just when we thought things were going to be perfect for her." She wanted to add "again," for the sake of Sean's father. But she couldn't. Things hadn't been perfect for Sheila during that whole volatile, ego-deflating marriage. Bill Callahan probably knew that, too, but neither of them was going to admit it.

Except that her eyes were open and she moved, Sheila could have been in a coma. Patrick and Rose arrived and she seemed to hear nothing they were saying. The instinctive cry for her mother seemed to have been only a momentary thing. She did not sleep or eat and barely spoke. They told her, gently, of the funeral plans and she said nothing. When Bill Reardon phoned on Thursday evening, Sheila would not speak to him. It was Sally who again had to go through the grim story and try to explain Sheila's mental state. Bill's response was instantaneous.

"I'm on my way," he said.

Sally hesitated. "We don't know each other, Bill, but I'll speak frankly. When Sheila went into this terrible retreat from reality, I pinned all my hopes on you. She loves you so much. She was so happy a few days ago, planning her future with you. I thought you could bring her back to life. But now I don't know. I've seen depressions before, but never one like this. I'm not sure she'll speak even to you. She hasn't talked to her son or her mother or me. She just sits and stares into space. We're—we're afraid to leave her alone. She seems to have no will to live."

"She must live. Not just for her own sake; for mine, too. My God, she has every right to be in shock! Who wouldn't be, at a time like this?"

"It's much more than that, I'm afraid. I think it goes 'way back, Bill. I think she's going to need professional help and I hope she'll accept it."

She knew he thought she was dramatizing Sheila's condition. But that was because he hadn't seen this empty shell that was once the cheerful, communicative Sheila. Maybe he's right. Maybe when she sees Maryanne (if she will; so far she'd refused to) and when Bill talks to her and Tommy arrives she'll break down and cry and come back to us. "All right," Sally said. "Maybe I'm too close to it. Come to her, Bill. Maybe you *are* the answer after all."

"Has Tommy arrived?"

"No. They'll be here in the morning."

"Poor kid," he said, echoing Bill Callahan's words. "This'll be tough on him. His father and sister gone and his mother in the state she's in. I want to help that boy, Sally. I guess you know what he represents to me. Not just a part of Sheila, but another son of my own."

"I know. Sheila told me. It was a big part of her happiness, knowing how much you wanted Tommy. I'm sure she told you she'd planned to go to Palm Beach this weekend to tell him all about you."

"Yes, she told me again Tuesday night on the phone how happy she was, how hopeful that Tommy would be glad."

Bill remembered the lilting voice, the almost-girlish gaiety, the affectionate banter on the phone. He would not believe this was more than a natural, stunned reaction to tragedy. She was deep in her grief, but she'd come out of it, however slowly. He was more determined than ever that they'd start their new life as planned, wipe out the memories of the past. She was mourning deeply, understandably. But it was not possible that she could undergo a total personality change overnight, not even with a blow as terrible as this.

"I'll be there tomorrow," he said. "We'll pull her out of this, Sally, I promise you. You and Rose and Patrick and I. And Tommy. She'll cherish him more than ever now."

Sally didn't answer. You don't know Tommy, she thought. None of us does. He probably feels he's nothing to anybody. It occurred to her that probably he had felt displaced for a long time, had come to realize it only since Sean's death. All his life he thought he'd been overshadowed by his parents' admiration for Patrick, imagined he played second fiddle to a sister who drained their emotions. He'd never been the "macho boy" Sean had wanted. And even after his father died, he'd had less of Sheila than he hoped for, had been quickly "replaced" by Jerry Mancini. What would he think when he found out about Bill Reardon, his intended stepfather? Would this solid, loving man bring Tommy closer to Sheila or tear them farther apart? Yes, everybody used the right term: poor kid. Poor, angry, uncomprehending Tommy. She felt almost as sorry for him as she did for Sheila.

Chapter 30

Tommy slowly packed all his belongings. Everything he'd brought to Palm Beach and quite a few things he'd acquired in these past months. He wasn't coming back here. No point. It was only a few weeks until school closed. He was glad of an excuse to go home early. Glad to get away from his grandparents. They'd been good to him, almost too good, too solicitous, too anxious to be his "friends." They didn't know that kids didn't want their grandparents or, for that matter, their parents to be pals to them. It was like acting a part all the time, everybody trying to pretend that it was natural for him to be here, as though he was some welcome house guest instead of a "bad boy" in exile.

That's the way he thought of it, as exile. He hated Palm Beach with its hokey hibiscus bushes and its overdressed tourists. He hated the kids who went to school in a resort. A resort was for play, not for study. He found himself adopting an indolent attitude toward study, something, even in his worst moments in Cleveland, he'd never felt.

Yes, he was glad about a lot of things. Secretly ashamed of the fact, he made himself face it: He was not even all that sorry that Maryanne was dead. It seemed all his life the family had been obsessed with Maryanne, her complexes, her crazy behavior, her unpredictable "reforms" and almost immediate relapses that made Mom so miserable. She'd been one of the reasons his parents had fought so much. He could remember when he was ten or eleven, hearing them argue about what to do with her. When she'd finally left home, he'd been glad. But it hadn't ended even then. Sheila was always talking about her, worrying about her shacking up with Jawolsky, trying to get her back to Shaker Heights where, for Chrissakes, anybody could see she'd never belong.

He hadn't even been surprised when he heard about her suicide. It wasn't that he hated his sister, he just knew she'd end up dead. He'd figured it might be in a car accident, or maybe she'd o.d. on drugs or be killed by that crazy guy she lived with. But he knew something was going to happen to her because she wanted it to. He wondered why nobody else saw the self-destructive side of her. Maybe they did. Maybe Sheila did and couldn't face it.

Anyway, he couldn't be sad she was gone. She was bad news. Nowhere to go but down. She was hell-bent on making trouble, for herself and everybody else. It might have gone on for years, driving his mother crazy with worry.

What a bastard you are, Callahan, he told himself. Your only sister killed herself and all you feel is relief. Why can't you at least feel sorry for such a mixed-up girl? Jesus, man, she was part of your own family! He remembered how he felt when his grandfather told him and his grandmother about her. Bill had looked tortured and Jean had collapsed, sobbing. But he felt nothing, except maybe a sense of release. The way he guessed you'd feel if you were married to a woman you hated and couldn't divorce. Or like if you had a deformed child with no future.

Bill had said that Sheila was taking it hard, that they were not to be surprised if she barely knew them when they got there. Tommy didn't believe that. The not knowing them part, that is. He'd be able to comfort her. She'd be so glad to have him home. He was all she had now. There was Patrick, of course, but he had his own life, his career, Betty, and a baby on the way. It was Tommy Sheila would turn to. He'd be the whole focus of her life, the way he'd always hoped to be, the way he'd deserved to be all these years.

He wondered about the good news she'd planned to come and tell them this weekend. Thank God it didn't have to do with Mancini! Maybe it was money. Maybe his father had left more than they knew. If so, Sheila wouldn't have to work any more. She could be home, where she belonged.

Unconsciously, he began to whistle as he packed his bags. A bright, cheerful tune. Passing his door, Jean and Bill Callahan looked at each other and wondered.

I'm more nervous now, Bill Reardon thought as the plane landed in Cleveland, than I was when I first came here a few weeks ago. Then, I was afraid of a "public appearance." Now I'm scared of a private one. Strange to think he was walking into a world of strangers, all of whom soon would be part of his life. Aside from Rose, he knew no one. And not many of them even knew *about* him. So what? He didn't have to "pass inspection" by Sheila's friends or, for that matter, even by her family. He hoped her sons would like him but if, God forbid, they didn't, that still wouldn't change his plans. His and Sheila's. Since Maryanne's death, it seemed more important to him than ever that Sheila marry him quickly, make a new life, get away from all the old reminders. Maybe he could convince her not to wait until July. He wanted to take her away, take care of her, help her forget.

He dropped his overnight bag at the Hollenden, checking into a room that was almost identical to the one he'd had before. He smiled sadly, remembering the happy nonsense about the double beds. And his face softened as he thought of the big one they shared later in Bermuda. Maybe they'd go back to Bermuda right away, spend the summer there. Tommy could come with them. It didn't matter if Sheila's kid went along on the "honeymoon." They'd already had that.

Without even calling, he took a cab to Shaker Heights. The door was opened by an attractive woman about Sheila's age who smiled at him, "You're Bill. I'm glad you're here."

He took her hand. "And you must be Sally. How is she?"

She led the way into the living room. There was no one around. "Not good," Sally said.

He glanced around. "Where's everybody?"

"Various places. Tommy's up in his quarters and the Callahans are in their room. Pat and Betty have gone home to get a little rest. Rose is sitting with Sheila in her bedroom. I've asked friends not to come. I don't think they understand that Sheila can't see anybody. Or won't. But I really don't care."

"She'll see me," Bill said.

"Yes. Of course. I'll tell her you've arrived."

She disappeared and in a few minutes Rose came downstairs. He hadn't seen her in years and his first thought was how remarkably little she'd changed. There was the same strength, the same look of determination he remembered. As a kid, he'd always been a little intimidated by her, even though he knew she liked him. There was something about the way she'd always seemed so completely in charge, of Sheila and Sheila's father, of their whole lives. He was thankful for that ability now. When the going got tough, Bill thought, Rose was the kind of gutsy Irish lady who rose to the occasion. She could pull out all the stops when she chose—be pathetic, put-upon, and, he was sure, irritating. But when it came to a crisis, she'd be strong as a rock.

He kissed her lightly on the cheek. "I'm so sorry, Mrs. Price. I never knew Maryanne, but if she was anything like her mother, it's a terrible loss."

Rose nodded. "It's tragic, Bill." And then, almost as though she were thinking aloud, "All the more because they didn't really know how alike they were. Sheila was always a conformist and Maryanne a rebel. They both thought they hated each others' lives and yet, in a funny way, I think they almost envied them. The sad part was, they were never able to show their deep feelings for each other. I think that's what Sheila's realizing now . . . and feeling guilty, responsible, really, for letting that girl go to her death."

"But she wasn't responsible! We talked a lot about our past and our children. I know how she worried about hers. But she's too intelligent to think she failed any of them in any way!"

"I hope you can convince her of that. So far none of us has been able to." For the first time she looked uncertain. "I don't know what's going to happen to her now."

"We all get over things, Mrs. Price. No matter how terrible. You know that from experience. And, Lord knows, so do I."

"Yes. I heard about your wife and son, Bill. How you must have suffered!"

"The suffering didn't stop until I found Sheila again," he said. "Then I knew that life could still have meaning. That's what she did for me, and that's what I'm going to do for her." He paused. "You know we plan to be married. We'd set July. I hope to convince her to do it sooner."

"I hope you can. . . ." Rose's voice trailed off.

"But you don't think so."

She faced him squarely, the bright blue eyes boring into his. "You want the truth? I'm not sure she'll marry you or anybody after this."

He stared at her in amazement. "Oh, look here, Mrs. Price! I can imagine the state she's in, the shock, the grief, the self-reproachment. But we know that will pass. Maybe I won't be able to convince her to marry me earlier, but she'll marry me. She loves me."

"I'm sure she loves you. But something terrible has happened to Sheila. I want to believe, as you do, that time will heal. I do believe it, because God is merciful. And yet, looking at her now . . ."

"May I see her?"

Rose hesitated. Only moments before Sheila had said she didn't want to see him. Not him. Not anyone. Tommy was sitting alone in his room, bewildered by a mother who barely glanced at him when he came home. Even Patrick had finally gone away, frustrated by his inability to get a word out of her. Only when Sally had come up and said Bill Reardon was here did Sheila speak. "I don't want to see him," she said, turning her head away on the pillow. It was unfathomable. No one could reach into Sheila's mind, to uncover the demons that possessed her. It was much more than grief. It was kind of a deliberately self-inflicted madness, quiet, deep, understood by no one, probably not even by Sheila herself. If she's going crazy, Rose thought, she's taking us all with her. It must be stopped.

"Yes," Rose said, "you must see her."

She let him into the darkened room and left, closing the door behind her. He stood for a long while looking down at the woman he loved, a woman lying so still she seemed not to be breathing. He thought he'd never seen anyone so agonized, though her features were composed and her eyes closed as though she slept. He knew she didn't. He pulled a chair up to the bed and took her hand. She didn't stir.

"Sheila. Darling. It's Bill. I'm here with you. Don't be afraid, sweetheart. You're not alone. You'll never be alone again."

For a long time she didn't respond. Her hand lay limply in his grasp and her body was perfectly still. Then, finally, she opened her eyes.

"Why did you come?"

"Where else could I possibly be? You're my love, my life."

She shook her head. "I have no life left. No love to give. Nothing. It's empty. *I'm* empty. Go away, Bill. It's over. Everything's over."

"No. Everything's beginning. Just as we planned."

"I killed her."

"Sweetheart, don't say such things! You loved Maryanne. You did everything you could."

"I did nothing. I sat back and let her go."

"No, Sheila. You're wrong. You can't control another life. And you can't give up your own to right what you think is wrong."

"Can't I? I'm the sinner. The criminal. And the criminal suffers more than the victim." She seemed to rouse suddenly and her voice became strong. "I have no right to go on as though nothing has happened. I don't deserve to be stupidly satisfied when I let my child die. I've failed everybody in my whole life. Sean. Maryanne. Even Tommy. I'm less than nothing. A blind, selfish fool who's taken all and given nothing. No more. No more. I hate the Sheila Callahan who was. I loathe her. I'll bury her tomorrow, along with her daughter."

"Sheila, you're not making sense!"

"Yes, I am. More than I ever have in my life. I'm not a nice woman, Bill. I've been a hypocrite. I chose to see only what I wanted to see, pretended everything was the way I *wanted* it to be. I made up a marriage that was shallow and phony. I dismissed Tommy's cry for help as a 'boyish prank.'" She laughed harshly. "I even deluded myself that Maryanne was happy, that she was going to be a success as a singer. And I was angry that she didn't pay more attention to me. Sheila Callahan is loathsome, stupid, and vain. She's a jinx. But she's not going to ruin your life, too."

He gathered her into his arms. She was trying to take the failures of those she loved on to her own shoulders. It was the only way she could survive her grief, for now. It was pointless to argue with her, to tell her how temporarily masochistic she was. How irrational. He held her gently, as he'd sometimes held his own child, and he spoke softly and reassuringly.

"Rest, my darling. Remember there are perfect years ahead."

She didn't answer. She didn't believe it. She'd never known any.

She'd broken through the wall of silence, and now, with a sudden return to her old composure, she rose from her bed and moved forward into her life. But the composure was feigned. Outwardly, she was calm, kind, the "old" Sheila. But inside there was an emotional malignancy, a spiritual cancer that ate away everything she'd believed in. She felt it had killed her, though she still lived.

She went through Maryanne's funeral as she had Sean's with the kind of self-constraint that deceived everyone but Bill Reardon. Her family and friends took heart at the sign of her "recovery" and they thought again how brave, how extraordinary she was. They blessed Bill. He was, they thought, her salvation, staying close to her side, giving her not only emotional strength but even physical support. She held his arm at the church and the cemetery. They liked him, for himself and for Sheila. They did not know what had been said in that bedroom on Friday.

Only Tommy denied Bill the gratitude expressed by the others. He was scrupulously polite to his mother's old friend, but he exuded an air of possessiveness that said, more clearly than words, that Sheila was *his* responsibility. Unaware that she'd planned to marry Bill, Tommy accepted him as someone from the past, with no part in the future. And when Bill went back to New York on Sunday evening the boy had no idea that the man who left was heavy with disappointment.

Not that Bill had given up the idea that Sheila would marry him. But he saw that no words of his could bring back the woman he loved. Not yet. Still, he knew that beneath the self-condemnation, the exquisite torture of guilt, she was there and would emerge again. He'd wait. He'd seen too much grief, too much abandonment of hope not to know that in time the pain ebbed, the mind cleared, and self-preservation, now denied, would return. He'd had one more talk with Sheila on Sunday morning, an apparently fruitless talk. She'd said, more calmly, what she'd said before. She couldn't marry him or anyone else. She loved him, but she had nothing to give.

"I don't ask anything," Bill said. "Let *me* be the giver, darling. There's joy in giving."

"No. You'd soon tire of living with someone who felt nothing but disgust for herself."

There'd been more. More that made no sense except to Sheila's penitent mind. He didn't press her. He was too wise for that. He kept saying over and over how much he loved her, how much he needed her. She'd smiled sadly and stroked his hair and told him she'd give anything in the world not to feel as she did. She simply couldn't help it.

"Everybody else thinks it's just a matter of time," she said. "They think I'm already on my way back. Only that's not true, Bill. I can never come back."

He didn't argue with her. It was useless to keep going over the same ground. He kissed her lightly, as he would a sister, and went away without another word.

Chapter 31

Rose left, reluctantly, the following Tuesday. As she had the past August, she offered to stay on, really wanted to. But Sheila had, once again, assured her that she was able to pick up and go on.

"I must, Mother. I want to go back to work. Try to get back to normal. I love you. I may not show it, but I need you. I always will need you. But I can't lean on you or anyone."

"What about Bill?"

"We've postponed that, dear." Better to lie. She couldn't explain what she felt, couldn't listen to Rose's protestations that she was foolishly throwing away her life for no reason.

"Not for long, I hope," her mother said. "I know when you told me about you and Bill I said it was unseemly for you to marry less than a year after Sean's death, but things are different now. He's a good man, Sheila. A strong one. And you need each other. Don't make the mistake of losing him."

"You believe that's the answer to everything, don't you? Marriage." She did not say it unkindly.

"I know that when it's right it's the only way to live," Rose answered. "You may have thought I was not a loving wife, Sheila. It's not my nature to be effusively affectionate. But your father understood me. I've never had a truly happy day without him. It's no good being alone,

Sheila. Look around you. There are too many bored, useless, unfulfilled widows. Like me. I don't want that for you."

They're not like *me*, Sheila thought. The widows are like *you*, guiltless in their loneliness. They think they had good lives, that they gave everything to their marriages. Maybe they did. I only blinded myself to my faults. I won't do that again.

"We'll see," she said soothingly. "Bill's a wonderful man. He deserves to be happy. He will be."

Rose seemed relieved. She interpreted that as Sheila meant her to: that Bill would be happy with *her*. Not, as Sheila believed, he'd be happy when he found someone as generous and giving as his Eileene was, as Sheila had felt herself to be, until Maryanne's suicide showed her what a miserable failure she'd been as a wife and mother. I have only one chance to make up for some of it, Sheila thought, and that's through Tommy. I'm going to be the kind of mother he needs for the next few years, the kind he's never really had. It's the least I can do. There'd always been so much to distract her before. Sean and his demands, Patrick's education, Maryanne's problems, the short-lived but all-absorbing affair with Jerry, even her selfish involvement with Bill. Tommy had always been there, somewhere on the fringes, loved but taken for granted. Yanked out of his school, packed off to Florida, expected to adjust to everybody's needs, crying out for his own.

As they walked back to the car after seeing Rose off, Sheila put her arm across her son's shoulders. "It's going to be a good summer, Tommy. We're the July birthday kids, remember? The moon children. We'll do a lot of loony things together." Tommy's birthday was two days after hers. On the fourteenth he'd be sixteen. "Hey," she said, "you'll be able to drive the car. Legally. That's a milestone!" Then, involuntarily, she shuddered. Tommy felt it.

"What's the matter, Mom? You okay?"

"Of course." She couldn't tell him that at that instant she'd thought of young Billy Reardon. Nothing will happen to Tommy, she thought fiercely. Why am I so fearful of everything? Nonetheless, she said, "You've got to promise me, though, that you'll be very careful when you get your license. I know you're already a good driver, but there are such maniacs on the road. They're the ones I worry about."

He smiled. "Don't worry. I'm going to be the most careful chauffeur you've ever had. You'll think you're riding in a hearse." He looked stricken. "Oh, lord, I'm sorry, Mom!"

She patted his shoulder. "It's all right, Tom. Just a slip of the tongue. When I shivered I nearly came out with that old superstition that 'somebody was walking over my grave.' We'll say things like that from time to time. Bound to. Life's all mixed up with death, honey. We have to accept it without brooding over it, or watching every word."

"Yeah." He seemed very manly. "None of it's easy, is it? And I guess it gets harder as it goes along."

She slipped behind the wheel. "I'm not sure. Sometimes I think your age is the hardest of all. The most confusing. You know so much and yet so little when you're growing up. Not just you. Everybody. It takes a long time to discover priorities, Tom. In your teens, everything is equally important, and equally wrenching, whether it's a Saturday night broken date or a parent who doesn't seem interested enough in your problems. It's a tough time of life, caring so deeply about everything. I suppose that's why they say old age has its compensations. Most things aren't all that gut-churning any more."

He looked at her. "You're not old, Mom."

She kept her eyes on the road. "No, not in years, Tom. But I'm finally reaching the age when I'm beginning to accept the truth."

He looked puzzled. Sheila managed to laugh. "Wow, this is pretty heavy stuff we're into! There's been enough sadness for us both, my friend. Let's make a few good plans for the future. Together."

"I wish you didn't have to work, Mom. I mean, not only because we'd have more time together. I know how hard it is on you. You know, I hoped you were coming to Palm Beach to tell us Dad had left more money than we thought. I guess not, huh?"

"No, dear. No more than we thought. And I don't really mind working, Tommy. I like the store and it's good for me to be occupied. Much as we love each other, we couldn't really stand being together every minute, could we? I'd bore you to distraction! I want you to have your own friends, your own age. But nice ones, of course." They both knew what that oblique reference meant.

"No problem," Tom said. "But what *were* you coming all the way to Florida to tell us?"

"Nothing vital," Sheila said. "It isn't important any more."

"I don't understand you," Sally Cantrell said one Tuesday in June she and Sheila were having lunch.

"What's to understand?"

"Oh, come off it, Sheila! You're a different person since Maryanne died. You've completely changed."

Sheila continued to eat her salad. "For the better, I hope."

Sally slammed down her fork in exasperation. "See? That's exactly what I mean! You're so guarded, so damned noncommittal about everything! We don't talk any more, not really talk. We haven't in weeks. It's all calm and impersonal with you, no highs and lows, at least none that show. I used to feel we shared so much and now I feel you're keeping me and everybody else at arm's length. Betty says . . ." Sally stopped abruptly.

286

Sheila looked up with mild interest. "What does Betty say?"

"All right, I'll tell you. She and Pat are worried sick about you. They can't understand why you decided to break it off with Bill Reardon. Neither can I. For that matter, I think neither can *you!*"

"I still talk to Bill," Sheila said, evasively. "In fact I talk to him almost every day."

"Terrific. I talk to my butcher every day when he takes the meat order. What do you and Bill talk *about?*"

"Little everyday things. We're good friends. He's interested in Tommy, in my job. He tells me what's happening to him. He's writing another book."

Sally stared at her. "Sheila! Only weeks ago you were going to marry that man! He's still in love with you. What kind of game are you playing?"

"No game. I'm not going to marry anybody. Not ever."

"And Bill's accepted that."

"Yes."

"But he still calls."

"Yes."

Sally sighed. "I don't get it. I don't get any of it. You act as though you want to wipe out everything that ever happened in your life. All you do is work and spend time with a fifteen-year-old boy. It's unnatural, unhealthy. Betty says you've never even asked exactly how Maryanne died! You don't want the few possessions Patrick gathered to bring to you. That's *weird*, Sheila."

"She's gone. I don't need to know *how*. I know *why*."

"All right, why?"

"Because I failed her. The way I failed everybody. The way I'd fail Bill if I married him."

"Oh, my God! I don't believe this. I do not believe the way you're thinking! Failed her? Failed everybody? What are you talking about?"

"Just what I said. I never really tried to understand any of them. If I'd done better as a wife, Sean wouldn't have been the way he was. Maryanne wouldn't have run away from the things she could have believed in if I'd set a better example. Tommy wouldn't have become a thief and a liar."

Sally was openmouthed. "You really think those things are true?"

"I know they are. I have utter contempt for that Sheila Callahan, the smug, opinionated, cast-in-a mold creature who was."

"You prefer the lifeless one in the symbolic hair shirt? You like *this* Sheila Callahan who might just as well enter a convent and take a vow of silence?"

She gave a little smile. "You know, if it weren't for Tommy, I might do just that. I've thought about it."

Sally's voice rose. "Sheila, you know you're not making sense! All that talk about failure is ridiculous! I wish you could hear yourself. 'Sean wouldn't have been the way he was. Maryanne wouldn't have run away. Tommy wouldn't have become a thief.' I think you're enjoying this fantasy! I honestly think you like wallowing in self-hatred!"

People at nearby tables turned to stare. Sally lowered her voice. "Listen, Sheila, I love you. A lot of people do. If we didn't, we'd just let you go along indulging yourself. You're wrong, friend. Dead wrong. And deep inside you know it. You're beating yourself up over a string of tragedies, not one of them of your making. I'm sure you're hating yourself for Jerry, too. Turning the rejection of a worthless fool like that into another piece of manufactured evidence about your own 'failures.' My God, I've seen widows react in strange ways . . . take to drink, have their faces lifted, open itsy-koo boutiques, but I'm damned if I ever thought I'd see one weave a whole elaborate fabrication of imaginary guilts to justify her fears of being hurt again."

Despite the tirade, Sheila seemed unmoved. "I'm not afraid of being hurt again. I'm unhurtable."

"Like hell! You're the same sensitive, patient, caring woman you've always been. Even Jerry recognized that, rhinoceros-hided egomaniac that he is. That's why he was so drawn to you."

"No, he was drawn to me because I'm as rotten and selfish as he is. He's what I deserve. I'm what he deserves."

Sally made one more try. "Sheila, stop punishing yourself! Run like hell to Bill Reardon while he's still patient enough to put up with you!"

Sheila shook her head. "No. Whatever's left in me is for the only person who really needs it."

"Tommy."

"Yes, Tommy."

"Can't you see how out of proportion *that* is?" Sally begged. "In a few months, less even, Tommy will have had his fill of undivided attention from you. Oh, sure, right now he enjoys possessing you. He's making up for lost time. But it won't last, Sheila. He'll want his own life, too. Just like the others. He'll begin to disappear and you'll be really alone. What will you do then? Sit home and feel guilty that you've failed him again? My dear, you can't build a life around an adolescent. Even if you're mixed up enough to want to, he won't let you. He's nearly a man, Sheila. What do you want to do, keep him a baby forever, tied to the proverbial apron strings?"

"I sent him away once," Sheila said, "and he was lost and miserable. I'll never do that again."

"Nobody's suggesting you do that. He'll go of his own accord, because he's basically a selfish, normal kid. First he'll go to the people he *should* be spending time with, his peers. And then to college. He'll marry. And one day you'll wake up and be deep in middle age and alone and you'll wonder what the big renunciations were all about." Sally gave a hopeless sigh. "You just won't see it, will you? You're hell-bent on some kind of crazy atonement. You're begging to be punished. I don't understand, Sheila," she said again. "I'm no psychiatrist, but I know you're suffering from some kind of cumulative, imaginary guilt that must go back to the cradle. You seem to me like an exaggerated case of delayed shock with everything triggered by Maryanne's death. I think you should get help, honey. Professional help."

"I'm all right, Sally. I don't need a doctor. All I want is peace. No more doubts. No more torment. No more people who expect more of me than I'm able to give. I haven't been able to live up to what a lot of good people thought I was, what a lot of wonderful people still think I am."

Sally had never felt so frustrated. "You just want to be left alone, is that it?"

"No. I want to be close to my children and my grandchild when he or she arrives. I want to keep a dear friend like you. But no more emotional demands. No more schoolgirl dreams. I don't want any more decisions and any more peaks and valleys. I'm tired in my soul."

"So we're all to accept you as a nice, quiet, dull widow lady who's paid her dues."

"I suppose. If you accept me at all."

"I wouldn't buy that if you served it to me on a Tiffany platter," Sally said. "To tell you the truth, I'd almost *like* to buy it. But you're not through with your sacrificial stage. You'll figure out some new way to hurt yourself. It's terrible to hate yourself, Sheila, because then, unconsciously, you hate everybody else. All of us."

"You know that could never be."

"Do I? I didn't think you could ever be the way you are now. I always thought you were the best balanced, most in-control lady in the world. If I ever had a female idol, you were it."

Sheila smiled. "Past tense. You see? You've been fooled, too, by that old Sheila Callahan. The one who even fooled herself."

Sally found herself crying as she drove home alone. It's as though Sheila has ceased to be, she thought. It's like talking to a friend who's already dead. I think she wishes she were. I've never seen anybody so unhappy.

It was not quite true. Sheila was far from happy, but she did not feel as dead as she sounded, and she had no wish not to live. The give-and-take with Sally had distressed her more than she showed. Yet, in a way, it had been good to come out with everything, rather than hint at her thoughts as she did with Pat and Betty, or blurt out hysterical self-disgust as she had with Bill Reardon.

She relived the conversation with Sally. Not everything Sheila had said was true. She admitted that to herself. Even in her wildest moments of self-loathing she knew she'd been as good a wife as Sean Callahan could have hoped for. Probably better. She even knew she was exaggerating her guilt about Tommy's behavior. True, he'd taken something of a back seat in her life for the past few years, but he was one of hundreds of thousands of boys and girls who got into minor scrapes these days. She'd made too much of it, she supposed, unconsciously tying it in with her shame about starting an affair with Jerry so soon after Sean's death. Not that juvenile delinquency was to be ignored, but she'd acted as though Tommy had held up someone at gunpoint, or mugged an old man, or raped an innocent girl. Because she felt *she'd* gone wrong, she'd overreacted, to the point of sending him away, into a "normal" atmosphere. Was that what it was? Or did she simply not want to be reminded, by his presence, of how recklessly she'd behaved with Jerry? After all, Patrick had gotten into small scrapes when he was Tommy's age, too. Nothing this serious, nothing involving the police. But in Pat's case she'd given him what-for, stopped his allowance for a month, and not behaved as though she was responsible, as though her neglect of him was the cause of his "crimes"—crimes like truancy, or coming home drunk one night at sixteen. Because she felt guiltless about her own life then, she'd been able to handle his offenses sensibly and alone. And she *was* alone. Sean had always washed his hands of the children's problems. They were her department. And, Sheila thought, I coped. I even coped, in a strange way, with Maryanne, the most incomprehensible of her children, during her formative years, and without any help from Sean. It was not until I was literally alone, widowed, that I began to fall apart and do crazy, impulsive things. How strange that a husband, even one as undependable as Sean, represented a kind of security that enabled a woman to get through troubles large and small.

Perhaps if Sean hadn't died I could even have handled our daughter's suicide. It wouldn't have been all mixed up with self-accusation about the other things, because the other things wouldn't have happened. But Sean *had* died and she had tried to find herself in a strange new world and she had messed up everything, ending up hating herself and blaming herself for Maryanne's death.

That was the one thing from which she could not absolve herself. How could I have let her disappear as she did? How could I have selfishly enjoyed myself with Bill Reardon, not knowing where she was or how she was living? How could I have closed my eyes to my obligations?

Perhaps it made no sense, now, to renounce personal happiness as an act of atonement for that. No one understood why she felt she had a debt to pay. Not Sally or Pat or Betty, not Bill Reardon who continued to wait for her to "recover." Certainly not Tommy who knew nothing of the awful burden she carried. But Sheila clung stubbornly to the idea that she had failed her daughter. It was too late to make it up to her. The only act of contrition was self-denial and the giving of herself to the child who was left. Even so, Sheila thought, am I devoting myself to Tommy for his sake or because through him I'm trying to pardon myself? Am I concentrating on him because I can't bear to think of Maryanne whose needs I didn't answer? How she must have hated me! How resentful she must have been that I simply let her go with no more than a timid protest. I could have saved her if I'd really tried, if I hadn't been so involved in my own survival that I ignored hers.

It's why I haven't wanted to hear how she died. I refuse to let Patrick tell me how it happened. I won't even look at the things he brought home to me. I don't want to know any of it. Not how she did it, or where her few pitiful possessions were left. I want to pretend it never happened, even while I spend the rest of my life seeking forgiveness.

Bill would help me forget, might even help me forgive myself. He's so wise, so sensitive and strong. But he has his needs, too. He doesn't deserve to be saddled with a woman whose self-reproach will never end. Cliché that it is, I'm not good enough for Bill Reardon. And there's something else, too. I don't think I can take any more emotion. Love and passion are disturbing things, agonizing as well as joyful. I'm not up to the demands of being in love, with all the uncertainty and anxiety of it. I lied to Sally. I am afraid of being hurt again. And God knows I don't want to hurt, either. With me, Bill is vulnerable. I won't take advantage of that, for his sake even more than mine. That's why I've crawled into this shell. I don't want to care deeply about another man. Not ever again.

Chapter 32

       June and July passed in the way Sheila knew they would: one hot, identical day after another. There were certain changes, of course. She saw less of Sally, not because the friendship had ceased but because they no longer had the precious, easy rapport of friends who understood each other perfectly. Bill called less often, though still with the same sweetness and assurances of love. He did not speak of their future but on her birthday he sent her a huge oleander plant and a message that told her clearly he still hoped. The exotic flowers reminded her, as he intended, of Bermuda. And the free verse brought a lump in her throat:

> It was not a perfect year.
> But has there ever been a perfect year?
> Has there ever been a year
> When all the love and health and fame
> We wished for one another
> Ever came to pass?
> Yet, despite the disappointments
> Of these, our complex lives,
> We learn to make do . . . make better . . . make believe
> That better days will come.
> And if we continue to believe,

Who is to say that
The perfect year
Will not yet be here?

When she was in control, she called to thank him. "Those are beautiful words," she said.

"I didn't write them. I read them somewhere. I can't remember where, but I believe them, Sheila."

She didn't answer.

"I have something to tell you," Bill said. "I'm giving up the apartment in New York. I'm moving to Bermuda. Permanently. Or as permanently as anything ever is."

"I see," Sheila said slowly. Are you taking someone with you? she wanted to ask. Have you found the right woman to share all that peace and beauty? She wanted it for him, but she didn't want it to happen. Dog-in-the-manger was the trite expression for what she felt. Funny expression, she thought irrelevantly. I wonder where it comes from?

"I can't take New York any more," Bill was saying. "It's not our old city, Sheila. It's dirty and disheveled and used up, like an old whore. I can't breathe here any more."

"I thought you always wanted it to be home base."

"I did, when I had someone whose radiance blocked out the ugliness."

"Eileene."

"Yes, Eileene did that. And I thought you would."

She felt a mixture of relief and sadness. Selfishly happy that he still loved only her. Foolishly disappointed that he'd obviously resigned himself to never having her. What was the matter with her? That's what she wanted, wasn't it? For Bill to give up on her, to find someone else? Why did she feel such conflict? It would have been easier, somehow, if he'd told her he'd fallen in love, that he'd finally accepted her ultimatum because another woman had made it impossible.

"Sheila, come with me," he said. "You and Tommy. We'll be happy there. I've given you time to get things into perspective. Haven't we both suffered enough?"

For an instant she wanted to say Yes. She loved him. He was the solution to her loneliness, her lostness. But not to the lingering feeling of her unworthiness.

"I don't want *you* to suffer at all," she said. "Not over someone like me. I can't come, Bill. *My* suffering isn't over. I don't see how it ever can be."

"You know that doesn't make sense. Your penitence doesn't make the dead lie easier in their graves."

"No, I know it doesn't. But it makes me lie easier in my bed."

Frustration made him angry. "For the first time in my life, Sheila, I've lost respect for you. I could forgive you anything but this ridiculous martyrdom. You're too intelligent for that. That's what's so terrible. You *know* how unrealistic you're being and you *persist* in it!"

"I can't explain it," she said helplessly.

"Of course you can't, because there's no sane explanation."

"Perhaps not. But that's the way it is."

She heard love and sympathy creep back into his voice. "All right, darling. I can't fight it any more. If sacrificing yourself is the only way you can live with Maryanne's death, then that's what you'll have to do. But I'm wrung out, Sheila. I can't beg any more. If you ever want me, you know where I am."

Tommy wondered why he wasn't happy. He had everything he thought he wanted: his mother's full and undivided attention. They spent every evening together and every Sunday and Tuesday, her days off from the store. She hardly ever saw anybody else. Once in a while she had lunch with Sally Cantrell and sometimes they went over to Pat's for dinner. Lord, Betty was getting as big as a house! In less than a month he'd be an uncle. That sounded strange. He didn't think of himself as being old enough to have a generation following him.

Sheila couldn't do enough for him. On his sixteenth birthday she even bought him an old, secondhand car. He'd been surprised and delighted. He'd figured on driving the station wagon when she let him, but Sheila had smiled at his astonishment and said it was important for him to have something of his very own.

"All you kids want your own wheels, don't you?" she'd asked. "That's how you refer to cars these days, isn't it?"

"Yeah. Jeez, Mom, it's swell. Thanks a million."

"Out of sight, huh?"

He'd grinned. But he wished she'd stop trying to be his contemporary, using his language. For that matter, he thought, guiltily, he wished she'd stop being so attached to him. It put a responsibility on him, knowing she looked forward to being with him every free minute. He didn't know why it made him so uneasy. It was like he was some kind of symbol to her, like he was being used. He knew she was giving up everything for him. She couldn't really afford to buy him a car. And she couldn't afford to re-enroll him in University next term as she told him she had. He'd protested.

"I don't have to go back there, Mom! You don't have to worry. I'm not going to see those same kids at Shaker Heights High."

"I know that, but I want the same kind of schooling for you that your brother and sister had. You're just as entitled."

"But it's different now. We don't have the money. Heck, you haven't bought yourself a new dress in almost a year!"

"I'm loaded with clothes, silly. And we're making out okay, aren't we?" She'd hugged him. "We have each other, and we have fun. As a southern lady I once knew used to say of *her* son, 'You're my eyeballs.' I love you a lot, pal. Things that make you happy are no sacrifice."

He wondered what the hell was the matter with him. His life now was everything he'd dreamed of. There was no competition from anyone for Sheila's devotion. But it didn't sit right. Even *she* had said, a while back, that they couldn't spend every minute together, that it was good for her to be away at work. He realized she was right. They were together too much. She *has* to be bored with no company except a kid's, he thought. He felt himself actually blushing with shame. I know, because lots of times I'm bored with *hers*. That's what was wrong, of course. He didn't see people his own age. He felt obligated to stay with Sheila because that was so obviously what she wanted.

If only there was someone he could talk to. It was all so confusing. He wanted his mother to care for him, but she was enveloping him, swallowing him, drowning him in her love. He didn't even make plans with his old friends, the ones from University he now felt he'd like to see. He'd feel guilty leaving Sheila alone in the evening or on Sunday when she expected to be with him. Jesus, Tommy thought, things sure go to extremes in this family! Mom, Dad, Maryanne, me. We're all alike. Never doing anything in moderation. Only Pat seemed to be on course all the time. Maybe he wouldn't be, either, if it wasn't for Betty.

He wondered whom he could approach. Not his Uncle Terry, for God's sake. *That* square. Bob Ross? No way. Even Mom didn't see him much any more. Sally Cantrell? No, this wasn't the kind of thing you could talk out with a woman. Besides, she probably would report back to Mom. His only hope was his brother.

"How about if I go have dinner with Pat and Betty tomorrow night when you work late?" he asked Sheila one Sunday. "I mean, if it's okay with them?"

"Good idea. I won't have to worry about your waiting so late to eat. Why don't you give them a ring?"

He came back from the phone and said it suited them. Pat was off-duty and they'd be glad to have him.

"Fine," Sheila said. "I'll pick you up there." Then she laughed. "I forgot. You don't need to be collected any more, do you, now that you can burn rubber on your own?"

He hoped she didn't see him wince.

It wasn't easy to tell Patrick what was on his mind. It sounded so disloyal, so ungrateful. But when Betty lumbered off into the kitchen to prepare dinner, Tommy seized this moment to try.

"Pat, I've got a problem. It's kind of tough to explain."

"Would a drink help?"

"No. I've been off that stuff since I got busted."

Patrick hid a smile as he made himself a scotch. "Okay, Tom, what's on your mind?"

"It's Mother. She's . . . she's, Jesus, I don't know how to say this, but she's eating me alive!"

"What does that mean, exactly?"

"I'm not sure. I mean I can give you specifics. Like buying me a car and sending me back to University next term when I know she can't afford either. But mostly it's acting like I'm the only thing in her life. She spends practically every free minute with me. She's always planning Sunday outings, asking me what *I'd* like to do all the time. She even tries to talk the way she thinks the kids do." Tommy sighed. "I used to hate it when I thought she didn't pay enough attention to me. Now I'm bitching because I feel like a prisoner. Like . . . well, like she's trying to make up for everything she feels guilty about. I know that sounds crazy, but what's happening to me is exactly the opposite of the way she was with you and Maryanne. I mean, I always felt she loved you two more, but she still left you free. I guess it's because she had Dad. I don't know. It sounds awful, but she's driving me up the wall with so much concentration on me. I love her, Pat. She's one helluva woman. But I guess what I'm saying is that it just doesn't seem natural. I don't mean anything really sick, for God's sake, but she doesn't act like a mother, more like a girlfriend or maybe a wife. Hell, I feel so damned obligated all the time! She should be with her friends, people her own age. But all she wants is to be with *me*."

Pat wasn't really surprised. He'd been expecting something like this. "I guess she thinks you're all she has left now, Tom. You're still the baby at home. She's hanging on to what's left of a family. I suppose part of it's selfish, all right, but mostly I think she's trying to make up for all the attention she feels she didn't give you and the rest of us. Maryanne, in particular."

Tommy stared at the floor.

"But you're right, kid. Out of the mouth of babes et cetera. It's too big a load for you. She doesn't realize that, of course. She thinks she owes you. I'm sure she believes this is what *you* want."

"Yeah. I thought I did. It's not her fault. And there's no way to tell her. I can't hurt her, Pat. Not after all she's been through."

"I know. Damn it, I wish she'd married Bill Reardon."

Tommy looked up, genuinely surprised. "Reardon? The guy who came to Maryanne's funeral? Was Mom thinking of marrying him?"

It was Patrick's turn to be surprised. "You mean you didn't know? They were planning to get married in July. That's what she was coming to Palm Beach to tell you, the week Maryanne died."

"I thought he was just an old friend. She told me on the phone, months ago, that he'd come to Cleveland. He's a writer, isn't he?" Tommy frowned. "You mean they saw each other after he was here that time?"

Pat nodded. No need to go into the Bermuda trip about which Sheila had lied to Tommy and the Callahans. "Yes, they saw each other. They were in love, Tom. But after Maryanne, something happened to Mother. She called it off. She'd even put the house on the market, planned to move you both to New York. But she told Bob Ross to cancel it. I think," he said slowly, "she decided that Maryanne's death was somehow a sign. I guess it explains this fierce devotion, Tom. She's trying to be what she thinks a full-time mother ought to be. What she feels she never really was."

"Pat, I've never wanted that! I never wanted her to give up her life for me!"

"How could she know that, Tommy? You were pretty hostile when she was seeing Mancini. You even deliberately went out and got yourself into a mess with a gang of punks. Mostly, I suspect, to make her notice you. And you were angry when she sent you to Florida. You felt you were being pushed aside, right?"

"Sure. Okay. But that was different. Mancini's a heel. Everybody knew that. Everybody but Mom."

"Granted," Patrick said evenly. "But you were just plain jealous. Mom knew *that*. She also was afraid you were too attached to her, that's why she sent you to the grandparents."

"But when Mancini split, she took up with Reardon. That doesn't add up."

"Sure it does. At that moment, before Maryanne, Mom was *troubled* about you, but not *guilty*. When her daughter died, Mom lost her balance. Like I said, she decided she was at fault. Hadn't paid enough attention to her children. She called it off with Reardon and decided to devote herself to you, hoping, I suppose, to be forgiven for 'neglecting' you and Maryanne."

The brothers stared at each other. And then Tommy said, "I don't understand. How can people get so mixed up?"

"I don't know, Tom, but they do. Especially sensitive people like Mother." Pat made himself another drink. "Betty and I have seen what's happening. We know it's a bad scene for both of you. Funny. All of us thought at first that you were too possessive of Mother. Now she's too possessive of you. It's become her lifeline to salvation, this overblown crusade to make you happy."

"Then there's nothing I can do about it." The boy sounded resigned.

"That's not true. You're the only one who *can* do anything about it. *You've* got to make the break, Tommy. Start making dates, going out with your own friends, letting Mom know that you love her but that you're not a child who's content to spend his time at Mama's knee. You're the only one who can make her see that she has to have a life of her own. Other people have tried and failed. Bill Reardon, Sally, even Grandma Price. She won't listen. She's afraid to fail you."

Tommy was horrified. "I can't do that! Not after all she's done for me!"

"Unless you do, Tom, she's going to waste her life and yours. With the best will in the world, she'll make you feel so obligated you'll never escape. And she'll never be free to be a healthy, normal woman again." Pat felt sorry for the boy. "You're awfully young to take on this kind of load, but you're the only person who can cut her loose from this exaggerated sense of 'duty.' You have to do it. For her sake and yours."

"She'll be heartbroken."

"No. Disappointed at first. Maybe even suffer another bout of heavy guilt. But it's what she needs. Hopefully, she'll get Bill Reardon back. Level with me, Tommy. Would you hate it if Mother married again?"

Tom thought for a moment. "No. Not now. I'd have hated it six months ago. But if Reardon's the right guy, I'd be glad for her." He looked ashamed. "I guess I'd be glad for myself, too. You say she's broken off with Reardon, though. What if I start pulling back and she runs to somebody like Mancini?"

"I don't know," Patrick said honestly. "I guess it's a chance we'll have to take."

"Have a good time with Patrick and Betty?" Sheila called out from her room when she heard Tommy come upstairs.

"Yep." He started toward his own quarters.

"Come in for a minute, honey," Sheila said. "I'm just reading. Tell me about the evening. How's Betty?"

"She's okay. Says they're going to name the kid 'Dumbo' to match its size."

Sheila laughed. "I can't wait! It's so good to see them happy. It's so good to see *you* happy, Tommy."

"How about you, Mom? Isn't it important whether *you're* happy?"

"But I am, darling! Listen, what about a picnic tomorrow? We could pack a lunch and drive somewhere. Take our swim suits. Maybe find a nice cold little creek."

He hesitated. "Gee, I'm sorry, Mom, but I talked to some of the old gang from University today. They're getting up a ball game and then going to a drive-in later. I told them I'd join them." It wasn't true, but he'd go somewhere. He had to make a start.

She was quiet for a moment. "That sounds like fun. You haven't played baseball all summer. I'm glad you're going to see some of your old friends again."

She was a terrible liar. For a moment, Tommy weakened. "Listen, if you've made plans, I can cancel with the kids," he said. (I know, Patrick. You'd kick me in the ass, but *you're* not looking into those disappointed eyes.)

"Don't be silly," Sheila said. "I want you to do what you enjoy."

"What'll you do?"

"Me? I don't know. Maybe call Sally and have lunch if she's free. If not, no problem. I have a million chores."

"Well, if you're sure . . ."

"Of course I'm sure! For heaven's sake, Tommy, you're making a big deal out of this! I told you long ago you should be with people your own age."

He wanted to blurt out, So should you, Mom, but he simply said, "Okay. See you in the morning. Night."

"Good night, sweetie. Sleep well."

Maybe I've got this figured all wrong, Tommy thought as he got into bed. Maybe I've been imagining that she's sacrificing herself for me. Reardon might have backed out, for all I know. She might be pleased if I start going my own way. Now that he thought of it, Pat's explanation sounded a little dramatic. Could be Sheila was so shook up by Maryanne's death that she didn't want to see people. Maybe it was easier to be just with me. She's had almost three months to get herself together. She's probably as ready to be on the loose again as I am. Three months seems to be the magic number, he thought cynically. It was three months after Dad's death that she got involved with Mancini.

He gave his pillow a hard punch. You're just trying not to feel like a bastard, he told himself. You know damned well she saw right through you tonight. "Lifeline," Pat had said. It was true, Tommy had the awful task of cutting off the oxygen. And it *was* true. Unknowingly she was choking the breath out of both of them.

Sheila lay awake, too. Tommy's sudden decision to spend the day away from her had surprised her, alerted her intuitively that something important had happened. I wonder what my boys talked about? She could guess. She remembered that old joke about the mother who bragged how much her son loved her. How did it go? Oh, yes. The woman told her friends, "My son loves me so much that when he goes to the psychiatrist, what does he talk about? Me!" It didn't seem so funny now. She hadn't really believed the things she'd told Tommy about how they'd bore each other if they were together all the time. She'd been stupid enough to think they really could build a safe, secure, uncomplicated life together. No. Correction. She'd thought she could build such a life for *herself*, untroubled, selfless, all-giving. It was disgusting. She was far worse than Rose had ever been, trying to play on her child's sympathy.

And yet hadn't this been what Tommy had silently begged for?

Hadn't the desire for her attention been at the root of all his problems after Sean died? Hadn't it been somehow the motivation for Maryanne's rebellion long before?

She didn't know. She didn't know anything. She seemed to mess up whatever she tried. She read Tommy as well as he read her. Tomorrow's plans were an invention, but they were also the beginning of a new phase. Of that she was certain. Another rejection. Another mistake. She tried to feel glad he no longer had this crying need for her. It was good. Normal. No. It was her last chance slipping away from her.

Hating herself for it, she dissolved into tears of self-pity. I can't do anything right. I mean to and I'm such a miserable failure. I give too little or I give too much. And neither works. I try so hard and I'm such a worthless creature. Sally was right when she said I hated myself. Stupid, bungling, clumsy Sheila Callahan, that's me.

And though she did not know what Sally had thought driving home, she felt for the first time what her friend had sensed. She really wished she were dead. It would be easier for everybody. Mostly for herself.

Chapter 33

She'd been a widow for a year, but for the first time she felt like the stereotype. She knew now what it was to have a telephone that rarely rang, to eat alone—listless dinners on a tray in front of the TV set, listening to the litany of Watergate and watching the hysteria of game-show contestants. She felt the terrible lack of being a part of some-*one* or some*thing*.

Not that she was abandoned. Tommy's withdrawal this time was nothing like his earlier rebellion. He was scrupulously thoughtful, always telling her where he was going and with whom, even phoning her (as she had phoned Rose) when he was going to be out later than expected. And many nights he made it a point to be with her. They played gin rummy or visited Pat and Betty or took in a movie. He was really a good boy. If he pitied her he was careful not to show it. But he left no doubt that he had a life of his own, one in which she was an important but background figure.

She could have made things better for herself, if trying to pick up the "old life" could be considered better. She could have called the Rosses or Terry and Margaret and asked them to dinner, but she really had no interest in seeing them. Nor did she fancy herself in the "lone woman role," a hostess without a host, the unattached female trying to pretend that three or five at a dinner table was no different from four or six.

Bill was right. She was a woman who'd always need a man. Not just for the physical pleasure of one, but for a sense of completeness and orderliness it gave her. I'd make a lousy "libber," Sheila thought. Independence and self-sufficiency are admirable traits, but I'd rather be adored than "equal." Human nature is stronger than social revolution, at least for me. Being female in a totally feminine way doesn't keep one from being a person. Desirability isn't demeaning. At least I've never felt it to be. I don't understand angry women who take umbrage at anything that smacks of "inequality," whatever that means. Bill had respected her, as he'd desired her. He'd felt her his intellectual equal as well as his love. Until the end. Then her inexplicable behavior, what he called her "martyrdom," had been too much even for him. He couldn't cope with a whining, suffering woman who disliked herself more than she loved him.

Sometimes she thought of calling him, or writing to him in Bermuda. She could close her eyes and see every outline of that beautiful island, every inch of that warm, welcoming house, remember every detail of their lovemaking there. He'd told her she knew where to find him. She would, if only she could believe that she had enough to offer, that she deserved all he wanted to give.

She'd gone alone to the cemetery on the anniversary of Sean's death. It was utterly unlike her. She didn't believe in visiting plots of ground beneath which there was no one. It had always seemed pointless, even phony, an exercise in self-indulgence which did nothing for the dead. Yet this year she'd driven out and stood looking at the two graves and felt herself wanting to talk to their headstones, those chiseled-in-marble stand-ins for her husband and daughter. She wanted to ask "Why?" Why hadn't she been satisfactory to either of them? Where had she failed as wife and mother? She could accept Sean's death as she had accepted his life, a selfish comedy played out to the final curtain. No costar would have been big enough for him. But Maryanne's story was a mystery throughout, a baffling series of elusive clues that seemed to lead nowhere, a plot without a satisfactory conclusion.

Standing there in the hot sunlight, she wished she had Rose's faith in religion. What comfort it must be to believe utterly in God's will, to accept, with unquestioning sadness, the cruel decisions of the Almighty. But God hadn't taken Maryanne, as he had Sean. The girl had sought death and Sheila didn't know why.

To this day, she'd never had courage to ask Patrick about it. There must not have been a farewell note or he would have brought it to her. Or would he? She'd made it clear that she didn't want to hear anything about Maryanne, didn't want to know about her last days, didn't even want the mementoes Pat brought home. He'd tried to talk to her, but she'd shut him out, literally putting her hands over her ears.

"I don't want to know!" that stricken Sheila had said. "Nothing matters except that she's gone!"

302

"You're wrong, Mother. It's not a pretty story but it might make it easier to accept."

"No. I can't bear it."

"You're shutting out reality," Pat had said. "The unknown is always more terrible, more frightening. Please listen. You won't reproach yourself any longer if you do."

Sheila had turned on him angrily. "Won't reproach myself? How could I ever stop? The child's mind is the product of the parent's molding. Wherever it goes wrong, the fault lies with those who deformed it."

Patrick hadn't understood. "That's a lot of Freudian hogwash and you know it! Maryanne wasn't a child. She was a woman bound and determined to make herself and everybody else suffer. She was sick. In her head. I'm sorry, Mother. I loved her, too. But her screwed-up thought processes weren't your fault. We were all raised the same, and Tom and I have muddled through."

She'd calmed down a little. "I wish I could believe that, Patrick. But it isn't true. Maryanne needed something all her life. Something you didn't. Something your father and I didn't take the trouble to understand. We can't be excused for that."

She remembered that conversation now, three months later. I should have let Pat tell me about it, she thought. He really needed to unburden himself. I denied him that. I didn't want to hear. Perhaps I didn't want to be comforted. I suppose I still don't. That's sick, too, I'm sure. Everybody thinks it is. But they don't know what it's like. Pat had said he and Tommy had "muddled through." That wasn't quite accurate. Pat was all right, but Tommy was still in those pliable years, the same age Maryanne was when she began to show the first real signs of unrest. We didn't move in on the problem then as we should have. That's why I've been fearful about neglecting Tommy.

But Tommy was all right. He was stronger than she'd thought. He'd taken the initiative, this past month, in gently cutting himself free from her possessiveness. And he was right. At sixteen, Sheila thought ruefully, he's far, far wiser than I. He doesn't need protection. He needs love and understanding, and that I can give him, when he wants it. I've been pampering *myself* in every way, she realized. What a bore I am. What a miserable flop.

She was in the middle of fixing her dinner when the phone rang. Pat's excited voice told her that Betty was in labor. He was at the hospital.

"Is everything going all right?"

"So far, perfect. They don't think it'll be protracted and Betty's being terrific. Can you come over, Mom? We'd both like you to be here."

"As fast as I can make it. Give her my love."

It seemed a strange world, this busy, impersonal hospital that Sheila rushed into, yet there was something reassuring about the crisp efficiency of it all. She hadn't spent much time in hospitals. Her children had been born there, of course, and she'd visited ailing friends, but she'd never done a "vigil," waiting for someone to be born or, God forbid, to die. As she stepped off the elevator onto the maternity floor, she looked around helplessly and then approached the reception desk.

"Is Dr. Callahan around?"

A trim little nurse looked up at her and smiled. "He's off-duty. In fact, his wife is having a baby."

"I know. I'm his mother."

"Oh. He's in the delivery room, Mrs. Callahan." She grinned. "Observing, of course. Dr. Mancini is doing the big job."

"Dr. Mancini?"

"Yes. Mrs. Callahan's O.B. is out of town, unfortunately. Like most first babies, this one didn't stick to schedule. But you needn't worry. Dr. Mancini's the best. Your daughter-in-law's in good hands."

"Yes, I'm sure she is. May I wait in her room?"

"Of course. Second door on the left."

Sheila went into the empty room and sat quietly in a chair. She'd thought she could wait with Patrick, but she should have known he'd be allowed into delivery. Some hospitals even let nondoctor husbands in these days, she'd heard. She wondered idly whether that was a good thing: letting a man see what childbirth was really like. Sean would have run to the nearest bar if such a thing had been suggested to him. He hated pain. He hated anything even remotely unpleasant and troublesome. It occurred to her that maybe he hadn't even liked the nuisance of children *after* they were born.

Ironic that Jerry should be delivering Betty's baby. Fate again. Or timing. What difference? He might be a disaster as a human being, but he was top notch as an obstetrician.

It was almost an hour before Patrick came in, beaming. "They told me you were waiting here. We have a girl, Mother! A beautiful, healthy six-pound daughter!"

She hugged him. "I'm so happy, Patrick! Is Betty all right?"

"She's fine. Insisted on staying awake through the whole thing. Said she wouldn't miss a minute of it."

Sheila had tears in her eyes. My first grandchild, she thought. Another girl in the family. She'd been so anxious to hear the news she hadn't noticed another figure standing in the doorway behind Patrick.

"Hello, Sheila," he said.

"Hello, Jerry. Thanks for doing such a good job."

"It was a piece of cake. Betty did all the work."

"Don't let him fool you," Patrick said. "He's a master."

"*Past* master," Jerry said lightly. "I'm terrific. Everybody knows that."

His eyes were directly on Sheila as he spoke. She didn't turn away. "Yes," she said, "your reputation precedes you, Doctor."

Patrick caught the little interchange and ignored it. "Betty will be back in her room in a little while. You want to wait here, Mom? I'm going back until they bring her down."

"Why don't I buy you a cup of coffee instead?" Jerry asked. "I could use one. And it will be a little while before you can see mother and child."

Sheila hesitated. Then she said, "All right. I could use one, too. I was just starting to fix dinner when Pat called."

On the way to the cafeteria, Jerry said, "You haven't had dinner. I don't recommend the food here. Would you consider letting me buy you a real meal later, after you've seen Betty and the baby?"

"Thanks, but I don't think so, Jerry."

"There won't be any point in your hanging around the hospital."

"It isn't that, and you know it."

"Still angry with me?"

She shook her head. "I got over being angry a long while ago. I even got over being disgusted with you. There's been too much to genuinely grieve for since then."

"I know. Maryanne. I wanted to be in touch with you when I heard, but I didn't know whether you wanted to hear from me." Jerry idly stirred the coffee he'd brought to the table. "I also heard you were going to get married. Are you?"

"No."

He didn't ask why or what had happened. He simply said, "If you're free, I'd like to see you again, Sheila."

"Are *you* free, Jerry?"

"Yes. The divorce is final. Barbara got it in Mexico." He stared into his cup. "You were absolutely right, you know. It was a stinking thing to do, but I had to get her back so that I could be the one to end it. I'm not proud of that. It was vain and rotten." He gave a little laugh. "At least I know now how rotten I am. It's helped to take away some of the blind conceit. I'm no better than the man you knew, but I'm a little less in love with myself. If you'll let me see you again, Sheila, at least you'll know what I am. I won't be able to disappoint you this time."

She sat silently for a while. He was no good. He'd never be. But in her own opinion, neither was she. And she was so lonely. So terribly, unbearably lonely.

"All right," she said. "If you want to. Not tonight. I'm too tired to go out to dinner. But tomorrow evening if it suits you."

He seemed almost humble. "It suits me. Thank you. Really. If I believed in fate . . ."

"Maybe you should," Sheila said. "Maybe we deserve each other."

"What are your plans for this evening?" Sheila asked at breakfast next morning.

"Nothing special," Tommy said. "Why?"

"I've been asked out to dinner."

"Great! It's about time!"

"I'm not sure you'll be so enthusiastic when you hear who asked me. It's Jerry Mancini."

Tom didn't answer for a minute. Then he said, "Look, Mom, I'm not going to say I like him, but I've learned a lot in the last year. I haven't got any right to tell you who you should see. And you shouldn't *let* me."

She looked at him lovingly. "You've grown up so much, haven't you, Tommy?"

"I don't know. I'm trying to understand things, that's all."

"Darling, most of us never understand things. I'm three times your age, and God knows *I* don't. I don't think I ever will. But I was around when a new life came into the world last night and it made me realize how impossible it is to just exist without being part of the whole crazy scheme of things. I thought I could live *through* you, *for* you, Tommy. I was wrong. You saw it before I did. I was doing it for myself as much as for you. Maybe more. Anyway, I have to come out into the light again, even if it's with someone as unadmirable and temporary as Jerry."

He nodded solemnly. "I know. I want you to have some fun again. But . . ."

"But I'm not going to marry him," Sheila said. "I don't think he wants that. And I know *I* don't."

"Can I ask you a personal question?"

"Shoot."

"Why didn't you marry Mr. Reardon? Pat told me you planned to. I only saw him a couple of times, but he seemed like a nice guy. Did you change your mind because of Maryanne? I can't understand that, if you did. Or was it me, Mom? Did you think I'd mind?"

She didn't know how to answer him. She couldn't say it was both those things and more. He was only sixteen. He couldn't begin to comprehend the low opinion she had of herself, the certainty that Bill Reardon deserved a less selfish wife.

Sheila hedged. "*Would* you have minded?"

"I don't know. No. I think I'd have been glad."

"Why, Tommy? Because he's more suitable in age and temperament than Jerry?"

He thought carefully. "I'm not sure. That's part of it, probably. I guess when I came home from Florida I really saw you for the first time as a person, not just a mother. I just wanted . . . I still want you to be happy." He actually blushed. "I guess, after Dad died, I thought I could take his place. I mean, not *really*, but, you know . . ."

Sheila nodded. "Yes, I know. I thought you could, too. But you have a place of your own. A different one. Just as good. As I said, you recognized that before I did. But even before I fully realized how bright you are, Tom, I was going to marry Bill. It was Maryanne's death" (the word still came out with difficulty) "that threw everything out of focus for me. It's still out of focus, honey. I don't know what will ever make it sharp and clear again."

"Is it too late for you and Mr. Reardon?"

"Yes, love. But it's okay. As they say, it was nice while it lasted. And so many things are much better even now." She glanced at the clock. "Good lord, I'm going to be late for work and you'd better get off to school! You planning to see your new niece today?"

"Yeah. I thought I'd go over this afternoon. Terrific, isn't it? 'Uncle Tom.' How about that?"

Sheila gave him an affectionate shove. "Harriet Beecher Stowe would have loved you."

"Oh, boy! Talk about cornball jokes!"

She laughed. "Okay, Uncle Tom. Move your fanny."

"Where would you like to have dinner?"

"I don't really care. Anywhere you like."

Jerry thought a moment. "How about something off-beat? A real change of pace. We could do something crazy like go to Theatrical."

Sheila laughed. "Theatrical? I haven't been there in a hundred years! I thought it was only for advertising people and visiting firemen!"

"We don't have to go. We can go anywhere you like. Pewter Mug? Hollenden Tavern? Leonello's? You name it."

Neither of the last two, Sheila thought. She'd see Bill Reardon's ghost in every corner. At least Theatrical would be anonymous and non-memory evoking. She remembered the food as being quite good, though she thought of the place more as a supper club, with loud, continuous entertainment. Maybe it was a good idea. You could hardly hear yourself think, much less talk. She wasn't in the mood for a soul-searching conversation with Jerry. She just wanted to get out, to forget who and what she was, to stop feeling like a monument to monotony.

"No," she said, "Theatrical's a good idea. Let's try it. Why not?"

It was just as she remembered. An enormous place with tables on several tiers, a long, crowded center bar, one part of which was wide enough to accommodate an ear-blasting rock group, amplified beyond human endurance. They got a banquette table on the top level, as far as possible away from the music, ordered drinks, and Sheila began to relax. It was no longer exciting, nerve-tingling to be with Jerry, but he was attentive and flattering and he made her feel attractive. It was good to know you looked pretty, and that a handsome man thought so. She had no intention of starting up the affair with Jerry again, but she was glad to get out of the house, away from her own company.

He seemed to sense her feelings. He talked easily, almost impersonally, putting her at ease. I wonder if we can be friends, Sheila thought. Some women remain friends with their former lovers. She knew that. Jerry must know it, too. She hoped he accepted the idea. Or was he simply clever enough to know he couldn't push her? He was smart about women. Look how he'd gotten Barbara back, and she must have known him better than anyone. The hell with it. She'd learned her lesson. Or had she? Why shouldn't she use Jerry as he'd used her—physically, unemotionally, truly realistically this time? If he wanted to go to bed with her at the end of this evening, why not, if she felt like it? Sex was a good, temporary-forgetfulness prescription if one looked at it as a man such as Jerry did. There'd been a lot of bitter truth in what she'd said to him at the hospital yesterday. They did deserve each other. In her way, she was no better than he.

She realized he was speaking to her.

"Sorry. What did you say?"

"I said, you seem very different, Sheila. No less beautiful and desirable, but, well, less outgoing."

"Colder, you mean. Harder."

"No. I don't think you could be either. It's, I don't know, as though you've built a barrier against the world. Or against me."

"Or against myself."

"Maybe. But if so, I don't know why. You've suffered terribly, I know. But it seems more than that. More than grief. It's as though you've turned all the nightmares inward. What are you blaming yourself for, Sheila?"

"You're being silly," she said lightly. "I'm the same. Just more realistic. I'm a late bloomer. Takes me nearly half a century to find out that people are no damned good."

"You don't believe that."

"Sure I do. With me at the head of the list."

They were interrupted by the Captain. "Excuse me, madam," he said, "are you Mrs. Callahan?"

She looked up, startled. "Yes. Why?"

"The guitar player asked me to give you this." He handed her a scrap of paper, bowed and departed.

Jerry raised an eyebrow, "Mash notes from the band? What's all this?"

"I haven't the faintest idea."

Sheila unfolded the paper and read the few scribbled words:

"Mrs. Callahan, I'd like to come to see you tomorrow, if you let me. Please raise your hand if it's okay. It's important." It was signed "Rick Jawolsky."

Sheila went white. She looked in the direction of the musicians. They were so far away she couldn't clearly see their faces, but the guitarist was staring at her. She felt as though she were suffocating. Rick Jawolsky.

That loathsome creature who'd destroyed Maryanne! And then she remembered. It wasn't Rick who'd done it, it was Sheila herself. He'd want to talk about Maryanne. She couldn't! But as though her arm had no will of its own, she slowly extended it upward and saw him nod in response.

"Sheila! What the hell's going on?"

"Take me home, please, Jerry. I don't feel well."

"What's in that note?"

She tore it into pieces. "Something you wouldn't understand. I'd like to get out here now, please."

He was baffled and angry. "We haven't had dinner, for God's sake! What's the matter with you?"

She sighed. "That note was from Rick Jawolsky. The man Maryanne lived with. He wants to see me tomorrow."

Jerry stared at her. "Well you're not going to see him, for Christ's sake, are you? What do you need with that hippie?"

"I'm not sure," Sheila said. "I just want to go home now."

He'd driven her in silence and at the door she'd taken his hand and said, "I'm sorry I spoiled your evening, Jerry. It probably was a mistake anyway. I thought I could be something I'm not."

"I don't get any of this. Are you all right?"

"No," Sheila said, "that's just the trouble. I'm not. But it's nothing you can help."

"Shall I call you tomorrow?"

She shook her head. "I'll be in touch. Maybe."

Jerry walked slowly to his car, annoyed. A wasted evening. She's really flipped out, he thought. I suppose I should talk to Pat about her. He turned on the ignition. The hell with it. Flaky dame. She's probably menopausal. Who needs it? It was a stupid impulse to begin with.

Chapter 34

After she got Tommy off to school, she called the store and said she was sick and wouldn't be in. One of these days Miss Rawlings was going to run out of patience with her. She'd taken so much time off, she'd probably have to look for a new job. She'd be sorry. She liked this one, liked the store, her boss, and the people she worked with. And of course she needed the money, couldn't exist without it. But it wasn't as though she "goofed off" to nurse a hangover or go to a luncheon. Every absence this year had been for some important reason, good *or* bad. When she sneaked off to Bermuda with Bill. When she'd had to bury her daughter. Ecstasy in one case, torture in the other. Lies for the first. Total helplessness for the second. And now another lie for this absence. And a terrible dread of what Rick would say when he appeared.

She'd told no one about Rick's note. Tommy thought she really was ill this morning. He'd been sweetly solicitous, asking her if he should call Patrick or Mrs. Cantrell. Or should he stay home today to take care of her?

"No!" Sheila's voice was sharp with fright. "I mean, it's nothing, darling. I probably ate some rotten seafood last night."

"Did you have a good time?"

"It was all right," she lied. "Did me good to get out of the house. I was fine until I ran into those clams."

She hoped Rick would call or appear early. She didn't want him there when Tommy came home from school. It was tricky timing. Unless his pattern had changed, he slept half the day. She knew. She used to imagine, heartsick, Maryanne sleeping beside him all afternoon in that apartment in Ohio City. I wouldn't be heartsick now, Sheila thought. I'd be glad, no matter what she did, simply knowing she was alive. Oh, God, if time only ran backward! If Maryanne were a little girl again and I could do things differently. If only I could have made her *like* me. I wouldn't have asked for love. Just liking would have been enough. But she hated me. She couldn't stand the sight of me. She was too polite, too considerate to say so, but I know it now. Withdrawal was her way of showing her contempt for me and for my surrender to a dull, hypocritical life.

Stop it, she told herself firmly. You don't know anything. That's the whole trouble. You never tried to know.

But I will today, Sheila thought. Somehow I think Rick can explain Maryanne to me. I wonder why I'm going to listen to him when I've refused to give Patrick a hearing. Because Rick was my daughter's lover? Because he saw her in a way her family couldn't? Because she told him things she was never willing or able to confide in me? Was this ignorant, careless young man more understanding of Maryanne than I ever was? Probably, incredibly, sadly so.

It was a little after one o'clock when she heard a car stop in front of the house and, from the living room window, saw him jump out of a battered Volkswagen. She opened the door before he could ring. They stood looking at each other, not speaking until Sheila finally said, "Come in, Rick."

She was surprised by her own composure. All the night before she'd lain awake, wondering how she'd react when she came face to face with him. Would she weep? Scream? Beat on him, physically, with her fists? None of these. As though he were another casual visitor, she led the way into the living room and motioned him to a seat on the sofa. Then she sat in a facing chair, folded her hands and waited. He was far more ill at ease than she. Usually he sprawled. But now he, too, sat bolt upright, his hands twitching with nervousness. Suffer, damn you, Sheila thought. I'm not going to make it easy for you.

"I never meant to see you again," he said. "I don't think I would have, if you hadn't come in the club last night."

He hoped for some response, but Sheila made none. The goddamn woman was made of stone. Just like Maryanne. All that stinking politeness, that "good breeding." If it had been *his* mother, she'd have been yelling accusations at him or crying or throwing things. The only time he'd ever seen Maryanne really lose control was that last night. The night she slipped into the river. Even then, he hadn't thought she'd do any more than run back to the hotel and be mad at him for a few days before she had the abortion that any girl in her right mind would have had. Damned middle-class, suburban upbringing! They never really kicked it, no matter what they pretended.

Why doesn't he say whatever he's come to say? Sheila wondered. Why are we sitting here like strangers at a tea party? What is this important thing he had to see me about? She couldn't stand it any longer.

"Why have you come?"

He cracked his knuckles. The noise was explosive in the quiet room.

"I have something that belongs to you. Something of Maryanne's."

Hearing him speak her daughter's name made Sheila tremble. "I thought Patrick brought everything home," she said. "If he overlooked something, you could have mailed it."

Rick shook his head. "He didn't overlook anything. At the time, I didn't know this existed. And when I found it, I decided you shouldn't have it at all. It's a letter, Mrs. Callahan. She wrote it a couple of weeks before she died. It's to you, but I don't think she ever intended to send it. It was stuffed way in the bottom of one of her suitcases. When I read it, it sounded so crazy I figured why the hell put you through more reminders of her? The way I looked at it, the sooner you forgot, the better. I thought I was doing right. I swear to God I did. That's why I didn't send it to you. And then, last night, when I saw you out with that young guy, I said to myself, why not? She's okay. It's been months. She can handle this."

Sheila was hardly breathing.

"You see, Mrs. Callahan, I didn't figure there was any point in rehashing everything. I mean, I was pretty sure Patrick told you about the pregnancy and all that stuff. I thought it would hurt you to read about how remorseful Maryanne was, though Christ knows I didn't think she was so full of guilt she'd take a dive off a bridge! That didn't seem her style. She was always cool, except when she'd come here. When she'd get back from visiting you—like around the holidays last year—she was a crazy lady. All mixed up. One minute hollering about the uptight Shaker Heights phonies and the next saying how lucky all of you were to live such untroubled lives."

Sheila hardly heard the last part of Rick's speech. The words ran together. Pregnant. Guilty. A "dive," as he so crudely put it. She felt the sweat run down her legs though her hands were ice cold. What was that he'd said later? About Maryanne being like a crazy lady when she'd been home. About being mixed up. She stared sightlessly at the young man on the couch. The look of her frightened Rick. He'd never seen anyone so stricken. Her face was deathly pale and she gripped the arms of her chair as though she would fall out of it if she didn't. What had he said that produced such a reaction? She looked like she might have a heart attack. Jesus, that was all he needed!

"Mrs. Callahan. Mrs. Callahan!"

She seemed to come to with a start.

"Are you sick? Should I get help?"

She gave a tiny shake of her head. "I'll be all right in a minute. But I think you'd better go."

He stood up and handed her a thick sheaf of papers. "Here's the letter. Do you want it?"

Hardly knowing what she was doing, she accepted the pages, not looking at them, not looking at him. "Thank you," she said inanely. "It was kind of you to come."

Rick stared at her. They never forgot their damned manners, did they? A minute ago he thought she was dying. Now she was kissing him off with that boarding-school politeness. He was out of his depth with her. Just as he'd known, even when he was dominating her, that Maryanne had the kind of class that would always make him look crass and stupid. He hated women like these. Hated the men they married and the children they bore. And yet he felt sorry for Sheila. Surprised, he heard himself saying, "You may not believe this, Mrs. Callahan, but I really loved Maryanne, in my way. She didn't love herself, that was the trouble."

A strange expression came over Sheila's face.

When he'd gone, Sheila sat for a long while, not moving, feeling somehow as though Maryanne was literally waiting to speak to her. She knew it was more than just a letter she held. She had Maryanne's life in her hands. All the things, Sheila felt sure, her daughter could never bring herself to say. Slowly, fearfully, she unfolded the paper and saw the familiar, careful, well-trained handwriting. Even the sight of it was painful. I can't avoid knowing any longer, Sheila thought. Rick told me what I wouldn't let Patrick say. And now Maryanne is going to tell me more. She began to read.

Dear Mother,

I don't know exactly why I'm writing this because probably I'll never have the courage to send it. Not courage, really. Probably not enough bigness of spirit, not enough genuine humility to confess what I feel and what I've been at such pains to keep from you most of my life. And yet it is kind of a confession, I suppose. If I went to Church I'd be able to tell it to an unseen presence behind a curtain. Perhaps that would help, except that I've never felt anything but scorn for those who "confess"—as though spilling one's guilts takes them off the shoulders of the sinner and deposits them onto the listener. With priests it doesn't matter, I guess. They hear so many things that the outpouring must take on an impersonality that doesn't touch them for long. They must look at souls the way doctors look

313

at bodies, don't you think? With professional interest, some humane concern but no real involvement. But confessing to a person close to you is the kind of selfishness I really hate. It's wrong to burden someone you love with knowledge they needn't have. I always felt that way about Dad. I always resented him for making sure you knew about his affairs, as though he couldn't handle his guilt so he dumped it on you. *His* wrongdoing became *your* problem. You had to be strong so he could bear being weak. From the time I was old enough to recognize what he was doing to you, I was filled with disgust for him and determined never to be like that. He used you to exorcise his devils. Perhaps he didn't want to be bothered with them. More likely he was too inadequate and too insecure. Unable to cope, but knowing *you* could and would.

Funny to think of Dad as insecure, isn't it? Outwardly, he was so flamboyant, so dominant, so bloody independent. In a way, he was a "rich man's Rick"—all extrovert on the outside, all uncertainty beneath. There was no overt resemblance between the men we lived with, yet they were very much alike. We gravitated toward weakness, or attracted it. The only difference is, you handled a bad scene with dignity and love and endless compassion, while I used masochism and bitterness and self-delusion.

Why do I keep using the past tense when I speak of Rick? I don't know. He's still very much here. I'm the one who's not. In body, yes. In spirit, no. I think I despise him. I think I'd leave him for good, except that I'm carrying his baby. He doesn't know yet. I know what he'll say: "Get rid of it." What will *I* say? I don't know. I keep wondering what *you* would say in these circumstances. But that's academic. You'd never be in these circumstances. You would not know how to be ugly and sordid and full of hate. Just as you wouldn't be shocked or moralistic about me. You'd be my mother.

I wish I could sit down with you and say the things I feel about you. I wish I could tell you how much I love you, how much I admire you, how proud I've always been of the person you are. The person I'd like to be. I know, even now, if you were reading this you'd not be outraged by my pregnancy, any more than you've been angered by my rebellious, hostile, stupid way of life. You've been hurt because I've made my love for you seem like hate or, at best, indifference. You've tried so hard to understand me and I've blocked you. Deliberately. Knowing I could never approach the qualities that are yours, I spat on them. And on you.

All my life I've wanted to be like you, Mother. Generous in your affection, undemanding in your claims on any other human being, sensitive to the right of every person to make his own way, to reach for his own values. We tried to talk about values once, remember? I knew you were holding out your heart to me then. I wanted to take it. For a little while I thought I deserved it. But I didn't. I don't. As long as I live, I never will. I'm "Daddy's girl," God help me, riding roughshod over those I love most because I'm afraid they'll see how small I am if I really let them get close enough. How jealous I am of you, Mother! How envious of your strength, your warmth, your reality, your lack of phony righteousness! And how I've loathed myself for not being the daughter you should have had . . . the one who could have let you know how grateful I am for all that you are, and for all that you tried to be to me.

We are parent and child, an accident of birth that hardly counts. It's what comes later that matters. I've respected you always, comforted to know that you were there. Yet I felt competitive to you, even while I knew that it was an unnecessary contest that I had no ability—or need—to win.

And if I worshiped you as a child and a girl, how much more I've come to appreciate you now that I'm a woman! The way you stood on your own feet, emotionally and financially, after Dad died, the way you faced loneliness when you'd never known a moment alone before. The way you're still so proud of all of us: Patrick, Tommy, even me. The way you did not play the "poor little widow" game, milking the situation to gain attention from us kids who were all too self-involved to see how tough it's been for you. Pat's been good. He *is* good. And Tommy's going to turn out okay. Forget those terrible things I said about what you were doing to him. How you'd make him a "Mama's boy." I was striking out at you again, as I have so often. And you, gentle lady, didn't recognize the bitchiness that I saw and hated in myself. My scorn for all you represent to Tommy wasn't scorn at all. It was a longing to love like that, like Tommy does, and be open about it. In these last years I became as different from you as I could . . . or so I tried to make myself and the world believe. I sneered at the "nice things of life," the home and husband and children. I worried you because I knew you'd never worried your own mother. I punished you to punish myself. I've succeeded in both.

My love for you is much more than the love of a daughter for a mother. I love you as a woman, as the embodiment of womanliness in its best sense. I like you as a person, as I've liked few other people in my whole damned messed-up life. I care for you as my friend, see you as my longed-for confidante. And yet I cannot *say* these things to you. That's the saddest of all. My fear of being sloppy-sentimental, that thin shell of defense against your recognition of my hatefulness —these keep me silent. Except in this letter which you'll never read.

But writing it lets me put down all the things that I say over and over to you in my head. It is my therapy, my confession, perhaps even my absolution. You see? There I am. Thinking only of myself. Wonderful Maryanne. Selfish in everything she does.

I am blessed to have been born to you. Whatever happens, you are the finest thing in my life. And now that there is life inside me, I would wish for it a mother like mine. Poor little thing. No chance. I'll destroy it, as I destroy everything, one way or another.

Queer, what release it is to put things tidily on paper, even if no one ever reads them. You've given me so much, including this need for orderliness which is the least of your gifts. I've even fought that, too. You are neat, so I'll be messy. You are outgoing, so I will be sullen. You can love and show it. Can I love? Yes. I love. Can I show it? No, God help me, never.

Unless someday, for some reason, you do see this letter. And then you will know the Maryanne who always wanted to be. The one you tried so hard to draw out. The one who fought you every inch of your patient but bewildered way. The one who loves you as much as she loathes herself.

Whatever happens, I want *you* to be happy. I want it more than life. If there's a God, He'll make you happy. For me.

Maryanne

Sheila was sobbing openly, helplessly, by the time she finished reading. Maryanne had known what she was going to do when she wrote this letter. Had she hoped it would get to her mother? Sheila didn't know. She'd never know. All she knew was that through the terrible pain she felt the first surge of peace. The peace Maryanne wanted her to have. For in writing down her thoughts, her "confession" to absolve herself, she unknowingly had lifted a terrible burden from the heart and conscience of Sheila Callahan.

Maryanne's letter did not miraculously terminate all Sheila's feelings of guilt, for surely there must have been some way to have reached the girl if she'd only known how. But it did take away the unendurable feeling that her child had hated her. If Sheila believed she was still at fault, Maryanne had never felt that, and for this her mother was humbly grateful. If only we could have talked, she thought for the thousandth time. If we could have seen each other as two imperfect, well-meaning people, perhaps we'd have found a way to cross the bridge between the generations, to understand what drives and motivates all women, irrespective of their ages or circumstances.

It hurt to know, after the fact, how Maryanne felt. And yet it also healed. It brought a kind of resigned acceptance, a peculiar, helpless consolation. And it brought home a strange truth, or perhaps one not so strange at all: I've been as alien to my mother as Maryanne was to hers, Sheila realized. I've given lip-service love, without expressing genuine liking. She suddenly wanted to see Rose before it was too late. To tell her how much she cared, how much she regretted the lack of closeness between them. In my own way, I've rebelled against my mother, too, Sheila thought. I tried to be as different as I could. She dominated her husband while I lived unprotestingly with a tyrannical Sean. She demanded respect from her child while I sought only crumbs of affection from mine. Even as a widow, I was determined not to act like her. My matter-of-factness, my refusal to go through the conventional portrayal of bereavement was perhaps my unconscious way of showing how unlike her I thought myself to be. And, like Maryanne, I've always wished it could be different. Does Rose feel far removed from me? Am I almost a stranger? Does she think I don't need her? Does she believe, like most widows, that nobody, including children, gives a damn?

She thought of the women she knew who'd lost their husbands. So far, except for Sally's divorce, most of the couples in her "social set" were still together, happily or not, by habit or choice. But some of the women at the store were widows, clinging to their jobs as much for contact with people as for the salaries. Sheila had talked to most of them in the past six months. Theirs was a resigned boredom, relieved only by an occasional visit to or from their children, the highlight of their lives. They lived through their children and grandchildren, discussing the good marriages their daughters had made, the fine careers their sons had chosen, the scholastic achievements of their grandsons, and the popularity of their granddaughters. Was it a make-believe world? Were they putting up a front, pretending they're important to these dutiful but indifferent offspring? Is that how Rose felt as she ate her solitary dinners, watched her favorite TV shows, played her predictable bridge games with the few cronies she had left? Is that how *I'll* feel?

She was overreacting, she knew. Family relationships weren't the way the women's magazines portrayed them, the way old-fashioned movies or new-formed television shows like "The Waltons" showed them to be—full of nearness and tenderness and understanding. Life was merely a situation involving people who might not even care to know each other if they hadn't happened to be related. Nobody owed anybody anything. She must remember that always. It was no good being angry because your husband had been careless enough to die and leave you alone. Or resentful because your children claimed their right to separate lives. Or remorseful, as she was now, that she'd had so little time for Rose. Sensibly, she knew her mother was as imperfect as she. And they'd been apart too long to live together again. But at this emotional moment, Sheila felt a need to see and talk with Rose. I don't really know her. I've never really tried. In a way, I *am* like Maryanne, though I chose a different kind of

317

rebellion. And maybe Rose is like I was, aching to be in touch with her daughter and, fearful of rejection, unwilling to intrude.

We're both alone. There must be something special we can give each other. Some feeling we can share before time runs out. I want Mother to approve of me, Sheila realized. I suppose, in the end, that's what all children want. No matter how grown-up we pretend to be.

Chapter 35

She called Rose and said she'd like to come to New York the next Saturday night and spend Sunday with her, if it was convenient. The unlikely idea made Rose instantly suspicious.

"What's wrong?"

"Nothing's wrong. I'd just like to see you. It's been a long while since we really talked."

"And you're spending all that money to come here for one day?"

"I wish it could be longer, but I can't take time off from work. I've missed too many days already. Anyway, Mother, we can cover a lot of ground in twenty-four hours, even with time out for sleeping."

"You're keeping something from me. I'm sure of it. Nothing's happened to the baby, has it? Or Tommy?"

Sheila felt the old irritation welling up. But what did she expect? Whenever she unexpectedly called Rose it *was* usually trouble. And except for that one time, years ago, when Patrick was small and Maryanne was an infant, she couldn't remember any voluntary visits to her mother. Rose had always come to Cleveland for holidays and birthdays. And deaths. It's been years since I've been in New York, except at the airport, Sheila realized. And to think that a few months ago I thought I'd be living there by now.

"Everything's fine, dear," she said. "I'm just, well, lonely for another woman to talk to."

319

"What about your friend Sally Cantrell?" It was not asked with bitterness. Rose was genuinely and understandably surprised by this sudden overture. "Is she out of town?"

"No. Sally's here. But it's you I want to talk to."

"I'm flattered." Rose couldn't keep the slight sarcasm out of her voice. Then she felt ashamed. "You know I'll be happy to see you, darling. I'm delighted you want to come."

Yes, I do want to, Sheila thought as she hung up, and I'm not entirely sure why. Except that I must talk to someone about Maryanne's letter, someone I can trust to understand. Dear as Sally was, she'd not be able to identify with this need to grapple with the mother-daughter relationship. She'd be warm, sympathetic, patient. But she had no children of her own. How could she understand Sheila's need to share this evidence of a child's love, this revelation that both soothed and agitated? Sally would analyze, cite case histories of classic love-hate relationships, discuss, in intellectual terms, Maryanne's father-resentment and mother-envy. It would all be true, but it was not what Sheila needed. Rose was far less worldly, less intelligent and "modern." Rose was, in fact, completely "old-fashioned" in her reaction to everything. She'd cry over the letter, not dissect the psychological implications. And that's what I need, Sheila thought. Some honest, sloppy, gut-feeling sharing.

There was nowhere else she could get it. Tommy was too young to understand why she could be so sad and relieved at the same time. Patrick would take a doctor's view that Maryanne was disturbed, poor, sad girl. Even Betty, with her natural gentleness and her professional training in psychology, would try to explain the twisted mind of Sheila's child. I don't need textbook platitudes, Sheila told herself. I need blind love and, yes, the restorative power of middle-class emotion. I need someone to feel sorry for me. I'm tired of being a faceless thing, brave and sensible. I want to be me. My mother's child. Not somebody else's mother or friend or lover. I'm lost. And I need to run home.

She drove over to see Betty at the hospital. Pat was there and after they'd visited with Betty a while, Sheila asked him to go with her to the nursery where they could see the baby through the big glass window. As they walked down the long hall which smelled of medication, disinfectants, and flowers, Sheila told him of her plan to visit Rose. She didn't mention the letter, but she did tell him that Rick Jawolsky had come to see her that afternoon. Patrick was furious.

"That sonofabitch! What gall! How dare he show his face? What in God's name made him come to see you?"

She explained about dinner with Jerry. "I'm sure that's the last I'll see of Dr. Mancini," she said calmly. "Running across Rick threw me into such a state of depression that all I wanted was to go home. Jerry probably thinks I'm crazy." Sheila gave a little laugh. "I'm not sure he's wrong. I think I must have been temporarily mad, thinking I could forget myself with him again. I've been running away from myself for more than a year, Patrick, and it's unbecoming. I'm a forty-eight-year-old widow who'll probably never marry again. Why can't I resign myself to what most women like me learn to accept? I'm lucky. I'm self-supporting, occupied, have two great boys, a marvelous daughter-in-law, and now this angelic grandchild. I even still have my own mother. What do I expect out of life—champagne and sequins?"

"You're wrong. You're still young and beautiful. You've gone through a hideous year. It would be enough to throw anybody into a tailspin."

"No. Pat, I'm trying hard to be realistic. I want to find peace."

"And *Rose* is peace?" He sounded so incredulous that Sheila laughed.

"Not really. She's just part of the self-acceptance process, I suppose. Hot or cold, love, she's my parent. There's an attachment that never goes away. Now that you're a father, you'll begin to know what that means." Sheila took a deep breath. "Rick told me Maryanne was pregnant. My poor child. If only she'd felt able to come home. If only she could have had a child of her own."

Patrick was silent for a moment. "Even *his?*"

"Yes, even his. You'll think I've taken leave of my senses, but I believe in his own way he loved Maryanne."

"Mother! He wanted her to have an abortion! I suppose he didn't tell you that."

"Yes, he told me. But I think he'd have changed his mind if she'd been in any fit mental condition to discuss it with him. I wish Maryanne had had her baby, with or without a husband. I wish she'd felt sure enough of my love to know I'd have welcomed them with open arms."

Patrick looked at her suspiciously. "What else did you gather from Jawolsky's visit?"

"I know *how* she died, as well as *why.*"

"Goddammit, you didn't have to have that whole nightmare to live with! I wanted to tell you everything at first, and then I realized you didn't need that, too. I was glad you didn't want to know. Your instinct was right."

"Only at the time. It's better that I do know. It's real, now. I can comprehend a little more. There's nothing worse than asking yourself over and over again, 'Why?' I'll never know the desperation that drove her, Patrick, but at least there's one thing I can hang on to, for whatever comfort it can bring. I've finally accepted the fact that Maryanne's death was her final choice. Her right. I'd even like to have the things you brought back from New York."

She's keeping something from me, Patrick thought. Whatever it is, it's painful but at least it's released her from that terrible, numb anguish.

"Mother," he said gently, "what about your own life? What about Bill Reardon?"

Sheila shook her head. She repeated what she'd told Sally. "I'm through with peaks and valleys." She smiled. "I've had more than enough of them in my life. I'm too tired to climb and too afraid to fall. I can't offer Bill what he needs—the laughter, the adventurous companion, the care-free partnership. It's too late, Pat. I won't be a man-crazy, middle-aged woman. I don't have to be constantly ecstatic. It's too much to handle."

"That's hard to follow, Mother."

"Is it? Maybe for you. You're still so young." They'd reached the nursery and stood looking at the tiny little person in a bassinette marked "Callahan." Sheila smiled. "She's adorable. Jennifer. Such a pretty name."

"You know we wanted to call her after you."

"I'm glad I talked you out of that, sweet as it was of you. One Sheila Callahan is enough. More than enough! Besides, I can't stand all those pointedly Irish names." She smiled up at him impishly. "Tell you a secret, son. If it hadn't been for your father, I'd probably have named you Ramon and your brother would have been Isaac."

"Thanks a *lot!*"

"I'm teasing. What I really think is that people shouldn't be named after other people. That's why we never had a Sean, Jr. Or a Sheila. Children deserve their own identities, from birth on. God save me from the 'juniors' or the 'little Sheilas'!" She looked at the baby. "You be your own woman, Jennifer," she said. "And be a good one."

The cab pulled up in front of Rose's apartment building and Sheila, carrying her overnight case, jumped out. All the way in from the airport, she'd felt excited. There really was nothing like the New York skyline at sunset, the buildings all tall and rosy, cutting a powerful, jagged slash across the sky. New York was hard and impersonal, but it was awe-inspiring and stimulating like no other place in the world. It could be lonely, but what place could not? She was strangely happy to be here. There'd been only one moment of panic, as she stepped into the cab and gave her mother's address. "Do we have to cross a bridge to get there?" she asked.

The driver turned and gave her a strange look.

"I . . . I don't like bridges," she said lamely.

"You ever been here before, lady? Manhattan's an island, surrounded by water. Whatdya think I am, Moses parting the Red Sea?"

"I just meant . . . isn't there a tunnel or something?"

Another nut, the driver thought. "Yeah, there's the Midtown Tunnel, but that's goofy. It's way out of the way and it'll cost you more than if we took the . . ."

She interrupted him. "I don't mind the money if we just don't have to go over a bridge. Please."

He shrugged. "It's *your* ride. Jesus!"

She felt ridiculous. Over water. Under water. What difference did it

322

make? She didn't even know what bridge Maryanne had chosen. She just didn't want to see one. Not now. Not yet. Bridges and Maryanne. The girl crossed one to get to Ohio City. She'd dropped off another to end her life. And she'd burned them all behind her. For God's sake, Sheila, pull yourself together! By the time she got to the West Side she was calmer, eager to see Rose. She clutched her purse with the letter inside. She hated Rick for having read it first, but he didn't understand it. Her mother would.

It was almost nine o'clock when Rose opened the door, but she was fully dressed, immaculately coiffed, looking as though she was waiting to go out. Sheila was so surprised that her first words were strange ones.

"What are you doing all done up, Mother? Why aren't you comfortable?"

"It's one of the things you learn when you live alone, Sheila. Not to let yourself go, slopping around in some terrible old robe with your hair uncombed and no make-up on."

It was such a ludicrous conversation in the doorway that Sheila burst out laughing, and in a second Rose joined in.

"Will you listen to me?" Rose said. "You're not even in the door and I'm talking to you like a child who needs instructions!"

"Will you listen to *me?*" Sheila said. "Commenting on the way you look before I've even said hello! Hello, Mother. I'm so glad to see you."

"Hello, Sheila dear. I'm so glad you're here."

They hugged each other. They'd never been much for physical contact. Always that tentativeness, that reserve between them. It wasn't that way with Daddy, Sheila thought again. He was a cuddler, a tickler, a loving enveloper. I remember his embraces so well now, but I was always like Mother. More stand-offish with my kids, with none of the uninhibited, exuberant gathering of them to me that came so naturally to my father. Funny how bits and pieces of memory came into your mind at unexpected moments.

"Have you had dinner?" Rose was asking.

"Yes. On the plane. Horrible, as always."

"Hungry?"

"No, but I'd love some coffee if you have some."

"I can make it in a minute. It'll be Instant, I'm afraid. *I've* given up coffee. Keeps me awake at night. Doesn't it bother *you?*"

"No."

"Strange. It gives insomnia to everybody else I know. Well, if you're sure . . ."

While Rose was in the kitchen, Sheila sat looking around her, surprised that so little had changed. It was the same apartment she grew up in, a little seedier, but virtually the same. She could almost see her father sitting in his old Morris chair, reading his evening paper, occasionally looking up to give her a conspiratorial wink as Rose complained about something unimportant. How relaxed he'd been. She'd asked him once, when she was nearly grown, how he was always able to keep his temper when Mother was so testy. He'd just smiled and said, "People have different ways of showing love, baby. Your mother fusses because she wants everything to be perfect. For me. For you. It annoys her when it's not. That's why she seems so impatient. You have to look beneath the surface, Sheila dear. Your mother loves us. We're her life. And she thinks life should be flawless."

She hadn't really understood it then. It seemed a poor excuse for Rose's constant nagging, but now she saw her mother through her father's eyes. To him, she'd always been the epitome of the good wife and mother, the beautiful young girl who'd married him and had his child. What seemed incessant carping to Sheila had been, to Frank Price, signs of how much Rose cared for them both.

She looked at her father's photograph flanked by so many others on a side table. They were all there. Sheila and Sean on their wedding day. Patrick and Betty on theirs. Sheila and all her children. Tommy at his first communion. Maryanne when she graduated from college. Rose's world. One still to be fussed over and scolded because it was not the way she wanted it to be. No wonder they all dreaded her visits. They couldn't see her as Frank Price always had. They didn't see that the preaching, the interfering, the humorless concern was the only way Rose knew to tell them how much she loved them all. But her son-in-law and her grandchildren hadn't understood that. Even I never did, Sheila thought. And to this day I'm not sure Daddy was right. He indulged her, bolstered her conviction that she knew what was best for everybody, did her bidding and was blind to her faults. Maybe it *was* her way of expressing love. But maybe that love also had a great degree of early selfishness and later self-pity in it. I think she believes life cheated her, that it's cheating her still by its refusal to be perfect.

For the first time since she'd read Maryanne's letter, Sheila had qualms about Rose's reaction to it. Maybe I was wrong. How could she understand my imperfect daughter? Maybe she won't see the pathos and heartbreak, but only her disappointment in a grandchild who didn't live up to Rose's expectations. Maybe she'll blame me for failing as a mother. Don't let that happen. I don't need her blame. I couldn't stand it. I have enough, self-inflicted.

It might be better not to show her the letter at all. Nonsense! "Your mother loves us. We're her life." She could hear her father saying those words. And they were true. Sheila had come begging for comfort and closeness. Rose would recognize that. She'll reach out to me at last, Sheila thought, as I always wanted her to. As I should have with Maryanne. We can still do it, Rose and I. She'll understand. From the wisdom of her years and the goodness of her heart, she'll fulfill my childish needs. We'll cry together and I'll be her little girl again.

As Sheila sipped her coffee, they went over the events of the past months. Rose knew them all. Sheila talked to her on the phone every Sunday, but she wanted to hear them all again. Tommy was fine, getting so tall, doing so well in school. Yes, her job was all right and she was managing financially. The baby was beautiful and Betty would be home Monday.

"Whom does Jennifer look like?"

"Winston Churchill, of course," Sheila teased. "Don't they all?"

Rose wasn't amused. "I certainly hope she looks like Patrick."

"For heaven's sake, why? Betty's a lovely-looking girl."

"Patrick is far more handsome. Besides, they say that girls who look like their fathers are born for good luck."

Sheila laughed. "Mother, you don't believe that old wives' tale!"

"I don't know. Sometimes I wish for your sake you didn't look so much like me. Maybe you'd have been luckier."

Sheila was uncomprehending. "Luckier?"

"Oh, come now, darling. Sean wasn't anybody's idea of a perfect husband."

There was a little silence and then, because she couldn't resist, "You certainly sang a different tune at his funeral," Sheila said.

"That was a terrible, emotional moment. I was in shock. You were very rude to me about it at the time."

"I know." Sheila remembered what she'd vowed more than a year ago. She wasn't going to say she was sorry when she had nothing to apologize for.

"And, of course, dear," Rose went on, "you haven't been lucky since his death. No money. Tommy getting into that terrible trouble. Getting yourself mixed up with that dreadful young doctor. Poor child, you weren't even lucky enough to keep Bill Reardon. Sheila, I know you haven't postponed marrying him. He's backed out, hasn't he?"

The question wasn't meant to hurt Sheila. It never occurred to Rose that one couldn't say anything one thought to a member of one's family. It was "for their own good," because she cared, deeply, about what happened to them. Even her mourning over Sean's death had been more anxiety about Sheila's future than over the end of her son-in-law's life.

Sheila understood Rose as she never had. Rose longed for the same closeness her daughter did. And they were never able to express that. Just as Maryanne and I never could, Sheila thought. That's why I'm here, hoping we can find each other while there's still time. Let me try to understand her. Let me not listen to what she *says* but what she *means*.

"Bill's living permanently in Bermuda, Mother. He didn't back out. I did. After Maryanne, I couldn't think straight. You saw that when you were in Cleveland. You were wonderful. It made me realize how much I needed you."

"That's what a mother's for, Sheila. To be there in time of trouble."

"No, it's much more than that. I know that's what you must think. I guess that's what I felt about my own daughter. That she only needed me when she was in trouble. I didn't know how she felt about me until a few days ago." Sheila took the letter out of her purse. "I'd like you to read this. It says everything better than I ever could."

Rose read the long letter slowly. "Did she send you this?"

"No. I'm not sure she ever meant me to see it. Rick—the man she lived with—brought it to me."

"Poor, lost, fallen soul." Rose wiped the tears from her eyes. "How she must have suffered! I've prayed every day for God to forgive her sins. I've even found solace in the belief that she was taken from us before she could bring more shame on herself and her family."

Sheila stared at her. "Taken from us! She wasn't taken from us! Mother, she killed herself!"

"Don't you think I know that, child? Wasn't Patrick in this very room when he told you she was gone?" Rose came over and put her arms around Sheila. "I'm glad you let me share this. I've been praying for the wrong person, haven't I? It's you who's felt like the sinner, isn't it? Well, you're wrong, Sheila. You've been a good mother. Not a saint. None of us is that. But you did what seemed right and natural to you, for your child's happiness. The way we all do. And we make mistakes because we're human. But we can't spend the rest of our lives wishing we could take back the things we did or didn't do. Don't you think I've had a hundred regrets about you and me? Hindsight is such a waste unless one learns something from it. I've learned, dear. Learned more tonight than I have in almost fifty years. I feel this is a letter that but for the grace of God you could have written to me. Do I presume too much, Sheila? Isn't that why you really wanted me to read it?"

Sheila was crying, too. "Yes. I've never been able to tell you how much I really admired you. How I've always loved you and felt stupidly competitive. The way Maryanne did. I didn't want either of us to die not knowing that."

Rose held her close. "Baby, baby. I haven't been able to say the things you need to hear, either. What fools we are. We love each other so much and we're not as big as our individual selfishness. I've nagged and carped and disciplined and alienated you because I wanted nothing bad to ever happen to you. So unrealistic of me. So selfish, really. I know you never understood. Because I never really understood what I was doing. But neither of us is to blame, Sheila. Love gets all mixed up with other things. Protectiveness, frustration. It comes out wrong and we don't know how to set it right. I suppose I knew how difficult I seemed. I never saw you as a woman. You were always my child, my charge. Certainly you could do nothing but misinterpret this inability to let go. It wasn't until you felt you'd failed that you began to understand I've always considered myself a failure, the way you've been seeing yourself in relation to Maryanne. Thank God we've brought it all to the surface at last. Maryanne did more than erase your pain with this letter. She opened the eyes of two generations."

Sheila nodded. "Daddy always understood how much you loved us. He tried to explain it to me once, but I couldn't understand you or myself. I never have, all these years."

"Your father was an extraordinary man. Sometimes I was jealous of his ability to be so open, so sentimentally exposed. It was never my nature, Sheila, though I often wished it could have been. You're not really like me, but I suppose in these last few months you have been. You thought you didn't offer enough to Maryanne. That you didn't know how to reach her. That you couldn't save her from the inevitable. That's the way I've always felt. Hating myself because I knew how much I loved you and sure, most of the time, that you didn't even like me. It's a curious parallel. We're such different women, and yet we've suffered the same agonizing sense of inadequacy." Rose moved back to her chair. "I'll never be the kind of mother one reads about in books. I'm not the idealized creature on the greeting cards. But I want you to know I'm grateful for the best present I ever received—knowing my daughter loves and respects me and forgives me my errors. You learned that from Maryanne and you shared it with me. I won't change, Sheila. I'm too old for that. But now at least I can rest easy, knowing you understand what my kind of love is all about."

"What a shame I had to wait so long to grow up," Sheila said.

"No, what a blessing you finally did. What a blessing we *both* did. Your father would have been so happy to hear us talk like this together for the first time. He was always so proud of you."

"And he loved you so much, Mother."

"I always knew that. Even when I was in doubt about your affection, I never doubted his. He knew how I adored you both. I never had to say it. He had a worldful of love and compassion and patience to share with us, Sheila. You and I understood that, even if we didn't understand each other." Rose looked at her tenderly. "You've come full circle. It's been a hard journey, dear, but worthwhile. I think you're free at last. Free of your guilts about Maryanne. About me. It's time to take up your life again, little girl. Go find that good man you sent away. It's never too late for a fresh start."

"Go find Bill? How do I know he still wants me?"

"He'll want you." Rose smiled. "Remember," she said with a trace of irony, "Mother always knows best."

Chapter 36

For a split second when she awoke there was the
disorientation that comes with realizing one is not in the usual room, the
usual bed. It took Sheila a few seconds to remember where she was. The
bedside clock said ten-thirty. She couldn't believe it. She never slept that
late. Even in Bermuda she'd awakened early, conscious of Bill beside her,
eager not to lose a minute of the day with him. It wasn't difficult to analyze why she'd slept so long and well. She'd enjoyed the most untroubled
rest she'd had in months.

Lying there, Sheila appraised the night before. She'd always been unfair
in her assessment of her mother. What Rose had said was true. She hadn't
had much "luck"—if that's what it was—in her marriage and in the year
since. Rose knew and was troubled and helpless. And there was something
else Rose sensed. Her daughter *would* be able to share her life with another man. Sheila'd known that, really, since Rick brought the letter. The
knowledge had only been confirmed by Rose's unexpected self-disclosures
and her comforting, unselfish support.

I've been on a pointless hunger strike against happiness, Sheila thought.
That's over. I'm going to take life again, in sensible bites, savoring the
deliciousness of being alive. I'll never really get over Maryanne, but if I
failed her in life, the least I can do is be faithful in death. The last thing
she wrote was that she wanted me to be happy. For her. I'm not the

328

paragon she thought I was, God knows, but I'm worth something. I'm almost worth what my parents believed me to be, what Rose still thinks I can be.

Last night was a revelation. I came looking for something, maybe nothing more than the solace of sharing bereavement with one who's been through it. I didn't anticipate the near-apology I found, nor the understanding and respect. Respect. That's where it was. I really had no respect for Mother until last night. I've not done much to deserve hers. What had Bill said in their last conversation? "For the first time I've lost respect for you." I should have listened. What he really was saying was, "You've lost respect for yourself."

She slipped on a robe and went into the living room. Rose, fully dressed, was reading the Sunday *Times*.

"Good morning," Sheila said cheerfully. "How does it feel to have the laziest daughter in America?"

"I'm glad you slept well, dear. Or did you lie awake half the night?"

"No, I went right off. It was the best rest I've had since I can't think when. How about you?"

"I don't need much sleep these days. One doesn't, as one gets older. It's marvelous you can still sleep like that."

Sheila smiled. A few months ago she'd have been irritated, reading into Rose's remarks another put down, another attempt to equate her widowed daughter with her widowed self. She'll never really change, Sheila thought. She doesn't even know what she's doing. It's a reflex. Rose's little barb was unconscious. She was well named. A beautiful, elegant flower with thorns that pierced if you got too close. She'll say little things like that all her life, but they won't hurt me now because I know she doesn't consciously *mean* to hurt.

"I'm a good sleeper," Sheila agreed. "You been up long?"

"Since seven. I've even been to Mass."

Yesterday I'd have bled from the little prick of reproach, guilty that I hadn't gotten up and gone to church with her. I'd have been conscience-stricken that I wasted three of our precious hours together. But not today. She's just being Mother. I wonder if she realizes the implied criticism. No, of course not. It's simply her way. She said she was too old to become different. But to me she *is* different. We both are. She won't forget our talk any more than I will. I must learn not to take every word she says as criticism, to misread the things she doesn't know are insensitive. Or do I simply *think* they are? Am I so defensive that I imagine her every comment is a finger pointed at a naughty child?

"That was a good talk we had last night, Sheila. I feel very peaceful about things today." Rose smiled. "I even knew where to concentrate my prayers this morning."

"Thank you, darling. I need every one of them."

She was disappointed that Sheila was taking a midafternoon flight back to Cleveland. "Must you go so early? I'd planned to call the girls and ask them to drop over this afternoon and meet you."

"The girls?"

"My bridge club. You've never met them and they've heard so much about you and your family. They're always bragging about their children. I'd like them to see what a lovely daughter I have."

Sheila's eyes misted. "I'm sorry. I didn't know. I'd love to meet your friends, but I must get home and get ready to go to work tomorrow. I'll come again soon. That's a promise."

Like a good child, she obediently ate the big breakfast Rose insisted upon preparing for her. She'd have loved her usual toast and coffee, could hardly choke down the waffles and bacon that were so proudly presented.

"You don't eat enough," Rose said. "You mustn't get too thin, Sheila. After a certain age, women look old when they're all skin and bones."

Zing. The unwitting reminder that she was no longer young. Knock it off, she told herself. Remember what you've learned about your mother and yourself.

She left earlier than she had to, telling herself she wanted to walk a little in New York, telling Rose she was going to take the bus from the airline terminal and should allow extra time. Neither was true. Despite her new feelings, she was eager to escape, not yet sure enough of her ability to deal with Rose's all-too-honest, well-meaning tongue. I don't want to hang around and spoil it all. I don't want to lose this good, warm feeling for a woman whose opinionated pronouncements are subconscious pleas for reassurance that she'd been irreproachable, infallible in her roles as wife and mother. They parted warmly at the front door.

"I feel terrible not going to the airport with you," Rose said. "You always go with me when I leave Cleveland. In fact, you always meet me, too, which I didn't do for you."

"Darling, that's different." No need to say one felt a duty to see ladies of Rose's age on and off airplanes, help them with their bags, see that they didn't have to fight for public transportation. No need to point out that she was nearly thirty years younger, that the roles were now reversed. No reason to strip Rose of her dignity by pointing out that I feel I'm the mother and she's the child. Strong, independent, stubborn as she is, I feel protective of her, sad for her.

"I don't see why it's different," Rose said.

No, of course you don't. "It's just that *I'll* be happier if you don't have to make that tiresome trip to the airport. It's a bore. Next time *I* won't meet *you*, okay?"

They embraced each other. "I'm grateful you think you have a lovely daughter. It means a lot to me."

"To me, too, Sheila. You'll be all right?"

"Yes. Now, I'll be all right."

She was glad that all morning they'd not mentioned any of the old problems again. They hadn't brought up the future, either. Rose took it for granted she'd "straightened Sheila out" about Bill.

Carrying her overnight case, she walked down Central Park West and across Fifty-ninth street. Unknowingly, she was headed east on the same street Maryanne had walked. Deep in thought, she passed Madison Avenue, Park, and Lexington. Ahead she saw a bridge, but there were no mystical vibrations, in fact, no fear, this time, of crossing any bridge. She hailed a cab at Third Avenue and said, "Kennedy Airport, please!"

"You wanna take the Queensboro Bridge?"

"Whatever way you think best."

It was not until they were rumbling across the bumpy old span that Sheila wondered whether this was The One. There was a pang, but she willed herself to stop dramatizing. She didn't know exactly where Maryanne died. She probably never would. It was only important that she'd finally laid her to rest. She'd stay alive in Sheila's heart, but not as a tormenting ghost, a specter of accusation.

"I did the best I could, Maryanne."

"You say something, lady?"

She hadn't realized she'd spoken aloud.

"Nothing," she said. "Pay no attention."

Crazies, the driver thought. The town was full of them, talking to themselves. Funny, he could usually spot them. This one didn't look the type. But who could tell the yo-yos from the sane ones these days? He kept an eye on her in the rearview mirror, but she seemed calm. Calmer than most.

She was still calm when she reached her own house later that afternoon. There was no sign of Tommy, but for the first time in more than a year she realized that she did not have the unreasonable rush of fear about where he was or what he might be doing. He was simply out. Period. As simple as that. He wasn't a man, but he was no baby. Sixteen-year-olds weren't in this age of early maturity.

She called the hospital to see how Betty was and was told that Mrs. Callahan had been discharged that morning. Delighted, she called the apartment and Patrick answered.

"How was New York? How's our Wild Irish Rose?"

"Surprising, as usual," Sheila said. "But good surprising. I'm glad I went. I learned a lot."

"Oh?"

"Too complicated to go into now, but it was a worthwhile trip for me. And for her, too, I think. I'll tell you about it sometime when we sit

down to talk. How's Betty? And Jennifer? I'm so glad they're home! I wasn't sure it would be before early in the week."

"Betty's great. I had to practically drag her out of that lying-in wing. She was getting impossibly spoiled."

It was said with teasing affection, and Sheila felt warmed by the love in her son's house.

"Tom's here," Patrick went on. "He came with me to schlep home potted plants and things that Betty refused to leave behind. You want to talk to him? You want to come over?"

"No, thanks, dear. Just tell Tom I'm back and give Betty and Jennifer a kiss for me. I'm kind of pooped from the trip. Think I'll take it easy and maybe see you tomorrow evening if that suits you."

"Sure. Any way you want it. We were just about to fix a little supper, Tom and I. Okay for him to stay?"

"Of course."

She was actually relieved not to have to cook tonight. She'd scramble an egg for herself, climb into bed early. She thought of calling Sally to chat, but decided she really was tired. Too tired even for a long phone conversation with her friend.

An hour later Sally called her. "Hi! I've been calling you on and off all day. You been at the hospital? How's everything?"

"Everything's fine. Betty's home. But I haven't been there. I went to New York yesterday."

"New York? You didn't tell me you were going! What happened? Bill Reardon get in town?"

"No. I went to see Mother."

"You *what?* What on earth for? She isn't sick, is she?"

"No, she's in good shape. I just had a crazy yen to see her." Sheila hadn't told Sally about the letter and she was reluctant to tell her even now. She didn't know why. Sally was her dearest friend, her closest, almost her only, confidante.

"Boy, that is a wild impulse! In all the years, I've never seen you rushing toward Rose!"

"I know. If anything, I've rushed the other way. But I guess instinct is a strong motivating force, Sally. I've been so miserable. It seemed as though Mother might understand my erratic behavior about Bill, my guilts about the children, all the things I couldn't seem to sort out."

Sally grunted. "Don't tell me. I can imagine what happened when you tried to talk to that self-involved lady!" She began to imitate Rose. " 'You've lost your religion and let your children lose theirs. You weren't firm enough with Maryanne and you let Tommy run wild. You had that shameful affair with the doctor and now you've let Bill Reardon get away from you.' I can hear it now. I'll bet she even told you that you lost Bill because you were so sorry for yourself. That grief bores men. A whining

woman turns them off. Or maybe she told you that unattached men never marry women their own age, that you should reconcile yourself to that and become a resigned widow like herself. What on *earth* made you think you could talk out your problems with Rose? My God, Sheila, she'd be the last woman who could understand!"

"It wasn't like that," Sheila said slowly. "Not at all like that. I was afraid it was going to be. But she was marvelous. Compassionate. Even aware of how little love we've been able to show each other."

"You're putting me on! Rose? Compassionate? Aware? Are you sure you went to the right apartment?"

"I know it's hard to believe, but it was a Rose I'd never seen before. I think she was only waiting for me to make the first gesture because she didn't know how to make it herself. It was a wonderful experience, Sally. I'm grateful for it. That may sound syrupy, but I mean it."

"Sheila, that's all swell, but don't build up another fantasy in your mind. You're clutching at any sign of affection these days. Sure, Rose loves you. But she's no different than you've always known she was. You're so eager for reassurance that you think any momentary, emotional softening is something that's always been there, just waiting there for you to discover it. I'm not knocking Rose. She means well. But at forty-eight, you're not about to become a child again, establishing some storybook rapport with your mother! If you had a good visit, that's terrific. But don't think she won't be the same old Rose when you see her again—full of doleful predictions about your future and platitudes about a widow's lot."

Sheila didn't answer for a moment. Then she said, "Maybe you're right, Sally. Maybe one day Rose will say all the things you expected her to. I hope not, though. I hope I've grown up enough to appreciate the side of herself she showed me last night. And the side of myself she made me see. Anyway, it was good. It helped a lot."

"Well, I'm glad of that. Even if it doesn't last. Want to have lunch Tuesday?"

"I'd love to, but I thought I might go over and help Betty. She'll probably need a hand with the apartment and the baby and that's the only day except Sunday I have."

There was a trace of exasperation in Sally's voice. "Good grief, we're not going into the grandmother syndrome now, are we? You have to have some diversion, Sheila. Lord knows you have little enough."

"Sally, I *want* to do it! I'm not taking on a lifetime role! I just thought I could be useful for a week or two! You know I'd love to have lunch. I'm dying to see you. But this Tuesday I'd like to be at Betty's. Maybe we could have dinner one evening instead. You free?"

"Sure. There are no Jerry Mancinis or Bill Reardons knocking at *my* door. You name the night."

"Wednesday?"

"Fine. Want to come here or go out?"

"I don't know. I'll talk to you during the day Tuesday."

"Good enough. Sheila, I hope you're not angry about what I said about Rose. I just don't want you to be disappointed again. You've been let-down so much lately."

"I know. Of course I'm not angry."

She wasn't. When she hung up, she was sad. Sally was her dearest friend. She'd been the soul of kindness through all Sheila's troubles, the first one there to soothe and comfort. But a terrible realization wouldn't go away. Sally was jealous. The words she'd put into Rose's mouth, the stabbing phrase about men hating "a self-pitying woman," the belief that the marriageable ones weren't interested in anything but young girls, the idea that Rose would suggest she resign herself to widowhood—those weren't Rose's thoughts, they were Sally's. That's how *Sally* felt. Much as she cares about me, she's angry that she's found no one, good or bad, to care for her since her divorce. That sarcastic mention of Jerry and Bill. She's bitter about her manless life, about the young thing who stole her husband. But most of all, she can't comprehend the feeling of a mother for a child. She's never known that feeling. She can't believe it exists. She probably feels she's speaking for Rose, but she's really speaking for herself. That's how she sees me. Self-pitying, whining, unwilling to believe that a man can love me, bewildered that I must spend the rest of my life alone. She's had reason, God knows. That's the way I *have* been. But that's not how I really am. That's how Sally is. And she presumes I'm just like her.

No, Sheila told herself. You're wrong. The things you're thinking about Sally are unworthy of her devotion to you. She's been good and dear and close. She doesn't want me to go on as I have. She doesn't want me to share her cynicism and her misery. I'm being unfair to her. Sally would never intentionally hurt me.

And she hasn't, intentionally. She's like Rose, thinking she really is the character she tries to project. But between the two women the role-playing was reversed. Rose still doesn't know how much love she withholds. And Sally has no idea how much unrecognized envy she harbors. I love them both. And I know them better than they know themselves.

Chapter 37

There was very little sleep for Sheila that night. Tommy came in about nine o'clock, looking happy and full of enthusiasm for his niece.

"She's a terrific baby, Mom. I never liked them much. Little babies, I mean. But Jennifer is super! She's pretty and so good. She never even cries."

Sheila smiled. It was reassuring to have the "old Tommy" back—warm, sensitive, affectionate.

"You're taking this uncle business pretty big," she teased. "You'll spoil Jennifer worse than I will."

He grinned back. "I doubt *that*. You have a good visit with Grandma Price?"

"Super," she echoed. "See you in the morning." She was wide awake, thinking about them all. Her family was all right. She could do nothing for those who'd gone. It had been a hideous year. It would never be really right again. It couldn't. But the terrible cloud of confusion was lifting, chased away by the instinct for self-preservation. It's the first law, Sheila thought. And the right one. I want my life back. I'm entitled to it.

At midnight, she got up and took Bill's old letter from Ireland out of the drawer where she kept it. She went to her desk and painfully, uncertainly, began to paraphrase it.

"Cleveland. . . . A Sunday night in a quiet suburb where families are together and people love each other and it's a million miles from Bermuda. I sit here remembering the beautiful sea reflecting the faces of the reunited . . . the gentle words spoken softly, gratefully in a kind of passionate wonderment . . . and how lovely Cat's Corner treated me, for ecstasy, for peace, for hope. The sunshine, the memories of striding purposefully toward the eighteenth tee . . . feeling foolishly young, driving through the streets of Hamilton in a horse-drawn carriage like some silly tourist-bride on her honeymoon . . . and being close in a quiet room, feeling safe in the arms of the man I love.

"And how I yearn for the oleander and the hibiscus . . . the sunshine and showers . . . the wild little cats in the woods and croaking frogs glowering along the road . . . the mad, young, laughing things on their motorbikes . . . so recklessly unaware of the preciousness of life, hurtling, confident, down the 'wrong side' of the road.

"And a man and a woman, finding each other through the deliciousness of mental and physical exploration . . . and reliving the past and anticipating the future . . . and so certain that nothing cruel could come between them. Dreaming of days and nights, weeks and years together.

"So much do I think of those five miraculous days . . . as though I'd lived a dream, visited another planet, some sparkling dot in the galaxy of lovers' worlds. . . . And how unknowingly changed I was by it all . . . and how sadly lost, for a time, was the wonderment, inked out by the unthinkable, the unacceptable. The soft breezes of happiness became the cold winds of anguish . . . and the woman who swam and sunned and sang became bitter and tormented and blind . . . with rage and hatred of man and God.

"How I long to make that voyage to love again . . . for now I can . . . knowing that the best place to be is with the one who utterly fills your heart. No, not even the *best* place. The *only* place. Forever.

"All these things I remember . . . and want . . . and more and more."

She sealed the letter and sat staring out the window into the blackness. It was dark, but there was light somewhere. She prayed it was waiting for her.

Whatever her brusqueness, her businesslike manner, Kitty Rawlings had a streak of intuition that sometimes surprised even her. She'd known from the start that Sheila was not destined to be one of the "permanent" members of her staff. She'd stayed a year, which was almost more than the buyer expected. She'd been conscientious, hard-working and, in spite of a few absences, dedicated to the job. But Sheila was not, by nature, a "liberated" woman who felt unsatisfied in the home. Nor was she simply a bored widow needing something to keep her in contact with people.

336

Kitty half-smiled. Sheila worked because she needed money to live. Not an unadmirable motive, but once the necessity disappeared, so did the "career urge."

Funny. On this Monday morning, she sensed that Sheila was on the verge of making a change in her life. She wasn't sure why she felt so certain. There simply was something different in the way Sheila looked, a new kind of serenity and, yes, recovery. She hadn't looked that way since her daughter's funeral. Kitty had gone to it and realized that Sheila hardly knew she was there. Hardly knew anybody was there, for that matter. So sad, losing the young girl who'd left home. She must wonder where things went wrong, where *she* went wrong. That's how women were. When things went amiss, they looked at themselves in an effort to place the blame. Sheila had seemed to cower at the funeral, almost as much in shame as in sorrow. As though she were apologizing to the dead girl and to the people who looked at her with the sympathy she must have interpreted as reproach.

But, watching her move around the department, Kitty saw a different Sheila. Even her posture was more erect, her manner more confident. What has happened? her boss wondered. Maybe Bill Reardon, who supported her at the graveside, had something to do with it. Whatever, Sheila had regained her dignity and her will to live. She was going to make some move.

Kitty wasn't surprised when, a little past ten o'clock, Sheila appeared in the office and asked if she might see Miss Rawlings alone.

"Of course. Natalie, excuse us, will you? And please close the door behind you. All right, Sheila. What's on your mind?"

"This really isn't easy. You've been so kind to me, so patient, you and everyone in the store. I've loved it here. I was so lucky to get this job, unskilled as I was. I've learned so much and I'll always be grateful to you."

Kitty waited. She'd heard similar speeches before when people quit. The least she could do would be to make it a little easier for this nice woman.

"You're trying to tell me you're going to leave us, is that it?"

Sheila nodded.

"I hope it's for something good," Kitty said. "A better job—or, preferably, a nice man."

"I don't have another job. I couldn't find one I'd like more. As for a man, I'm not sure. There is someone, but I don't know whether he'll have me."

The buyer raised her eyebrows.

"I know," Sheila said. "You must think I'm crazy. You know I need to work to live, and I'm walking out on my income. As for the man, well, it's Bill Reardon. You probably guessed that, seeing him at Maryanne's funeral. We were planning to marry. I called it off. But I've written to him, hoping with all my heart he'll give me a second chance."

"I still don't quite understand," Kitty said. "If you're not sure about Bill, why quit now? Aren't you being a little premature?"

"Probably. But there's more. I've got to start over, in all directions. Even if it doesn't work out with Bill, I've got to change everything I do. Maybe I'll sell the house, leave Cleveland, get some kind of job in another part of the country. I don't know. I really don't. I just know that I have to breathe new air, see new faces. I'm sure it doesn't make any sense to you. It won't make sense to *anybody* I tell. I just have to run. But not really *away* from things, *toward* things." Sheila gave a little laugh. "I told you it doesn't make sense except to me. I know I must shake up my life, tackle something different before it's too late."

"Have you discussed this with your family?"

"No. I sat up all night thinking about my life. The sameness of it. The predictability of it. I felt myself growing older and duller and more grandmotherly. And I knew I needed—though I hate the word—a challenge."

Kitty shook her head. "I hope you're not making a mistake, Sheila. I can grasp some of what you're feeling, some of the unwillingness to accept that cliché about 'lives of quiet desperation,' but you must be practical, too. Level with me. You're banking on marrying Bill Reardon, aren't you?"

"I guess so. I want it so much I can't believe it won't happen. But if it doesn't, I still have to move outward."

"You're a nice woman," Kitty said. "I don't know whether you're doing the right thing, but I know you must try it while there's still time. We'll all miss you. You've been a great addition. There isn't one of us who doesn't wish you well." She sighed. "When do you want to leave?"

She hadn't really thought that far. Bill would have her letter on Wednesday or Thursday. If he wanted her, he'd call. If he didn't call, she was still determined to cut the old ties, free herself from memories and reminders, from the house, the job, even the friends. There was no one to think of but herself and Tommy. Not even Tommy, really. He was on his own, emotionally. He could stay in school, probably live with Pat and Betty if need be. He'd be perfectly happy without the "obligation of Mama," maybe even relieved not to feel responsibility for her.

"The end of the week if that's convenient," Sheila said in answer to Kitty's question.

"Okay. Once again, I'm sorry to see you go, but I can glimpse what you're feeling. You'll make it, Sheila. You're a very gutsy dame." She paused. "I probably haven't seemed too friendly, but that's the way it has to be in business, you know. There's a line that can't be crossed between socializing and coworking. It interferes with the day-by-day operation when things get personal. But I like you. I hope you know I'm your friend. And if you need anything, holler."

Sheila was touched. "Thank you. You know how much I admire you and . . ."

Kitty stood up, a gesture of dismissal, once again the organized executive. "Sure. Well, back to work, right? Got to sell books and enrich all those dear little lives out there. Good luck, Sheila. Hope you enrich your own."

It was sheer lunacy, what she'd just done, Sheila thought as she left Kitty Rawlings' office. What on earth had come over her, quitting her job, talking about moving toward some "challenge" as though she were a kid with no sense of responsibility? Why couldn't she gracefully settle into the life that seemed to have been mapped out for her—that of a dignified widow with children and grandchildren, an aging mother to consider, a nice house and a pleasant job, and peaceful acceptance of what everybody expected? It's the damned Irish in me, she thought. It's that stupid restlessness that she supposed had originally drawn her to the unpredictable Sean and which now made her long for an exciting, ever-changing life with Bill Reardon.

Kitty was right, of course. She *was* pinning her hopes on Bill's wanting her. He *must* still want me, Sheila told herself fiercely. He must believe that I'm once again the Sheila he knew for a few days in Bermuda. Please God, let him call and tell me so. But if he doesn't, I still have to go on to other things. I can't sit here, stagnating, accepting crumbs of friendship and dutiful expressions of respect from my family. There could be another thirty years of that passive, impossible boredom. No. That was a trap into which other women often fell, a prison built of timidity and inertia. It was like meekly waiting for death. Life isn't going to come to me at my age. I've got to go out and find it, at least fight boredom and loneliness with some kind of action.

She told no one what she'd done. She knew why she kept quiet about it. She hoped to be able to tell them, within a few days, that she was going to be with Bill. The thought of facing her children and her mother with the idea that she was "going adventuring" without a plan, or announcing she was determined to shake up her life without knowing how —was a prospect she dreaded. But she'd do it, if she must. She wasn't going to be a Rose, or even a Sally, accepting on the surface and raging inwardly at the unfairness of life. She had no idea what she'd do. But the doing was all-important. She was through with useless tears and unproductive guilt, with the endless, anxious effort to please, to be perfect for those who expected it. Most of us spend our lives trying to live up to somebody's image of us, and failing miserably, Sheila thought. It's unreal.

It was strange. She should have been frightened about the giant step she'd taken, worried "what people would think," but she suddenly felt free and eager. She remembered something her father had once said. "Don't ever worry about what people will say, Sheila. They don't pay your rent. They don't put food on your table or serenity in your soul. Be your best, my dear. Never complain and never explain."

She'd thought it odd at the time, but she knew now that he was talking about his own life. People considered Frank Price a "hen-pecked" husband, a self-effacing, unresisting appendage to Rose. He knew what they thought and he didn't care. He knew he was his own man, inwardly stronger than those who criticized him for being weak. And Rose knew it, too. She knew exactly what to expect of him and she was never disappointed. Not like me, who always felt I had to live up to everybody's expectations. And when I couldn't, I fell apart.

No more. No more feeling I've failed because I can't be the extension of everyone else's ego—the "superior being" they'd like their child or wife or mother to be. No more trying to meet other people's goals for me. No more shamed feeling of being less than what's demanded. Perhaps that's why Sean and I managed to hold a marriage together. We really asked very little of each other, so there was no terrible drive to please.

I can't be a human sacrifice, Sheila realized. And then she smiled. Who the hell asked you to be? You only *imagined* they did.

Betty looked forward to her mother-in-law's arrival the next day. Things were going fine. She felt well and strong enough to handle Jennifer who really required very little care. She'd found a cleaning woman, to be replaced later by a nurse when Betty went back to work. She was content and happy. And curious. She wondered what Sheila meant when she told Pat that her visit to Rose had been "good surprising." Betty had always recognized the underlying hostility laced with love that lay between Rose and her daughter. Neither woman had ever really comprehended, and would have rejected the idea if they had. Was it possible that at this late date they'd seen each other as women?

"You look beautiful," Sheila said when she came in. "Your new role agrees with you."

"How about that nice, flat belly?" Betty said, patting her middle. "Not as flat as it should be *yet*, but it's sure great to see your toes again! How are you, Sheila?"

"I'm good, honey. Where's my granddaughter?"

They stood looking down at the baby who slept peacefully in her bassinette beside Pat and Betty's bed.

"That's the prettiest sight in the world," Sheila said. "I gave her a message in the hospital. I told her to be her own woman." She put her arm around Betty. "And with you for a mother, she will be."

They tiptoed out of the bedroom.

"Now," Sheila said, "what can I do for you? I came to be useful as well as to visit."

"Not a thing, except keep me company. Tell me what's been happening to you."

I wish I could. But not yet. Of them all, Betty would be the most understanding of this desperate urge for a new start, but Sheila would wait until they were all together, a "family council" to hear what she prayed would be good news. Instead of revealing her decision for the future, she decided to talk about the past. "I had a marvelous visit with Grandma Price. As I told Patrick, I learned a lot."

"Really? In what way?"

Sheila weighed her words. "I came to *like* her for the first time in forty-eight years. We didn't talk as relatives; we talked as people. I never really thought of her as a person with sensitivities and fears, Betty. She was always just 'Mother.' Expecting too much of me and making me feel unhappy when I disappointed her. I'll never really achieve the fairytale goodness Rose wants for me. The same wishful kind Maryanne expected of me as her mother. And the kind I felt she should have given me because she was my daughter. It was like a light bulb going on over my head when I realized that. All those painful, emotional dreams we entertain! The ingrained inflexibility of parent and child. The stupid sense of duty. The effort to avoid the real facts of life. What sadness our unrealistic longings bring us in the end!"

Betty sat quietly, saying nothing.

"I saw for the first time," Sheila went on, "that love has no right to be demanding. The more you expect, the more responsibility you put on the one you love. I don't mean that people, parents really, shouldn't hope for the best for their children. They should just see them as human beings, nothing special, full of inadequacies and human failings. Our children aren't supersouls because they came out of our bodies. They shouldn't be made to feel obligated to please. And by the same token, our kids shouldn't expect us to be surrounded by some supernatural halo because we're their mother and therefore above reproach. I'll never really understand Rose. Nor she me. Maryanne and I had the same problem. But I know now that it's not a unique problem, as I thought. That's the way it is in this life. We have to love with open eyes, which doesn't diminish the strength of it at all. It just makes living with ourselves bearable."

"And you're able to live with yourself," Betty said. "That's a good thing, Sheila. An important thing. Guilt is so all-consuming. Some people make martyrdom a life sentence. Maybe even come to enjoy it, in a way. I'm glad you're not going to do that."

"I'm glad, too. I didn't think I could ever hope again." Sheila smiled. "I'll tell you something I probably would never have courage to tell anyone else. I talked to Maryanne when I was in New York. Driving over a bridge, maybe over the very last place she stood, I told her out loud that I'd done the best I could. Maybe it wasn't right. Maybe it wasn't enough. But I can't change that now. I've tried to do right by everybody I love. All of you will have to accept me as I am, Betty, because that's the way I have to accept myself."

Betty spoke softly. "Don't you know we do? Don't you know we like you just the way you are?"

Chapter 38

Driving to Sheila's for dinner on Wednesday evening, Sally hovered between annoyance and uneasiness. Annoyed that her friend had insisted on cooking for them. It was so silly. She worked all day. You'd have thought she'd have leaped at the chance to go out to a restaurant as Sally's guest, as had been suggested, or even come to the Cantrell house where they could have been served by the housekeeper. But no, Sheila seemed determined to be at home.

"You're always taking me out to dinner," she'd said when they talked on the phone Tuesday night. "Once in a while I like to reciprocate."

Bloody foolish pride, Sally thought. Can't stand anything that smacks of dependence or "charity."

"Well, then, come here," Sally had said. "At least you won't have to cook."

"No. You come here, Sally. Please. I enjoy doing dinner and I had a chance to do all the marketing today. It's no trouble, and we won't be disturbed. Tommy's invited to his girl's house for dinner, so we can relax and eat whenever we're ready."

"His girl's house? I didn't know he had a girl."

"Neither did I until this morning. You should have seen him at breakfast. He was so sweet. All awkward and embarrassed about telling me he was 'going steady' with little Faith Stewart. She's a darling child. I know

343

her parents. Tommy's been taking her out since he went back to University."

"Isn't he a little young to 'go steady'?"

"Maybe, but I doubt it's a permanent arrangement. Anyway, I much prefer to see him spending his time with Faith than tearing around with a bunch of wild boys, getting into trouble again."

"Let's hope he doesn't get *her* into trouble. Lord, the things you read these days about pregnant high school girls!"

Sheila laughed. "Honestly, Sally, you sound like Rose! Tommy's going on seventeen. It's about time he took some interest in the opposite sex." She paused. "Anyway, I trust my son. I'm glad he's showing all the normal instincts for his age."

She couldn't help thinking of that long-ago talk with Maryanne, that frightening conversation in which the girl had warned her about hanging on to Tommy, turning him into a homosexual through his excessive maternal attachment. The letter had dispelled that thought. It had been one of Maryanne's many confused efforts to hurt her mother. Still, Sheila was glad that Tommy had so firmly established a world of his own, almost entirely divorced from her. It would make the actual break easier when it came. He must know all about sex, she thought, though we've never discussed it. Of course he does. Kids aren't innocent these days. He's probably already had some experience. The idea was hard to imagine, but it likely was a fact. He wasn't a baby any more. Not even a little boy. In a couple of years he'd be in college. She had to stop thinking of him as anything but a young man.

"Anyway," Sheila went on, "we can talk about that and a lot of other things tomorrow evening. Come over about seven-thirty?"

"Okay, if you're sure that's what you want to do."

She was sure. She wasn't going to leave the house any evening this week. At any moment Bill could call. He could receive her letter tomorrow or the next day. God willing, he'd phone immediately. And if he didn't, well, she'd have to survive that, too. Like Maryanne, she'd burned her bridges. Strange, but she didn't feel frightened. I'm in touch with myself again, Sheila thought. I have a sense of who I am, even if I don't know where I'm going.

When Sally arrived, she still had that uneasy feeling. Some change had come over Sheila. She couldn't put her finger on it. It was in the tone of her voice, the lack of acquiescent agreement with everything Sally said. She'd felt it Sunday night when Sheila came back from New York. She felt it again last night when they talked about Tommy. Maybe it was good. It was time Sheila came out of her shell. Yet Sally had a hunch that her friend had come to some kind of crossroads, and things would never be quite the same again.

There was no outward sign when she was greeted warmly at the door. Sheila seemed the same, a little nervous, perhaps, as though she were waiting for someone or something. And her eyes unconsciously strayed toward the telephone as they sat and talked. Otherwise, she was the same soft-spoken, fond woman she'd always been. Indeed, more like the one who'd been Sean Callahan's wife, composed, gracious, candidly charming. The depressed, lost, frantic Sheila of the past months seemed to have gone away. But the replacement wasn't really the "old Sheila." There was a new firmness about her, a kind of quiet determination that Sally had never seen. It was not unpleasant, but it was unsettling. Forthright as always, Sally spoke her mind bluntly after dinner, after they'd gone through the superficial, amusing chitchat and gossip that usually was their pattern.

"What the hell's going on with you, Sheila?"

"What do you mean?"

"I'm not sure. You seem different. It's nothing specific, just something I sense. You're more, well, private. I have this crazy feeling of being a stranger. Like you're weighing your words with me. Look, if I've annoyed you, say so. Are you angry because I was snippy about Rose the other night?"

"No, of course not. Nobody could have been more impatient with her over the years than I. You had every reason to think she might react that way. I was surprised myself when she didn't."

"Then what is it? Did you resent my crack about Tommy getting that little Stewart girl in trouble?"

"Don't be silly."

"Well, something's changed, and if it's my fault, I'd like to know. We've always been so close and I have this odd feeling that you've moved away and left no forwarding address."

Sheila was genuinely surprised. She thought she'd been doing a good job of hiding her new attitude, but she'd always been a rotten actress. *Of course* she'd resented Sally's remarks about Rose and Tommy. Try as she would to overcome it, the feeling that her friend had a streak of bitchiness persisted. She'd shown it on Sunday and again last night. But it wasn't really Sally who made her feel (and, apparently, act) like someone else. It was this irresistible urge to be free of the old ways, the old demands, the old constrictions. She dared not confide that she'd already recklessly quit her job, that she was determined to start over, probably somewhere else. Sally couldn't be trusted not to pass on the news before Sheila was ready to announce it. Sadly, she felt, too, that Sally couldn't possibly understand this risk-taking. Not Sally with her love of material things, her insistence upon security, her determination to live as she always had and punish Fred Cantrell by making him pay for it forever. But Sheila had to give some answer to her friend's probing.

"It's not your fault," she said. "I've just begun to see things differently, that's all."

"What things?"

"Myself, mostly. Rose. The kids. My job. My whole stifling future as a widow."

"And where does all this heavy thinking take you?"

"I'm not sure."

"You've changed your mind about Bill Reardon again, haven't you?"

"Yes. I was wrong to send him away. But that's only part of it. Part of a whole series of regrets. I'd like to undo that mistake, Sally, but I don't know whether I can. Any more than I can undo a lot of others. But I'm not going to sit around brooding about the past. That much I know. I'm whole again, for the first time in more than a year. Maybe for the first time in my life."

"I wish I knew what you were talking about."

"I'm sorry, dear, I can't really explain it. I've come to terms with myself about Maryanne, or at least my culpability for that tragedy. I've learned to accept Rose for what she is. Tommy is a joy again. Pat and Betty and the baby are safe and happy. Everything is better than it's been in a long time, except for this awful, urgent restlessness I feel. I have to change the pattern before I become a dreary, withered-up old lady in a rut. I don't want to be just somebody's mother or 'that nice little woman who lives in Shaker Heights.' There's a whole world out there and I've seen so little of it!"

Sally stared at her. "I think you need a checkup. Sounds like you're starting change of life."

Sheila smiled. "That's exactly the right phrase for it. But not in the medical sense."

"Then in *what* sense, for God's sake? What choice is there for women like you and me? We're single, overaged females. I have the advantage of money and you have the advantage of family. We're past the time of 'restlessness.' We've *had* our lives, Sheila. Can't you accept that, as I have? Can't you relax and reconcile yourself to it?"

"No, I can't!" Sheila was angry, fighting back. "It's all very easy for you to say. When you get bored you can pick up and go on a shopping spree in New York. You can afford to travel and entertain or lie in bed all day if you like, having someone wait on you hand and foot! You can get your kicks out of flirting with our friends' husbands and alienating the wives. You don't have a responsibility in the world. Never *have* had! You don't know anything but freedom. How can you understand that I've *never* been free? You don't know what a precious commodity that is, because you've always enjoyed it. Damn it, Sally, I want to think about *myself*, too! But not like you do. Not with that acceptance of a lonely life or that fatalistic resignation you speak of so casually!"

Sheila stopped, aghast. What was making her say such terrible things to the best friend, the only friend she had? Sally was only trying to be realistic, helpful, and Sheila had attacked her as though she were an enemy.

346

She put her hands over her eyes to blot out the sight of Sally's disbelieving face.

"Oh, God, I'm so sorry. I didn't mean all those things, Sally. I don't know what's come over me. I didn't mean to hurt you. I'm jealous of you. Not just for the luxuries you have. For the adjustment you've made. I wish I *could* accept. I wish I could count my blessings, as Mother would say. But I crave more. I want to feel things again. Not just sorrow and guilt as I have in the past. And not the kind of passive abandonment of hope that you and every other person in his right mind thinks I should accept. Maybe I'm crazy. Maybe I'm chasing a dream, not even knowing what dream it is. But I can taste selfishness and I like it. I'm probably shallow and awful, but I'm tired of being tied to everybody and everything. I've been a prisoner long enough."

Sally wasn't angry. "I had no idea how you felt," she said quietly. "I thought giving was a necessary part of your nature. It's one of the things I've always envied about you—that seemingly endless supply of patience and selflessness. I suppose we've all taken advantage of that and pushed you to the breaking point. I don't know what you're going to do, Sheila, but apparently you must do it. And whatever it is, I hope it's as wonderful as you deserve."

"Oh, Sally, I don't know what I'm doing!"

"Sure you do. You're deciding that Sheila Callahan has a right to life, liberty, and the pursuit of happiness. *How* you do it is something else. You're right you know. About me and about yourself. I'm a taker. You're a giver. Neither of us will basically change, but you've earned your chance to *get*."

"I've thought some things about you that weren't very nice, Sally. I apologize. You don't deserve them."

"The funny part is," Sally said, "I probably do."

Thursday and Friday passed with an ominous silence from Bermuda. And as each hour of the days and nights went by, Sheila's resolve began to weaken. For all her high-flown speeches about wanting a different kind of life, she was frightened by the thought of striking out in some new direction. She still hadn't told anyone outside the store that she'd quit her job. She'd given no indication to Tommy that his whole life was about to change with hers. Sometimes she felt as though she were standing to one side, looking curiously at some desperate woman who didn't make sense. And yet she was impelled toward a fresh start, certain it was now or never.

The only positive action she'd taken was to tell the children that she'd appreciate it if they could all be together on Saturday night. Betty said it was fine, and why didn't she and Tommy come over for dinner? Her youngest looked momentarily unhappy when his mother accepted. Saturday was a big night when you were sixteen. He had a date with his girl, but the urgency in Sheila's voice told him this was important to her.

"Sure, Mom." And then, "Something special on your mind?"

Sheila looked at him. He was always so attuned to her moods. She hated to admit it, even to herself, but her youngest really was her most-loved child. There'd always been a special bond between them and this past, tormented year had put them through tests that proved their unshakable devotion.

"Yes," she said. "There is something kind of special. That's why I need the Family Council."

"You're not sick, are you?"

"No, darling. I just want to talk about where we're all going. Where *I'm* going, really."

He didn't seem especially surprised. "You're pretty unhappy, aren't you?"

She wouldn't lie to him. "Yes, Tommy, I am. And I have to do something about it."

He nodded. "Anything you do is okay with us. You don't have to worry about your kids. All we want is for you to be happy."

Echoes of Maryanne. How blessed I am to have children who care.

"We'll talk it all out on Saturday," she said. "I need your help. Yours and Pat's and Betty's."

"You got it," Tommy said.

She knew that was true. Whatever seemingly foolish path she decided to follow, they'd support her. It would all be so simple if Bill would call and say he wanted her. Then Tommy could be with them, if he liked. If not, she'd give the house to Pat and Betty and ask them to live there with Tommy and Jennifer. They needed more space now. They'd have to move anyway to have a room for the baby and they couldn't really afford a bigger apartment. Tommy could stay in his school, be with his girl, benefit from the guidance and example of his brother. She was sure he'd rather do that than go trundling off to Bermuda with her.

But it seemed less and less likely that she would go to Bermuda. Or anywhere else with Bill Reardon. There'd been no word from him, though surely he had her letter by now.

He's not going to call, Sheila decided, feeling a terrible emptiness. Why should he? He'd offered her everything, been patient beyond belief and she'd sent him away. What did she expect—that she could change her mind any time she felt like it and he'd come running back?

So if there was to be no Bill, what then? She'd still go through with her plan about the house, and she'd move to New York, get a job, try to find some new interests. She'd not live with Rose. Neither of them truly wanted that, but they could see each other from time to time. Maybe Tommy would come to New York with her? No. He'd hate it. He was happily settled. He could visit her often and she'd come back to Cleveland to see them all. God help me, Sheila thought, what makes sense? What will I say Saturday night?

Her knees were shaking as she walked into the book department at Higbee's on Saturday morning. It was her last day in this familiar place, the last hours with the women who'd been so kind to her, the final contact with the only real security she felt. She wondered if she was early. The place seemed deserted. As she was putting her money from the tube room into her cash register, Dottie Parker came up behind her.

"Miss Rawlings wants to see you in the office, Sheila."

"Okay. Thanks."

As she approached the cubicle in the rear of the department, she heard voices, and when she walked in, they were all there, Kitty, Natalie, the whole staff. Even, she noted with surprise, the two employees who normally had Saturday off. There was coffee and Danish spread out on the buyer's desk and a big banner on the wall that said, "Good Luck, Sheila!"

She was speechless, and then she began to cry, noiselessly, her shoulders shaking and the tears streaming from her eyes. Kitty handed her a Kleenex.

"Hey! You're not supposed to weep! You're some guest of honor, you are! Here we go to all this trouble to give you a lavish send-off and you thank us by bawling into the buns!"

The others laughed nervously and even Sheila, drying her eyes, managed to smile at Kitty's nonsense.

"I just didn't expect . . . That is, I'm so taken aback. I mean, nobody ever gave me a surprise party before." Sheila faltered. "I don't know how to thank you. Not just for this. For everything. You . . . you've saved my life. All of you. I don't know what I'd have done this past year without this place and the kindness you've shown me."

There was an embarrassed silence. Someone sniffled loudly and even Dottie dabbed at her mascara. It was all sweet and sad and warm. They were like a little family, bidding good-by to one of its members, wishing the departing one well, hating to see her go.

"Not too late to change your mind," Kitty said. "I haven't hired a replacement. Of course, if you decide to stay, *you'll* have to pay for the coffee and cake. I mean, that's the *least* you can do!" Once again, she'd rescued them. "No, huh? Well, in that case, we might as well drink to your health and happiness before this witches' brew gets colder than it already is."

Good luck, Sheila, they said. Here's to your happiness. To your health. To your future. Don't forget to come back and see us. We love you. We'll miss you. They didn't say, we'll worry about you, but she could read it in their eyes. Apparently they knew she had no plans. Perhaps

349

many of them felt as she did—that there was more to life than a well-traveled path to and from work, more than the anxious wait to be noticed by children and grandchildren, to contemplate, patiently, the end of the world. Maybe some of them *had* thought of going to look for adventure. Or perhaps they were more sensible than she, recognizing the stirrings of discontent as normal, passing pangs, being grateful for their hard-earned independence, knowing they were lucky not to be a burden to anyone.

She'd never know. She simply knew she loved them, these dear women with their kind, patient ways, their fondness for other human beings, their eagerness to be useful. They lived in a world of other people's stories set down on the printed page. Yet they were more realistic than the make-believe tales they sold.

The little party was brief and determinedly merry, but it just didn't come off. They were truly sorry to see her go, concerned for her future, pretending envy and secretly glad that they knew where they belonged.

Why can't I be like them? Sheila thought. Why don't I stay here, enjoying this affection, accepting the safety? But she couldn't. Secure as this life might be, there had to be something more.

Chapter 39

       The jet sped toward New York and the woman in seat 14B sat back with her eyes closed, the events of the past week unreeling before her like a private movie.

Just a week ago she'd left Higbee's feeling scared and a little foolish, dreading what she'd say to her children that evening, wondering what lay ahead for her, despising her adolescent longings.

And then the miracle. For that's surely what it was: a miracle. She and Tommy had been out the door, on their way to Pat's, when she heard the phone ringing. She'd raced back, her key fumbling in the lock, praying she'd get there before the caller hung up. Praying most of all it was the call she'd waited for.

"You sound breathless," Bill said.

Sheila almost laughed aloud. Such an ordinary beginning to maybe the most important conversation of her life. "Tommy and I were on our way to Pat and Betty's. I came racing back when I heard the phone. How are you, Bill?"

"All right. And you?"

"Pretty good. How's Bermuda?"

"Same as ever, last time I saw it which was a week ago. I've rented the house. I'm in New York. Got here last Sunday."

Last Sunday. She was leaving New York last Sunday, maybe at the very time he was arriving. Crazy coincidence. What if they had bumped into each other at the airport? And then she realized that he'd left Bermuda before her letter arrived. He didn't know how she felt. He hadn't called before because he hadn't received those begging words. Why was he calling now, after all these weeks?

As though in answer to her unspoken question, Bill said, "I couldn't go off again without saying good-by and seeing if you were okay."

"Go off? Where are you going?"

"Believe it or not, Ireland. I've leased a rambling old place in County Cork. Kilbrittain, to be exact. They call it a castle, but you know how the Irish romanticize everything. I haven't seen it. It may just be a big house, but it looks great from the pictures. Anyway, it should be a good place to work on the new book, and my accountants say it has tax advantages for me."

Sheila was stunned. And then, almost irrelevantly, "I wrote to you in Bermuda last Sunday night. You didn't get my letter."

His voice was very quiet. "No, I didn't. Want to tell me what you said?"

She hesitated for a fraction of a second. "I said I loved you and I asked you if you still wanted to marry a woman who finally has taken a good look at herself." Sheila waited. Maybe he's not going to Ireland alone! Maybe he's already married one of those women in Bermuda who were so mad for him. Dear Lord, don't let me make a fool of myself again. And don't embarrass Bill. It seemed minutes before he answered.

"Sheila, are you sure? I love you. I want to marry you more than I want anything in my life. Leaving Bermuda was really because I couldn't stand it there without you. Everything reminded me of you and I was so sure we'd never be together again. I was convinced you'd never be able to stop blaming yourself for everything tragic in your life."

"I have stopped. It's a long story, but I'm me again. Maybe even a little better me. Wiser, at least. And able to respect myself. Even able to earn your respect again, I think, if you'll let me."

"Darling, you never lost that. Not really. I was so angry with you. I wanted to shake you, but I couldn't reach you. I love you as you are, just as you must love me with all *my* weaknesses. And there are a lot of them, you'll discover. I'm a different kind of Irishman from Sean, but in my way I'm also volatile and unpredictable. I'll adore you and take care of you. I'll probably even be faithful to you. But you're not getting a guy who'll live a neat, predictable life. I'm a wanderer, a seeker, and dreamer. But I'll try to make you happy, Sheila. You and Tommy."

She'd never felt such joy. "I want you as you are. I want both of us as we are. Separate but indivisible. Tell me when and I'll come to you. Alone. Tommy's young, but he's able to stand on his own feet. He'll need the knowledge of me, of us, but without our constant physical presence."

She paused. "He's very grown-up for his age, Bill. He's young Tom Callahan with a girl of his own, friends, and a brother to be near. And he's not the return of Billy Reardon, darling. It wouldn't be fair to ask him to be a replacement."

"Sweetheart, you know best. We have a lot to talk about. When can you come? I'd planned to leave a week from Monday. Can you manage by then?"

"Yes. Any time. Anywhere. Just so I can be with you."

"We'll get married in Ireland. There's this little church I know, with a priest who's the reincarnation of Barry Fitzgerald. And we'll have a celebration at the local pub and drink Irish whiskey and oh, Sheila Price Callahan Reardon, how I'll make love to you!"

She found herself smiling as the plane droned on toward New York. Everything after that had been like a golden dream. The children were genuinely happy for her. They'd moved into the house as she planned. Even Tommy had shown mature understanding on Saturday night when he heard her news. She'd been afraid, for a moment, that her youngest would feel rejected again.

"Bill would be so happy if you'd come with us, dear," she'd said. "You know how welcome you are. I want you and so does he. It might be interesting living in Ireland for a while."

He'd patted her cheek as though she were the child. "I know you want me, Mom. I know we'll always have each other, even when I'm grown up and married. You're not abandoning me. I know that worries you, but it shouldn't. I love you. But I like it here. It's where I belong. Ireland'll be swell for summer vacations, but I don't want to live anywhere else right now. I don't *need* to start over. Heck, I haven't even *begun!*"

She'd smiled, knowing he was right. "I'm so proud of you, Tommy. Of all of you. I wish Maryanne could have known how proud I was of her, too."

"I think she did, Mother," Patrick said. "In spite of everything, I think she always did."

Only a week ago, Sheila mused, I was running in all directions. Now I'm headed straight as an arrow.

The middle-aged man beside her coughed lightly. Sheila opened her eyes.

"You live in Cleveland?" he asked. "Great town."

"I used to live there. Yes, it is. Great."

"Live in New York now, huh?"

"No." Sheila smiled at him. "My home's in Ireland."

"Ireland! Sonofagun! What's it like there?"

"Up with Desmond and O'Brien and down with Cromwell."

"Huh?"

"Nothing. It's just a line from a letter someone wrote me long ago."

"Oh. I see. Isn't there a lot of fighting going on in Ireland?"

"Unfortunately, yes. But not where I'm going. Where I'm going there's nothing but love and peace."

"Well, you're a mighty lucky lady."

Hear that, Rose? Maybe I haven't been unlucky. Misguided. Stupid and self-pitying. But not really unlucky. Not with Sean or Maryanne or Tommy. Not even with Jerry Mancini. I've learned from them all, hurt them and been hurt, loved and hated, left them and been left by them. Experience teaches and tempers, even when it's bad. People make their own luck, my darling Rose, by tolerance, caring, and the will to survive.

She licked her lips like a little girl. She could taste happiness, anticipation. Life is a lollipop for grownups. Sweet and sour, sometimes almost unbearably delicious, sometimes cutting your tongue with its sharp edges. But you hang on to the stick, savoring every precious lick while it lasts.

And it could last a long, long time.